Mahogany Slade

Mahogany Slade
Black Saint Records
blacksaintrecords@gmail.com
Cover by Lee Heidel, Heideldesign @ 2012
ISBN: 978-0615680217

ISBN: 0-6156-8021-6
ISBN-13: 9780615680217

Mahogany Slade

Stephen Robinson

Dedication

This book could not have been written without the following people:

Alan A. Russell, who long ago introduced me to Flannery O'Connor and Joyce Carol Oates, among others, without whom I would never have met Janet Tomalin.

Charlayne Hunter-Gault, the former Myers Hall resident who helped make it possible for Brad Carlton and Janet Tomalin to meet in Athens.

Erin Kennedy Urban, who through many drafts over many years always believed in Brad and Janet and never let me forget them.

Acknowledgements

Thanks to all who have contributed: Debbie Hoodiman Beaudin, Robert Brown, Claire Callow, Caroline France, Lee Heidel, James Longo, Marjorie Miller, Renee Perez, Zach Ralston, Kathryn Robinson, Larry Robinson, C. Trent Rosecrans, Melissa Bower Smith, Christopher Urban, and Dan White.

"All this happened, more or less."
—*Kurt Vonnegut*

FALL QUARTER '92 PLAYLIST

U2, "Mysterious Ways"—Brad
Public Enemy, "Can't Truss It"—Heather and Andy
The Beatles, "You Know My Name (Look Up the Number)"—Janet
Ella Fitzgerald, "Night in Tunisia"—Brad and Janet
Magnapop, "Merry"—Jennifer and Gwen
Bernard Herrmann, "Prelude and Rooftop" from Vertigo—Brad and Janet
R.E.M., "Drive"—Brad and Heather
Paul Wallace, "All I Need Is the Girl" from Gypsy—Brad
Wayne Newton, "Danke Schoen"—Brad and Janet
Helen Gallagher, Thelma Oliver, and Company, "Big Spender" from Sweet
Charity—Janet
Sonic Youth, "Crème Brulee"—Andy
PJ Harvey, "Hair"—Heather
Julie Andrews, "The Shady Dame from Seville" from Victor/Victoria—Brad
and Janet

1

The first time I saw her she was tying her shoes. I watched her through the window of the Science Library as she gracefully knotted a pair of black Oxford heels. She wore a black short-sleeved blouse with gray high-waisted trousers and a matching fedora. Two groupies — one brunette and famine thin, the other blonde and corpulent — trailed after her as she melted into the Georgia sun.

Numbers are not my strong point, but 9, 14, 1992 has remained lodged in my memory and not just because it was my first day of college. Over time, it has taken on anthropomorphic qualities, and unlike the Biblical Elijah, it actually turns up at my door — each year, slightly different. I've found it sad, hopeful, morose, bracing, and distant. On its most recent visit, it managed to encompass all those feelings and a few more simultaneously, so I've decided to pour it a glass of wine, pull up a chair, and confront it once and for all.

I'd wandered into the Science Library that day by accident, and the events of my life prior to that moment were equally aimless. I'd graduated in June from a run-down, poorly funded institution that no one would ever call a magnet school. In fact, it had long since slid off the refrigerator door of public education. The guidance counselor, who proudly displayed a signed photo of Strom Thurmond on her desk, said I was one of a handful of my graduating class who was going to college at all. When she offhandedly asked me what I planned to study, my answer was a confident "Journalism," punctuated with a silent "I guess."

My particular talents for writing and observation made journalism a safe, practical major. The high school newspaper had been a solo effort on my part. I'd also won the prestigious Frances Carrington Hubbard Evans Journalism Scholarship. Her family had lived in South Carolina since the early eighteenth century, so every scholarship winner honored tradition and attended a school in the Palmetto State. Tradition had not worked out that well for the Carltons — the undistinguished line that produced me — so I ignored it and instead enrolled at the University of Georgia.

I was the first black winner of the scholarship and the first member of my family to attend college. Such distinction is more cause for embarrassment than celebration. Along with $10,000 a year, which covered my tuition and housing, the scholarship included a paid summer internship at my hometown newspaper the *Greenville News* where my mentor, Melinda Miller, was evidence of benevolent extraterrestrial life. The french-vanilla blonde blinked half as often as most people and once told me with a straight face that I had a "kind aura."

My experience so far confirmed I had an aura but one somewhat less than kind. A force field that radiated several feet outward, it prevented anyone from sitting beside me in the cafeteria or on class field trips.

"I so envy you," Miss Miller said during lunch on my first day. "When I was eighteen, I spent the summer hitchhiking across the country. It's such a great age. You'll never have another year like this."

I answered phones and ran errands until late July when I filled in for the obituaries writer, who'd just resigned, presumably upon realizing how morbid his job was. I did get his office all to myself, which was nice for about half a day until Miss Miller cheerfully informed me that Mrs. Evans had died there in 1977.

"I can still feel her presence!" she said before leaving me alone in her tomb.

Classes at the University of Georgia started on September 21, but my college life truly began a week earlier when the residence halls opened. My parents, having read and understood my *Welcome Week* brochure as one does stereo instructions, agreed that the "normal" thing for me to do was to arrive early and make new friends ("new" incorrectly implying the existence of "old" friends).

We left Greenville in silence in my father's 1980 Pontiac Bonneville and arrived in Athens no more communicative. The dormitory I'd selected was Myers Hall, which my parents found peculiar because it had neither air conditioning nor an elevator (my room was on the top floor). However, I'd enjoyed the photos of the brown and white building that resembled an eighteenth century manor house with hipped roofs the color of asphalt and parapet-gable wings on either side.

French windows lined the front of Myers; three of which were surrounded by decorative pilasters and octagonal lanterns. Perhaps my favorite feature was the tower with a pointed spire on the roof that gleamed white in the sun.

The move itself was not labor intensive. My belongings fit into one suitcase that was older than I was. It had gone on to see very little of the world compared to the others displayed next to it at the store where it was purchased, and as I considered the random, uncontrolled outcomes of life, my parents panted behind me as we went up to the fourth floor.

"It's not like this place has air conditioning and the other dorms have elevators," my father grumbled. "Didn't Russell have both?"

Russell Hall was one of the high-rise dorms on west campus — steel and concrete eyesores that looked like they'd been assembled from a model kit of modern despair.

"I bet everyone else stayed there," my mother said between gasps for air.

It had been my parents' life ambition for me to be like everyone else, and I'd always regretted that they ended up with me instead of anyone else.

My room's single window looked out onto the quad, a vast lake of grass with three other dorms along its coastline — Soule to the south, Mary Lyndon to the east, and Rutherford to the north. Throughout the day, girls sunned themselves on blankets and boys slapped volleyballs over white nets.

"You don't seem excited," my mother observed with alarm. "You should be excited." She turned to my father. "Shouldn't he be excited?"

"I'm excited," I said unconvincingly.

"You should be excited," my father stressed. "This is the most important time of your life. The choices you make will stay with you forever."

My father was never very good at generating excitement.

My mother wore a plain black dress — either to mourn my childhood or in preparation for some relative's upcoming funeral. She was the youngest of ten, so funerals were as close as the Carltons came to attending the theatre.

She wiped her eyes with a handkerchief and stood outside in the thin gray hallway with a flickering overhead light. Then she insisted I pose for a picture with each of them. Because I am an only child, no pictures exist of me with both my parents. Flipping through a family photo album, you might think I'm the product of a broken home, a not unreasonable conclusion.

My parents left me to my future, and I decided to explore the city where I'd live for the next four years. When considering colleges, I recall someone commenting that Athens, Georgia, where the University does not so much reside as dominate, was the "Santa Fe of the Southeast." I'd never been to Santa Fe so I found the phraseology appealing in a faintly romantic sense. It wasn't until years later when I'd actually visited the New Mexico city that I learned it was also absurd: Santa Fe is nothing like Athens.

I didn't own a car, but the University campus was easy enough to traverse on foot. I was raised in a neighborhood with no sidewalks, where my mother's 1982 Buick Century transported me from school to our house or some other appropriate place like a dark gray hearse. The sidewalks on campus felt paved in yellow brick, but I didn't know what to ask for from any wizard I met along the way. I got as far as the Arch — three somewhat foreboding black iron pillars topped by an open half-moon, it separated the campus from downtown. I stood behind it and stared down College Avenue. There was not much of a downtown where I grew up — at least at the time — so the eyeful of lively restaurants and shops appealed to me. But I didn't cross Broad Street and instead retreated back to campus. That's how I wound up stumbling into the Science Library.

Later that afternoon, I wandered along Sanford Drive to the Tate Student Center, which seemed large enough to contain all the houses in my neighborhood on each of its many levels. There was a movie theater on the third floor of Tate, but the only thing playing when I entered was an instructional short advising me how to make friends with my roommate, even if he's a drug fiend, a slob, or a kleptomaniac. I went outside to sit on Tate's concrete steps with its view of the Plaza, where it felt like the entire student body had assembled for a gathering to which I'd not been invited. It was not an unusual feeling, as familiar as my uniform of neatly pressed khakis and blue dress shirt, which I'd continued to wear even after my mother stopped selecting my clothing for me.

"You're not having a good time."

The voice was soft and warm, slow-moving with a bit of a splash and without a trace of any accent that might link it to a specific place. I turned to the source of the melody and briefly thought the September afternoon heat had induced a mirage. The young woman from the Science Library stood perfectly straight on the landing above me, her arms folded behind her back and her right leg swinging in front of her otherwise still form like the pendulum on a grandfather clock.

"I can always tell when someone's not having a good time," she claimed. "My parents would send me out at parties like an early warning device."

I took off my glasses and shook them as though the wires were loose. When I put them back on, she was still there. The bright, caramel-apple face looking at me was a spectacle of symmetry: Every feature assembled perfectly but not in any fixed or routine way, so you were compelled to return to it, to see if there was anything you'd missed in the frivolous seconds you squandered blinking. Floating on this oasis was a pair of white-framed rhinestone-studded sunglasses. They fitted over a nose that curved slightly upward — not arrogantly but like she'd just smelled a pie baking in the next room, causing her ripe lips to dampen at the prospect of a slice.

She sat next to me, crossing her long legs at the ankles and working out a cramp in her right foot. There was a simmering reddish-brown glow in her round cheeks, as if she were blushing and you were possibly the cause. It pulled you in and enticed you to say something — anything — that might result in a smile from those still-moist lips.

"How are you?"

She either ignored or answered my question with a shrug. She cocked her head toward Tate Plaza. "Everyone out here is having a good time. It's hard to relax." She folded in half and touched the tips of her shoes. "What's your name?" she murmured into her knees.

I mumbled something close to what appeared on my birth certificate.

"Brad," she repeated, giving the word a lyricism that had never before existed.

She stood up while readjusting the fedora topping her bed of black curls, and before I could say or do anything to convince her otherwise, she descended the steps as though riding an escalator. Her direction was uncertain — she seemed to pass through the crowd like they were the mist from a waterfall — but it was distinctly away from the observed "good time."

I couldn't possibly expect to see her again. Thirty thousand students attended the University; I'd once considered its size a plus. The odds of another meeting were miniscule, but I couldn't forget that face or the voice that had rendered my favorite songs arid and dry. I half expected sand to pour out of my Walkman when I opened its case. So, although not the least bit rational, I spent the next few days drifting through areas I thought she might find suitable to "relax."

An obvious choice was North Campus, an arboretum with a ceiling of trees and walls of classical, Greco-Roman buildings and where sidewalk shores bound seas of deep grass. You were far enough from Tate Plaza and Sanford Stadium that the chants of "go dogs, sic 'em" could fade away, and amid the pastoral stillness, you might briefly consider yourself a great scholar. My pursuits weren't quite so academic when I sat on a bench outside the chalk white New College building (it was about 170 years old but, as such things are relative, was still newer than the Old College building). My headphones blocked out the sound of temporally displaced hippies playing Hacky Sack nearby, as I waited with rising anticipation for a woman in rhinestone-studded sunglasses to emerge like a maelstrom from the still waters surrounding me.

I took quick breaks during my vigil for gloomy meals at one of the dining halls. Snelling and Oglethorpe were closer to Myers, so I was probably lost when I wound up at Bolton, which was just across the street from Creswell Hall — a grotesque high-rise dorm that seemed to forever cast a T-shaped shadow on the building.

Bolton was the largest dining hall and thus had the most expansive cereal selection. Students sat at what looked like dissection tables where autopsies were performed. The white students dined on the first floor, and the black students ate downstairs. No segregation laws were required for this arrangement — it was self-imposed. I carried my tray with its bowl of Cap'n Crunch to the second floor, with the international students, and timed how long it took for my lunch to turn soggy.

Wednesday evening came, and I sat through a screening of *The Fisher King* at Brumby Hall, an all-girls dorm at the top of an imposing hill. Most of those assembled were freshmen boys, who'd scaled the hill in hopes of more than stale popcorn. I ate my complimentary bag without considering that a woman in a fedora might appear in the Rotunda, the large, circular room where the movie was shown on a big-screen TV, but I nonetheless felt disappointment as the credits rolled that she hadn't.

I lingered needlessly for a few minutes — standing on the cold terracotta floor and looking somewhat lost as my listless eyes surveyed the Rotunda's dome, which crinkled like a white paper fan.

Two blondes approached me. They dressed identically: gray Georgia T-shirt, Adidas track shorts, and black-and-white sandals.

"Hi," Blonde No. 1 said. "We noticed you sitting by yourself during the movie. So we came by to say hello. We're having a little get-together tomorrow night, and we're wondering if you'd like to come."

Blonde No. 2 smiled vacantly.

"It'll be fun," Blonde No. 1 promised. "We're just going to hang-out for a while, you know, and discuss Jesus and the kind of man he was."

I was relieved to have some explanation, no matter how potentially sinister, for their friendliness.

"I know it's short notice," Blonde No. 1 said. "Don't say yes. Don't say no. Just drop by if you can. It's really informal. We live in Soule. Our number's 1919. Call us after eight, and we'll let you in."

Two white girls giving me their phone number and suggesting an after-hours rendezvous should have aroused some degree of interest in me, but it only made the situation more eerie. I raced back to my dorm. A certain face and voice still whipped through my mind with a gale force, so when I stopped outside the front door of Myers to wipe the sweat from my forehead, I was amazed to see their owner flowing gently through the lobby.

She held her panama hat in place with one hand while the rustling from a standing fan rippled her ankle-length dress. As she crossed the hall, a beast — all black skin and muscles — pounced at her from behind a couch, grinning carnivorously as he stalked her.

"Hey, sis, I remember you," he said. She didn't stop; in fact, her pace quickened as if his very existence offended her. "You were in my Orientation group."

"Was I?" She'd just defined the rhetorical question.

"Oh yeah, I wouldn't forget you. Say, some friends and I are about to head downtown, and... "

I thought I saw icicles form on her sunglasses.

"I don't know you, and I don't like strangers."

He had no hope of altering this classification because she immediately ascended the stairs. I finally opened the door. Only 400 people lived in Myers — that was all I could think — and *she* was one of them.

I'd dutifully purchased my textbooks for the quarter already, and I spent the better part of the next few days reading them in the Myers lounge. There was a steady stream of movement in the valley between the north and south wings, but by Saturday, it seemed hollow and dry. There'd been no sign of her.

I was finished with my textbooks at this point and was more prepared than perhaps any incoming freshman in the University's history. I ventured over to the University Book Store in Tate Plaza and splurged on a hardback collection of poems by E.E. Cummings, where I thought I'd find more relevant answers for what I felt than I had in anything else I'd read that week.

The door to my room was wide open when I came back shortly before 1, and a tall, broad-shouldered fellow was plugging in a computer. Once he noticed me, he grabbed my hand and squeezed it tightly.

"How ya doin'? I'm Barry."

I knew this already. University Housing had sent me a mini-dossier on him during the summer. Barry was a sophomore biology major from Smyrna and presumably had no need to spend the past week feeling welcome.

A polite but superfluous exchange occurred during which we asked each other things already fully covered in the dossier.

Barry ran his fingers through his hair, which was weighed down with the greasy kid stuff of 1950s teen movies. I was glad we shook hands prior to this.

"You have a TV?"

"I don't watch TV," I replied.

"Wow. Well, I've got a small set at home. I'll bring it up next week."

His tone irritated me. I didn't mind his having a TV, but he shouldn't make it seem as if he were doing me a favor.

"You must get up early." He sat with a creak on his unmade bed. "We got here about 10 and you were up and out already." There was an awkward silence; the room shrank the more I contemplated having to see him every day for thirty weeks.

"Hey."

A girl with hair like overcooked spaghetti stood in the doorway — her torso obscured by two Styrofoam containers.

"I parked in a staff spot," she said. "Do you think I'll get a ticket?"

"Nah," Barry reassured her, taking the top container. "They don't start giving out tickets until Monday."

"Oh good." Her drawl reminded me of the Confederate flag hanging in the room across the hall. "Daddy'll kill me if I get another ticket."

Barry introduced us: Her name was Susie and when she heard mine, she curled her fingers at me and repeated, "Hey." It now felt like I had two roommates, and the way she cuddled up to him on his bed reinforced the impression that I'd see more of her.

Barry popped open his plate. The aroma of grease and a foul imitation of chicken filled the room.

"You know, I shouldn't eat this," she whimpered. "I heard there are 3,000 calories in each meal."

"Yeah, well, you better watch it." He dipped a chicken finger into a cup of brown sauce. "You're getting fat." He pinched her nonexistent hips.

"Stop it!" Susie giggled, exposing her dental history. She still wore braces, which made me wonder if she were even old enough to drive alone at night.

This was a good time to excuse myself. I returned to my armchair in the lounge and read Cummings for a while until I heard a girl call out, "Jesus H., Razinski, is this really where you live?"

I felt a chill, and I thought for a moment that Myers had suddenly installed air conditioning.

"It's not so bad," her companion defended through a full mouth. "There's a computer lab."

"Whatever. Just grab your stuff and let's go."

I was halfway through *somewhere i have never traveled, gladly beyond* when a green-nailed hand snatched the book from me.

"Shit, this is really Cummings. I thought you were reading porn under there."

Looming over me was hair the color and thickness of the most aggressive ivy. It surrounded a stately, brick brown face, which was marred only by a nose ring and a cigarette jutting from a mouth that looked like it had just tasted something unacceptable. Slightly obscured by the climbing vines of green were deep panes of icy blue that allowed their owner to inspect and scrutinize — as they did to me now — but without revealing to you anything taking place within.

It seemed unlikely that this face had been confined to an office, a checkout line, or anywhere else indoors during the summer, but it was less likely that its rich color came from lounging on a beach. For instance, the equally brown arm that now held my book boasted a confident firmness. My guess was it had spent the past few months swinging a baseball bat or a tennis racket or some other instrument of leisurely yet spirited exertion. A white tank top with the words "FUCK THA POLICE" attempted with moderate success to contain the unyielding structure facing me.

I thought the only appropriate reaction was to introduce myself.

"You have a frat boy's name," she said with amused contempt. "And wardrobe. You didn't rush, did you?"

Her companion had bounded down the north stairwell in time to interject, "Only assholes rush. Anyone who rushes is an asshole."

Although his voice had left puberty, his speech was still stuck in the vocal cracks of adolescence. He was tall — well over six feet, and his white T-shirt and knee-length blue jean shorts hung limply on a body where weight departed quickly for fear of loitering. They were the only unenthusiastic things about him. His ungainly arms and legs, even his thin, sloping nose and vertical shoot of curly dark hair were a blur of movement. He was constantly shifting positions — not from nervousness but more out of an insatiable curiosity, as though the wonders of the age would reveal themselves if he suddenly sat on the end of a chair... or maybe on its armrest... or maybe just stand for a second while jumping in place. This contrasted with the girl next to him whose gestures were so subtle and assured she didn't appear to move until she'd already done so. It was like passing a store you thought was always in a certain spot but was now down the street.

"Carlton reads poetry," she said, nudging her companion's bony elbow with my book; he repeated my last name and then exclaimed, "Oh, like that guy from the *Fresh Prince*!"

I replied that I'd never seen the show. The girl's thin lips turned upward.

"We're going to Atlanta." The imperious tone of her voice had me practically standing at attention. "You should come with us."

I'm not sure why I left with her. Romanticism, as well as basic self-preservation, should have kept me safely in the Myers lounge waiting for... something to happen, but I must have had a bit of the rapscallion in me that afternoon because I thrilled at the notion of doing something my parents could not have approved of less. This is the motive for the best decisions anyone makes in college.

I walked parallel to her on the pavement, as she tramped through Myers's small park of a front lawn while her companion, who introduced himself to me as Andy, stared hypnotically at the tattoo of a rabbit on her right shoulder blade. I thought it improper to examine more closely, but it looked like the rabbit was dead.

She reached into the pocket of her camouflage pants and snaked out a set of keys to a dark blue Porsche illegally parked next to a fire hydrant. I briefly suspected the car had been stolen, so I sought to allay my fears with an offhand comment.

"Nice car."

"Graduation present," she said. I wore mine on my feet — an unfashionable but serviceable pair of sneakers. "You're riding shotgun, Carlton, and because this is Georgia, you'll be carrying an actual shotgun."

She tossed my book in the back with Andy, who stretched across the seats to accommodate his height. I'd barely fastened my seat belt before she tore down Lumpkin Street.

My abductor's name was Heather — at least that's what Andy called her. I initially thought it was in jest. Heather was so normal a name that I imagined someone going so far as to alter herself with green hair and a tattoo would start first by changing it.

Her full name, I learned, was Heather Jordan Butler Aulds. I discovered this from a glance at her driver's license when she asked me to rummage through her bag for a certain CD (Public Enemy, I think, or N.W.A. — either way, I found it unlistenable). The dramatic formality of her name shocked me less than the fact she actually had a license. She was an appallingly reckless driver: We made it to Atlanta in just under an hour, which was only possible if you ignored all traffic laws and a few related to physics. The music didn't help: She'd periodically join the angry voice vibrating through the speakers and gyrate in her seat, her hands abandoning the wheel as I mentally prepared for a head-on collision. Seemingly unconcerned about his own mortality, Andy exchanged high fives with her during their shouted utterances of "bass," "gang bang," and "motherland."

I had passed my driver's test on the eighth attempt — hand-eye coordination was not one of my more prominent traits — and drove like someone's elderly grandmother, halting, nervous, with both hands on the wheel and the radio turned off. In contrast, I suppose Heather was less reckless than in complete control, like a stunt driver during a car chase scene.

The trip itself was sufficient exercise of whatever whim of Heather's had motivated it. Once on Euclid Avenue, she rolled her eyes and declared, "What a dump." Andy compared Atlanta unfavorably to Chicago, which he believed was the greatest city in the country — far better than New York, which was all "flash" and no "substance."

"You're thinking of L.A.," Heather corrected. "Possibly Miami."

"No, I meant... "

"New York is more dirty and mean," she said with finality. "Sort of skanky, actually."

I'd never been to Los Angeles or Miami; my New York experience was limited to a school trip five years earlier, so I was more than pleased with Atlanta that afternoon. The Little Five Points neighborhood in particular had the bohemian flair of the Greenwich Village I knew from movies, and compared to where I grew up, the streets teemed with the excitement of Times Square.

Heather lit a cigarette and spoke into a cupped hand she held over her mouth to guard against a rare but pleasant breeze.

"Where you from, Carlton?"

Specifically, I was from Piedmont, South Carolina and more specifically, an area within it called for no discernible reason Moonville, but generally all part of the county of Greenville. I decided to answer with the slightly more impressive generality.

"Oh." She was not impressed. "Not much now but up and coming. They're building a BMW plant."

The three of us wandered around in that youthful way that is defiantly oblivious to time. Eventually, hunger directed us to Planet Bombay, my first exposure to Indian cuisine. The food was as spicy as Heather's mouth. Every other word was a vulgarity, which, combined with her boisterous tenor, had me half-convinced we'd be asked to leave. She spoke like someone fluent in a language that wasn't her own and impressed with her mastery of it.

Andy Razinski, meanwhile, was an open book that screamed its contents into your ear. This was foreign enough to me to generate a consistent sense of discomfort. He made a lot of chest-thumping statements that I presumed were intended to impress Heather — either romantically or the way a puppy attempts to curry favor with its pack leader.

At one point, he asked me if I'd read Nietzsche. He said the name of the German philosopher as if he were a Founding Father, someone even the most average student should know intimately.

"No, I haven't," I said, slightly startled by the forcefulness of his question.

"You should read *Thus Spoke Zarathustra*," he insisted. "For a start. It speaks to people like us." He included Heather, who was as engaged in our discussion as someone at a bar casually checking the score of a game on the TV.

"Razinski was raised by hippies," she said after seeming to realize we were still there. "That's where all the philosophy comes from. It's a waste of perfectly good pot."

The waiter had chosen that precise moment to bring the check. He looked at me as if I might be Heather's supplier. Andy continued:

"You know, basically Christians are herd animals." This drew stares from the next table, which Andy ignored. "It's as true now as it was then. You see it here with the Greek system, the way people join things, this need to belong to a collective."

His fervor reminded me of the two girls I met after *The Fisher King*.

"Yankees are usually atheists." Heather smirked at me from across the table. "I think it's the weather."

Andy was from Schaumburg, Illinois — just thirty miles north of Chicago but still what Heather derisively called "the 'burbs." He had confused her constant flippancy with earnestness, so he continued his efforts to convert her to his way of thinking.

"What's your major?" Andy asked me suddenly, draining the last drop of Pepsi from a glass almost as tall as he was. Heather and I each sipped ice tea.

"Journalism."

"Jesus H., Carlton. The J school here's like fucking DeVry," Heather snorted. "I'm surprised they don't make you wear uniforms and nametags."

This annoyed me.

"What are *you* studying?" I asked.

"History" was her response. "Like my mother before me."

"What will you do with that?" I was genuinely curious. I didn't see her as a teacher, and a history degree didn't seem to offer many other alternatives.

Heather shrugged, as if it was of no consequence to her.

"For Karen, it was just an MRS degree." Her parents were the only people she seemed to call by their first names. Her face grew suspiciously solemn: "Maybe I'll discover a new century."

"History is not very existential. You're focused on the past, rather than the present."

"You're a fucking philosophy major," Heather said, not even bothering to raise her voice. This field of study, which I didn't even know existed until that moment, seemed less tangible to me than history. "Whatever, Razinski, we know you're basically pre-law."

This bit of stark reality seemed to silence Andy for a second — though I had no reason to believe it would last long. Neither did Heather, I think, because upon noticing the darkening sky through the window by our table, she declared it was time to leave.

Heather paid for our meals with a platinum credit card that gleamed so impressively on top of the check it could have been accepted as currency itself. I recall Miss Miller commenting once that she'd "sworn off plastic... at least until I get back to zero." There apparently had been a "misunderstanding" involving an "ancient" student loan.

As Miss Miller had done multiple times over the summer, Heather waved off my attempts to pay for my share of the bill. "No worries," she said as though she'd given me a stick of gum.

"We should do something," she said listlessly as we walked down Moreland Avenue. Boredom lay in the dark shadows and back alleys and the only cure was the varied storefronts we passed. "What do nice young people do?"

Heather suddenly turned and entered a tattoo parlor. They were about to close, but Heather convinced them to remain open long enough to give her a third tattoo — this one on her waist and in the shape of a black panther. I'd never before witnessed first-hand the persuasive effect of freely offered money.

Andy and I stood in a corner and watched this bizarre piece of performance art. At least I stayed there until Andy started up again on Nietzsche, herd animals, and slave morality — all very sophisticated gibberish. I excused myself and sat on a stool next to Heather, as the tattooist completed his work. She chain-smoked Marlboro Reds during the procedure, which despite my limited knowledge of the process struck me as unwise.

Attempting to pass the time and still hungry after dinner, I ventured to learn more about the girl I'd just met a few hours ago. I only got out of her that she was born and raised in Atlanta before she insouciantly declared, "You ask very probing questions, Carlton."

The day had encouraged me to respond, "That's why I came to DeVry."

Heather's laughter forced the tattooist to stop until she settled down. The resulting profanity directed at me felt somewhat like applause or a bawdy welcome mat.

She dropped Andy and me off at Myers just after midnight. As her Porsche disappeared into the darkness, I realized my book was still in her backseat.

Walking from the parking lot to the quad, Andy suggested we exchange numbers, and he explained how he would mentally store mine by thinking of it as "fourteen ninety three" rather than "1-4-9-3." "I never have to use the phone book," he boasted. His way was the mark of a lateral thinker, the other the province of the linear thinker. He had a whole complex theory about the inflexibility of linear thinkers through which I politely smiled and nodded. I wasn't sure if he was a lateral thinker because that was the superior method or if he only thought it was the superior method because he was a lateral thinker.

On our way inside, I happened to notice a red glow coming from the third-floor window just beneath mine on the south wing. I remember absently waving goodbye to Andy while standing there gazing at it with the same intensity that he'd given Heather's shoulder blade on several occasions throughout the day. At the time, I couldn't have told you why I was so drawn to it, but I didn't go back to my room until it was gone.

2

My father had defined my mornings for as long as I could remember. He'd never missed a day of work and was never late, and such discipline was instilled in me. We were up each morning at 6:45, dressed and eating a breakfast of cold cereal by 7:15, and out the door for school and work by 7:45.

I suppose I should have fled such regimentation at my first opportunity. Yet I wound up arranging my schedule accordingly, so my day began at 7:50 a.m. and ended three hours later. Empty desks surrounded me during my first two classes, but attendance rose moderately for my 10 a.m. class, History 251, which met in a mammoth lecture hall in the city-block-spanning Journalism Building. From the back row, I could barely make out the professor, which wasn't a great loss because he only told bad jokes while his teaching assistants passed out the syllabus.

Midway through class, the lady in the rhinestone-studded sunglasses slid into the desk next to me. I stared at her for a moment in astonishment before averting my gaze. I was probably asleep. The lecture was certainly dull enough. But my face never burned so fiercely in my dreams.

She rested her head on her closed hand and watched the stage like she'd wandered into a play during the second act and didn't understand why she couldn't follow the plot. No evidence existed of her enrollment in this class — or any class. There was no backpack slung across her shoulder, no space in her purse for notebooks or textbooks, no copy of her schedule clutched tightly in her hands. She could have just wandered in off a movie set, secretly conducting research for an upcoming role.

Her tan ballroom shoe struck a percussive beat against the bottom of my desk. She turned suddenly and spoke to me as if resuming a lengthy conversation.

"This is boring. He's boring." The professor had just made a painful joke about the Civil War. "Aren't you bored?"

Boredom was not the emotion I experienced at present. I started to speak, but she halted my words with a raised hand. Mimicking a magician about to perform an elaborate illusion, she pulled at the sleeves of her short crepe jacket to demonstrate there was nothing up them.

"Wanna see a magic trick?" she whispered and then added with an expressive wave of her hands, "Let's disappear."

Those same beige hands pulled me from my seat. There was little stealth involved in our vanishing act — she laughed all the way out of the room, and I cast anxious glances behind us in fear that the TAs were in pursuit. Once we were safely outside, I senselessly offered her my newspaper as protection from the dissipating drizzle.

"A little water never hurt anyone," she said as an Orbit bus screeched to a halt in front of us. "I took one of these this morning. I got so lost. But I'm always lost."

She apparently held no grudge against campus transit because she boarded while flipping and then unflipping the curved brim of her hat. I followed her to the back of the bus. She smoothed out her knee-length tulip skirt as she sat down.

The University's color scheme extended to its transportation — the seats were bright red, the window frames jet black. We'd completed half a lap around campus before I could conceive of anything to say that wouldn't expose me as a complete fool.

"How was your summer?"

She was looking out the window, so her reflection spoke to me.

"Why would you want to know that? You didn't even know me this summer. You might as well ask me how my tenth birthday was."

Taken aback, I extemporized, "So, uh, how was your tenth birthday?"

Turning away from the window, she pulled off her sunglasses.

"Divine," she answered softly. "My family and I saw *42nd Street*."

Her eyes were wide, deep, and dark — blacker even than the lenses of her shades and with a thin burst of flame along the rims. Her eyelids were heavy from the weight of lashes that swayed like the fronds of a palm tree. The only reason I could think of for a woman with eyes like those to always wear sunglasses was that they were less for her protection than for yours.

After reminding myself this was a conversation and not a reverie, I confirmed with her that she'd seen the show on Broadway, and then, helpless against those eyes, I started talking about myself, which I never do.

"I went to New York for the first time in June of '87," I babbled. "It was a Beta Club trip. We saw *Cats*."

She made a face and patted my hand consolingly.

"I can't stand that show. They don't look like cats. They don't act like cats. It's just so bizarre. Anyway, we wouldn't have bumped into each other. I'm rarely in the city during the summer."

"You're from New York?"

She tapped her nose, then closed her eyes and rubbed her temples with her index fingers.

"I know what you're thinking: You're wondering why I came all the way down here for school." She ended the swami act and shrugged. "Your guess is as good as mine. I didn't give it that much thought. Sometimes, you just need to get away."

She spoke of college as some sort of vacation resort, where there was no pressure to build a foundation for the future. I envied anyone who could regard the whole experience so lightly.

She removed from her purse a leather-bound address book, the kind a lawyer might use. Thumbing through the pages, she stopped at the one dated exactly a week ago.

"Here's what I wrote about you."

I stared at the entry in a mild shock. It read:

Met a boy today. Seems very sweet. Wonder what he'd bring to a potluck dinner? Of course, I think potluck dinners are molto tacky.

She pushed back a yawn with her cupped hands; her nails were bright purple.

"You don't know my name," she said without segue.

She wrote in a decorous, cursive hand under the day's date: *Janet Tomalin, You Know My Name (Look Up the Number)*. Ripping out September 21, she folded the page and tucked it neatly inside my shirt pocket.

"Aren't you going to reciprocate?"

I had trouble remembering my number now. I concentrated.

"It's 1-4-9-3," I said — first in my head, then out loud.

"Fourteen ninety three! You better call me!" she chanted as if reciting a nursery rhyme. She slid her sunglasses back on with the thumb and forefinger of each hand. "I think this is your stop."

We were back where we started. I got off the bus and watched it lurch forward into the fog, her white hat peeking through the pane glass window. It's very disorienting when your day climaxes so early.

"Hey, B., what's up!"

Andy Razinski, his backpack slung over one shoulder, moved aggressively toward me from across the street.

"How's the first day, man?"

"Not bad."

"My Intro to Philosophy class is incredible! My professor is so existential. She just railed against society for an hour."

"That's great."

He was full of the restless energy of someone eager to return to class — to learn still more and challenge others with that knowledge. If I were capable of looking at myself from Andy's vantage, I imagine I'd see the yearning expression of someone who wished he was back on the Orbit bus.

He steered me around with the back of his hand.

"Let's go to Heather's. She should be up by now."

I asked him where on campus she lived.

"She's not in the dorms, B." He would continue to call me "B." although no syllables were saved in the practice. "She has her own place at River Mill."

River Mill was a modern apartment complex not far from the Journalism Building, close enough to campus that residents could hear their lectures through an open window.

Heather's Porsche rested in its parking space like a leopard on a tree branch, ready in an instant to strike with a whip-like movement. Andy banged on her door. No answer. He knocked again and shouted, "Hey, Heather, it's us!"

A muffled roar came from inside: "It's open, dammit!"

Drawn curtains darkened the room. The only piece of furniture was a black leather sofa that I didn't think was more than a few weeks old. Green-nailed toes waved at us from the armrest. We sat across from Heather on unpacked boxes.

"What happened to you?" Andy asked.

"Parties. Plural," she mumbled into a black throw pillow. "Got in at 6 this morning."

"You didn't go to class?"

"What the hell for, Carlton? They only pass out the syllabus." She rose with trepidation, her plaid bathrobe conforming to her compact frame. Steadying herself, she announced, "Need food."

She shuffled off into her bedroom and returned ten minutes later wearing ragged blue jean shorts that were higher, more revealing, and overall more effective than Andy's. Competing with the shorts for attention was a white T-shirt with a crude drawing of a ten-gallon hat and the inscription *Never Trust a Cowboy — Bono '92.*

Andy shot up. "Should we do the Luau at Snelling? It's all you can eat."

"Jesus H.! You live in the dorms and you're on the meal plan? You are high-lariously freshmen."

This was Heather's first year, as well, but I got the feeling she never did anything for the first time.

Throwing on a ten-gallon hat of her own, Heather herded us from River Mill to downtown. I felt strangely secure in the hands of our wrangler as she guided us to a benign destination for cattle — The Grit, a vegetarian restaurant on Prince Avenue.

We sat in slightly kitschy dinette chairs around a square table in the center of the room. Andy's restless eyes followed a zigzag pattern on the tiled floor to the day's specials listed on a black chalkboard above the bar.

"The menu looks more appetizing than what's on it," he complained. "I don't understand vegetarians. It's natural to eat meat. We're carnivores."

"Omnivores, Mr. Wizard," Heather retorted. "The public school system has failed you."

Andy quickly changed the subject, leaning forward to ask me what I thought of my roommate. I told him I hadn't formed an opinion.

"He can't possibly be worse than the dumbass they gave me. This morning, he comes out of the bathroom, rubbing his belly, and says, 'Doncha hate it when you have to shit after taking a shower? It just ruins it.' Who the hell wants to hear that first thing in the morning?"

"As opposed to hearing it now?" Heather said with disgust.

"Yeah, well, he's a fucking psycho! His side of the room is covered with *Playboy* centerfolds and he has all these videos — girl on guy, girls on guys, girls on girls. And after he watches them, he goes into the bathroom and... I don't even want to talk about it."

Heather pounded a pack of cigarettes against her palm and said with no apparent sympathy, "That's what you get for living in a student ghetto."

Andy was two floors below me in a suite — two rooms united by a private bathroom. Personally, I preferred the relative anonymity of the hall baths, rather than intimately knowing the three other people sitting on my toilet and bathing in my tub.

"You know they deliberately set you up with opposites? It's supposed to be a 'learning experience.'" He snapped his fingers. "You know what I should do? Next year, I'll fill out my housing application so I'm the complete opposite of who I really am. That way, they'll give me someone normal."

"But what if everyone does that?" I asked.

He dismissed the idea. "No, they aren't that clever."

A pair of PanHellenics, blonde and brown, paused by our table. I'd noticed them earlier gently squabbling over whether this was the place that served burgers and milkshakes. Having determined by the menu that this was *not* in fact The Grill, which was in College Square, they were on their way out when they rubbernecked at Heather.

"Heather Aulds, is that you?"

She stared at the two girls with icy contempt.

"I barely recognized you," one of the girls said. "Your mom was at the house last week. She's really bummed that you didn't rush."

The other girl observed the tufts of green that extended from Heather's cowboy hat and crept over her face and shoulders.

"Are you like an art major or something?"

Heather lit a cigarette, and these two unpleasant reminders of her past wandered off along the plumes of smoke.

"Karen *really* thought I'd pitch my tent in a frat boy cafeteria," she said to us with self-amused scorn. "And she whines to the other Phi Mu-rons about how her only daughter ended a legacy of four generations! That's so like her."

Andy devoured his spinach quessidissimo with game bemusement. The lentil burger I ordered served mostly as practice for cutting techniques with my knife and fork. Later, a pen temporarily replaced a cigarette, a credit card receipt was signed, and we followed our cowboy out onto Prince.

Heather Aulds roamed downtown with the confidence of someone in her own backyard, occasionally stopping as if to mentally note, "Good place we have here," but I thought the streets and avenues we passed glittered with an unfading novelty.

I'd escaped, for the moment, a city of gray buildings and silent neighborhoods. Athens was a town of bright colors — sidewalks that sprouted green, leafy trees on every corner and red brick buildings where inside you could buy everything you wanted and nothing you really needed.

Shortly before 8, an unseen hand lit the ornate black candelabras along the streets that cast everything within their reach in a cool blue. Bars and clubs stirred from their daily sleep, and music stumbled rowdily out the doors. None of this ignited wonder in Heather's indifferent eyes. The present offered little that she hadn't viewed already in her past, so she forged ahead to the future, to what was new, a demanding hopefulness lingering forever in the crevasses of her glacial voice.

Over the next couple days, Janet Tomalin and the delicately penned challenge she'd given me swirled in my thoughts like a late summer squall. Her number was the key to a door I feared opening, even if inside promised a smorgasbord of delights, and I found myself watching the date on the page slip further into the past.

My roommate's cordless phone was never far from my timid hand, and I'd turn it over to him whenever his girlfriend called, which was often but welcome because it forced him to turn off the TV. This continued until 3:58 Thursday morning when the phone rang again, but this time I heard Janet murmur into the receiver, "Let's get dinner."

It didn't matter if it were 4 a.m. or 4 p.m. I rushed downstairs in under a minute. Janet faced the front door, staring intently at the falling rain and softly singing "Night in Tunisia." The rain splattering against the French windows, the ticking clock in the empty lobby, the tip-tap of her polka-dot heels with red soles... they all provided a fitting musical accompaniment. Sensing my presence, perhaps from my awed reflection in the glass, she stopped abruptly and greeted me with an eager wave behind her back.

As fascinated as Janet was by the weather, she dressed in defiance of it, her only concession to the elements a sailor pencil dress and nautical sun hat. We huddled underneath a $2.99 umbrella I'd purchased at the Kangaroo convenience store and continued to walk south toward a golden marquee with the words "Waffle House" printed in simple black letters.

We entered to a blast of fluorescent light and the odor of artificial syrup. Our damp clothes soon stuck to the plastic seat covers of a corner booth.

"Can I tell you something? Can I confide in you? I so need coffee right now. You wouldn't believe." She spoke so quickly I thought she was on her second pot. "Do you ever get really excited about life and then realize it's just the caffeine? It's really depressing, but that just means you need more coffee."

I attempted to wipe the moisture from my glasses with a napkin, as Janet consulted the yellow laminated placemat menu in her hands. After a moment, it fell from her face and she stated, disapprovingly, "You never called me."

She defined "never" differently than most people. It had been two days. I apologized regardless.

"I forgive you," she said graciously. "Food heals all wounds."

"Maybe I could buy you dinner… if that would be all right, I mean."

"Aren't you sweet!" She looked around and whispered, "I left my wallet at home."

I'd been hoodwinked.

The waitress took our order, inducing a giggle fit in Janet, who apparently had never before heard the word "y'all," at least not in person.

"I know what I want," Janet said, composing herself. "I'll have a big bowl of grits and a plate of hash browns. And *coffee*!" She pronounced coffee "caw-fee" and the giggle fits returned.

"May I have the same, please?"

Janet wrinkled her nose in distaste.

"Copycat!"

Something unusual had occurred. My attention, generally confined to the internal workings of my own mind, had extended to include the woman facing me. I added cream to my coffee and offered her the decanter. She shook her head, while humming along to a tune in direct conflict with what played on the jukebox.

"No, thank you, I don't support integration — in coffee, I mean."

"I didn't see you in class today."

"Oh, I dropped that." Her hand lobbed the subject to another booth. "History is such a bore. I mean, what do I care about the past? Or the future, for that matter? It's usually always unpleasant — from past experience, at least. Can you imagine being thirty? Gray hair, crow's feet, and liver spots?

Yuck. And I never want to be sixteen again. No, the present's where it's really at, kiddo."

"I suppose that makes sense," I said, although it didn't. "But you'll have to take history eventually. It's required."

"I don't believe in requirements," she snapped, fiddling with the stems of her sunglasses then adding, as if it explained everything, "You see, I'm an actress."

I had visions of her at auditions and in plays or even movies.

"How long have you been an actress?"

"All my life. I just love being able to escape, to become another person. Don't you ever just want to be someone else?"

"I'd settle for being someone first."

Her full lips curled into a smile then paused as if she'd remembered something vitally important; leaning perilously close to me, she asked with almost religious solemnity, "What's your favorite song?"

Perhaps sensing deliberation exercising rigorously in my mind, she commanded, "Don't think! *Anyone* can think," which resulted in my answering without hesitation, "'Happiness Is a Warm Gun.'"

Her reaction was like nothing I'd ever seen: She squealed, leapt from the table, clapped her hands, and twirled in the aisle before returning to earth. Hugging herself with barely contained delight, she said while laughing, "I'm *so* glad."

Sitting on her hands and swaying to a nonexistent breeze, she resumed humming the sad-yet-catchy melody. The jukebox could not compete. I wanted to tell her how lovely her voice was — a safe, non-lecherous observation, but I was afraid if I started complimenting her, I wouldn't stop.

Our food arrived, and she inhaled her meal in a matter of minutes. Her epicurean enthusiasm must have been contagious because I finished when she did.

"How were the grits?" I asked. I imagined this was the New Yorker's first encounter with them.

"Divine." She slapped her flat stomach. "I really must have Agnes whip some up for me when I'm in the city again."

"Agnes? Is that your mother?"

She looked confused. "Gosh, no, why would I call my mother 'Agnes'? Mother's 'Mother.' And not 'Mom.' That's what my brother calls her, and I don't want to step on toes. I'm not a usurper, you know. Agnes is our cook."

"That must be convenient."

She waved down our waitress for another refill of coffee.

"More than convenient, kiddo — it's critical. We'd all look like Ethiopians without her. Mother can't boil water." She set her sunglasses next to her fork like just another utensil. "Agnes has a daughter about my age, you know. And she has three kids! Can you believe that? Just last month, she got in this big fight with her young man — who's not the father of any of those kids, by the way — and he hauled off and decked her! He broke her nose! Agnes was just a mess about it. I tell you it's inexcusable, just totally inexcusable to cause someone else pain because of your own self-indulgence."

She chugged the contents of her cup without regard to its temperature.

"You're really easy to talk to," she said suddenly.

"Thank you."

Her tongue rotated clockwise behind her closed mouth.

"I'm not sure if I mean that as a compliment yet."

I paid the check while Janet "powdered her nose." Charmed that I knew someone who still used that expression, I listened to Patsy Cline on the jukebox until Janet's fingers danced a quick jig on my head.

"Ready to vamoose, goose?"

Outside, the rising sun heated the air as the storm subsided. Although there was no longer a need for an umbrella, Janet still walked close to me, her curly hair brushing against my face, and I felt a new sensation in the pit of my stomach. The hash browns might have been the culprit, but I doubted it.

3

Although I would like to remember those first few weeks in Athens as being composed entirely of early morning dinners with Janet, the truth was far less thrilling. I went to class every day and evidently was the only one doing so, aside from one other student, whose presence was more mercenary than academic — she transcribed the lectures for the Student Notes Service.

After class that first week, I would rush up seven stone slabs and enter the University's Main Library. The front of the building was a showcase of ancient Greece: A pediment rested on six rectangular columns and "Ilah Dunlap Little Memorial Library" was engraved into the entablature's frieze. I recall thinking this was an amusing example of Southern understatement. The library a half hour from my parents' house was a small room next to a barber shop that stocked mostly Danielle Steel and Stephen King and a few authors with different names but who wrote about similar romantic or horrific concerns. The "little" Memorial Library was a 146,900 square foot cotillion where I was properly introduced to Oscar Wilde, Truman Capote, and James Baldwin among other dance partners. I'd leave the library with my backpack stuffed with books and read out on a North Campus bench until the setting sun sent me back to Myers where the dance continued under the light of my desk lamp.

It took only a few days for me to discover that "Little" was not a quaint reference to the library itself but the surname of Ilah Dunlap's second husband, John D. Little. The library opened on November 19, 1953, a fact I retained because it was coincidentally the same day Melinda Miller was born somewhere in Colorado.

Miss Miller had advised me to write for the college paper and build a collection of clips unrelated to obituaries. A couple weeks had passed and I'd made no efforts in that direction, but it also occurred to me that after working at the *Greenville News* almost as long as I'd been alive, Miss Miller was still struggling to pay off her student loans and lived in a one bedroom apartment smaller than Heather Aulds's River Mill place. Journalism suddenly seemed less "safe" and "practical," but I felt caught already within the eddy of my declared major. So Thursday afternoon — my Waffle House meal still very much with me, I walked over to 123 North Jackson Street, which held the offices of the student newspaper, the *Red & Black*.

The receptionist, not looking up from her paper, which wasn't the *Red & Black* but the *Athens Daily News*, directed me to Jennifer Howard, the new writers' editor. I climbed a suspicious staircase to the main office. The floor wheezed with every step and I feared interrupting the receptionist's reading by falling through and landing in her lap. The only person in the wood-paneled room played air drums at her desk with a pair of pencils. I assumed this was Jennifer and introduced myself.

"Wow! You really want to write for us. That's super!" Her effusive reaction implied I was her first new writer. The carefully stacked papers and tidy rows of freshly sharpened pencils and paperclips indicated either extreme boredom or the early stages of obsessive-compulsive disorder. "You know, I was on the other side of that desk a year ago, so I know how nervous you might be."

"I'm not nervous."

"Don't be afraid to admit it. That's what I'm here for. I'll guide you through it. You don't have to be scared."

"I'm not scared."

She took this as an unintended compliment.

"Great! See, that's why I'm here."

"I'll take any assignment you might have," I said in my "Ambitious Young Go-Getter" voice. "I'm eager to get started and..."

"That's just a super attitude! Jump right in!" She handed me an index card. "I got this one yesterday, so it's just hot off the press!" She made a sizzling sound. "It's about students who put themselves through school by working really funky jobs. This is the number of one of the guys, and he should get you in touch with a few others. He's a real creep, by the way. Dated both me and my roommate at the same time!" She shook her fist. "But journalistic integrity and all that! He'll still get fair treatment here."

"Right," I said shortly. "When do you need this done?"

She continued smiling even while sipping coffee from Espresso Royale Café next door. "End of the week is fine. Take your time. And if you find you can't or don't want to do it, just call me — my number's on there, too — and I can reassign it. Good luck."

She never expected to see me again.

I made the phone calls and conducted the interviews the following day. I focused on a grad student who taught ninth grade during the day, attended night school, and worked weekends at the Baxter Street Chevron Station. Her students would come in every so often to make fun of her.

"Wow! You came back!" Jennifer exclaimed when I showed up Sunday with my story. "I always thought you would. There was just something about you that said, 'He'll be back.'"

She set me down behind her computer.

"OK, a couple of pointers: We don't indent for paragraphs here. Don't ask me why. Just relax and write it as best you can. When you're done, I'll help you with any changes. And if I do change anything, it doesn't mean there's anything's wrong with you."

When I'd finished, she read my piece with the glee of a proud parent, every so often mouthing a "wow" or a "super."

"I'm really impressed," she said. "And you're just a freshman? What kind of background do you have?"

I told her about my internship.

"That's so cool! Look, you wanted to eventually write for entertainment, right?" I nodded, and she led me by the arm into the next room. It felt like we were in a dinghy and transferring our weight from one space to the next caused the office to shift slightly. "You should meet our entertainment editor, Gwen Lupo."

Hiding behind one of the less outdated Macs was a frightfully malnourished girl. There was not an ounce of fat on her body, and what little gamey muscle there was in her arms and legs looked like it was acquired fleeing from predators.

"He wants to write for you," Jennifer explained to Gwen, who tugged nervously on a pale brown pigtail. "He's really good. I mean, his first story was just super. I think you should give him a chance."

"I understand I won't be able to start writing reviews right away," said Mr. Ambitious Young Go-Getter, "but I'm willing to work up to it."

"He has such a super attitude!" Jennifer cried.

"Well..." Gwen's country-fried voice circled the room like a frightened moth. "We do need some help with our CD reviews." She motioned to the stack of discs tottering in a wire metal bin by her desk.

Another girl entered the room, barely older than the others and still dressed for church. The morning's sermon was fresh in her voice, which seemed to broadcast serenity. Its soothing rattle even charmed Gwen out from behind her computer.

"Jennifer," she said gently, "do you have anything we can use for tomorrow?"

"Wow, Lori, I actually do," Jennifer replied — not quite convinced herself. She squeezed my arm, as if seizing onto tangible evidence. "He wrote this super feature, and I didn't even have to change a word."

Lori shook my hand with the intimacy of a hug.

"Welcome," she hummed. I expected her to try and baptize me. "I look forward to reading your work."

Monday, after I saw my story packaged between an article about tuition increases and another on the hazards of Drop/Add, I dialed Janet's number for the first time.

"Oh delicious!" she said when I told her my news. "Come help me pick out something to wear and we'll celebrate."

Those words sent me down a flight of stairs at speeds previously recorded only in Guinness. I passed other residents on the third floor hallway as a blur. Outside Janet's door, I attempted a reserved knock but managed only a surprisingly irregular thumping. She greeted me in a violet dress with sleeves extending to her wrists. It was the first time I'd seen her without a hat; her pitch-perfect black curls flowed in churning rapids along her face.

"Enter freely and of your own will," she said dramatically while making a sweeping gesture inside. A bunk bed and a red-velvet couch faced each other; a shelf — stuffed with tapes and records — sat underneath the window, and framed posters of Broadway musicals and old movies covered the walls like a thick and vibrant coat of paint.

"Where's your roommate?"

"She's with her boyfriend... *off campus*," she said in a stage whisper. "They practically live together. And whenever her parents call, I have to say she's out or in the bathroom, and then have her call them back from her den of sin. It's all very skullduggerous."

She pointed a bare foot at two pairs of silver shoes competing for intimate contact with it.

"So, what do you think? The open or the closed toe?"

Swallowing was suddenly harder than I remembered.

"The open toe's good."

"I'd hoped you would choose those! They're scrumptious!"

She placed her hand on my shoulder to support herself as she slipped them on. In front of me, a lava lamp rested on the windowsill. I recognized it as the source of the glow that had captured my attention the other week.

Her voice gently caressed my cheek:

"What are we waiting for, kiddo? I'm *fah-mished*!"

We had dinner again at the Waffle House, and Janet ordered pecan pie and hash browns, which she ate concurrently. Afterward, we sat out on a bench by the quad. The mugginess hadn't left with the sun, and it felt like the crispness of fall might never arrive. But as sultry as the evening was, I didn't want it to end — ever — and would have held onto it with both fists if possible. Instead, I employed less metaphorical stalling tactics and started asking Janet the questions most pressing in my mind, questions about her, about her life prior to my first glimpse of her, her no doubt exciting life in a city I'd visited all of once.

"Hush!" She pressed a finger against my lips, which almost silenced me forever. "You'll spoil the moment! Don't you just love the air? It's so different here. I can taste it — it's divine, like ice cream slowly melting."

A quiet moment passed during which I stared into the same patch of night as she, vainly attempting to discover whatever held her interest.

"I'm going to ask you a favor now."

I wondered what I could possibly offer her.

"The Tate Theater is showing my favorite movie on Thursday and I'd like you to come with me."

"What is it?" It was an irrelevant question. I'd sit through a John Hughes movie if she wanted.

"*Vertigo*. Have you seen it?"

"No, no, I haven't… but I'm sure I'll like it."

She smiled a smile that was for me only.

"I've seen it about a billion times. My father would take me whenever it played somewhere. It was *our* movie, no one else's."

Her invitation flattered me so completely I would have said something to spoil the moment for sure, but perhaps sensing that, she stood, stretched, put on her sunglasses, and went back inside Myers.

❀❀

Janet and I were at Tate a half hour before the film started Wednesday night; they were still cleaning up from the 6 p.m. show. All week, I'd deliberated over whether I should buy her ticket — would it appear gallant or presumptuous? I wasn't naïve enough to believe this was a date. Her friendship astounded logic enough without my pushing things further. I couldn't imagine she would be interested in me romantically. Unfortunately, I couldn't imagine being interested in anyone else.

She made my decision for me: She'd bought our tickets and was in line for popcorn before I'd even taken out my wallet. Inside the theater, we looked around the black-backed seats with red fillings for the best view of the screen, and there, in third row center, was Andy Razinski. He was alone, which made it impossible for me to not speak to him.

"Oh, hey B.," he said. There was a fleeting moment of shock as he realized Janet was not illusory. I saw him stare unabashedly at her endless legs, and after he rose quickly to provide an unobstructed path to our seats, I also saw him admire her equally full chest and backside as she sauntered past him. I should have found any excuse to sit elsewhere. Still, he *was* alone, and by this point, I'd already barged in on two of his outings with Heather. Rationally, I had no choice, but I regretted my enslavement to courtesy within five minutes of joining him.

"OK, now, the best movie ever, of all time, without debate, without discussion, is *A Clockwork Orange*."

Janet's sunglasses remained fixed on the ceiling. Andy leaned past me. "Don't you agree?"

"Does it matter?" she asked. "You said there was no debate, no discussion."

"Well, have you seen it?"

"Yes, I have," she said flatly. Then with emotion: "I hate it. I couldn't get past the first twenty minutes. It's so violent."

Andy shifted in his seat. "True, the first twenty minutes are pretty graphic, but it's worth it. It's brilliant. It changed my life. Before I saw it, my favorite movie was *Beverly Hills Cop*. I didn't know anything about film."

"And now you know everything?"

"No, that's not what I meant at all, I just…" He took a deep breath. "So, uh, what kind of movies do you like?"

"That's a rather personal question, don't you think?"

Andy didn't see why, so Janet pressed her hand to her heart and answered, "I absolutely adore *Victor/Victoria*. It makes me so happy."

"Really? You like that?" He frowned. "I respect your opinion and all, but I think musicals are just dung. The genre doesn't really lend itself to cinema."

"That's not a very nice thing to say on Julie's birthday."

No clarification followed, but I quickly deduced that it was the actress Julie Andrews whose birthday celebrations Andy's unsolicited critique had potentially diminished.

After Andy mercifully left to get snacks, Janet stood up straight in her seat and brushed away a stray piece of popcorn from her black turtleneck dress. She exhaled loudly, as if she'd been holding her breath.

"I, me, mine, he certainly has his opinions."

"He's a nice guy," I said in the least convincing tone possible.

"I'm sure he is." She bent to retrieve her soda from the carpeted floor and offered me a sip; I tasted her strawberry lipstick on the tip of the straw. "You have excellent taste. Well, almost." She tossed a kernel of popcorn into her mouth. "It's just that..." Her fingers curled around her black chiffon scarf. "Gosh, for the longest time, this was *our* movie." She made a florid motion with her arms. "And then, suddenly, it was just *my* movie. And I sort of hoped that it could be *our* movie again." She made another florid motion, but this one included me. "Oh well."

I was about to apologize, but Andy returned with a pack of Skittles and a Tab just as the lights dimmed and the shimmering red curtains parted. I paid more attention to Janet than to the movie, mainly because of her mood, which was better suited for a funeral and grew worse as the film progressed. Finally, when Kim Novak took her header off the top of the Spanish mission, she burst into tears and fled the theater.

"I'm so sorry." She crouched against the concession stand, wiping her eyes with the backs of her gloved hands. "I'm such an idiot."

"It's actually a tribute to the filmmaker when someone is so moved by a film that they cry," Andy said, placing a hand on her shoulder. Such statements could bring me to tears, but it was no tribute.

On our way back to Myers, Janet walked slightly but distinctly ahead of us, as Andy conducted a lecture on Hitchcock's dazzling use of color and mise-en-scène. The gray clouds lumbering above us appeared stuffed with rain, and we'd barely made it inside before a violent deluge began.

The Myers lounge was empty except for TV Guy, who'd taken root in a chair facing the lobby set weeks ago. When we arrived, he was watching *Star Trek: The Next Generation*. Janet flung her winter white coat to the far end of the couch. She hadn't spoken since we left Tate and her visible anger upset me so much I had to get away.

"I should probably go," I said. The Tate Theater popcorn was starting to make me sick to my stomach.

"Sleep tight. But be careful," she warned. "Bed bugs are vicious." As I left, I saw Andy sit in the empty space next to her on the couch. Wonderful, now I'd just compounded my offense by leaving her alone with him; however, I'd seen her brutally and decisively deal with someone in whom she had no interest. He wouldn't annoy her for long.

I was up all night composing and editing apologies in my head. I slept through class and didn't wake until the phone rang early afternoon. It was within arm's reach, so I didn't have to move from the fetal position to answer it. Andy began speaking before I'd put the receiver to my ear.

"Hey, thanks, man!"

"Sure," I muttered.

"Fuck, man, she's so... fuck!"

I didn't need to ask who the "she" was amidst all the profanity.

"Well, I, uh, was calling to see, well, look, you weren't interested in her, were you?"

"We're just friends."

"Oh, I figured, you know, that you were, you know... I mean, I always sort of thought, but I just wanted to make sure. Well, uh, I'll catch you later, OK? And thanks again!"

What was he talking about? Not that I cared. I got off the phone and pulled the covers over my head. The next time the phone rang, hours later, I let the machine answer.

"Hello, son, it's your mother. We're just leaving and should be there to pick you up in a couple hours. See you then. Goodbye."

"Fuck," I whispered into my pillow.

4

I spent the weekend in Greenville cleaning my room. I brought up boxes from the garage and filled them with everything that wasn't relevant to me at that very moment — high school notebooks, yearbooks, Christmas and birthday gifts, report cards and my old Cub Scouts uniform (my membership was a short-lived mistake). What remained were books, videos, CDs, and ten changes of clothes. Simplicity had been achieved, and I savored my new asceticism. I carried the boxes outside to the curb. My parents, shocked to see me throwing so much out, asked Oprah-inspired questions about my mental health. They also refused to part with the framed academic awards decorating the living room walls. I'd never make a clean break from the past as long as they were around.

An hour and thirty-seven minutes after I returned to Athens, Janet swept into my dorm room without any sign of lingering irritation. Swan-diving onto my bed, she slid the soundtrack to *An American in Paris* into the portable tape deck on my desk.

The sedate browns and grays in the room retreated without valor against the onslaught of Janet's brightness — her cardigan was green as a lake, buttoned to the top with a polka dot scarf peeking through, and the swirl of her lilac perfume made you forget that this eight by ten space had for decades now housed boys and their questionable hygiene.

She wiggled her feet out of her pumps with a playful grace. They spilled onto my bed as her eggplant-colored toes rapped against the headboard in perfect rhythm to the music.

"Hello," I said once she'd made herself comfortable. I realized in horror that my basket of freshly laundered clothes, revealing an old man's assortment of white briefs, was in her field of vision, but she was more concerned with my word choice.

"Don't say that!" she groaned. "It's so *boring*. The only good thing about salutations is the word itself: Salutations. Salutations." She puffed out her cheeks like a bullfrog and added a final, "Salutations."

I sat on the edge of my roommate's bed. He was still in Smyrna visiting his girlfriend.

"How was your weekend?"

"This is my favorite album right now… it's still going on, you know." I found myself racing to catch her train of thought, but I gathered she meant the weekend and not the album. "Don't tense the past just yet."

"Did you do anything exciting?"

I had to know. I assumed Andy had been delusional on the phone and that Janet wouldn't spend any more time with him than necessary, but I still had to know.

"Why are the lights on?" she protested, switching off my desk lamp. "It's much more relaxing in the dark. Sort of like a movie theater." She yawned. "I had dinner last night with Mr. Razinksi. Then we walked hither and yon. Hither's divine, but yon's rather dicey."

The revelation stunned me. I figured Andy was audacious enough to ask her out, but I never imagined she would accept. If my mind could pair her with anyone, it would be someone who mattered — a rising film star perhaps or a brooding musician or even Prince Rainier, certainly not a lanky know-it-all in blue jean shorts. This development should have either raised my opinion of Andy or lowered mine of Janet, but neither happened.

"He really likes you," I said, attempting nonchalance.

She grinned puckishly and turned on her side, supporting her chin with her fist. "Yes, I know. I'm well aware. All last night, you could just see him thinking, 'Can I hold her hand now? Can I hold her hand now?'" She stuck out her tongue and panted like a puppy begging for table scraps until she cracked up laughing.

"Do you like him?" The possibility remained that she'd only gone out with him on a charitable impulse.

Her lips puckered.

"Is he having you grill me for information?"

"No, no, we haven't talked about it. I'm just curious."

Satisfied, she rolled on her back and shrugged. So far, music, movies, and food were the only subjects I'd seen provoke more than indifference from her.

"He has very nice eyes… so many colors." The day's last bit of light appeared to skate on the surface of her sunglasses. "I like that."

My eyes were the same sober brown as my desk and bed, so I irrationally took this as an insult. She hugged my pillow, lying so still I thought she'd dozed off to the lullaby of rain against the window, and when she spoke again, it sounded as if she were talking in her sleep.

"What is...?"

Rather than provide a word — a mundane formation of letters, she bounded off the bed and threw out her arms to their full wingspan. I thought for a moment she might take flight.

She stood almost en pointe while gazing at my side of the room's one piece of decoration, which hung at the same line of sight but in a different frame of mind as my roommate's poster of a swimsuit model who looked hungry and angry. It was a blue tin sign with a picture of Marilyn Monroe holding a small white bottle. It read: *Marilyn Monroe says, "Yes, I use Lustre Creme Shampoo."*

"I found it at a flea market years ago," I said. "We were on our way back from..."

"Oh, I don't care about that," she said sharply.

It occurred to me now what she'd actually wanted to know.

"There were marathons of her movies on her birthday, which is the same as mine," I said — this was something I never thought I'd discuss with someone else. "It was always the best part of the day."

Janet turned away from the sign for a moment. Her smile had receded like the tide, but now there were new, unearthed wonders in her face.

"I like her... a *lot*. She's lovely." Janet resumed her study of Marilyn. "You know, the last time I saw *Vertigo* with my father, we had dinner afterward and walked around Central Park, and it was such a wonderful evening. Then he told me he was going away for a while." She hesitated. "He'd had an affair with some dumb blonde in his office. It wasn't the first. Not by a long shot, but Mother found out this time and made him leave."

"I'm so sorry."

Her voice tightened like a drum.

"Don't apologize for things that aren't your fault. It's too easy."

She misunderstood me. I wasn't apologizing for her father's infidelity but for my own blundering. I'd ruined *Vertigo* for her. I followed certain rigid rules of conduct because I believed they would navigate me safely through life and felt somewhat betrayed to learn they weren't so reliable.

"But all that's Ancient History 252; let's drop it. Besides, my father moved back in a few months later... it can't last, you know. He doesn't like The Beatles." She was talking about Andy now; the other subject was left at the station as her thoughts hurtled onward. "There's just no hope."

When her music ended, she took out the tape, touched up her flawless appearance in my mirror, and was gone as suddenly as she'd arrived, and not even Marilyn could make the room less gray, less brown, or less silent.

Despite my own hopes, Janet managed to overlook Andy's aversion to The Beatles, because they continued to see one another. After a dispiriting dinner one night at Bolton, I walked in on Janet and Andy on the couch in the Myers lounge, her red heels resting on his lap as he helped her study for an Italian test. This one sight, glimpsed in flashes as I raced up to my room, made me feel more alone than I'd ever been in my life.

I decided that the *Red & Black* might prove an adequate distraction from my self-inflicted torment, so I wrote a few more articles for the paper, whittling away at the stack of CDs by Gwen Lupo's desk. Pleased with my work, she hired me on staff as a stringer, which made me Jennifer Howard's one success of the quarter. She took me around the corner to Espresso Royale, and against a backdrop of chattering students, the warm gargle of an espresso machine and the resulting aroma of coffee, she confided in me all the secrets of the office, who was a "dork" and who was "super."

She explained to me that because the paper was independent of the University, the journalism school tended to look down upon it. The more traditional journalism students worked at the *Athens Daily News* or the afternoon paper, the *Athens Banner-Herald*, and the few students who saw themselves at the *Village Voice* or even *Rolling Stone* someday worked for the *Flagpole*, the alternative weekly — that left the *Red & Black* with an eclectic staff of the unhip and the unconnected.

"But everyone reads us for the crossword at least," Jennifer assured me. "If we're ever short on space and have to cut it, we get loads of angry letters." Her cappuccino had left a dab of white foam on her nose. "Still, no matter what, we're the easiest pick-up on campus!"

Her official *Red & Black* T-shirt proclaimed this, as well.

I'd seen Heather Aulds exactly twice since the first day of class. Both meetings began with a shouted "Carlton!" and took place outside a building on North Campus. In each instance, I was heading south to either Myers or Bolton and Heather's destination was eventually somewhere downtown.

The first time was the last week of September. She'd been waiting for Andy Razinski outside Peabody Hall, and when she called me over, she was standing by the paneled front door underneath its crown. It was one of those Athens days when rain felt imminent but never quite materialized. I had my umbrella at the ready and leaned against one of the columns framing the entrance. We spoke for a while, as the sun dripped a little off the fanlight and onto her green forehead. I discovered we liked few of the same things but found mutual amusement in almost everything.

Andy eventually exited the building behind a patiently attentive professor with wild gray hair, an ankle-length skirt, and a faded T-shirt bearing the image of a black spider. Whatever they'd discussed had taken his enthusiasm to its crest, and he started to excitedly roll off places we could go next — now including me in these plans as though I'd been part of them all along.

"Nowhere Bar's the only place I can get your Muppet Baby ass into tonight," Heather said. Andy was still seventeen. A slow yawn also included an invitation: "Coming, Carlton?"

The establishment was too dark and smoky to see anything beyond Heather's disdainful eyes above the flame of her cigarette. I felt Andy jostling beside me against the sticky bar and heard the crack of cue balls on a pool table elsewhere in the room. My soda tasted weak, as though there was little syrup left in the fountain; overall, the place smelled like the pitcher of beer Heather and Andy shared, which she described as "lukewarm piss." And that was the extent of my first bar experience.

The second North Campus run-in with Heather was the week after *Vertigo*. She yelled my name from Phi Kappa Hall where, having no interest in the literary society that met there, she'd nonetheless sought shelter under the building's triangle-shaped pediment during a sudden downpour. My umbrella was safe and dry in the Journalism Building, where I'd left it after history class, so I hurriedly joined her on the portico.

The shadow of the trees performed a fan dance on the brick façade as we talked. Heather planned to wait out the storm with her Marlboros and then go over to a bar called The Globe. She stated through an exhale of smoke that I should come along, but I was still dizzy from seeing Janet and

Andy together the other day — even while standing there with Heather, I could feel North Campus moving beneath me like a sickening carnival ride. The storm, somewhat like my self-pity, showed no signs of letting up, so a few minutes later, Heather and I both took off alone in the rain.

After those two chance encounters, I next heard from Heather deliberately. She phoned me the following Monday and asked me to accompany her to a listening party for the release of the new R.E.M. album.

"Razinski bailed on me," she growled. "You're up."

Hearing music in public had never appealed to me, but I figured it was something I should get over, as I'd almost successfully done with the hall baths at Myers. So I left my room and met Heather at the 40 Watt Club.

"Really thought you'd be a rasta or a hippie by now," she noted upon my arrival. "But you're still rockin' the khakis. Awesome."

She wasn't being sarcastic. Something about my inherent incongruity appealed to her. I think she viewed a black guy who wore unwrinkled khakis through the same ironic lens as a green-haired girl who drove a new Porsche.

Janet and I were perhaps the only students on campus and possibly the only people in town who weren't fans of the band, so the venue, which felt like you'd paid to enter someone's basement, was packed.

Andy's absence only served to remind me *why* he was absent, so I doubt I was very good company. In fact, Heather and I didn't say much to each other for most of the night. I tried concentrating on the music but I was either distracted or particularly obtuse that evening because I couldn't make sense of the lyrics.

I turned to Heather at one point to ask if the song playing currently was about the actor Montgomery Clift — the few lines I understood seemed to hint at it — but she was no longer there.

I found her and her cigarette outside, leaning against the numbers 285 painted on a wall that displayed fliers promoting future music acts. I thought I should apologize for being a lousy substitute for Andy — not the best feeling to have even if it was true.

"Can't believe Razinski's missing this," she said before I could speak. "Kind of fucking depressing anyway. Don't let musicians turn thirty." I guessed she was now referring to the album and not Andy. "It's all he's been talking about since we got tickets, but that Cosby kid he's dating suddenly decides they should 'stay in.' Bet she 'ate in,' too."

I didn't know Heather that well, and I realized that I also didn't know the full extent of her feelings for Andy. Was it possible she was jealous of Janet? If so, what were they putting in the water in this town? I wondered, as well, if her mood was just bruised pride that a higher power had broken the spell her shoulder tattoo once cast.

"What do you know about the princess?" she asked the cloud of smoke in front of her although the inquiry was directed at me.

I delivered a masterful evasion of the question, which caused Heather to snort derisively.

"Whatever. OK, I get it. You don't gossip. That confirms it: You're not a fag."

"I'm sure he's told you anything he'd tell me."

I regretted this as soon as I said it.

"He's told me things," she insisted. "But only enough to make me hurl. You know she calls him 'Mr. Razinski'? How pretentious is that?"

I thought it best to allow the irony to go unacknowledged. Not that there would have been time to pursue it: a swarm was migrating toward the club. It shared a collective tardiness; the actual listening portion of the listening party had just ended.

"Jesus H.!" Heather groaned. "Here come the alternateens."

If this flock of flannel had a leader, it was an otherwise nondescript young man who emerged from the group. He was not handsome: his ears were lopsided, his nose suggested a distant relation to Mr. Potato Head, and his eyes wandered lazily in opposing directions. His skin was apparently not on speaking terms with the sun, and his dark hair was neither curly nor straight. It just seemed to cover his head. Each feature on its own would have tipped him into ugliness, but assembled, they projected a misleading accessibility.

He lingered near us on the sidewalk, casually but with chilly precision. It took a moment for me to interpret this circuitous physical vocabulary as an interest in engaging Heather.

Neither overtly reacted to the other, but anyone with insight into the assertion of dominance would have recognized the waging of a social cold war. The weaker nation would be the first to issue a greeting.

"Hey, Heather, what's up?"

If his yielding first was a concession, the smile he gave her more than compensated for the initial setback. It was a brilliant smile, stretching the limits of his face and offering its target a heaping of frozen warmth. If a smile conveys that the recipient is of interest to the bearer, his demonstrated solely that you were of interest to others and thus to him. It was an honest smile under those circumstances and for some people more valuable.

"Cody," Heather said coolly.

"A friend and I heard the album at their office last week," he said. "I think it'll do well for them."

An alternateen slinked up to him; her wafer-thin arm, sheathed in black leather, slipped through his. "*To-om*," she said, lifting a thick eyebrow toward Heather. "*Are we going inside?*"

"Oh... sure, Dana," Tom said absently, her presence clearly a distraction. "We'll just let it cool off for a moment."

Dana pulled on the metal hoop in her right ear. She'd either lost the earring in her left at some point during the evening or hadn't worn one. Large gray eyes like an empty concrete pool stared at Heather.

"Hey, Aulds," Dana said with cold enthusiasm.

"Weichman," Heather said with no enthusiasm.

"We're totally coming to your Halloween party," Dana informed Heather.

I was retroactively flattered that when I'd accepted Heather's invitation, her reaction was more emotive than the table scrap she threw Dana:

"If you'd like."

Someone of importance had just entered the club, creating a buzz amongst the swarm. Tom Cody led them inside. Anyone else would have followed, but Heather simply said, "Let's go — this is much too hip for me," flicked her spent cigarette into the dark, and walked off with me down Washington Street.

On Sunday morning, when students congregated in the many white churches along Lumpkin, I sat at my desk in Myers and reviewed my journalism, political science, and history notes. I'd read them all fully and already committed their contents to memory, so like any other devotional text, they provided no new insights.

Shortly after 1, I heard a knock that I recognized as the opening beats of the overture to the *Chicago* musical. I knew this because someone had left a cassette tape of the 1975 cast recording outside my door with an elegantly written note reading, *"Nowadays" is my favorite. Let me know which one is yours, kiddo.*

That someone, smiling brightly, now stood in front of me.

"Fall's here," Janet announced, pushing up her white-framed sunglasses. "Let's revel in it."

"It's been fall for weeks," I reminded her. I expected to see Andy Razinski around the corner.

"Silly boy." She grabbed my nose and pulled. "It didn't feel like fall before. It was too hot. But today," she pronounced — her hands rising up slowly with her palms facing me, "is the official opening of *Fall!*" The name of the season appeared to materialize in flashing lights above her.

The calendar might have disagreed with Janet, but I did not. I followed her as she kicked, stepped, and rocked unabashedly through the quad, past Soule and past Snelling Dining Hall, which she called "Smelling" with a fresh giggle. I ate most of my meals at Bolton, which was a straight shot from the Main Library on the Russell Hall bus, so this was my first extended look at the Georgian-style building: Sash windows peered out of red brick, and four white columns screened the door. Trees on either side of the entrance waved their tufted branches like pom-poms.

"It is pretty," she conceded. Her fingers kicked, stepped, and rocked on my shoulder. "But the pizza is *awful*. That's unforgivable."

We rambled over Sanford Drive and along the quieter Cedar Street and then wandered off the pavement and cut over to Field Street. We walked along Tanyard Creek underneath Sanford Stadium. Janet's loose drop-waist dress was a bright hibiscus against the brown stream banks, slick gray rocks, and whatever color the water was — discarded food wrappers, soda cans, and I think an opposing team's player from Saturday's game floated along the surface. We quickly heeded the counsel of our noses and left. Heading north, we stopped in front of the tree-framed Main Library building, and I mentioned to Janet my earlier confusion regarding Mrs. Ila Dunlap Little.

"You should still call it Little Memorial Library," she insisted between giggles. "You shouldn't stop enjoying something just because you learn the truth about it." Her next words came quickly, like dominoes tipped over by her emphatic laughter. "I think I'll start calling it Li'l Ole Memorial Library. Mrs. Ila Dunlap's Li'l Ole Memorial Library." More giggles and then an urgent and intoxicating grasp of my arm. "This is my favorite place on campus."

"That's why they built it."

After a symphony of laughter, more boisterous than I'd heard from her, Janet said, "Up there... on the seventh floor..." An amber finger traced a column of windows dividing sunny brick before stopping at the top. "...they have tapes and tapes and tapes of old movies!" She whispered the words to me as though she were doubling the number of people aware of this magical, mystery floor at the library. "Tate is nice and all and has good popcorn, but they show a lot of dreary movies, too, and here you can come and just watch whatever you want to see... like *Gypsy*... and that's what we're going to see now because... oh, there's no Ethel... but there's *Natalie*... and I'll just make you a tape with Ethel's versions later."

By the time I'd fully processed what she'd said, we were on the seventh floor, in front of a TV set in our own private cubicle, and *Gypsy* was starting.

I left the library that day for the first time without a backpack bloated with books, which might have explained my sensation of walking on air. I turned suddenly to Janet and said, "'Mr. Cellophane.' That's my favorite."

Segues were unnecessary when I was with her. She smiled, fully comprehending my meaning, and took energetic steps forward on her right foot and slow steps backward on her left, her jump rope of a necklace swinging as if North Campus were the Savoy. Whenever she danced, I wished I could join her.

A thick cushion of leaves covered the lawn, which the wind had swept across the sidewalks, as well, and only the crunch of gravel or the soft pizzicato of dried grass under our feet revealed what was beneath the surface.

I imagined the red, green, and yellow leaves that flowed up the granite steps and through the Doric columns of the Chapel were silently demanding absolution in their final moments, and I realized the stark white building, which didn't alter colors through the seasons, could never relate to their futile appeal.

During this brief moment of contemplation, I'd almost wandered through the Arch's black iron posts before Janet gasped and pulled me back with both hands.

"You can't do that! Something terrible will happen. And you'd make such a good father."

She referred to the unorthodox campus legend that promised sterility to any freshman who walked through the Arch. The official story was that you'd never graduate unless you avoided the Arch until your sophomore year. I laughed and pointed out that it was just a superstition.

She swatted me on the head with her wide-brimmed hat.

"There's a bit of truth in every superstition and a bit of superstition in every truth." Her T-strap pump hovered over a red-freckled leaf; she gently picked it up and dropped it in her purse. "Let's spare this one, shall we? May it see another fall. I think it's terrible to only experience one."

We rounded the Arch on separate sides and united on the bricked sidewalk.

"Oh, there you are," Janet said, forcing the flood of black curls back into the restraints of her hat. She took my arm again, and ignoring the red light, we crossed Broad Street.

Eyes that had grown accustomed to the face of Manhattan devoured the quirky imperfections of downtown Athens. The multicolored Federal-style and Greek Revival buildings fit together like pieces from unrelated puzzles that a precocious child had creatively combined; it thrilled Janet like a finely detailed musical set piece.

She marveled at a three-story house on Broad and Thomas with elaborate paneled doors on the second and third stories that opened to nowhere but a sudden drop. Janet thought one building we passed had on a concrete paper hat and grimaced in the direction of Jackson Street through two rows of arched windows on its sorrowful, weathered face.

We paused further along Broad to look through the four pilasters encasing a restaurant with white tablecloths, stemmed water glasses, and serious conversations taking place between students and their parents. We turned onto College Avenue, and Janet pointed out a "scrumptious" white-frosted slice of cake resting above a green-canopied storefront that sold what she called "dreary and cruel ice cream" (the actual product was more successfully advertised as "smoothies").

Across the street, we encountered windows plastered over with a peeling and discordant wallpaper of concert fliers. A red sign flashed "Wuxtry" from the bare transom. Inside the record store, Janet and I explored the walls of vinyl, speaking to each other in whispers as if in a house of worship, before she "rescued" a Wayne Newton album from the bins. You were always rescuing music when you saved it from simply being on display, she explained into the fold of my neck. As I collected myself, the clerk in the *Speed Racer* T-shirt avoided actually touching the record when ringing it up.

We strolled down Clayton Street, and Janet sang "Danke Schoen" and smiled at a pair of dormer windows above us that lit up as the sky slowly became the color of the Tate Theater curtains.

"Great, I thought it would *never* leave," she remarked about the day, which had just slipped into a more comfortable evening. "Now we can be alone."

Janet wiggled her nose as we approached 233 East Clayton.

"I smell pizza!"

Leaves cascaded over the face of the building, partially obscuring the sign that identified the restaurant as "Rocky's." Janet pretended to gnaw hungrily on my shoulder as she led me toward the screen door; it slammed behind us — startling a waitress and resulting in a small puddle of pasta on hardwood.

"Oh, sugar honey ice tea!" Janet said with a sigh. "So much for an inconspicuous entrance."

We dodged tightly spaced tables on our way to a lime green booth in the far corner of the restaurant, which was decorated haphazardly — like an indoor yard sale that also sold pizza.

Our table was covered with a red-and-white plastic tablecloth. Dried wax coated an old (not vintage, just old) wine bottle with a candle fit snugly where its cork had once been. A waitress slouched over. For a moment, I thought she was about to join us but instead she asked what we wanted. We'd not yet been given menus, but Janet ordered a spinach-and-feta pie and a pitcher of ice tea.

A reddish-brown model train circled the restaurant on tracks attached to the wall. It whizzed past our heads as Janet whispered, "Choo! Choo!" This entertained us while we waited for our food and shortly afterward until Janet suddenly poked her fingers in her ears and grimaced.

"I hate this music!"

The offensive sounds belonged to the band Nirvana.

"I think Andy has this album."

I delighted in pointing out a key difference between them.

The light from our candle flickered against the backdrop of her eyes, and I enjoyed this rare glimpse of them without the barrier of sunglasses, but suddenly her plum-nailed fingers snapped out the flame.

"You know, nothing's going to change between us," she said not so much reassuringly but defiantly. All that was missing was her shaking a clenched fist at an oncoming storm.

"Nothing has changed," I said stupidly.

She had a habit, when considering something, of seeming to balance the issue on her nose like a brittle beach ball that would shatter if it fell to the ground. Her head tilted back, her arms folded, she was the image of faraway focus, until she'd suddenly jerk forward, and I could almost see the pieces of what concerned her scattered across the floor.

"You don't know my real name."

This confused me.

"I sort of thought I did."

"No, that's just my stage name." She helped herself to another slice of pizza. "I'm named after my grandmother, you know. And get this: She's Janet Jackson! And my grandfather's Michael!"

"You're kidding."

"Would I lie to you, kiddo? But they were Janet and Michael, first, I suppose. My middle name's Elizabeth. That's for an aunt I never knew. She died when she was eight. She had the worst case of chicken pox ever. They were all over her, even inside her." She spoke rapidly, as though attempting to outrace the morbidity of her story. "When I got them, I thought I'd die, too. Boy, what a copycat I would have been! To have my aunt's name and her death, but life's not that romantic."

"I've never had chicken pox." There were some advantages, I guess, to childhood isolation.

She stroked my forearm. "You haven't? That's divine! If you get them now, we could hole up in my room and listen to music and I could feed you vegetable soup!"

I immediately fantasized of ways to expose myself to the disease so this dream could begin as soon as possible.

"But you see the problem, don't you? Janet. Elizabeth. Tomalin. None of those are mine. They're just loaners. I wanted my own name. So I chose..."

She paused dramatically as if she were announcing the winner of an Academy Award. "...*Mahogany Slade*."

"It has the same number of syllables," I said and then realized I sounded deranged so I added, "Did it catch on?"

"I didn't *tell* anyone my name, silly. It only works if no one knows. That way, I can be my very own imaginary friend. And whenever I hear people talking about 'Janet,' I know they're talking about someone they don't really know, not the real me."

She cupped her hand over her mouth. "I just hate the way my breath smells after pizza. Excuse me."

She always carried toothpaste and a brush with her for whenever she ate. "Take care of your teeth, and they'll take care of you," she'd said when I'd asked her about it. I watched the train circle the restaurant twice before she returned.

"Let's do this again," she said.

"Sure."

"No, I mean it. Every Sunday, we'll have brunch at Rocky's — sort of like breakfast at Tiffany's but at a less gruesome hour." She defined "brunch" differently than most people, as well. It was a quarter to eight. "Come what may. Every Sunday. It'll be our place. Are you down, bro?"

"Totally, sis."

We soul shaked (poorly) and drank more ice tea while watching the train race over our heads. Much later, after the door had been locked behind us at Rocky's and we were halfway down Jackson Street, Janet hunched over and circled me with an imaginary switchblade.

"Wanna rumble, Daddy-O?" she said, identifying herself as a "Jet" (appropriate, given her initials) and me as a "Shark" (slightly less so).

I'd never had so much fun, but I felt guilty. She gave far more than I did or ever could, and I feared she'd eventually realize that and vanish as suddenly as she'd appeared.

5

Janet's birthday — an occasion more worthy of fireworks than July 4th — was on Halloween, and I agonized over what to get her. I spent Saturday afternoon at Big Shot Records in College Square among aisles of used CDs that stretched out endlessly like fields of plastic wheat. Lost for a moment in the relatively tiny musical theatre section, I harvested a copy of the original cast recording of *Sweet Charity*. I couldn't think of anything more appropriate. She'd seen the revival in 1987; her father's firm represented Debbie Allen, so they went backstage on opening night where the whole cast signed her program.

I wrapped her present in the front page of Friday's *Red & Black* and walked over to River Mill. The temperature seemed to drop with each step. It was the chilliest night of the year so far, which I suppose was appropriate for the holiday. I'd volunteered to help Heather Aulds set up for her Halloween party. I was attending mostly because I knew Janet would be there at some point, so I thought the least I could do was make myself useful.

Furniture — all new — had been arranged in a coldly efficient manner in the orbit of Heather's leather sofa. The hardwood floor could have used a vacuum and a mop but was otherwise presentable. Random personal items — textbooks, magazines, and scraps of notepaper — sat around the living room, looking as forlorn as an abandoned child. I pointed them out to Heather, and with a shrug of leanly muscled shoulders, they were banished to the bedroom.

We stood out on her balcony for a while, wrapped in sweaters against the cold, as Sugar's *Copper Blue* blasted from her stereo. Heather had put on a plastic hockey mask with a hole cut into the mouth wide enough to let her drink Guinness through a straw.

"It's almost civilized tonight," she said. "The frat boys and the Lilly Pulitzer crowd are all in Florida."

Soon we were laughing about the absurdities of Florida and the assumed absurdities of the next few hours, and I wanted to ask why she'd thrown the party in the first place — it didn't seem like her, but before I knew it, it was around 9 and the first shoal of revelers had arrived. They were eager, most were freshmen, and some even wore costumes... or at least, I thought they were costumes. It might have been in fashion.

I somehow thought standing behind the refreshment table would make me look less conspicuous, but it only made it seem like I'd been hired to cater. This was my first party, and I was the only black person there. No mask could alter that reality, so I placed mine next to the snack platter Heather had bought at Kroger.

"Dope set-up," a short guy commented to an even shorter guy. "Real mellow." Apparently, they were both named "Phil," but the one from Georgia maintained home state advantage so the other was called "Seattle Phil."

"Total party virgins," Heather declared of the two. Smoking through the jagged hole in her mask, she waved a Guinness under my nose. "C'mon, pop your cherry."

"No, thank you. I'm fine."

"Jesus H.! What kind of pussy are you?"

A little after 10, a bloom of guests — less eager and somewhat older — had spread over the surface of the apartment. Tom Cody and Dana Weichman were among them. Dana was in costume or so I hoped: A sparkling dress draped her ironing board frame. Ruby lipstick made her wide mouth more clown-like than sensual and clashed with the natural reddening from the cold at the tip of her long, hefty nose. Her hair, the color of a bruised eye, remained in a bun and preserved the severity of her appearance, in spite of the attempted frivolity of her party piece. She lolloped over to Heather in high heels that exaggerated the height difference between them.

"It's short and strappy," Dana said with a cow-milking motion of her arms, which were so pale I thought for a moment she was wearing extremely long white gloves. She slathered a defensive layer of irony on her ensemble: "Can you believe people dress like this?"

"Yeah," Heather replied, "it's hard to believe."

"Just saw Donkey at Chameleon," Tom said. His costume was a dinner jacket with a ruffled shirt and blue vest.

"Go Figures were playing after, but we *figured* we'd *go* to your party instead." Dana laughed. Heather and Tom did not. "We might have to skip out later, though, for the rest of Five-Eight at Club Fred."

"We'll see," Tom said. "I'm not crazy about the new album."

"Tom preferred *Inflatable Sense of Self*," Dana explained, "but I think *Passive-Aggressive*'s their best."

Heather excused herself once the front door opened again, and Janet and Andy entered, fused at the hand. Andy introduced Janet to the now unmasked Heather with the same grace as early man returning victorious from the hunt.

"Well, well, well, Tomalin," Heather said with Guinness-spiked scorn, "I was beginning to think you didn't exist."

"I don't," Janet replied, spotting me from behind her sunglasses and pointing in my direction. "I'm a figment of his imagination."

Heather raised her right arm. "Might I offer you some libation?"

Janet scrunched up her nose, as if Heather were holding a dead rat. "Oh gosh, no, thank you. I don't drink beer."

"Jesus H.! What kind of pussy are you?"

"Do you have any wine, by chance?"

"Why, Lovey *dahling*, I believe we do," Heather said through gritted teeth. "It's in the kitchen, *dahling*. Why don't you come along with me, *dahling*, while I pop open a bottle, *dahling*?" She turned to Andy and said in her normal voice, "At least I know what kind of pussy you are."

"When did you get here?" Andy asked me.

"Around 7. I helped her get ready. She's been drinking almost non-stop since then. I think she's pretty far gone."

"No way, it takes more than that to knock out Heather. Her tolerance is probably up there with Keith Richards. She says only sorority girls get drunk anyway. They think if they don't remember it, they're still virgins."

I suspected that somewhere on Andy's bookshelf was a copy of *The Quotable Heather Aulds*.

"You know today's Janet's birthday, right?"

I nodded.

"What did you get her?" I wasn't about to discuss this with him, but he proceeded without an answer. "I got her *The Portable Nietzsche*. I've been after her to read it."

Andy scooped up a handful of chips and joined Janet on the sofa. As I fumed at the sight, a lobotomy victim mistook the sleeve of my shirt for a napkin and wiped salsa from her mouth.

"Hey," she asked, "do you know where the bong is?"

Three months ago, I could not have answered her question — I didn't know what a bong was. Such were the benefits of higher education.

"It's in the bedroom."

"Coolness. Hey, do you live in River Mill, too?"

"No, Myers."

"Really? How can you stand it?"

From the refreshment table, I watched Tom Cody circle the apartment talking to Heather. Dana followed, tossing out rejoinders to their backs. It was a dysfunctional conga line. The three eventually ended up on the balcony, where they discussed music and bands and the people in those bands as Heather inched closer to the ledge.

I went into the bathroom to clean my shirtsleeve. One of the freshmen from earlier was lying in the tub, bouncing a tennis ball off the wall. When I left, I saw Janet sullenly examining her reflection in the hall mirror as if it were a painting done in a style she didn't appreciate.

"Don't worry. There aren't any gray hairs yet."

I'd surprised her; red wine trickled down her black dress. I clumsily apologized and almost offered her my shirtsleeve.

"This old thing?" she giggled. "No harm done."

"Happy birthday."

"Too little, too late, kiddo." The Elvis clock next to the mirror gyrated to the tune of half past 12. "I was waiting all day by the phone for you. I guess I'm just yesterday's news."

I didn't want to see her until I had just the right gift. What a dumb thing to do! Now, she thought I'd forgotten.

"I'm sorry, I... "

"Oh, don't apologize. Mr. Razinski told me you were busy making all this possible." She sipped her wine and made a face indicating that Heather either tried to poison her or served her something from a box. "It's quite the little jamboree."

"So, are you eighteen or nineteen today?"

"Goodness gracious, someone has a lot to learn! You're not supposed to ask a lady her age." She sighed. "But if you must know, I'm neither. I'm twenty."

She was the oldest person I knew who I didn't call "ma'am" or "sir."

"Does that surprise you?"

"Oh no," I lied. "You, uh, well I mean, you don't look it."

My absurdity made her giggle.

"I try to stay out of the sun."

"I got you a present."

She leapt with joy, spilling more wine on her dress and sending her top hat to the floor. "You did? Gimme!" She ripped away the *Red & Black* wrapping paper and squealed, "*Sweet Charity*! Thank you so much! You are so sweet!"

She kissed me softly on the cheek just as the music stopped. I couldn't tell if the CD had ended or if I'd gone deaf. I only knew I wanted to kiss her in front of everyone. I wanted to hold her. I wanted to be alone with her and experience the warmth and fullness I always felt when around her.

"Carlton," Heather called out from behind the kitchen counter, "you sure I can't get you anything?"

"No, I'm not sure. Give me a beer."

"Attaboy! We'll get you out of those khakis yet." The silence caught her attention. "Someone play something!"

Janet eagerly obliged and, with a gleeful clap of her hands, inserted the just-opened *Sweet Charity* CD into Heather's stereo, which almost seemed to resist at first but eventually relented. Once the brassy opening of the overture began, there was a shared look of puzzlement on the faces of the other guests. Heather, however, neither noticed nor cared as she pulled out bottles from her liquor cabinet.

"Let's get some soul in you, Carlton, but your first drink *cannot* be beer. It just wouldn't be Christian." She rubbed her hands together. "I'm making you a Slow Comfortable Screw Up Against the Wall Mexican Style."

While I wondered how many of my admittedly forgettable childhood memories this drink would erase, Janet shucked off her heels and folded her legs up under her on the sofa. Andy's long, thin arms drew her close to him, her head fitting comfortably underneath his chin.

Heather put her creation in my hand. I downed it and immediately transformed into a Tex Avery cartoon, steam blowing out my ears, and my eyeballs spinning in their sockets. I oozed into a chair. My stomach burned. I thought I was dying, but the pain was only physical now.

My eyes cleared enough to see Janet nuzzling Andy's neck, her fingers raking through his curly black hair. "I love this song," she whispered in reference to "Big Spender," which was playing now.

"Uh huh," he replied. She could have told him the apartment was on fire.

She untangled herself from him and stood, swinging her hips to the music. The sinuosity of her body was spellbinding, and my eyes tasted every sensual meander of her hips and chest. I wanted her — it was as simple and as feral as that — and I could think of nothing but what I'd do once I had her. I felt sick and ashamed, disgusted with myself... and so I motioned to Heather for another drink.

I woke up the next morning in Heather's tub. The previous occupant had taken the tennis ball with him, but it appeared that I'd passed out sitting upright and holding a glass of water.

"Don't worry, Carlton, I didn't take advantage of you. I was a gentleman." She lay on the tiled floor beside her tub. "I thought you'd be dancing on tables, but you just sat in the corner, not saying anything — just like you are sober, but paralyzed from the waist down. You have the makings of a good drunk, though. When it came time to pray to the Porcelain God, you went straight into the toilet, no fuss. I was impressed. I'm going to go fix you my surefire hangover remedy. It's the same thing they gave Socrates but a little stronger. Oh, and I think Razinski had his sexual Bar Mitzvah last night. He and Tomalin were all over each other. And he might want to think otherwise, but he was the only one being deflowered. I can spot a virgin a mile away and he was the only one in that couple. Anyway, don't die on me before I get back. The vinegar and honey's about to come to a boil, and once I add it to the prune juice and Southern Comfort, you should be as good as new."

I wasn't. Hours later, Heather poured me into her car and drove me back to Myers, where she helped me up the stairs to my room. Delirious from alcohol poisoning, I vowed never to drink again, as I blamed my current state entirely on the "slow, comfortable screw." I did manage to regain partial mobility in time to join Janet for an 11 p.m. "brunch" at Rocky's.

"Is he going to be OK?" our waitress asked as she refilled Janet's ice tea.

"Gosh, I hope so," Janet said. "He just had a li'l too much fun at a li'l ole party last night."

"Just make sure to take him outside if he starts to get sick. And do it on Jackson, so it doesn't hurt our foot traffic."

Janet sopped up the remaining sauce from her half-order of pasta with a slice of bread. "You know, kiddo, I should call Miss Aulds and let her know how great her little soirée was. I had a divine evening."

"She suspects as much." With an extreme effort, I lifted my head from the red-and-white tablecloth. "She thinks Andy probably had a divine evening, too."

Janet's glass stopped halfway to her mouth. Her sunglasses could not blot out the anger spilling over them. She sat back in the booth, silent and perfectly straight to the point of rigor.

My hangover had caused me to behave so crassly I didn't recognize myself. I was constructing an apology when a stranger stopped at our table to speak to Janet. He was tall, thin with hunger, and based on his unkempt reddish-blonde hair, patchy goatee, and scruffy clothes, I thought he was going to ask her for spare change.

"You're in my Italian class, aren't you?" he said instead. "With Signora Cooper? 1:15 p.m.? You sit in the third row?"

The only encouragement for him to continue was a slight smile offered in his direction.

"I'm Scott. You're Janet, right?

There was no movement above her neck, but her smile almost nodded. I looked up from the uneaten slice of pizza on my plate, now ice cold, and noticed a small girl with burnt orange hair standing impatiently by the screen door — frigid air from the street squeezing past her. Swathed in a flannel shirt and a dour expression, she grimly watched the superficially benign exchange at our table.

Scott commented on Signora Cooper's apparently challenging class, and Janet responded with a series of nodding smiles. She didn't actually speak until Scott casually suggested they prepare for the midterm together. Her answer was not immediate: She took a sip of ice tea and dabbed each side of her mouth with her napkin. I stared at the grease that had coagulated into viscous pools around the mushrooms on my pizza.

"Sure," Janet murmured. "Why not?"

Scott returned to the small, dour girl. They left Rocky's with what remained of Janet's anger. She turned to me with a smile.

"He seems nice," she said. "Very studious."

She drank the rest of her ice tea in one quick gulp, patted her chest and said "aaah!" and then went to the ladies' room. I avoided watching the train this time because its journey around the restaurant only made me queasy.

Growing up, I lived across the street from my high school, and when football season arrived, I could hear the chorus of exultation emanating from the stadium every Friday. My parents urged me to attend a game, but I considered my room the ideal location to appreciate the event. That was one of the constant predicators of fall, my favorite season, which always symbolized newness and the illusion of change.

Janet dubbed the weeks between Halloween and Christmas "Movie Season," because of the unique time warp effect in which you could enter a theater with the sun against your back and exit into darkness. We took full advantage of the season and the Tate Theater became our private clubhouse. Quite often, we were the only people in the red-and-black seats, munching popcorn, and sharing a large soda. That was the case when we saw *Funny Face*, and after the film let out, we found ourselves in the middle of a small uprising in the Tate Center.

Students were whooping and hollering, and only a few morose khaki-clad onlookers appeared out of place for the first and most likely only time in their lives. I suddenly realized it was election night, and we had a new president. I began to explain the riotous scene to Janet, but she'd already glided through Tate's sliding doors. She hadn't deserted me; she just assumed I'd be right behind her, a not unreasonable expectation. She could be remarkably single-minded: She hadn't ignored the crowd. It simply didn't exist because it failed to interest her. Politics were too grounded in realism to be romantic like a song or a film, and the future of the country moved her far less than the current tune on her stereo.

However, Heather and Andy were very much a part of the whole "Choose or Lose" movement. Heather, her car bumper emblazoned with a Clinton/Gore '92 sticker, had cast her ballot not so much for the future, but against her upbringing. Her family (the Jordans, the Butlers, and the Aulds) were all lifelong Republicans who defected from the Democratic Party in the early 1950s. Andy's parents had marched for civil rights and against the war in Vietnam; they'd seen Jimi, Janis, and Sly at Woodstock. His mother, a college professor, wore jeans to the office (my mother neither owned a pair of jeans nor worked outside the home), and his attorney father still decried "suits" and refused to wear one himself. His parents had failed him completely by not providing anything for him to rebel against.

My political science professor wanted us to write a paper comparing Bill Clinton's victory to John F. Kennedy's in 1960, as well as contrasting the political and social climate of the early '60s and '90s. I finished the paper on the night of Andy's eighteenth birthday, a drizzly Thursday two weeks before Thanksgiving, and as I conjured up images of Camelot, my roommate cooed to his girlfriend on the phone:

"Yeah, baby, yeah, I love you too. Yeah, I know you know I do. Yeah, I know you know I know you do. Oh, hold on, I've got another call. Hello? Oh, hi. OK, I'll tell him." He cupped his hand over the receiver. "Hey, Andy wants you to meet him in the lobby." He flipped back to his girlfriend. "Hey, baby, I'm back. Yeah, I missed you too, baby. Yeah, I know you know I did. Yeah, I know you know I know you know I did."

I didn't appreciate the summons, but I preferred it to the baby talk. Leaving Myers, Andy and I walked unusually slowly down Lumpkin before coming to a dead stop at the Kangaroo convenience store. Outside, Andy zipped up his jacket at the behest of the November chill. Staring morosely at a can of Tab, he suddenly emptied the contents onto the pavement.

"Janet and I broke up." His voice was as thick and hesitant as stale syrup. "It was my idea." He paused, reconsidering his words, because they made no sense. Who would willingly give her up? "We had dinner tonight at the Last Resort – it's my birthday, you know." I hadn't. "And right after they take our order, I ask her, real casual, about this guy Scott. When Heather told me that she'd seen the two of them together, I just thought she had the wrong idea. But Janet just leans back and says — so cold I get brain freeze — that she and Scott *are* going out."

This wasn't news to me. Earlier that week, on my way back from history, I'd watched Scott open his car door for Janet in the Myers parking lot.

"I didn't say anything; I couldn't. And she started talking about *Sweet Charity*. I guess she eventually realized how upset I was, because she said, 'We were never exclusive.' And I'm like fucking ballistic, you know? She's gonna fuck some other guy, and I'm supposed to be able to deal with that? And she says, 'You know, you're being very possessive.' And I'm like, 'Of

course, I am. I don't want to share you!' So, I tell her it's either him or me —
it's all or nothing."

The drizzle had now graduated into a shower. His face soaked, Andy
continued:

"So, she says, 'You're being silly.' And I ask her, 'Don't I mean something to you?' and she tells me, 'I never lied to you. I told you I couldn't be
serious.' And she had, but I thought that, maybe, I could... oh I don't know.
Anyway, I tell her that I needed it to be serious, that I couldn't stand the
thought of her with some other guy, and well, we broke up. We did the whole
'let's still be friends' bullshit, and I paid the check before the food even came
and got out of there."

I didn't know what comfort he expected me to provide. I think he told
me all this because Janet and I were friends and, in a way, it was like confess-
ing his pain to her. Still, when I compared it to my own eighteenth birthday
a few months earlier — trapped in an Olive Garden with my parents, I
couldn't feel sorry for him.

The streets were still damp and the bare tree branches still moist when
I walked over to Baldwin Hall the next morning to drop off my paper. My
professor flipped through my eloquent drivel and waved it in front of me to
emphasize how impressed he was. I'd done so well in his class he was distressed to see I was wasting my time majoring in journalism.

"It's a dinosaur, son. No one reads newspapers anymore." He patted
down the three remaining hairs on his head. "You've got too much potential
to bother with a dinosaur."

Six months ago, everyone was more excited about my future than I was.
Now, my future involved riding a professional dinosaur until it collapsed.

"I know, I know, it's your dream, right?" He shook his head. "I know
where you're coming from. I moved to New York when I was your age to try
acting, but then LBJ escalated, so I had to get my ass in college or have it
blown away. I don't regret my choice, though. Anyway, just promise me you'll
give it some thought."

I said I would but knew already there was nothing else I'd rather do. I
hadn't realized how attached I was to my dinosaur.

I left Baldwin Hall and marched through sodden leaves to Baldwin
Street (whoever Mr. Baldwin was, he couldn't have enough things named
after him). Instead of turning onto Sanford for my history class, I decided to

continue on humble Baldwin Street. Passing by Park Hall, I glanced up at the square tower on its roof and imagined I was reading Joyce in the domed cupola. I kept walking, no direction in mind, until somewhere along the perky sorority houses on South Milledge, I noticed a midnight blue Porsche trailing me. The car horn blared as it pulled up beside me; its driver leaning over to speak through the open passenger's window.

"Hop in," said Heather Aulds in the now familiar tone of voice that never stooped to make a request but was never so crass as to bark an order. It was just *understood* to provide the only reasonable course of action.

"So, Razinski called me last night. He's a fucking mess. You probably know the whole sobby story. Jesus H., to fuck someone over on his birthday! She's an asshole with a capital bitch. See, I knew that chick was a skank from day one. She didn't fool me with all those 'goshes' and 'divines.' I saw her at Depresso last week with Scott Waldorf. It was so obvious — just like her. I had to tell Razinski. I didn't care if he hated me or not."

I briefly considered swinging open the car door at the next red light, provided Heather actually stopped, and making a run for it. The last thing I wanted to do was talk about Andy Razinski. If he was still recovering from having flown too close to the sun, Heather seemed more than capable of tending to him. The way I saw it, Scott had Janet. Andy could have Heather. And I'd have my go-nowhere newspaper career. Everyone was a winner!

"He didn't believe me," Heather continued, "or he wanted to believe they were 'just friends.' Bull to the shit. Whatever. I get it. He had to wait for her to drop the bomb on him. That's how it goes."

A North/South bus almost collided with us, and Heather's fist punched the horn as if she saw Janet's face in front of her.

Then she pressed the clutch on my emotions, shifting them from unspeakable annoyance to pronounced guilt. Her next words, more softly and deliberately spoken, indicated that the overall point of our trip was not to discuss Andy's heartbreak but to confirm with me that she and I were fine despite my relationship with Janet, for whom she held significant antipathy.

Actually, that paraphrase might not fully reflect Heather's sentiments. Her exact words were:

"Look, I don't care if you're friends with... her," she choked on the word, "or not, but just let her know that I'll break my foot off in her ass if I ever see her again."

That bit of business behind us, we drove again to Atlanta, this time bypassing Little Five Points for the city you see on TV — Lenox Square, the CNN Center, and the cold granite of the towering NationsBank Plaza. We must have taken a wrong turn into the antebellum South at some point, because it seemed we were now touring the soundstage of *Gone with the Wind*. Through my window, I saw a showcase of houses, mansions actually, that stunned the eye with their defiant existence in the twentieth century.

There is a definite voyeuristic rush in viewing splendor that, by all rights, should be alien to you. I felt such a rush every time I saw Janet, and a similar sensation overcame me now, as I glimpsed grounds that would embarrass state parks and estates that were architectural redwoods. Except for slight, almost imperceptible, differences — the way a photocopy is never an exact duplicate — they were all uniform, as if uniqueness would diminish their grandeur. Heather, her arm poking out the window, stabbed at one such palace with her cigarette.

"That's where they grow rich white girls named Heather." She added morosely, "Takes a lot of fertilizer." Silence for a moment and then she said, "Time for a palate cleanser. Feeling funky?" I considered how to answer her question as she cranked up the volume on her car stereo, jarring the street's mortuary silence. "You like Prince?"

"Sure." I'd actually only heard half of one song.

"Not good enough! You like your parents. You fucking *love* Prince!"

She started to dance behind the wheel again, her throaty vibrato filling the car. Either my will to live had lessened or I'd begun to trust that she wouldn't kill us both.

We'd listened to Prince's entire output between 1982 and 1987 before arriving at the Trawler Seafood Restaurant near Charleston, South Carolina. There wasn't much on the menu that either of us ate, but we were content to share fries, drink ice tea, and watch the moon dangle over Shem Creek.

"You're blonde," I said suddenly.

"Oh shit! Are my roots showing already?" They were. I knew ivy wasn't her natural color, but I never expected blonde. All previous stereotypes went out the window. "Time for more Manic Panic. You know, I dyed my hair the day before I graduated from Westminster. Spencer was pissed like you wouldn't believe. He said, 'How could you do this to us, Heather?' Like he and Karen are the ones graduating from Klan Academy. I told him, 'Spencer, if you painted the house red, it wouldn't change anything. It would still be a museum inside.'" She smashed out her cigarette, effectively ending her digression into the distant past of high school. "Let's get out of here. The night, my friend, is embryonic."

We ran around downtown Charleston until a little after midnight. On our way back to the car, we cut through an alley that apparently belonged to a rather surly feline, given the way it hissed at us. I backed away instinctively, bumping into a trash can.

"Poor baby," Heather said with uncommon tenderness. She dropped to her knees and held out her hand, and after a brief introduction involving a suspicious sniff and a peremptory purr, she swooped up the creature into her arms, stroking its soiled fur in an attempt to soothe it.

"You're not going to take that thing back with us, are you?"

She rubbed noses with the animal before replying, "Of course. I can't resist strays."

"It could have rabies or some other disease or..."

"Just open your heart to little... little..." She realized the creature had no name, at least no appellation to which we were privy. "What should we call her?"

I never had pets growing up and lacked any practical knowledge in naming them. This made Heather all the more insistent that I should help her find one for her new companion. We tossed out suggestions to each other: I veered toward the traditional ("Chloe," "Tiger," "Spot") while Heather was more unorthodox ("Polly" or "Jean" or "Harvey," all three names inspired by the musician we'd listen to on the ride home).

"How about Fido?"

"That's a dog's name," she said. "You really do suck at this."

We'd put the still-unnamed cat in the backseat of Heather's car when, mostly out of desperation, I offered "Charleston."

"You want to name her based on where she's from? Is she a blind blues musician?" She paused. "Whatever. Fine, we'll go with Columbia."

I asked why the state capital was preferable. She replied with a shrug that when she was younger, she'd already had a cat named "Charleston," which she demonstrated by breaking out into its eponymous dance.

Columbia slept peacefully in the back of Heather's Porsche as we barreled down I-26. I must have shared that sense of security because when I closed my eyes after the last song on the PJ Harvey CD, I didn't open them again until we were pulling into Myers.

6

Melinda Miller phoned the first week of December to see how my quarter had gone, what "vibes" I had about finals and to let me know how much she looked forward to my return the following week. The call propelled her from mentor to friend — something I didn't notice at the time. I was too busy being depressed. I didn't want to go back to Greenville. I didn't want to endure three weeks without Janet.

I was in love with her. The one pleasant moment in an otherwise tedious Thanksgiving break was a dream that placed me sometime in my post-graduate future, where I was a columnist for a major metropolitan newspaper (perhaps the *New York Times*, but I'd never been inside the *Times* office so it looked remarkably like the *Greenville News*). Sitting at my desk, typing up a sure-fire Pulitzer Prize winner, my phone rang and Janet was on the other end, inquiring into my desires for supper. I woke up from the dream suddenly — slightly trembling, her name warm on my lips — yet perfectly relaxed and eager to return to it.

I'd never imagined my future before that night. Like a terminal illness, I thought it was something that happened to other people. Perhaps love was a heated union between hope and optimism, one that gave color to the days ahead.

Our last night of the year together began appropriately enough at the Tate Theater, where we saw *Singin' in the Rain*. The flickering lights played melodious notes on her face, which furrowed with a concentration unrelated to the film itself. Her arms folded pensively, her eyes overcast, a storm brewing within them — she made the passive act of watching somehow achingly beautiful.

The evening resembled in actuality how I always felt when around her. The streets were deserted except for us; finals had hit campus like a hurricane, confining most students to their rooms. Her voice, a husky murmur, warmed the chill air with a medley of songs from the film. She flowed through the streets, dancing to the music she herself created.

"What do you want for Christmas, kiddo?" She pirouetted with a grace that could only come from childhood ballet lessons. "The sky's the limit."

"I haven't really thought about it." I never did. My parents always gave me the generic hot item of the year. They'd bought Transformers and G.I. Joe figures for me even though I didn't play with toys. I'd received a Nintendo although I hated video games. Whatever was "in" this year for people my age would be presented to me Christmas morning.

"You're going to make me guess, aren't you?" She smiled at me and the world suddenly had an unquestionable meaning and purpose that would just as suddenly vanish whenever the smile faded. "OK then: I'm going to find something that has your name written all over it!" She curtsied as if taking a bow before an audience. "I can't believe you're leaving tomorrow."

"You are, too, right? That's when the dorms are closing."

Andy had returned already to Illinois; Heather, who was remaining in town until the week of Christmas, had offered to let me stay with her and Columbia, but the newspaper expected me.

"Well, that was the plan originally, but Mr. Waldorf has a show at Frijoleros next week and insists I stick around for it. He thinks I'll be good luck." She put on a cartoon-like voice: "He don't know me very well." She shrugged. "Anywho, I'm bringing my old kit-bag to his place. But don't you worry, kiddo. I'm not getting *married* or anything. No, this is just for a few days, and then I'm off…" She hesitated. For a moment, it sounded like she dreaded going home as much as I did. How was that possible? It was New York! "You know, this is just the oddest place to be."

"The intersection of Clayton and Jackson?"

"No, silly, I mean in our lives." She started to speak quickly, communicating her thoughts before they also went away for winter break. "It feels like so much has changed, but then we'll go back home and it'll be like we never left, everything's the same, but it won't be, not really. Don't you feel like everything is different now?"

I thought about this. I stood only a few inches away from the woman who was everything missing in my life, yet six months ago I'd never met her, never seen her, never imagined someone like her existed and, if so, would ever treat me like I mattered somehow in her life.

Glancing down at the pavement, I replied, "I don't know. I think things have a way of always staying the same, deep down."

She pulled back the skin on her face with her palms, wiggled her fingers, and crossed her eyes. This stranger stated, "It's like what John says in 'All You

Need Is Love.'" She was apparently on a first-name basis with the late musician. "Nothing matters in the end. It's all a waste of time. Of course, if nothing matters, you can't really waste time, can you?" I believed this was the most cynical interpretation of the song possible, and it warmed my heart. Janet returned with a sigh and a release of her stretched-face. "I don't think love is easy, though, even if it's all you have. Sometimes you don't even have that. It's worse when you think you do but don't really." She took my hand and we crossed the street against the light. Reaching our destination, she shouted, "Olé!" and posed briefly like a matador. I laughed, but her face suddenly turned serious.

"I know a lot of people hate me, but I don't care," she said in the insistent way that only confirmed she did. "But I never want you to hate me, kiddo." Her voice had the flavor of a command but it quickly sweetened. "Because I don't think I could handle that. Hey, look, we're at Rocky's!" We were. A sure sign of approaching winter was the lack of patrons — townie or student — sitting at the outside tables. "Now, I know it's not Sunday, but how about brunch? It'll be our last of '92."

Our arms linked, we bypassed the empty tables up front and found our regular booth in the back, where the lights and music were softest. For the first time in my life, I knew what I wanted and not just for Christmas.

My mother had rearranged my room when I returned to Greenville. She did this frequently. I resented it at first but soon realized it wasn't a hostile act but her way of combating boredom. I shouldn't begrudge how she filled her days. The room was more hers than mine, anyway. I'd read of childless women who will decorate an ideal room for the son they wish they had. This is what my mother did. A poster of Michael Jordan loomed over my bed; Whitney Houston stared at me from the door. She'd plastered the latter over a poster of Annie Lennox, one of my favorite singers but — much like me — too androgynous for my mother's tastes.

I no longer had to write obituaries. I covered the cops beat now. They'd fired the former police reporter when he suggested the assistant news editor needed a "good fucking."

"What's going to happen to Toby?" I asked Melinda over lunch. She'd taken me to a restaurant across the street to celebrate my "promotion." The last time I ate there was during a dinner for high school journalists. The college-aged waiter spent the evening poking fun at me, the sole male, in an effort to impress the female students. I felt sorry for him now. I couldn't fathom being that cruel to someone. I certainly couldn't live with myself if I did.

"He'll be fine," she assured me. "He's going back out West, I think. Honestly, though, I won't miss him. He's the biggest jerk I've ever met. Karma finally got his ass." She cut into her chicken with perhaps more force than necessary. "So, what's up? I felt something different about you on the phone but seeing you again confirmed it: Your aura has changed."

"Has it?" I asked patiently.

She grabbed my hand. "Absolutely. It's much larger now — almost swollen... and *inflamed*."

"Should I see a doctor?"

She shook her head.

"Not necessary. Just tell me about her."

"What makes you think there's anyone?"

"You're in love!" She clapped her hands. "I knew it!"

I didn't bother to deny it. Maybe Melinda wasn't just the office flake stuck with babysitting the intern. Maybe she really did have second sight.

"How did you know?"

She shook her head like Katharine Hepburn. "Hey, I was eighteen once, sonny. Centuries ago. Horse and buggy age, actually." Her voice snapped back to thirty-nine when she realized, "Jesus, Nixon was in the White House."

That night at dinner, my mother handed me an envelope with the seal broken and the contents stuffed hastily back inside. The return address was where I'd sent Janet's Christmas present.

"Why do you always open my mail?" I exploded. "Why? It's an invasion of privacy!"

"I know what this is," she said slowly. "Those hormones are acting up."

"What are you talking about?" I asked incredulously. "Puberty's over! This is as good as it gets."

She stared at me, not really sure what had just happened. I'd never raised my voice at her or anyone before. I preferred to express anger through the distance of the printed page. That way I wasn't present to see the impact on someone else. Looking at my mother, I could only see the black-and-white Homecoming photo of her from high school. That was a little more than twenty years ago. There was some gray in her hair now; some lines in her face, just like Melinda Miller. The two couldn't be more different. I could still see youth in those unblinking hazel eyes. My mother, even when I was a child, always seemed to be that indeterminate age that was somewhere just past being alive.

As I made my melodramatic exit from the table, I heard her remark to my father, "Gifted children are always difficult. I saw this on *Oprah*. They're easily disturbed."

"He just needs a girlfriend," my father replied. In other words, a "good fucking" would do wonders for my disposition.

I slammed my door shut and plopped onto my bed — instinctively in the location it had been prior to my mother moving it across the room. I landed on the floor, where I opened the envelope and found a card, letter, and cassette tape. I read the letter first.

Lovey-dovey, I've had the blues. "So what!" you (and Miles) say? "So what!" I say. It's my mantra. Mother's gallery had an opening this weekend. Hundreds of caterwauling ladies screaming, "Oh, how darrrrlinnnnng!" The worst of the bunch came over for cocktails. Mother wanted me to stand up straight and smile, like one of her pieces (glitter and be gay!). My brother's always been better at that than I am. I hid in my room. I wish you could hide with me. I miss you terribly, kiddo — even though you aren't lost. I'm just greedy. I want you near me. You're like that wonderful sweet tea I discovered down in Jor-juh. You're so refreshing. Oh, where am I going? What I'm trying to say is thank you. Thank you for being so kind to me the past few months. It's meant more to me than I can ever tell you. The cruelty of others faded away because you were so kind. You may forget all about me someday, but you were kind to me and I'll never forget that. See you in '93 — Mahogany.

A lipstick kiss straddled the signature. I reread the lilac-scented letter until I knew every word. An angry growl from my stomach reminded me my tantrum had cost me dinner. I folded the red stationary and moved on to her card. It had been specially designed for her family. The front was a photo of them frolicking in the snow in Central Park. Written in gold across the top half was "Merry Christmas from the Tomalins!" Inside was a standard salutation from James, Abigail, Janet, and Abraham, affectionate enough for relatives and professional enough for business associates. On the facing page, they all sat in what I assumed was their exquisitely furnished living room,

dressed in evening wear. Their signatures adorned each of them like pieces
of jewelry.

Janet wore a long, black gown, which fit her mood. Her father stood
over her, his hand on her shoulder. Her brother, in the chair next to her,
held her hand. Her dark eyes stared out of the photo itself. I met her gaze,
tracing her image with my finger. You'd suspect her sullen, unsmiling face
had been superimposed over the cherubic elder child of this happy family.
Some people, and I'm one of them, cannot lie to the camera. Every picture is
a post-modern reflection of Dorian Gray. The camera had a way of revealing
carefully hidden truths. The shameful fact was I'd been so absorbed in how
she made me feel that I had no idea what she was feeling.

Angry with myself, I played her tape. There was no song listing; she'd
just written my name over and over in different colors of ink. I listened to
her music while pondering the wan face in the photo. I'd heard most of the
songs before, but they possessed a new meaning now. What had once been a
monologue was suddenly a dialogue. She'd selected songs she loved with me
in mind. I listened to her tape, through my headphones, until I fell asleep.

Christmas Eve, I covered a story in which a man accidentally shot and
killed his pregnant wife while cleaning his gun and another in which a trac-
tor trailer decapitated a man on his way home from Christmas shopping at
the mall. The photographer and I arrived at the scene to discover the man's
brain, perfectly preserved somehow, lying in the middle of Haywood Road.
The photographer snapped some photos of it, which we couldn't print, so he
made copies and handed them out to everyone at work. I took one home,
figuring Heather would enjoy it.

"Merry fucking Christmas," I could hear her say.

My parents and I ventured out in a downpour for our annual Christmas
Eve dinner. It was such a farce. We never exchanged more than a half-dozen
words each year. We were a potluck family. You could pick three people at
random, from the five billion inhabitants of the planet, and there'd be more
natural intimacy between them.

After dinner, I retreated to my room, the Christmas lights in my window bathing me in a red glow. I couldn't sleep, so I overheard my parents
discussing me downstairs.

"He hasn't been himself lately."

"He didn't eat a thing at dinner."

"He said he doesn't eat red meat anymore. Now, where could he have picked that up?"

"Probably at school. There are all those weird new ideas out there, and he's young and susceptible. I saw it on *Sally*."

"Well, I just hope he's not, you know, experimenting."

"With drugs?"

"No, with, you know, *experimenting*, going down the wrong path."

The phone rang shortly after midnight. My mother's pleasure in saying, for the first time, "Son, your friend's on the phone," diffused any anger she might have felt over the late call.

I smuggled the portable into my room. I half-expected it to be Heather. Her card — with Santa bearing a chainsaw in one hand and the head of a toddler in the other and that instructed me to have a "Bitchin' Christmas! Ho! Ho! Ho!" — came the other day. It wouldn't be unlike her to crank call me on Christmas morning and pretend to be the Virgin Mary, who'd just suffered a miscarriage.

"Merry Christmas, kiddo."

I couldn't agree more.

"I hope it's not too late to call," she said uncharacteristically. She was usually cheerfully oblivious to such "dreary" things as time. "But I just had to hear your voice."

"Where are you?" I asked. Sounds of revelry littered the background, as if she were calling from the middle of Times Square.

"Oh gosh, I'm ensconced in my boudoir," she replied over The Ronettes' version of "Sleigh Ride." "My parents have these Christmas parties every year, and they always go on until they feel they've adequately impressed everyone. Did I tell you my brother is a freshman at Columbia? He's already declared his major. He's all focused. Not like anyone you might know. Anyway, he brought his latest young lady tonight. He just adores her. He thinks she's sooo beautiful and exotic. She's Italian, you know, so I tried out a few phrases on her, and she just looked at me like I was the dumbest thing alive, which is all right, I suppose, as long as she doesn't think she's prettier than me, because she's not! He may go for that sort of thing now, but soon he'll be back to those thin, pouty blondes of his." She hiccupped and giggled uncontrollably for a moment. "I'm sorry. I think I had too much eggnog. Ho! Ho! Ho!"

Her voice was more potent than eggnog, putting us on even footing.

"I got your present, kiddo. You are so sweet. It's already on my wall." I'd given her a framed *Vertigo* one-sheet. I'd worried that she'd take it the wrong way, that it would remind her of that bad day she'd had four years ago.

"I really enjoyed your tape," I said, refraining from expressing just how much it meant to me.

"Why, thank you — now quick, turn on HBO! They're showing *Victor/Victoria*."

"We don't have HBO."

"Shoot! And I so wanted you to see it."

"Maybe we can watch it together sometime."

"Oh my... that would just be *divine*." She sighed, and I imagined her balancing a beach-ball sized consideration on her nose. "I don't have anyone to kiss on New Year's Eve. Abe will be smooching his little signorina, but I'm lipless." She chuckled. "Just got these big ones of mine and no one to share them with."

"I don't think you'll have much of a problem finding someone, if you wanted to, you know."

"It would have to be *just* the right person," she murmured encouragingly. "What about you?"

Her voice overwhelmed me. I was seconds from telling her I loved her, hopelessly and irrevocably. I didn't care if I lived in a world where that emotion wasn't allowed. Maybe I could escape just by verbalizing how I felt.

"Janet, I, well, God, I don't know how to say this, but I..." I breathed deeply. "It's just that I think I'm..."

"Oh dear. Oh dear. Oh dear. You're not going to tell me you're gay, are you?"

My mother entered the room, mouthing the word, "Sorry," and unplugging the Christmas lights.

"No, no, Janet, I'm not."

"Oh thank heavens! *Obviously*, it wouldn't be problem if you're gay. Everyone's gay... at least in our neighborhood or at least our building... well, maybe just our floor. But now we don't have to worry about all the associated *drah-ma*. I hate drama. I prefer light operas... like ours. *Some* people might think you're gay just because you never talk about girls, but I know it's because you're a gentleman and that's what I adore most about you!"

I realized I couldn't see anything in front of me. I felt around in the dark for my bed. I don't remember the rest of the conversation. We talked until morning filled the room and my mother began loudly clanging pots and pans to announce the arrival of breakfast. My parents and I went through the usual Christmas chores before driving to my grandmother's house in Anderson. I hid in an empty room and read a book, waiting for the day to end. I could hear my relatives in the living room, going on and on about how smart and quiet I was, how I didn't eat red meat or pork, and how success lay in my future. They all thought I was gay, too.

WINTER QUARTER '93 PLAYLIST

The Beastie Boys, "So What'cha Want" — Heather and Andy
Miles Davis, "Fall" — Brad and Janet
Vigilantes of Love, "Keep Out the Chill" — Tom, Dana, and Eddie
Nirvana, "Lounge Act" — Evelyn
The Woggles, "My Baby Likes to Boogaloo" — Heather
Franz Waxman, "The Creation" from *Bride of Frankenstein* — Brad and
Janet
John McMartin, "Sweet Charity" from *Sweet Charity* — Brad
The Afghan Whigs, "Rebirth of the Cool" — Heather
Betty Hutton, "It's Oh So Quiet" — Brad and Janet
Barbara Cook, "Glitter and Be Gay" from *Candide* — Janet
Pylon, "Cool" — Baldwin and Reed
Throwing Muses, "Red Shoes" — Jaye
Simple Minds, "Alive and Kicking" – Brad and Janet

1

Snow fell overnight the first weekend of Winter Quarter, a prank of nature on a north Georgia town. When I looked out my window on Saturday morning, the Myers quad was covered in a white icing that stuck to my now very off-white sneakers as I walked downtown. The addition of a crewneck sweater and my grandfather's tweed jacket to my khakis and blue shirt provided adequate protection against the mildly chilled air, but I still passed parents carting balls of quilted down with a child safely if uncomfortably tucked somewhere at the center.

Students spoke with hushed, hopeful tones of cancelled classes, but as the temperature slowly rose, the spikes of ice hanging from the tree branches dripped steadily, like someone had left on a faucet, and I knew the white finish on the shrubbery and lawns would all soon melt away, perhaps somewhat cruelly, into gray ponds and marshes that we'd hurdle over on our way to a cavernous lecture hall Monday morning.

Of course, I would not participate in this obstacle course until just after noon, when my first class started. I was so enamored with Janet in November that between a movie at Tate or on the seventh floor of the Main Library or a meal at Rocky's or the Waffle House or any number of the spectacular diversions she provided, I'd forgotten to register for the upcoming quarter and wound up playing the collegiate roulette wheel of Drop/Add. I'd allowed fantasy to intrude upon reality, which was very unlike me. Although I'd subsisted on a steady diet of fantasy as a child, it was all carefully proportioned and sugar free.

I'd found myself on a sudden fast, however, as Janet and I hadn't spoken since Christmas Eve. Perhaps I feared she suspected what I was about to confess. It was a humiliating prospect, but regardless I needed to see her (and wanted far more but that would have to remain buried under the snow along with fall). I reached this abrupt conclusion while leaning against a marble pedestal on the North Campus lawn. The pedestal used to hold a sundial, which some person or group had stolen because it was somehow considered easier than buying a watch. I had an oblique view of Demosthenian Hall, and hours later, we parted on favorable terms, its green shuttered windows and cheery, pale yellow face having patiently tolerated my mawkish internal debate.

Dinner was two slices of soggy cheese pizza at Mellow Mushroom, a small, dark restaurant, whose only illumination were the psychedelic murals that screamed at you from the walls. I reviewed my check under the light of a kaleidoscopic mushroom and walked out onto Broad.

Twilight offered a sky as colorfully rendered as stained glass, and on the sidewalks, paths had been cleared for pedestrians, but the ice hills packed against the buildings displayed the rakish footprints of those who couldn't resist leaving their mark.

My desire to see Janet was now intense and urgent. Cutting through the Tate Center parking lot, I'd almost reached Lumpkin when a frozen missile struck me square in the face.

"Boo-yeah! Girl's softball pitcher of the year: 1985 – 1987. You never really lose it."

I shook off ice from my glasses and once my vision was no longer obstructed, I saw Heather Aulds standing in the pale blue glimmer of the parking lot lights. She wore a gas station attendant jacket with "Floyd" stitched on the chest, and her green hair was tucked into a gray stocking cap. There was a gloved wave from someone underneath a down coat and a thick wool hat with ear flaps who identified himself as Andy Razinski with a shouted, "What's up, B.!"

There was evidence on their coats, pants, and hats of an extended snowball fight that Heather had, perhaps unsurprisingly, won definitively. I'd never been in a snowball fight, though you could argue I was currently embroiled in one, so I was unsure of the appropriate protocol.

"Am I supposed to hit you now or something?"

"Sure — but you'd have to catch me off guard and my guard will always be up. It's all about being the first to strike. That's why guys like virgins."

A brief détente was struck as we caught up with each other. Although I did not reveal to her the cause of my Drop/Add travails, Heather nonetheless found great amusement in the result.

"You have the ultimate frat boy schedule," she declared.

"I think it's awesome that you got everything at the last minute," Andy said. "It's really existential."

"Jesus H.! You think taking a dump is existential."

"I'm hungry," Andy announced through his gloved hands.

"Awesome segue," Heather said. "You were speedballing burgers and fries at Allen's all afternoon... oh well, at least you've got your appetite back after breaking up with It."

Heather refused to refer to Janet by name, which suited me because I could separate her in my mind from the person they hated so much.

Andy paced us, shaking his fists as he spoke, like we were his sparring partners.

"Yeah, you know, it all happened on Christmas. I felt like shit, and I was renting *Home Alone* to dumb fucks at Blockbuster. Anyway, my break finally comes around and I'm starving. And nothing's open! Not a single goddamn place! What a bogus, evil holiday to starve me to death and close down every damn thing in town!"

"If only there was some subtle notification that this obscure holiday was upcoming," murmured Heather from the hood of a stranger's car where she lay curled up as if on her living room sofa. "People could plan."

"And I'm sitting in the break room eating shit from the vending machine, my stomach growling like a pit bull, and I realize that she represents all this. All this fakeness and bullshit and a partridge and a pear tree. That's her. She's dead – like all those sell-out Christian puppet jobs — DEAD! So, I'm thinking, 'fuck her!' Fuck her and her Disney-watching, no-meat-eating, red-wine-drinking, 'how divine'-saying, Billy Joel-listening, Debbie-Gibson-Tiffany-'I-think-we're-alone-now'-acting ass. Fuck her!"

"She doesn't like Billy Joel," I corrected.

"So, fuck The Beatles or The Smiths or whatever that shit is she likes!"

"Let's leave Morrissey out of this," Heather commanded.

I almost pointed out that Janet didn't listen to The Smiths, either — if she even knew who they were — and that the only similarity between that band and The Beatles was their shared nationality but decided against prolonging the topic.

"Look, B., I'm sorry to bust on her like this, but you just don't know her like I do."

The apology offended me more than his tirade. The implication that he knew Janet better than I cut deep, mostly because I suspected it was true. I remembered what Heather had told me the morning after her Halloween party.

"Take my advice, B. She's not worth your time. She's a fucking wackjob. Off the hook with no dial tone, line disconnected."

Heather hopped off the car, placed the back of her hand to her forehead and remarked, as if reading from Jane Austen: "Whenever a boy and girl break up, no matter the circumstance, his explanation is always the same: She. Went. Nuts."

"I should have listened to you, Heather. You were right about her. You were right all along."

"Yeah, well, don't suck *my* dick. Just stop taking orders from yours."

Andy thought it wasn't "existential" to wear a watch, so he would often ask me, after glancing skyward and realizing the answer wasn't in the stars, "Hey, B., do you know what time it is?"

"11:47."

"Tate's showing *Akira* at midnight. You guys wanna come?"

"Isn't that a cartoon?" Heather asked.

"No, it's Japanimation."

"I should be getting back," I hawed. "I have some studying to do."

Heather dusted snow off her bottom before also declining.

"Sorry, I prefer *live* entertainment." She winked at Andy. "Let's leave our friend to his... studies." She said this scornfully, as if knowing it wasn't true. "We'll order some Gumby's, put on *Check Your Head* as high as it will fucking get, knock back some pony necks, smoke some very good grass, and chill for the night. Not necessarily in that order."

Walking through the quad, I saw no indication from Janet's window that she was at home, but I knocked on her door and announced myself anyway. Eventually, a voice wailed from inside, "Oh you, you, you. I'm dark tonight. Come back tomorrow for the matinee."

"I just want to talk to you."

"You would!"

Her sigh almost buckled the door, which she unlocked but didn't open. I let myself in. Cigarette smoke, forbidden in the dorms, infiltrated my nostrils. The absence of hacking and coughing suggested this was not a newly acquired habit. She'd doused the lava lamp, so I was careful not to trip over anything lurking in the dark. I could make out shapes well enough to see Janet apparently levitating like a Zen master in the middle of the room. Once my eyes fully adjusted, I could tell she was actually sitting cross-legged on a black beanbag.

"So, state your business, kiddo."

I slumped to the carpet.

"I don't know. We haven't talked since we got back and..." It occurred to me that we were sitting in the dark. "Is something wrong?"

"Everything's wrong," she said hoarsely.

I'd never seen her this down, but suddenly, there was a rush of levity, as if summoned from the deepest reserves.

"Sour cream. Sour patch. Sour grapes... or something like that," she said. "I think I'm going to end all my sentences with 'or something like that.' It adds a nice ambiguity to things... or something like that."

"Did you go out in the snow today?" I asked irrelevantly. "It was lots of... fun."

"Fun?" she repeated as though the word was freezing water I'd dumped over her head. "No, it wasn't *fun*... it was beautiful. That's why I'm here... well, actually, I'm here because Dr. Botsis gives a mean C-section. What was I saying? Oh... I mean... I just never go out when it snows. It's just so white and pure and everyone just tramples through it making it all black and filthy. I won't be a party to it."

She presumably couldn't even stand to look at the natural end of a snowfall. She faced away from the window, and dark curtains, pulled tight, blocked out the view of the quad.

"I need more coffee... or something like that." My eyes followed her shapely outline across the room; she filled her oversized mug and an additional one. "Do you want coffee?"

I accepted the offered mug, and its contents left flaming claw marks down my throat.

"What's in this?" I gasped.

"Un poco de brandy," Janet answered after a hearty gulp. "It's like a roller coaster — up and down. I should've served drinks earlier. I'm not a very good host. The music's even bad."

There was no music at all, just an insistent howl against the window.

"Maybe this will help," I said boldly. Inspired by Janet's Christmas present, I'd made a mixtape of my own for her. She snatched it from my hands so quickly some of her coffee seared my khakis.

"Thank you," she whispered.

The rattling window pane and the slight crackling of the curtains, almost like a low flame, merged seamlessly with the first song's dusting of drums and crisp trumpet solo, but soon there was a heartbreaking vocal: Janet started to cry; tears falling from her eyes like the warming ice on the trees.

"Oh," I said nervously, "it gets better."

She laughed.

"You know nothing about me," she said after a while. "That's a good thing. But I know nothing about you, either. That's a bad thing. I want to know everything. You probably think that's not fair. But it is. You've seen everything you need to know. It's all right here in plain sight. When Abe and I were little, Mother would dress us up like matching dolls and say, 'What pretty little children I have!' Then I got old enough to talk and 'Whoa, Nellie!' I didn't mean to be difficult. Really, I didn't. I just felt different or differently or the most different. I think it all comes down to whether you like the truth or if you prefer to be deluded. I've picked both and been wrong each time." She made the "game over" sound from a video game. "Maybe it didn't matter what I chose. Maybe I'm just a big weirdo — like Gonzo."

"You're not a weirdo," I insisted. The brandy dulled the irony of some-one like me trying to convince someone like her that she wasn't weird.

"You are *such* a liar."

"No, I'm serious. I know I'm not the best authority, but you always make sense to me. Sometimes... all the time really, the whole world is strange, so you feel as if you're drifting, not connected to anything, but..."

"Get out."

"I'm sorry?"

"You need to leave," she said firmly. "You see... the song's changing."

I couldn't see anything and understood even less, but I heard the trum-pets melt away.

"Please. It's just... your tape is *perfect*, and I should listen to it alone so it stays that way."

She floated above the carpet on her beanbag raft as the music continued, and I could feel, if not see, her dark eyes staring at me as I left the room.

My "frat boy schedule," as Heather called it, freed my mornings to work at the *Red & Black*, where I'd been promoted to full staff writer on the entertainment desk. I would swing by Espresso to pick up a bagel and coffee and type my CD reviews amidst the calm of the office before noon. This routine ended when one morning around 9, a young man shambled into the room, finishing off a breakfast that consisted of a meatball sub and a large soda. He was about my height but looked like weight had been packed in his trunk for a growth spurt that would never take flight. His shirt and even his faded jeans were wrinkled, as if washed on a Shar-Pei setting.

When he saw me, he slammed down his soda proprietarily on Gwen Lupo's desk — she would not be in until that afternoon, and her computer was envied for its ability to respond to basic commands. Cramming the last bit of sub into his mouth — remnants of meatball lingering on his stubbled chin — he extended his broad, thick hand toward me. It drizzled grease near my shoe. I responded with a polite wave.

"Eddie Munster!" he proclaimed.

The senior film critic, his byline appeared regularly in the paper. I also recognized his voice: He co-hosted a campus radio show called *The Film Thing*. He pulled up a chair. Our postures were matching question marks. "I was in here yesterday and the frat boys were driving me crazy!" The sports desk was located in the same room as entertainment. "And Gwen starts going on about how clean the copy is for the CD reviews. And I ask her, 'Who is this new music writer I'm hearing so much about?' She says, 'I've only seen him once or twice. He comes in during the morning, but I never have to change a word!'"

Eddie and I settled into a discussion of movies that continued every day as we worked across from each other in the pushed-over phone booth of a room. The following week, he invited me to see *The Crying Game* with him as his guest. Although I expected to enjoy his company, my shrewder side saw this as an opportunity to begin reviewing movies, which couldn't come any sooner considering the reputation I'd earned, thanks to my mostly scathing CD reviews, as the "guy who hated everything."

One morning after work, a surprise shower sent me scurrying into a shop on Broad; a toy horse hung from a metal pole outside and galloped endlessly on a square treadmill reading "Almanac." Once the fog cleared from my glasses, I spotted Janet's reflection trying on hats in a full-length mirror. A black headscarf was tied under her chin — perhaps to avoid a jealous outburst from any hat she might have worn into the shop.

"Oh, there you are," she murmured. "I'll be done in a sec. If you're very patient, I'll buy you lunch."

"I have class in ten minutes."

"Oh. That." Her nose wrinkled. "I don't know about this one." She tossed the hat back on the rack and selected another one. "This one's divine, though. But then so is this one." She sucked in her lips with an alluring petulance. My eyes saw no difference between the two bell-shaped hats — maybe one had a darker ribbon. "I'll just get them both. Mother would always have a fit when I did that. 'You have to learn to make choices!' Then I'd say, to her horror of course, 'Why? I don't like choices.' My father would laugh and say, again to her horror, 'Whatever Janet wants, Janet gets!'" She pointed at me possessively. "And, kiddo, I want you. My roommate got a TV/VCR for Christmas. She's never home, but we can't just let it go to waste. I hate waste. Let's rent *Damn Yankees* tonight. I'll make popcorn. How domestic of me."

"I'm sorry. I can't tonight. I have plans."

Her lips evaporated. Her expression gave me a rough idea of how the first person to see an eclipse might have reacted.

"Oh." One of the hats in her hands fell to the floor. I went to retrieve it, but she waved it away. "I don't want it anymore." She wondered aloud, "Now, who's going to watch *Damn Yankees* with me?"

"Why don't you ask Scott?" I churlishly suggested.

She twisted the price tag of the remaining hat between her red-nailed fingers.

"I'm asking you."

I was a fool to resist her, but this was important to me.

"I'm sorry, Janet. It's work."

She wandered toward the register, her reflection vanishing from the mirror. She whispered, "Boy, does *that* sound familiar."

"I'm seeing *The Crying Game*. I might even get to review it."

A white lie because no such offer had been made, but I thought if I couched my refusal in professional terms, she'd be less offended.

She might even be happy for me. Instead, her sunglasses looked at me reproachfully.

"It's an ugly movie," she stated, shoving bills into the cashier's hand. "The girl is really a boy. It's unforgivably cruel to pretend to be someone you're not."

And she was gone. Like the storm, she never announced her arrivals or exits. I'd never heard her utter the words "hello" or "goodbye."

"What a bitch!" the cashier exclaimed. "I wanted to see that movie!"

The Crying Game ushered me into the much-fantasized world of film criticism. I'd experienced the perks of the press when covering city council meetings with Melinda Miller but nothing like this. A flash of our *Red & Black* IDs set us apart from those who paid to see the film rather than the reverse.

"Hey, I'm gonna get some snacky-wackies," Eddie Munster said, sounding like a Blue Meanie from *Yellow Submarine*. "Save a seat for me, OK? Third row center."

Eddie had the same obsessive seating requirements as Andy Razinski, whose size twelves I tripped over in the desired spot. Heather slumped next to him, idly working the day's crossword from the *Red & Black*.

"Hey, B.!" Andy indicated the empty seat next to him. "Come join us."

"Actually, I'm here with a friend."

"Jesus H., not…"

"Great. Someone's got our seats. I'm gonna have to get tough." Eddie spoke through a tub of popcorn and a large soda. He elicited an instant good will by virtue of not being Janet.

"I read your review of *Last of the Mohicans*," Andy said after I introduced them. "You called it a 'tour de nothingness.' I loved that!"

Heather's haughty blue eyes casually dissected Eddie. This was how she said "hello."

Eddie clutched his food to his chest as if she'd tried to steal it. "I feel like some Jujubes." He shouted to the people in the row behind us, "Anyone want some Jujubes?"

His spindly legs sped out of the theater. I followed him as he bypassed the concession stand, dumped his food in the men's room garbage, and locked himself in a stall.

"You didn't tell me, man," he muttered, his voice an instant echo. "You didn't tell me."

"Tell you what?" I asked.

"That she was, I mean, she was…"

"I'm sorry." I always apologized when I didn't fully comprehend something. "I didn't know they'd be here tonight, but…"

"You still never told me," he repeated, logic not swaying him, "that she was… she was…"

"A girl?" I suggested.

A brief silence and then, "Yeah, yeah, they freak me out, man."

I wanted to point out that he managed to work with Gwen without suffering psychotic episodes but realized Heather was probably more intimidating than someone who wore her hair in pigtails and dotted her "i"s with hearts.

I leaned against the stall. I was having a conversation with someone sitting on a toilet. Life demands that once you realize the absurdity of a situation, you will gain an audience to it. At that moment, someone walked in on our heart-to-heart, his fly unzipped in preparation for the urinal. He grimaced at the sight, zipped himself up unrelieved, and stumbled out, mumbling, "Fucking faggots."

"Eddie," I pleaded. "We should go. The movie's about to start."

"No way, man. No way."

"You're acting like a little kid!" I shouted at him through the stall. "And you're being rude. She doesn't have cooties."

Eddie only rambled further about how I "didn't tell him." Disgusted, I gave up and left him to his panic attack. Apparently, there existed someone more socially maladjusted than I. A chilling thought I took with me back to third row center.

"Where's Eddie?" Andy asked as the previews ended.

I decided to spare Heather's feelings, although I suspected she wouldn't care.

"He had to go home. He's not feeling well."

"Shit," she said, almost sounding disappointed. "I was really in the mood for Jujubes."

Leaving the theater, wondering if I'd have to forcibly retrieve Eddie from the men's room, I felt a tug at the end of my jacket.

"Hey sorry, man!" Eddie had watched the movie from the worst seat in the house — last row, far right. Sensing my annoyance, he smiled awkwardly and patted me on the back. "How about that secret, huh? Didn't see it coming, did you?"

"Not at all."

"Why don't you review this one?"

"Me?"

"Yeah, yeah, Gwen said you were interested in writing film reviews, and, well, I think you'd do a great job."

"You really don't have to... I mean, I understand."

"No, no it's not that." He squeezed my shoulder. "I was gonna suggest it all along. Big surprise for after the film. Besides, I could barely see it. You had the better view, my friend."

I caught up with Heather and Andy, sitting together on a bench in the Georgia Square Mall. Heather absently guzzled Jujubes.

"So why exactly do Yankees call food 'nosh'?" she asked Andy.

"I dunno. I don't think it's a Midwest thing — although my grandmother always said it."

She slapped him playfully on the shoulder.

"What good are you then!"

Eddie's guilt was far-reaching. When I saw him next, he offered to sponsor me for membership in Cinematic Arts, the organization that programmed all the movies shown at the Tate Theater.

He embraced me like a long-lost relative when I arrived for my first general meeting in a second floor room in the Tate Center. Ash gray carpet spread across the floor, and members sat in pews of plastic seats that were as sturdy as a McDonald's Happy Meal toy.

"I'm so glad you showed up." He ran his hand through a thatch of hair that had no intimate knowledge of a comb. "Travis is making noise about not letting staff writers join CA."

Travis Richards had replaced Lori O'Brien as news editor when she was promoted to editor in chief at the start of the quarter. Travis also hoped to fill her current position in the fall and was not at all discreet about the "big plans" he had in store for the *Red & Black*. Lori *very* discreetly implied that this would ensure he'd never get the job — the paper's board of directors, the shadowy group of adults who selected the management staff, did not enjoy change.

Still, the mere possibility of having to choose between writing film reviews and serving as CA president tormented Eddie Munster, who was married to the organization in all but the legal sense. Meanwhile, the makeup of the group itself was slowly changing.

Tom Cody had joined CA in the fall. His roommate was a film student and a longtime member. Cody didn't contribute much to the meetings, usually content to sit in the back with his roommate and watch over the proceedings with ironic detachment. He had suggested *Pete's Dragon* as a possible midnight film, but it didn't get past the first round of voting.

More of Tom's friends were present this quarter. Many I recognized from Heather's Halloween party. They supported putting "fun" movies on the schedule like *Ghostbusters, Ferris Bueller's Day Off,* and *E.T.* — movies they'd be content to watch on TV and most likely wouldn't bother to see at Tate.

"We don't want to be exclusive," said Patty Elmhurst, who chose her friends based on when they went to their first R.E.M. concert.

Dana Weichman had seen R.E.M. at Moonshadow Saloon in 1985. Not even Patty could beat that (Fox Theatre, 1986), so Dana had solid support behind her when she recommended *Ice Castles* for the Weekday schedule.

"It's a great date movie," she said.

Eddie attempted to convince Dana that *Marriage Italian-Style* was a preferable date movie, but of the two, Dana had actually been on a date so she had slightly more credibility.

The small, dour girl from Rocky's also joined CA that quarter. She scorched the floor on her way to me once the general meeting concluded.

"That bitch friend of yours stole my boyfriend!"

The room had not yet emptied, so this crazy girl's outburst drew curious eyes upon us, which ranked high on my list of experiences I preferred to avoid.

"You know, when I met Scott he was nothing. He wasn't even playing anywhere. He met everyone important through me!"

"Does that always happen to you?" asked a wild-eyed Eddie Munster.

"Not usually."

He shook his head.

"Now all we need is for your weird friend to join."

Eddie's behavior at *The Crying Game* had been so embarrassing he only seemed able to justify it by labeling Heather "weird." Although she certainly met many of the qualifying characteristics for that description, my Southern-bred chivalry wouldn't let it go unchallenged.

"She's not weird."

This startled Eddie. I thought I'd offended him by disputing his lopsided version of events, but a smile soon broke across his whiskered face. He slapped my shoulder with more gaiety than he'd expressed during the past hour.

He leaned in to say something as Dana Weichman trudged past us in black work boots; Patty Elmhurst and a thick, curly haired girl completed the caravan. Dana had sat two plastic seats over from me during the meeting (two and a half if you considered her gamine figure), but she hadn't acknowledged my presence — even when I'd handed her the sign-in sheet. Now, she paused to give me a slight two-fingered wave. As I wondered what triggered the sudden change, Eddie shuffled off, perhaps in search of a bathroom.

2

The area of downtown Athens spanning west to Pulaski and north to where Dougherty curves into Prince was no larger than a few square blocks, but its presence in the collective imaginations of musicians — either current, soon to be, or never will but nonetheless hopeful — and their devotees loomed larger than Sanford Stadium.

Although more traditional students, either through timidity or general lack of interest, never wandered past the Georgia Theatre, many others yearning for kinship or relevance or a little of both would descend on the stretch of Washington Street that Heather Aulds contemptuously called the "Alterna-mall" — a strip of bars, clubs, and even the requisite tattoo parlor extending from the 40 Watt and providing a convenient one-stop shop for alternative culture.

Dressed in their finest tattered clothing, they came ostensibly for the music and were welcomed if they knew someone who created it, even if the connection was as far removed as a poor family relation.

Winter was when you could witness the preening of those who had successfully molted the appearances and personas of high school over the course of Fall Quarter, and the young girl at the 40 Watt with the fresh tattoo from next door might go so far as to claim an extensive, deeply affecting (and only slightly affected) history with the band currently playing on stage (she happened to know the classmate of the roommate of the drummer) and would vehemently deny ever having cheered on the Georgia Bulldogs with anything approaching zealotry in the distant, long ago days of September.

If my recollection of this musical arcade is thorn-covered rather than rose-colored, I must confess a lingering bias stemming from Janet's having dated a prominent member of the coterie. Scott Waldorf was rarely a subject of discussion between us, and I fought off, often unsuccessfully, any painfully vivid thoughts of scenarios involving them that were, I was certain, incomparably pleasurable for him.

And then came that Sunday afternoon at Rocky's when she'd plucked an olive from my slice of pizza and announced, while chewing it entirely on the left side of her mouth, "I want you to come with me to the Shoebox next Wednesday."

Scott's band was performing, and their dreadful music and lyrics were not worth a British penny, so I hadn't the slightest idea why Janet wanted me to go. I considered resisting again, as I had her far more appealing offer to see *Damn Yankees*, but I knew my reward for saying yes was seeing the half smile on her face reach its full, ecstatic potential. So I agreed, almost eagerly, and on a blustery evening with February lapping at our heels, I accompanied her to the "Alterna-mall."

The Shoebox was an aspirational name for the club, which was tiny, narrow, and dank. Janet's Bordeaux court shoes were probably not the best choice for a venue without seating, and she'd occasionally take turns standing on one foot while slipping the other out of its patent leather casing.

Dana Weichman and Tom Cody were three hipster rows down from us. Her black hair was released from its bun and fell in waves over the top of her leopard fur coat. She looked at the stage through red-framed sunglasses while tugging on her lone earring. People-watching was how I passed the time because Janet and I were both too soft-spoken to hear each other over the music, which vibrated through us like a small, sonic boom.

Janet stifled a yawn with a swig of Heineken (the bartender had served my baby-faced companion, no questions asked). She rubbed her hands back and forth over her nearly empty bottle as if it suffered from hypothermia.

"When does your boyfriend go on?"

Her face soured.

"I'm a little past the boyfriend stage," she snapped. "I'm not sixteen anymore."

Scott Waldorf came over to us through clouds of smoke. The crazy girl followed closely behind, elbowing other patrons out of the way as her short legs attempted to keep up with him.

"Hey, babe, glad you could make it!" He kissed Janet full on the mouth, and my hands unconsciously clenched into fists.

Scott introduced the crazy girl to us as "his friend Evelyn." The platonic categorization caused her to glare at Janet with unconcealed rage. Evelyn turned away from her, a silent promise made to resume her contempt momentarily, and her mold green eyes inspected me.

"You write for the *Red & Black*, don't you?"

Although she was just a foot away, I had to yell my response.

"I hate that paper," she shouted. "They're such jerks there. They said Scott's band was 'Magnapop-lite'!"

"I don't really have much involvement with the live music coverage," I explained. "I review CDs, but I'm actually starting to write film reviews now."

This didn't satisfy Evelyn.

"Yeah, well, they don't know anything at the *Red & Black*! Besides, The Movie Dope's better anyway."

The Movie Dope was the film critic for the *Flagpole*. His reviews were short and acidic — much like their admirer.

With practiced ease, Scott lit Janet's cigarette with a red Bic, while Evelyn fussed with matches from the bar. The sight was humiliating enough to be contagious. I would have offered to help if I didn't fear searing my fingers.

"I gotta go tune up, babe. I'll see you after the show." They kissed again, this time exchanging saliva, and Evelyn's face collapsed like a rotting peach.

The first band had ended whatever it was trying to do, but the people around us kept speaking at their previous high volumes. Evelyn's baggy flannel shirt and Janet's fitted blue cardigan faced each other.

"Oh, Miss Wilson," Janet said coolly, igniting her with each word. "Mr. Waldorf tells me you're a journalism major."

Evelyn's hair and face were the same color as she spat out, "I'm P.R."

"That's right," she remembered as if this detail were part of some long-ago conversation that had slipped her mind. "But they're both in the same department or something like that."

Evelyn's eyes blazed with the image of Scott and Janet alone together, discussing her like she was his ugly male friend from camp who still wet the bed. Unlaced Doc Martens took an unhinged Evelyn to the bar.

"I hope you're having fun," I said, feeling a bit sorry for Evelyn.

"I'm sure I don't know what you're talking about," Janet murmured with self-amused politeness. "I'm just being friendly."

An altercation was taking place. Evelyn pounded both fists against the bar furiously as the bartender calmly shook his head at her.

"What the hell you mean you can't serve me? I'm here all the time!"

"I know, I know, Evelyn, but they've been cracking down on us. You gotta show me ID."

"All the bands my uncle gets to play at this dive, and now you won't give me a goddamn beer?"

A slight wave of one ginger pinky in the bartender's direction and Evelyn's age was no longer a concern. He obediently reached into the cooler and slapped a Heineken in front of her. Bristling with the awareness of her benefactor, she snarled, "You know I only drink PBR."

Scott and his band were on the black curtained stage now. Once their aural assault on the audience began, my sanity demanded I depart the material world momentarily, and my eyes found a nice spot to stare at on the grimy concrete wall. Janet pursed her lips and sucked in her cheeks, her eyes glazed over, which might have meant she was really into the music or contemplating a change of nail polish.

I kept enough of a toehold in reality to know when to clap at the appropriate times and to hear Scott say, "This'll be our final song tonight. It's called 'JET.'"

"JET"? I almost laughed. Janet Elizabeth Tomalin — he'd written a song about her.

"Her smile could defeat gravity..."

I thought it best if I zone out again, but before I did, I saw Evelyn, who seconds earlier had been on her feet, screaming and cheering like Scott's own personal pep squad, plummet to the floor at terminal velocity.

Unlike the rest of his set, this particular song managed to engage Janet's full attention, but her tight mouth conveyed the restrained anger of someone acutely aware of the irrefutable dishonesty of the words being spoken to her.

"You were amazing, just amazing, you just keep getting better! I'm so proud!" Evelyn exclaimed after the show, clinging to Scott like static.

He shrugged off both her and her accolades, turning instead to Janet to ask, "What did you think, babe?"

Janet wiped her sunglasses with a cocktail napkin, smudging them even more.

"It was... nice," she replied, still focused on her task. Her lukewarm review was less motivated by honesty — she'd practically slept through the show after all — than her well-concealed distaste for his "tribute."

Scott torturously extended the evening and led us around the corner for drinks at the Manhattan Café. The lighting inside was a dark red, like someone was developing film. We sat in ramshackle furniture facing a gallery of unleveled and bizarre artwork. Smoking twenty-five-cent Camels from the bar, Janet started to name the paintings, and as she sipped from her snowflake-patterned Old Fashioned glass, the titles became more abstract: "*Old Lady by the Light Bulb... Angels Inviting Cross to Banjo Practice... Topless Woman Who's Still Hiding Something...*"

The electric logs in the fake fireplace projected a slasher film on Evelyn Wilson's matte white face as she proceeded to get wino drunk on PBR. I tolerated Scott's hand on Janet's thigh about as well as a root canal without anesthesia, and when she pointed out a cast-iron lamp hanging from the wall and expressed, almost through tears, her fervent desire to take it back to her room at Myers, I felt an overwhelming helplessness that sent me from the table.

I sulked on a barstool next to a pillar separating the counter from the ceiling. Sometime later, Evelyn stumbled over carrying a bag of popcorn. A trail of kernels followed her, and when she gripped my arm for support, she left behind a residue of nutritional yeast on my corduroy jacket.

"You're friends with Heather Aulds, right?" she slurred.

"Uh-huh."

"I'm... I'm surprised. You know, she thinks she's" — she said this derisively enough to only mean Janet — "a big phony."

Heather also thought the same of Scott.

More framed pictures were scattered over the tobacco brown wall behind the bar. They became more unbalanced to my eyes the longer Evelyn spoke.

"Look... the thing is... the *truth* is... she's no good for him, and," she added grudgingly, "he's probably not right for her, either."

"Uh-huh."

"Hey... I know you're interested in her. You have to be."

"We're friends," I said for no good reason.

"C'mon!" Evelyn exclaimed. "She's not exactly the kind of girl guys are friends with, you know? Wouldn't it, like, wouldn't it... you know, work out for both of us to sort of, you know, push them apart? I mean, we'd be doing them a favor!"

What a pathetic creature she was! I pictured the two of us conspiring together, like characters from a bad '80s teen flick, to split up Janet and Scott while "I Go to Extremes" played in the background. I couldn't help pitying her — so painfully in love and with Scott Waldorf of all people — but my pity quickly turned reflexive as I watched Scott put his arm around a laughing Janet and realized that I had more in common with Evelyn Wilson at that moment than anyone else.

I didn't drink anything more intoxicating than water that night, but my head still pounded from the experience days later when I met up with Heather Aulds and Andy Razinski for a quick dinner at Taco Stand downtown.

This was an entirely different Athens from the one I'd glimpsed at the Shoebox. The people around us eating their quesadillas and nachos were dressed in the fashions of Lumpkin and Milledge: There were non-ironic displays of school pride — red sweaters with barking bulldogs and gray jerseys that reminded the wearer of the state in which they currently lived. I wondered where they'd go once they finished their meals and whether they were even aware of the disparate culture swarming around them. Or did it exist merely as the green-haired girl in the corner of their eyes — a spot of local color in a town known for its tailgating?

The three of us waited for our orders by the drab bar; there were tables available, but Heather had determined that we would not stay.

"This is what happens when you don't card," she said with a contemptuous shrug. The group sitting at a booth against the brick wall shared pitchers of margaritas and watched the TV overhead. They cheered loudly whenever a goal was scored.

Heather had a fake I.D., which claimed she was twenty-four and from Louisiana, but tonight she sipped ice tea through a straw — perhaps because there was no sport in anything stronger.

Andy interrupted my contemplation of the tin ceiling to point out a skinny bald man standing underneath a flashing sign for "Zenith Radio."

"Is that Michael Stipe?"

I confessed that I wouldn't know the R.E.M. singer if I saw him. This amused Heather, who pulled back a mane of green from her face as if parting thick drapes. Blue eyes colder than the late January air made a summary judgment.

"He looks homeless… so maybe. Why the fuck do you care? You have the albums. Leave him be."

I'd placed our orders so when they were ready, my name rang through the small rectangle of a restaurant. There was minor confusion as two barking bulldogs also approached the register. I wasn't wearing a red sweater, so it was sorted out without much difficulty.

We carried brown paper bags, dripping grease on Broad Street, to the North Campus lawn where we picnicked on burritos and chips and salsa under shivering stars.

"It's so damn cold," Andy complained. "Have you noticed how cold it's getting?"

"You do realize you're from Illinois, right?"

Heather lay on her back, her entwined fingers cradling her head and her slender legs folded against her chest.

"I didn't come to Georgia just to hang out with the *Dukes of Hazzard*!" Andy said. "I could have gone to Northwestern. I thought it didn't get cold here."

"January is the coldest month," Heather remarked. "One is the loneliest number. Beer before liquor, never sicker. Red on black, safe for Jack."

She stood up with one full-body shrug.

"It's probably eighty in Jacksonville, but Florida's the worst state in the union. Texas isn't much better. All the best places are cold. See what you started? Now we're talking about the weather. What's next? The government?" Standing on the toes of her combat boots, she pitched her crumpled paper bag into the trash; it bounced off the rim, landing on the frosty grass. "Jesus H., I'm throwing like a white girl now."

Andy dug into his backpack and pulled out a clipboard. As he did this, I scooped up Heather's discarded bag and dropped it into the proper receptacle.

"Before we leave, can I get you guys to sign this?"

"What is it?"

"It's for the lady who cleans the hall bathrooms in Myers. I walked in this morning and she's in there scrubbing up from when some guys had gotten smashed and smeared crap all over the walls."

"Jesus H.! That's disgusting. Frat house rejects."

"I know! University Housing is just gonna let it slide. So I thought I'd start this petition. If I get enough signatures, it might shame them into actually going after who did it. It can't be that hard to find out who it was."

"I don't live in your — quite literal — shithole, Razinski."

"Yeah, right, sorry."

He handed me the clipboard. I stared at it for a moment, not enjoying suddenly remembering that my aunt had a similar job.

"You know what the worst part is, though?" Andy added. "The whole time she's doing this, she's singing this hymn about 'going down to Calvary' or something. She's cleaning up human excrement, and she's singing fucking Bible hymns! It's humiliating."

"It gets people through hard times." Heather shrugged. "That's what Alma says, at least. I personally am a conscientious objector to hard times."

"Who's Alma?" Andy asked.

"Funny story, that." Heather said. "About four years ago, I sneaked out with some friends to… I don't even know what for. I think it was just in protest of this ridiculous lockdown Karen had me on because it was finals week. I'm going to ace everything anyway and she has me confined to barracks? Please. So I bolt. I come back well after midnight through this path my brother discovered to get to the part of the house where our rooms were without our parents knowing. He called it the Underground Railroad. He used it all the time. Anyway, I'm inches from my room and I look up and Alma's staring right at me. Now, Alma's been with Karen's family forever. Karen even insisted Alma come down from Louisville with her when she married Spencer. So, I figure I'm totally busted. But Alma just takes me into my room, sits me on my bed, and proceeds to tell me what feels like a goddamn bedtime story at first. Basically, back in '62, Karen and her friend Pam 2: Electric Boogaloo…"

I thought that name demanded an explanation.

"Pam 1 was born in 1920," Heather answered. "Pam 2 was born in 1942. I always called her Pam 2: Electric Boogaloo. As you might imagine: total lack of amusement. All right, so Karen and Electric Boogaloo are tight. And their families venture down to Atlanta for some second cousin, once removed's wedding. They both had only recently come out, and they're seated at the same table as the Carter twins from Virginia — Beverly and Carroll. After the reception, Electric Boogaloo gets the idea to pinch a bottle of champagne and take the party up to Beverly and Carroll's room."

"Holy Shit!" Andy exclaimed. "Your mom and her friend hooked up with twin girls at a Georgia wedding in 1962?"

"No! Gross! This was Atlanta, not Savannah! Beverly and Carroll were guys!"

"But you said they'd just come out."

"Into *society*, ya dizzy deep-dish pizza you! Anyhow, the next morning, Karen and Electric Boogaloo sneak back down to their room — taking the stairs, with their shoes in their hands — and just inches from the door is, you guessed it, Alma. She'd just started working for Grandma Jordan a few weeks earlier. She's barely more than ten years older than Karen and Electric Boogaloo herself. Her big job that morning was to make sure they didn't oversleep and miss the breakfast for Mr. and Mrs. Second Cousin, Once Removed. Now she's caught these two geniuses in a society page scandal. Karen and Electric Boogaloo are freaking out. They're thinking to themselves, 'How do we make this go away?' Of course, Electric Boogaloo is a Southern Lady. She has no money on her. But Karen is more resourceful. Dylan probably wrote 'Rainy Day Women' about her. She grabs her purse, pulls out two hundred dollar bills, presses them into Alma's hand and says, 'Is there something you wanted to tell us?' Alma doesn't say anything at first. Then she answers, 'You girls need to get changed. The breakfast is starting in ten minutes.' And that's that. So, I'm no dummy. I know what the score is. I calmly take out my wallet and say — cool as ice: 'Cash, check, or credit card?' Alma doesn't say anything at first. Then she just shakes her head and answers, 'It's not gonna be like that between you and me, Miss Heather.'"

"That sucks! What happened?"

"I was grounded. Until — actually, I think I might still be grounded. Even after acing all my finals like I *knew* I would. Whatever. Worst thing was having the Underground Railroad shut down on my watch. But my brother was cool with it. He said I should find my own way out."

"Did you?"

"Working on it."

"You know," I said, unable to contain my cynicism. "You could have threatened to tell your mother what Alma told you."

Heather looked stunned.

"Yeah, if I was a total dick. I'm not a narc. Especially not for Karen. Besides, Alma has balls. I respect that."

Heather quietly snatched the clipboard from my hand and signed her name.

3

After introducing me to Mahogany Slade in the fall, Janet soon became reluctant to mention her again as the weather cooled. I'd asked once if she'd prefer I call her Mahogany, as she felt it was her "real name," and she responded, "Oh don't call me that, honey, just call me." Pause. Then *that* giggle, which erased all inconsistencies and contradictions. "Or maybe I'll call you."

And she did. Often. I relished our Rocky's brunches because there was a clockwork certainty that I'd see her every Sunday; the rest of the week, I'd never know when she might appear at my door or tap me on the shoulder as I browsed through albums at Wuxtry. After she'd shared with me the seventh floor of the library, we'd frequently watch movies together. She once smuggled in popcorn from Tate when we saw *Charade*.

If a constant sense of anticipation within me was her goal, she possessed expert showmanship. A moment that has rent-controlled housing in my memory involves my usually routine journey from the *Red & Black* to my noon class.

One day, shortly after the night at the Shoebox, Janet suddenly appeared next to me, dramatically imitating what I've been told is my very deliberate and hurried walking pace.

"I'm going to play you in the movie. 'I am *very* serious.' How am I doing?"

"Oscar nomination, for sure."

She was far too gorgeous to ever effectively portray me, even if using the Method.

"Where are we going?"

I told her.

"Ugh. Sounds gruesome. Are they going to make you dissect frogs or something like that?"

Such brutality was unlikely. The class was geology — rocks for jocks, as it was known, which was appropriate because the majority of my classmates, when they showed up for the occasional test, were athletes.

She glanced at me sideways, deliciously mischievous.

"Isn't there something you'd much rather do?"

She then grabbed the textbook in my hands and hurled it into Jackson Street where a car promptly crushed it. The driver was not pleased.

Janet laughed: "OK, that really was supposed to just be for dramatic effect."

"That wasn't my geology book."

Janet laughed harder.

"I think I can salvage it, though." Taking my first opportunity as traffic calmed, I ran into the street and rescued my wounded — but not fatally — geography book (this was not an academically impressive quarter for me).

When I returned to the sidewalk, all I was aware of was Janet's laughter.

"You know I'm not letting you go to class, right?"

The frogs who were in no real danger from me perhaps slept easier as Janet and I spent the afternoon on the seventh floor. That's when we watched *Bride of Frankenstein*, which was and still is my favorite movie.

"I feel sorry for the Bride," she said while passing me contraband popcorn from her purse. It was fresh, which shouldn't have been possible as the Tate Theater didn't open again until 3. "All those men expect her to be what they want." She paused, as though she found the characters as real as I did. "I don't think Frankenstein's a monster, though. He's just hurt, heartbroken, and lashing out."

After I'd walked her to Myers's third floor then made the significantly longer trek to the fourth, I discovered my phone ringing as soon as I entered my room.

"Just calling to tuck you in, kiddo."

We'd often stay up all night on the phone. She'd sometimes call right after we'd seen each other, or a few hours later to "catch up," or after an agonizing few days when I hadn't seen her at all.

"Oh, there you are," she'd whisper with delight at locating me.

I was once bold enough to suggest, when my roommate was absent, that she come up to the fourth floor or, as her roommate was never around, I could come to her.

"Gosh, no, sweetie, I'd have to get dressed."

After a long silence, my voice returned with a shaky, "Yeah, so, yeah, uh, this is probably more convenient then."

I'll never forget her voice. It was like the song that played during your first kiss — every word an overture that commanded attention and promised thrilling entertainment ahead.

It was a delightful contrast to the many days we would spend not saying anything at all, especially in the afterglow of an early afternoon Tate feature when we'd stumble down to the Waffle House, which had what Janet believed was the best coffee for when it was cold and the best ice tea for when it was hot. That determination, as far as I can recall, rarely had anything to do with the actual weather. She would lean against my shoulder in the booth, sipping her drink through a straw (not always a logical extension of her choice of beverage), and silence never looked so appealing.

I pause here to detail this because I don't want to give the impression that my time with Janet after our Christmas Eve conversation had become at all fractious. In reality, at least as we defined it while together, our relationship only deepened. Our highs reached a level where the lows were barely visible or memorable.

I am not intentionally forgetting Scott Waldorf. However, if Janet herself resisted calling him her boyfriend, I could resist thinking of him as anything other than the saltpeter that prevented me from gorging on her.

It is also how I wound up spending more time at Cinematic Arts. I'd joined all four programming committees: Weekday, Weekend, Midnight, and Foreign, which occupied many Janet-less afternoons. I also saw a lot of Eddie Munster, who worked part-time as a projectionist at the Tate Theater. I don't think I ever introduced him to Janet — perhaps fearing another *Crying Game* meltdown — but I would sometimes go up to the projectionist's booth on my way back from work. We'd usually just talk movies — the "dreary, serious" ones that I could never discuss with Janet. However, more often, the topic was the gradual but steady decline of Eddie's beloved CA.

"No one cares anymore," he sighed.

"Maybe they do," I suggested, "but just about different types of movies."

"No, no, I don't think they *care*... at all."

During one Weekday meeting, as Kelly Bryant nominated *Can't Buy Me Love*, Andy Razinski came over and sat next to me.

"Eddie sponsored me," he explained. "He says he's recruiting true believers."

Eddie had previously mentioned this latest tactic in his battle against the alternateen infiltration. Andy and I were his only disciples so far.

Andy surveyed the assembled crowd.

"I'm surprised Heather won't join," he said. "It looks like her kind of people."

Superficially, perhaps, but despite Tom Cody's Pygmalion efforts to impart hipness upon CA, Heather's disapproval for Eddie Munster's organization wasn't about to change. The name of the group itself even bothered her.

"*Cinematic Arts?* It's just film club — call it what it is."

It was becoming harder to justify the high-handedness of the "Cinematic Arts" title when Dana Weichman managed to get *The Cutting Edge* on the Weekday voting list. Eddie had moved for an immediate cut of the movie but didn't rally enough votes. If the median age of the films from Fall Quarter was twenty-five, we were on our way to producing a not especially bright toddler for Spring.

"The two of us should form a film union," Andy declared.

"Is that like film club?"

"See, if we agree to always vote on each other's films, that'll be two guaranteed votes. It makes them more likely to pass."

That actually made sense. Andy had a full list of movies he wanted on the schedule — *A Clockwork Orange* at the very top, but I only had two I was eager to see make the cut: *Victor/Victoria* and *Bride of Frankenstein*.

Eddie bear-hugged us after the meeting. "It's great you guys are both here." He said to me, "Did Andrew tell you about his film union idea? Genius."

Tom Cody, his hands stuffed in his pockets, walked past Andy and me on his way to Eddie.

"Not into *The Cutting Edge*, huh?"

Eddie stared at his Converse sneakers.

"It's, you know, a really new film."

"I haven't seen it," Tom said, "but Dana seems to like it."

"Yeah, I get that but a big part of what we do is educational, so we try to expose people to films they wouldn't ordinarily see."

Tom could sense that Eddie was uncomfortable with even the mildest degree of confrontation, and his widening smile almost consumed him.

Tom suddenly set the full force of that smile on me.

"You know Heather Aulds?"

I confirmed that I did. I found I was asked that question at least once each CA meeting. Her name was like a hipster pass — good for one acknowledgement from someone more popular than you.

"She's something else, right?"

I wanted to hand him a napkin to wipe his mouth. I realized now that he'd remembered me the way that you recall the uneaten vegetable that shared the same plate as a top sirloin.

"Sure," I said coldly before turning back to Eddie Munster, who had disappeared.

A few weeks later, as I sat in a lecture hall with other bored geography students, I shuddered with the uncomfortable sensation of being watched. Whenever I turned around, a black girl three rows behind me would frantically preserve her anonymity with a quickly raised textbook.

University Housing's rather lax policy of giving out your number to anyone who knows your full name eventually led to an awkward phone conversation with her.

"Hey, what's up?" Her obvious attempt to lower her normal speaking voice made her sound like she had a cold.

"I'm sorry, may I ask who this is?"

"Oh... I'm Mariah."

I doubted anyone other than the singer was named Mariah.

"So, whatcha doin'?"

"I'm reading *The Beautiful and Damned.*"

I was also anxious to return to it.

"Is that Jackie Collins? Hot stuff!"

She accosted me after class the next day when I stopped at the water fountain.

"So, what's your status?"

"My what?" A stream of water struck me in the corner of the eye.

"Your status. See, I know this cute girl who really likes you." Even I wasn't naïve enough to fall for the "I know someone who likes you" ploy. "Are you seeing anyone? Are you taken?" She nervously clutched her books to her chest, and I tried not to think about the inevitable pain my answer would cause or how the darkening above her upper lip came closer to a mustache than anything I'd achieved.

"Uh, yeah, yes, I am," I said without thinking and without lying.

"Oh." She tried to remain cool and not seem too disappointed for her "friend." She was about to rush off when something caught her attention.

"What happened to your textbook?"

A black tire track ran diagonally across the cover. It occurred to me that I'd already answered her question.

Later that day, I discovered that my normally empty mailbox held an envelope mailed from outside Myers but with a Myers return address. Inside was a formal invitation written in a familiar decorative script:

Miss Janet Tomalin requests the pleasure of your company, kiddo, at 8 p.m. Wednesday, February 10, 1993.

It happened to be 6 p.m. on Wednesday, February 10, but whatever other plans I might have had, Fitzgerald included, were quickly forgotten. At the requested time, I knocked on her door. Miss Tomalin struck a provocative pose — one hand on a round hip and a cigarette smoldering between two fingers on the other as she openly sipped from a martini glass.

"You're lucky I'm not an RA," I said.

"I knew it was you, silly." She pulled me inside by my chin. "You have a very *serious* knock." She giggled. "I'll have to do something about that."

Her dress was a cloud cover of white then a soft but steady snowfall against a dark blue sky. It was shorter than anything I'd ever seen her wear — ending a few inches above her knees.

"You're the first one here. You win a door prize." Her raspberry lipstick burned my cheek and melted my knees; I clutched the arm of her red velvet couch for support. "Actually, no one else is coming. I just wanted to get you here alone." She winked, and I very much wanted to spend the night in this room, with her, alone. "Just teasin', squeezin'. The girls will be here soon."

The girls were Nell Quinn and Patricia Campbell, who weren't so much Janet's "friends" as roles cast. She'd met them both on her first day in Athens and hadn't made another friend since.

"I love your music!" Patricia exclaimed. People who refuse to dance do so to avoid looking like Patricia, who cut the air like a knife while trying to cut a rug. All sharp edges with no trace of feminine softness, there appeared to be no way to embrace her without puncturing a lung.

Janet chain-smoked clove cigarettes as she played with the blinds from her perch by the window. Nell, built like a snowman but with a paler complexion, bummed one from her and proceeded to gargle smoke. I patted her on the back.

"I'm really getting the hang of it," she assured me. "You should have seen me last year."

It's a given that at some point in high school a girl will obtain The Bad Perm. Nell, unfortunately, brought hers to college with her and looked like Harpo Marx.

Cosmopolitans circulated the room and by the second round, Patricia and Nell had become utterly captivating within their own minds.

Patricia poked her finger in my shoulder like a hypodermic.

"See, now, see, now, I'm drunk…" I nodded in agreement. "But, you, you're not."

"Maybe I am drunk, but you think I'm not because you're drunk."

"That's possible, yes, yes, that's possible."

Throughout the night, Nell and Patricia kept after Janet to show them her photo album. She finally relented, climbing off the radiator and retrieving the album from beneath the mattress of her bed.

"That's me at the family reunion in Boston. Gosh, I was sooo fat!"

Patricia dismissed the comment with a slurred, "Stop, stop, you were beautiful, beautiful! I wish I looked like that at fourteen! I wish I looked like that now!"

One photo showed Janet's unsmiling face drowning in an ocean of blonde.

"That's Betty, Gwyneth, and me at Spence." She lowered her voice, as if Gwyneth were in the room. "The poor dear really needed to do something with her hair."

Nell recovered from her latest coughing fit long enough to compliment Janet's ebon curls.

"Why thank you, Miss Quinn," Janet said, fingering a strand and pulling it into view for a quick inspection. "It needs cutting, though. It's turning into a regular jungle."

"Gosh, I wouldn't change a thing about your hair. It's simply beau… divine."

"And this is my brother and me in Washington Scare Park." Janet cocked her thumb back like a trigger, aiming her finger at each photo as she fired her comments. "And, gag, here's Betty and me at Corney Island." There was a slight tremble in her voice — a rumble in the back of her throat — that I, having my fair share of it, immediately recognized as repressed rage. "And that's me at my sweet sixteen." It was the album's last photo. The twenty or so pages remaining were all blank, waiting to be filled, as though her life had stopped at her sixteenth birthday party.

"That's... that's not all, is it?" Patricia protested. Janet patted an exaggerated yawn as she buried the album under her mattress.

"Yeppa deppa, Miss Campbell, that's all she wrote. Show's over. Nothing more to see here." She stretched as she rose to her feet. "This trip down memory lane has just drained me dry. I'm too pooped to pop."

This was her polite way of kicking us out. I offered to walk Nell and Patricia back to Reed Hall seeing as how they could barely stand up.

"You're... you're really great, kiddo," Patricia said. It occurred to me that being called "kiddo" had a very limited appeal.

Janet drained the last drop of Nell's Cosmopolitan and whispered in my ear, "Come right back."

I took Nell and Patricia out the back (an encounter with the front desk in their condition didn't seem wise). Their arms draped around my neck and mine wrapped around their waists to keep them upright, we walked up Sanford to Reed.

"Maybe you should stay at Janet's," I said reluctantly but prodded by pangs of conscience. "You could get in a lot of trouble if the RAs see you like this."

"Don't worry, don't worry, the guy at the front is a cutie, a cutie," Patricia said. Nell had fallen asleep on her feet. "We'll just you know, you know..." She tried to wink seductively, but it just looked like she had something in her eye. There was so much wrong with this plan I didn't know where to begin.

"I can call Janet from a payphone, and she'll open the back door for us." Patricia waved away my concerns.

"We've got it covered, kiddo!"

I gritted my teeth.

"Good luck."

Janet was more than a little tipsy when I returned. She gulped down the drink she'd made for me that I'd left unattended all evening.

"*You*... are staying over." Leaning back with her hands on the window-sill, she kicked off her "Judys" (her term for any pair of "divine" red shoes). They bounced off me as she laughed naughtily. "Where's my tape, buster?"

We'd begun a weekly mixtape exchange in January. I communicated things to her through the song selections that I could never say otherwise.

"It's in my room."

"You're not getting away that easily. We'll just listen to the one you made last week." She appeared to glow at the memory of it. "You included 'Sweet Charity'! One of my favorites!" She hummed the tune as her arms twisted above her in a Fosse-inspired rhythm. "And you had that silly rule about not including title tracks."

The song, which I'd never heard before meeting Janet, expressed so fully how I felt about her that none of the rules I'd accumulated over the years like barnacles mattered anymore.

She pressed play on her stereo, as the moonlight streamed through the window and onto her like a spotlight. She appeared to ride its adoration to her bed on the top bunk. I tried unsuccessfully to find a comfortable position on the mostly decorative red velvet couch.

"So, Mr. Waldorf and I are no more," she stated matter-of-factly, punching her body pillow into shape. My smile, hidden in the darkness, had defied gravity and now touched the sky. "And it was all premeditated. But what could I do? This always happens. It's inevitable." She repeated the word, stressing each syllable. "In-ev-i-ta-ble. I think everything is. When I was a little girl, my grandmother would always tell me not to 'mess around with them boys.' I should have listened to her. I like being single, really I do; I'm just not very good at it. I can't live without the applause."

Five seconds later, she was talking about eating somewhere called Tom's Diner with her brother, then an extended comedy monologue about a rude counter girl at Wuxtry. Around 2 a.m., I fell asleep, and when I opened my eyes hours later, I immediately questioned their functionality. Janet lay next to me, her long body pressed against mine, her limbs wrapped tightly around me. I dismissed this as a dream until she murmured into my chest,

"Go back to sleep, honey. You were having an awful nightmare, so I came down to help you through it."

Sleep was impossible now, not with this woman lying next to me, my lips so close to her lilac-scented hair. Against my will, morning flooded the room as I drowned in a wild optimism. Maybe it could always be this way.

4

The night before Valentine's Day, I tossed and turned for hours on top of my sheets. Around 5 a.m., a battering ram of a knock drew me to the door. Two great globes of blue confronted me until my eyes adjusted and I recognized Heather Aulds in the hallway.

"How did you get past security?"

"What is this, the Pentagon? I just walked right in."

Two weeks had passed since I'd last seen her, during which there'd been no magisterial summons sent through the phone or through Andy Razinski for me to meet her somewhere downtown. This was how she'd made social arrangements, so her actually turning up at my door surprised me almost as much as her appearance: She'd dyed her hair black and evidently taken up recreational insomnia — her eyes were stagnant from lack of sleep. I could hear my mother's voice miles away: "Drugs — all those rich white kids are on drugs now. It was on *Oprah*."

I clutched her arm the way I imagined a friend would when about to ask a difficult question.

"Are you sure you're all right?"

She yanked away from me.

"Jesus H., I just changed my hair! I'm not on the pipe. C'mon, I feel myself getting tackier the longer I stay here."

Still dressed, I pulled on my jacket and followed her down the stairs.

"So, where've you been?"

"Just got back from Stately Aulds Manor." I couldn't tell if this was a direct answer or expert misdirection. "I'm now the proud aunt of Miss Carrington Fay Baker Aulds. I saw her last week. She weighs in at a whopping nine and a half pounds. My sister-in-law's terrified she'll be a porker and is already planning diets. Do you know I was almost named Carrington? Dodged that bullet. It's an old family name, but Karen's cousin, Heather, died in some freak accident just before I was born. I was her consolation prize, I guess. From the photos I've seen, she was Queen of the Face Lifts. She looked like Pat Nixon. When she was my age, she almost married a Catholic, but her folks threatened to cut her off so she married a plastic surgeon. Very practical. Then she has an allergic reaction to the anesthesia before a routine nip and tuck and she's dead at forty-two. That might qualify as irony."

A couple kissed heatedly at the bottom of the stairwell, obstructing the back exit. Heather pushed through them, her arms covering her face, as though they were on fire.

"Jesus H., get a room," she complained. Morning crept up on the quad. "So is this when vampires have to hide in their coffins or do they have another few minutes? It's never consistent in the movies."

We walked an ungodly distance, up the paved mountain that is Baxter Street, to an International House of Pancakes. Heather ordered a short stack, but my stomach was too pensive to accept food.

Once the waitress — dressed curiously like a flight attendant — flipped shut her notepad and left our table, Heather quietly stared into the empty space a few inches to my right. This was not unusual. She often could remain silent for long periods — her lofty expression commanding you to entertain her in some undefined way.

Andy's constant, restless physical and verbal movement served this function better than I. But he wasn't here to pepper us with actions and words, so the two of us sat and drank coffee without a syllable passing between us until Heather suddenly declared to that fascinating space to my right, "You think I'm a real bitch, don't you?"

I stirred the cream in my coffee.

"No, of course not."

Her unsmiling face shifted slightly to make eye contact.

"But you don't think anyone's a bitch really. You're too nice."

"I don't think I'm all that nice."

"Yeah, you jerk off twice a week and that makes you the next Dahmer." She arranged her knife and fork on her plate to indicate she was finished — good table manners even at IHOP. "I'm just trying to get an honest appraisal of myself, but it's impossible when no one really knows you."

"You're not dying, are you?"

"Will you stop being so considerate? I'm just kind of fucked up right now."

I asked her what was wrong as she tied her black hair into a ponytail.

"Did I tell you about my brother?"

With her hair pulled back, I had an unobstructed view of her eyes for the first time.

"You told me you had one."

"Chris was the family shame and my personal hero. He gave me my first cigarette." She lit one now in tribute. "He came here in '85. Dropped out in '86. Spent a year in Argentina. Spent a year in Amsterdam. Spent a year in rehab. Now, he's married to Miss Tennessee – literally. She came in fourth in Atlantic City back in '89. No matter what I do, Spencer and Karen think I'll turn out like Chris. The worst I can throw at them, they just shrug off. It's all a phase I'll outgrow — like Chris, but that's not gonna happen."

So, that's what this was all about. She was afraid of waking up normal one day. I wished I could empathize.

Our waitress, red bows in her sandy hair, refilled our coffee.

"Hey, it's Valentine's Day!" she informed Heather. "Where's your red?"

Heather smiled contemptuously.

"I'm on the rag. Does that count?"

Our waitress didn't think so. She slammed the check down between us in disgust.

"You know, Saint Valentine is also the patron saint of epilepsy. Something to think about." The wind whipping through the parking lot buffeted Heather's wan face. "He refused to renounce that nunsense he believed, so it was Hammer Time — they beat him to death with clubs and beheaded him on February 14. Excessive, I think, but you know those Romans. Somehow, Hallmark got involved. Chicks can find a way to get candy out of any occasion."

"Are you and Andy doing anything tonight?"

I don't know why I still thought — even then — that something was going on between them.

Heather looked at me like my head was a pancake.

"What? Razinski?" She laughed, but it was a nervous laugh. That was an emotion I had never seen from her. Her cigarette, glowing red at the filter, dove from her flicked tongue to the pavement. "Think if I start now, I should be dead-ass drunk in time for *Jeopardy!* What is... Maker's, Alex?"

It was undeniably morning. The sun shined bright in the frigid sky. Heather and I split in opposite directions. I scoured the greeting card section of every drugstore I passed, leaving each one a little more depressed. What was wrong with me? What was I doing?

Hours later, seconds to noon, I sullenly scanned the selections at Barnett's Newsstand on College Square, hoping for inspiration from Hallmark. My eyes caught Eddie Munster standing next to the comics rack; a copy of *Daredevil* covered his face, but there was no mistaking his weather-beaten Converse sneakers and red-ink-stained jeans. The patron saint of procrastination prompted me to say hello.

"Hey, Captain!" He'd taken to calling me "Captain." "How are you on this glorious day?"

"Fine, I guess. I'm sorry I wasn't around this morning. I had a lot to do."

Eddie laughed.

"Who can be bothered with work on today of all days!"

"Oh," I said, reining in my surprise. "I didn't know you were seeing anyone."

"Captain, it's not about *who* I'm seeing, it's about *what* I'm seeing." He began to dance — although it looked more like an epileptic seizure. "I'm projecting *The Double Life of Véronique*, my friend. Are you coming or are you coming?"

"I don't think so. I have a lot on my mind, and..."

He grabbed my face like the Don in a mafia movie, his bushy eyebrows furrowed in concentration. "May I give you some advice?"

I nodded.

"'The readiness is all.'"

"I beg your pardon?" He hadn't released his grip so this came out all in mumbles.

"The Big Ham, Act Five, Scene II. Hamlet's about to go fight Laertes. He knows he's gonna die, but he doesn't care. All that matters is that he's ready."

His words camped in my head. When I returned to the card rack, I chose one with Munch's *The Scream* on the cover. The inside was blank and would spare me the humiliation of prepackaged platitudes.

I hopped a city bus downtown. I rode in the back, miserable, until late afternoon, eventually disembarking at a random stop. I froze on a cold metal bench across from a children's playground. When I was a child, I had the same view of the playground as I did now.

The card in my coat pocket demanded an inscription. Three simple words would be the most effective, but those three words said so much. They weren't a boomerang, intended solely to garner a similar response, but rather a passionate exhortation of two words — "thank you." Ultimately, however, as night chased away the playing children, I cowardly settled for another three words — "Happy Valentine's Day."

I came back to Myers to find my roommate staring mooneyed at his girlfriend, her straw-colored head in his lap. He giggled as he stroked her belly, which was distended and reminded me of starving children. He'd told me how they planned to get married during the summer and then move into Family Housing in the fall. He didn't seem to realize his life was over.

"Happy Valentine's Day, baby!" he cooed.

He kissed her forehead and continued rambling on in baby talk to her. I couldn't stay in this room. I muttered a gruff combination of "hello" and "goodbye" and retreated to the lobby.

A thin girl in a tight red dress formed a small island on the floor. A pair of red heels rested in her lap, and even her finger and toenails were a bright crimson. Her hands stretched outward, practically scratching at the air, as if struggling to dig through mounds of dirt someone had heaped onto her.

"I can't believe he did this. Today of all days." She wasn't talking to me, although I was the only person there. "I mean to pretend like he's sick and can't go out when I know he's seeing that fat tramp Teri. And tonight, he's taking her out tonight. What an asshole."

So, this is what heartbreak looked like. The good news was that I could never hurt anyone on such a level. I slumped in a chair and counted the soda stains on the carpet.

"Oh, there you are," Janet murmured from the lobby steps. She wore a dark begonia evening dress and a velvet coat; her perfect face was made up in a manner that delivered Manhattan to Athens if just for one night.

Her card burned against my chest.

"Can I talk to you? I mean, before you go out?"

She laughed breathlessly. "Before *we* go out, kiddo. And you can talk to me about whatever you like — as long as it's not the hips."

We walked hand-in-hand to DePalma's Italian Café. I know it was just the contagious thrill from the woman beside me, but the glittering, black-and-white sign out front seemed to glow as spectacularly as a marquee on Broadway.

A rather disconcerting line had formed outside; I was about to suggest we try someplace else, but Janet strolled up to the hostess and gave her name. "I made reservations." She looked genuinely shocked by her actions. "I made *plans*. See what you do to me?" She reached into her evening bag. "I also made you this." It was another mixtape. "Valentine's Day edition." Just as she was about to put it in my hand, the heat of an idea fogged her sunglasses.

"Wait here a second." She walked over to someone dressed like a manager. Smiles were exchanged and soon her tape played throughout DePalma's wood-paneled rooms. "Now everyone knows!" she said as she returned, and we laughed our way to our candlelit table.

She was right. There was something so intimate about the tapes we made for each other. The patrons might have thought they were just hearing Frank Sinatra, Betty Hutton, Barbara Cook, and Fred Astaire, among others, but for us, playing the tape in the restaurant was like skinny dipping.

"You're not wearing red," I remarked.

She scrunched up her nose, half-offended. "I hate red." I suppose aside from her "Judys," she didn't wear the color that much. "Besides, doesn't everyone look better in black and white? I think that's why I adore old movies."

The framed posters hovering on the walls above bottles of wine might have come from her Upper East Side bedroom, and our dinner's soundtrack only added to the intimacy. She shared some of her pasta with me — tortellini with a mascarpone cream sauce served to me on her fork. I told her I loved her multiple times over the evening, but I seemed to suffer from a speech impediment that always made the words come out as "Pass the bread, please."

During dessert, I noticed that she suddenly seemed distracted, frazzled, as if she were putting off something very important. I was about to ask if anything was wrong, but perhaps sensing the question, she held her honey face in her hands and smiled at me, obliterating my concerns. She did that so well.

We were the last people to leave DePalma's that night. I'd gone to pay the check while Janet was in the ladies room, but the person dressed as a manager ripped it up and said, "Happy Valentine's Day!" I left a tip equal to the cost of our meals and pocketed the mixtape that she had given him earlier.

We wandered down a street that flowed red with girls in dresses, blouses, or sweaters that marked the holiday. Some were with dates — boys in hastily knotted ties or ill-fitting suits. Others charged defiantly forward in groups to enter bars with drink specials devoted to their individual sorrow.

Janet managed with masterful ease to light a clove cigarette while never releasing my hand. I should have looked ridiculous next to her. I wore the same khakis, blue shirt, gray sweater, and wool jacket that had been perfectly acceptable for my IHOP breakfast with Heather. Yet whenever Janet smiled at me, I felt like I was in a top hat, white tie, and tails.

Dinner had left me completely full and satisfied, but I feared I was so replete with joy that I was failing to act. I liked to think that Scott Waldorf was off somewhere with Evelyn Wilson making terrible music together. Janet was here with me and all I had was some lousy card that didn't come close to saying how desperately I wanted her.

"You're *so* serious!" Janet whispered. "And, oh, so quiet..."

She was close enough to me that the surrounding red faded into the night. It was just us now by the Arch. I was so stupid with love for her that I might as well have emptied DePalma's wine cellar.

"I got you something."

It cost me her hand for a moment, but I reached into my jacket pocket for her card. Her full cheeks darkened — the only glimpse of red on her — as she read it.

"Beautiful boy, darling boy! Thank you so much!"

She hugged me, and I knew I never wanted to let her go.

"Do you ever feel that our friendship isn't real, that it's just a glorious dream?"

She'd just verbalized what I thought whenever I saw her.

"Sometimes."

"That's just because friendship like ours isn't well-documented." She still smelled of Crest toothpaste. "Come with me."

She pulled me through the Arch with a daring wink. After passing through a white, stone-columned portico, we climbed up the exposed stairway in the Academic Building to a wooden bench on the second floor that overlooked Broad Street and the north lawn; the people on the streets resembled small red puddles, evaporating slowly as the night progressed.

"I like to come here alone and just think." She paused. "I shouldn't do that, of course. It causes so much trouble. Nice girls shouldn't think too much; they'll remember why they aren't."

The P.A. system at Peppino's Pizzeria down the street screamed, "Number 64! Number 64! Get your pizza!" as Janet performed a bit of slight-of-hand; a red envelope appeared, as if from nowhere, in her lap, clutched tightly in her clenched fists.

"I don't know if I should give you this."

I'd never heard her sound unsure of anything; even her insouciant dismissal of certain matters had an air of confidence and assurance.

"You didn't get me the exact same card, did you?"

She laughed, relishing the action like a gift.

"I really like you, kiddo. I wish you liked me."

She knew. My feelings were as apparent as the full moon that night, and she wanted me to spare her my clumsy, inhuman attempts at love.

"I do like you, Janet."

"No, you don't. You don't really. You couldn't possibly." Perhaps sensing her discomfort, a cloud moved in front of the moon, blocking its rays so I could only see her dark profile. "I've done a lot of awful things. I still do. I'm not a very good person."

"That's not true," I said more forcefully than I'd said anything.

"How do you know what's true or not?" she snapped, but she sounded less angry than curious, as if I could solve a riddle that tormented her. She stared at her black leather heels, which, despite the cold, she wore without hose. She rarely wore stockings or hose because they were "too constricting."

"I want to tell you…" She stopped speaking and instead began humming The Beatles song of the same name.

She lit another cigarette. The humming ceased, but when she spoke again, her words were small, barely audible. I moved closer to her on the bench.

"When my father left, everything just sort of — how can I put this? — fragmented, like a mirror breaking. All was in confusion in the Tomalin house. Have you ever thought something was perfect and then learned that it wasn't, that it didn't even come close? Nothing made sense anymore, and it *had* before. I think that's what no one understands. It was like a grand movie, and I was Dorothy in Kansas. But then my life twisted up, became so subjective I couldn't tell what was real and what wasn't. All of a sudden, my parents had *never* been happy, and every memory I had to the contrary was some elaborate illusion. My family abandoned me, but *they* claimed I locked myself in my room and wouldn't come out. I ate all the time and got gross and fat, but then I collapsed at school, and the doctors said I was twenty pounds underweight.

"My father still took me out for dinner and to see shows, but it was all so hollow. I used to feel like the most beautiful girl in the world when I was with him, and now I felt like the ugliest. I spent a lot of time in the bathroom. Do you like baths? They're divine. I would just sink beneath the water and not hear anything or see anything, and the best thing is, when you're down there, you can't tell that you're crying. I wanted to stay submerged forever, but I had to keep coming up for air. I found a way around that, though. I took my father's razor and sliced open both my wrists. Time meant nothing."

She said this so casually I thought she was joking, so perhaps to convince us both, she raised her arms into a slender shaft of moonlight, exposing two, thin scars, each one running vertically down the underside of her wrist. I'd never noticed them. Maybe my eyes refused to acknowledge a flaw. I'd known Janet only a short while by the objective, non-emotional way time is measured, but the thought of a world without her seemed incomprehensible.

"I woke up in the hospital. My brother found me. I must have given him quite a fright, what with all that red water. I spent the next year someplace... odd. I don't remember saying anything the entire time I was there. I wasn't trying to be rude; I just couldn't get a word in edgewise. They told me I was dead drunk when I did what I did, which was silly because I'd been thinking so clearly. They told me I was desperately malnourished, but I just wasn't hungry. They whispered to each other about my various problems and hang-ups and how awful my hair looked, while I listened to *The White Album*. My family would visit me, and I would think how odd it was that *I* wasn't with them as they stared all sympathetically at this mute girl with bad hair. But, you know, I'm really not into sympathy; to me, it implies pity, which in turn implies superiority. I prefer empathy, but that doesn't exist. We are all alone, unhappy.

"A year later, I went home. At least that's what they told me. I still don't believe them, though. I mean, the idea of spending a year in that awful place is just too horrible to bear. Besides, I couldn't have listened to *The White Album* that many times. I'm convinced it was only about an hour and a half. Time is all relative anyway, like when you rent a bad

movie and fast-forward through the dull spots. My first day home was like
that. All eyes were on me, like it was my comeback special or something
like that. The first thing I said was, 'I'm starving,' and Mother made me
a peanut butter and jelly sandwich. That was about all she could handle,
and it still wasn't as good as when Agnes made them. And before I could
finish it, I was sitting in my therapist's office and he was poking and
prodding me and trying to see what went wrong. I was trapped in time —
except I kept moving forward. I could never go back, and I tried so hard.
The past is so elusive. We don't mean to, but we're always burning our
bridges behind us. One moment, I'm back in school, with everyone whispering behind my back like little flies buzzing, and the next, my father's
moving back home permanently. So, maybe I'm wrong. Maybe you *can*
repeat the past."

She smiled but not from joy. It was a smile of prepared disappointment,
a perverse pleasure in forecasting unhappiness, like the cynic who always car-
ries an umbrella.

"You can run away now, kiddo. No hard feelings."

"Why would I do that?"

She hugged herself and rocked back and forth on the bench.

"Everyone does eventually. You scratch the surface, and there's nothing
there. So, I'm saving you the trouble."

Her heels received her full scrutiny as she continued to sway nervously
in her seat. She looked like someone who'd decided on a course of action,
considered it and debated it, and now couldn't go through with it. My hand
grasped her foot, a playful gesture that disguised all intimacy.

People spend their lives trying to create the illusion that they are not
alone in their unhappiness. I pulled her to me, her mascara running down her
face and smearing my sweater, and our illusion was complete.

The next morning, a red envelope lay on the floor of my room a few
inches from the door, my name written in large, affected letters across the
front. I opened it and laughed out loud. She *had* gotten me the exact same
card. On the inside page, she'd written:

You're my brass band, honey. I could listen to you all day. You're my savoy
truffle – sooo fattening but I could just gobble you up. — JET.

A space of a few lines separated this paragraph from another, written
with a different pen and in a shakier script:

Hey, kiddo, you're a doll for putting up with me last night. I had a little too much wine and one thing led to another and, well, forget everything I said. Love you lots, but not vacantly. — Mahogany.

She regarded the previous evening as an emotional one-night stand and would prefer I erase those hours from my memory. She helped me forget my past, so it seemed fair to return the favor. I placed the card in my history book, between the same two pages I'd slipped the folded sheet of paper she'd given me months ago. History 251 had been otherwise uneventful except for that one amazing day. It is the one textbook from college I still own.

5

The days immediately following that night with Janet were an uncontrolled indulgence in each other's company. We were inseparable, and I was never happier. Geography and geology quickly became foreign subjects to me as we whiled away afternoons at Rocky's or took the Orbit bus for multiple trips around campus. We'd share the headphones of her Walkman and listen to *My Fair Lady* or *Candide* ("sooo divine!").

"If I have a girl, I'll call her Cunegonde." Then in an earnest whisper: "Or a boy, I suppose. It's a flexible name, don't you think?"

As I savored this ongoing party for two, I was also invited to a much larger one. Heather Aulds called me the first week of March and said if I had no other plans, I should "shake my rump" with her at Gina Sloane's "bash" that coming Saturday.

The previous "bash" with Heather's "alternateen" friends that I'd attended had not made me eager for another. However, over the phone, I sensed something in her dignified drawl that sounded as though she were asking me a favor, so I headed over to her place after discussing Kurosawa with Eddie Munster in the Tate Theater projection booth.

The floor of her apartment was carpeted with clothing, like a boutique changing room. PJ Harvey and the latest edition of the *Flagpole* entertained me as Heather became a blur of various outfits.

"You look fine," I would say when asked my opinion.

"You're no help at all!"

I'd never known her to care this much about her appearance or, well, anything for that matter. She was almost content with a green, wool sweater and maroon corduroy pants when Andy Razinski entered, finishing off a slice from Peppino's, and remarked, "You look like a Christmas tree!"

We both expected an obscene riposte, but instead she receded into her room, changing into a black version of the same outfit. She violently loaded us into her car shortly after 10 and headed west — far away from the comforting confines of downtown and well outside the orbit of campus transit.

Heather's Porsche eventually entered an actual neighborhood with houses and backyards. Here, students could escape the regulations of the dorms and enjoy all the freedoms of adulthood while still conducting themselves according to the established rules of a playground.

Gina Sloane lived by herself in a single family home that was one baby step removed from the dreamlike doll house she probably had as a child. When we arrived, the party had spread like beer from a spilled bottle onto the front and back yards.

Heather ignored everyone we passed during her grim trek up the driveway. She moved as though Gina lived in an isolated hut on top of a mountain that required us to scale to its peak. I thought I saw dapples of sweat on her forehead, as if she were burning up from within on a night that had dipped below freezing.

Music fled the house when Heather pulled open the front door. Down the long hallway and into the living room, guests played musical conversations, rotating from person to person with the chain of discussion remaining mostly intact.

Heather's eyes absorbed the crowd with gloomy disappointment. For a second, I thought we might turn around and leave before anyone noticed we'd arrived, but two blondes in matching turquoise sweaters marched toward her — one of them stating with cool reproach, "Aulds, you're such a ditcher! You ditched us."

Their presence took a moment to register with Heather, who was looking at everyone else in the room but them.

"No, no," she replied, "I told you I might drop by."

"Ditcher!" insisted the blonde on my right. "You were supposed to roll with us!" She pointed her Guinness at the blonde on my left. "Isn't that right?"

The blonde on my left nodded and then exhaled cigarette smoke.

"We roll together."

The two, who Heather called Baldwin and Reed, shared her aggressive pose, chilly supercilious gaze, and gruff, commanding voice. They even had the same bronze skin that served, in the last days of winter, as a prelude to spring and a visible reminder that summer never had to fade for the select few. My glasses must have been defective, though, because I thought they looked nothing like her.

Baldwin and Reed herded us into the living room with aggressive shooing motions. Reed collapsed on a lime green sofa from the 1970s that slithered in half-moon circles against the wall.

Gina Sloane was an art student, which was reflected in a taste for eclectic furniture and found objects that littered the room in a deliberately random way. I was seated somewhat ludicrously in an old barber's chair facing a wall painted to resemble red bricks; it was covered with CDs, records, and tapes on distressed wood shelves that ran in a zigzag pattern. Andy had landed on the half-moon next to Baldwin and Reed. Heather stood behind me as though she were about to give me a trim and silently sipped from a bottle of Bass Ale.

"Oh, Aulds," Reed said, "have we told you how much we love the whole Morticia Addams look?"

Baldwin nodded and exhaled more cigarette smoke.

"We love it."

"I was going to shave my head — you know, as a political statement — but it's way too cold," Reed said. "But if you're done with it, I could just pinch your green."

"Just don't go goth," Baldwin warned Heather. "It might seem like a good time, but those people live in dorms."

Heather reminded me that night of a stately home whose owner no longer had the resources to maintain. As there was no further need to keep up the façade, glimpses of riotous festivities could be seen through the brilliant windows if someone was curious enough to stop and take a look. Every so often, it would seem as if she might invite me inside, but just as the lights were at their brightest, the windows would abruptly shutter, and Heather would dart off toward a destination known only to her.

During these absences, Baldwin and Reed appeared to view Andy and me as personal items of Heather's she'd left behind, and they kept a casual but otherwise disinterested eye on us.

Reed tapped the ash from her cigarette into an abandoned plastic cup on an end table that at some point in its past had been a sewing machine stand. Doing the same was a curly haired girl whose potato-shaped head sat precariously on her narrow neck. I couldn't place her, but she looked familiar enough that I thought I should offer her a mild wave from the barber's chair, which encouraged her to speak.

1124 Stephen Robinson

"You're in CA, right?"

I nodded and now recognized her as Debbie Tyson, who generally followed Dana Weichman around Cinematic Arts like the dust tail of a comet.

"How do you know Gina?"

"I don't."

It occurred to me that this might be a serious breach of party etiquette. I considered cutting short my hair appointment and trying to find the host.

Reed, who was occupied in an absorbing game of Cat's Cradle with invisible string, said, "She went to Westminster, right?"

"No, Lovett."

Baldwin reacted like she'd uttered an obscenity.

"God, that's almost as bad as North Atlanta."

"Yeah, well, I don't know her from Lovett," Debbie said. "I went to Dunwoody."

This did not impress Baldwin.

"Oh, I heard people wound up there."

"Does Heather know her?" Andy asked.

This confused Debbie, who pointed to Baldwin and Reed.

"Which Heather?"

"Wait? Your names are also Heather? That's just like..."

"We know what it's fucking like, Razinski."

Our Heather had come back with another Bass Ale, which she now guzzled like it was root beer. Reed, who used Andy's twitching leg as an armrest, turned to her and asked, "Do you think there'll be any decent boys here tonight? There's a serious boy problem so far."

"It's awful," Baldwin confirmed. "Just dud after dud after dud."

"I hope Cody shows up."

The thought pleased Baldwin.

"Yeah — especially if he brings Joe and Robert. They're yummy."

"Joe and Robert are rehearsing with Stan."

"Stan said they might come over after."

"I like Stan," Reed said as if she were the only one who could justify his existence. "He's sort of Cobain-y, which is cool. Joe is more like that guy from The Cure, which has its place."

Baldwin nodded and gestured for a moment with her cigarette until she found the appropriate descriptor.

"He's... *different*... but not too much."

"Robert doesn't have a thing," Reed noted somewhat sadly. "He's just himself... that's his only problem."

"Those guys aren't coming," Debbie said definitively. "Only Cody can get them to put down their instruments, and Dana said he's not coming."

"Really?" Reed said coldly. "Because Weichman is *so* on top of Cody."

Baldwin laughed literally and concisely: "Ha."

"What I meant, of course," Reed clarified with a smirk, "is that Cody does his own thing." She looked at Heather, who had just returned from another quick tour of the house with yet another Bass Ale. "You wouldn't mind if Cody went stag tonight?"

Heather opened her mouth to speak, but the same unknown compulsion pulled her from her seat with great force. I got up, unconsciously tearing away the nonexistent barber cloth covering me, and followed her past scattered pockets of self-importance into the kitchen, which was larger than my dorm room, and then out the screen door to the backyard.

Some people outside had determined to entertain themselves by testing to see how long they could keep their beer bottles balanced on Gina Sloane's fence before they toppled over. Extra points were awarded if the bottle and its contents fell out of sight onto her neighbor's side. Heather's black hair and clothes had vanished into some private gathering of the night's, so I'd turned to go back inside when I heard someone on the porch say:

"Hey, *Bleach* is the best thing they ever did. *Nevermind* is just pop crap. All kinds of people like it. I was walking down Lumpkin the other day, and I heard it coming out of a frat house! If I were you, I'd be ashamed to even own it."

The voice was like rancid milk, so I knew it was Evelyn Wilson before I even saw her lecturing someone with a shaved head (winter had not stalled his political statement). She emphasized her points with violent waves of her PBR can.

"See, what I'm saying is if I can hear it on the radio or buy it at Walmart, I don't wanna know about it."

"So you support local music?"

"Obviously — until they sell out. That's the whole tragedy of Seattle. We can't let that happen here."

"What about R.E.M.?"

Evelyn raised a hand to God.

"Don't get me started!"

But it was too late. I left her to rail against music listened to by more than a dozen people. The barber chair waited for me in the living room. No one else had been foolish enough to sit in it. Andy was talking movies with Debbie Tyson... or trying to, at least. She had little to say on the topic, and it occurred to me that she might have joined CA simply because of the people who already belonged. It could just as well have been an organization dedicated to cooking or crochet; the flame was less important than the moths.

Baldwin and Reed sat wearily on the lime-green couch. Their hands on their stomachs, they looked as if they had stuffed themselves on a three-course meal of disappointment.

"This is a bust," Reed said suddenly and with such finality that she might as well have painted a chalk outline around the occasion. "It's like my father's garden, and my father's garden is... demoralizing."

"I told you Cody wasn't coming," Debbie said.

"Yes," replied Baldwin, making eye contact with Debbie for the first time that evening. "No one interesting came."

Heather had returned, more diminished than when she'd left. Andy was attempting to persuade Debbie to vote for *A Clockwork Orange* at the next Weekday meeting when she glanced up at Heather, who was barely a member of the conversation, and suggested that she join Cinematic Arts.

"It's not my thing," Heather said dismissively.

"Because of the movie nerds, right? They make such a big deal out of everything. I felt the same way at first, but it's much cooler now that they've started to leave. It's fun."

Reed unlaced her right boot and slipped it off to massage a green-socked foot.

"I like movies," she announced. "I saw a movie last month."

"The one with Madonna," Baldwin confirmed.

"See? We should totally be in film club, but let's do it after the movie nerds are gone."

"Don't wait too long," Debbie warned. "You don't want to be new school. See, I'm old school... like Cody and Dana."

No one commented on the absurdity of Debbie's statement. Baldwin and Reed rose from the couch with stretches and yawns as if getting out of bed.

"Should we just leave?" Baldwin asked.

"If no one cool's showing up, who cares what we do?" Reed pointed out. "We could have fun."

Baldwin and Reed's departure provided an opportunity to extricate myself from the barber's chair and go sit on the couch. Heather stood so still next to the end table that someone might have confused her for one of Gina Sloane's found objects.

Andy's restlessness had sent him dancing out of the room, and as soon as he'd gone, Debbie Tyson took a sudden and possessive interest in my arm.

"You're friends with Eddie Munster, aren't you?"

I nodded.

"Yeah, I saw you two going into the projection booth before *Throne of Blood* last week," she explained — then leaned in close enough for me to smell the sour cream and onion chips she'd eaten. "So, what's his deal?"

Eddie — who I'd define as a "movie nerd" with nothing but disdain for Debbie's terminology — had apparently conveyed mystery through his eccentricity. Debbie played with her rust-brown curls as she waited for a response.

"I don't think he has a deal," I said, now to my horror paraphrasing Heather Reed. "He's just himself."

"That's kind of hot."

Disturbed beyond description, I successfully negotiated for my arm's release.

It was then that I looked over and saw the columns supporting Heather begin to buckle. She clumsily gripped the end table — tipping over the red cup of ashes, downed her drink, and with a renewed strength and determination went into the other room. I was right behind her until she suddenly stopped and, to my astonishment, ran into a hall closet.

"She can't piss in there," a drunken girl next to me insisted. "People keep trying to piss in there." She paused. "I pissed in there."

Her confession startled me long enough for the closet to have opened and allowed its occupant to melt into the crowd. I set off in pursuit, but another girl in the room called out my name.

She wandered over to me in red Chuck Taylors. I think she liked the color because her hair was a collection of different shades; scarlet, magenta, auburn — they all struggled for dominance like competing wildflowers. Her face — clear and white — had a bubbly quality, and her thick, round-framed black glasses seemed to constantly ride the wave of her smile.

"Hey! I've wanted to talk to you all night."

"Oh." Then: "Why?"

She laughed.

"I think you're great. I *loved* your music reviews, and your editorials are hilarious."

That explained it: I'd started writing a column for the Op-Ed page of the *Red & Black*. My photo (unfortunately) ran with it. I thanked her for the compliment. She took my hand and smiled, her glasses cascading down her nose.

"I tried to say hello earlier but whenever I went into the living room, it looked like you were holding court."

"Oh… is that what I was doing?"

She laughed again.

"I'm Jaye."

I introduced myself before I remembered she already knew my name. It was a strange sensation that hasn't lessened with time.

"I'll let you get back to your friends, but it was great meeting you."

She let go of my hand and smiled; her red shoes carried her along Gina Sloane's hardwood floors into the kitchen and out the screen door.

I decided to wait for Heather back in the living room. If the pattern held, she should slump back in fifteen minutes or so with another beer. In the foyer, Baldwin and Reed danced robotically to something guitar-driven and loud, and Andy was engaged in a tragically futile wooing of a stunning creature with purple hair.

I spoke casually, as that was the only possible way, with Debbie Tyson, a half-moon separating us, for a few minutes before she left… either the room or the party, I'm not sure. Glancing at my watch, I saw that Heather had missed at least five scheduled appearances. I was about to assemble my search party of one when I noticed Evelyn Wilson by the fire brick wall appraising the music in our host's collection.

"I can't believe she owns *this*. It's so MTV."

"I kind of like *Pretty Hate Machine*," responded someone I recognized as a member of Scott Waldorf's band.

Evelyn shrugged. "I'd excuse it if she didn't just leave it out here for everyone to see. *Flaunting* it. It's OK to like something, I guess, but do it in private."

"Do you know when Scott's going to want to rehearse again?"

She replaced the CD and sighed, her featureless face collapsing.

"I don't know, Mike. I don't know. You have to understand the influence he's been under. My baby's just lucky he got out when he did."

Her "baby" had been dropped like a negligent mother's child. Janet had erased groveling, despondent, emasculated messages from him, begging her to see him, with a casual press of a button while she asked me what we should have for dinner. Evelyn was the sloppiest of seconds.

"God, that slut did a number on him. What's worse is that we can't even be together yet. I mean, I need him so bad, but I have to think about my health. I won't even consider it until he gets tested. There's no telling what he picked up."

A stranger, bearing an uncanny resemblance to myself, leapt from the couch.

"How dare you!" he sputtered violently at the stunned Evelyn. "How dare you say that kind of crap about her! You don't know a thing about her!"

Evelyn sneered. "And you do? Scott used to wonder where Miss Teenage Whore was when she wasn't with him. He just assumed she was with you, and he knew you didn't have the balls to try anything. But you know where she really was? She was downtown giving free rides to anyone who wanted to hop on. She never cared about Scott. He's lucky she could remember his name. Hell, he says she even forgot once or twice! So, basically, my heart was ripped out because that bitch was bored. Bored, goddammit! I'm sure I'm not the only one she ever did this to but I'm the first who fought back. There's not a bartender where it matters who doesn't know her on sight! Don't believe me? You ask her. Scott did. Ask her about the townies at the Manhattan who were up for a little jungle fever! Ask her about Scott's roommate! His fucking roommate! You must feel special, being the only one she hasn't fucked. But let me give you some advice: If you ever get tired of being her beard and want to get in her 'divine' pants, buy her a drink. From what I hear, that's the only prereq."

She'd just defaced a work of art because it was beautiful and transcendent and she was not. I couldn't speak. Pride demanded I not betray my pain to those rotting green eyes and that smirking mouth. Taking my silence as submission, she turned to Mike, dismissing me with a withering "you're still here?" look.

My hand clamped around her pale arm. The sudden, unexpected contact shocked her, and she tried to twist free.

"You're crazy!" I exploded. "I always knew that. But you're stupid, too, if you expect me to believe a word you've said. You're not capable of understanding why she's above you in every possible way, so all you can do is run her down! I don't think much of Scott, but I pity anyone who has to spend more time with you than I have. You're disgusting! You don't even deserve to say her name."

Now it was Evelyn's turn to fight back tears. She regressed to childhood — her snotty, puerile childhood.

"Janet! Janet! Janet!" she shouted. "Janet! Jan..."

My mind, along with Mike, fled the room.

"Ow! Goddammit! Let go of me!"

I regained control of my body, releasing her arm as if it were on fire. The spot where my hand had been now blazed red.

"Psycho!" she screamed. Coming from her, this was quite the insult. She emptied the contents of her PBR over my head and ran out of the house.

Andy came in from the other room.

"Hey, B. I hear something's going down in... Wow, what happened to you?"

I wiped the beer from my eyes.

"I think we should go."

I then set off to find Heather. I tried the backyard first — more out of a need for fresh air than a hunch I'd spot her amidst the trees and bushes that were more fascinating than the lingering guests. Yet that's where she was, hidden outside the reaches of the porch light and propped up against a withered tree that used all its remaining strength to support her slight body. Her hand still held the Bass Ale that had delivered the knock-out punch.

"We need to leave," I said, paranoia setting in. I could almost hear the police, squad car sirens blaring, coming to pummel me into submission after Evelyn tearfully revealed the details of our altercation.

The commanding arrogance in Heather's eyes had abandoned her, leaving behind a selective blindness. Nothing else was worthy of their focus except for what they now seemed to desperately crawl toward. I turned and followed them straight to Jaye, whose dark clothes melted against the fence as her hair simmered in the wind like a cold flame. Clouds of smoke, chased by icy breath, left her mouth in short bursts. Heather's experiencing so natural an emotion as infatuation made the source of it impossible to perceive as unnatural.

I peeled her off the tree and took her around the house to the street where we'd parked. Leaning against her car, Andy took one look at Heather and exclaimed, "Holy shit, she's wasted!"

I tossed him her keys.

"Can you drive stick?" I asked.

Andy nodded in confirmation. He entered the driver's side and made the necessary height adjustments to the seat. I climbed in the back with Heather, her hair spilling like oil over my lap. She shriveled into the dampness of my shirt to escape the toxic light from a passing car.

"You smell like beer," she moaned.

"It's my new cologne."

I joked because I was worried about her and because my ears still ached from Evelyn Wilson's deranged assault.

"Looks like it's time for B-E-D," Andy said.

"Don't wanna go home," she insisted. "Just drive."

And so we drove off, perhaps as demoralized as Heather Reed in her father's blue garden.

We stopped at a gas station for water, which I forced into Heather's reluctant mouth while we sped out of the city and onto the interstate. Three hours later, we were in Chattanooga, Tennessee, parked near the Walnut Street Bridge. The lights that dotted the bruised-blue scaffolds dimmed with the brightening of the sky.

Heather was in the eye of inebriation now and able to form sentences with careful deliberation. Leaning against the railing, I wrapped her in my coat and silently observed the undaunted progression of water underneath us. Behind us, Andy bounced spastically on top of a metal bench in a desperate gambit for warmth.

Reaching for my hand on the railing, she began to tell me about Jaye Goetz, who first disturbed Heather's universe when she recited *Love Song of*

J. Alfred Prufrock for extra credit in their English Lit. class. Jaye snapped her fingers as she spoke to prod her memory, and her lips curled sensually around each word. Heather wrote an incredibly passionate essay about *Prufrock* — so much so it felt as though she'd drawn Jaye's face in charcoal.

The feelings she had were new — not just for Jaye but for anyone, and the brakes were severed on them when at Noel Hartigan's party a few weeks ago, her eyes floated over to Jaye's delightfully lopsided face (her nose and mouth seemed to veer in opposite directions, like oncoming vehicles avoiding a collision).

She hadn't been able to talk to her then, but she'd resolved to do so at Gina Sloane's. She knew Jaye was coming. She heard her mention it in class with an enthusiasm Heather had never felt about a party until this one.

"I told myself that tonight I'd do something. I didn't give a fuck if she laughed in my face or screamed like I was some kind of freak. But what if she didn't? That would mean... it would mean... something. A lot, actually. God, the Manic Panic washes out, you know? But *this*... this is... and yet it's the first thing I've ever really wanted. You get this feeling in the pit of your stomach, like you're hungry but a little different. I feel like that all the time now. But every time I got close to saying something, I had a beer instead. And then my legs stopped working."

She slumped next to me, exhausted. She'd passed through the eye of lucidity. Her skin matched the algae on the rocks below. I held her by the waist as she doubled over and deposited the previous evening into the blue-green river.

6

The following week, at the Olde Spaghetti Store on Broad Street, March moving forward with regimental austerity, Andy Razinski slurped pasta from a wooden bowl and told us about his film project.

"OK, so my script's about a relationship between two college students who would normally never even meet: A black guy from the South Side of Chicago and a white girl from Dalton, Georgia. The black guy's named Damon Andrews — my nod to Richard Wright's *The Outsider* — and the white girl's named Beth Cross. She's a conservative Christian and he's this left-wing militant atheist, a true rebel in the Camus fashion. They meet at a Tate showing of *Rear Window*, and there's this intense passion between them. She can't resist him. He challenges her and appeals to the part of her that's buried underneath all the Christian bullshit but that's still alive and thinking. In the end, though, she doesn't have the courage or strength to stay with him and instead winds up with some khakis-wearing good ole boy." He finished off his pasta. "It's a tragedy, but I think the right audiences will get it."

"The Christian girl's last name is Cross?"

Andy appeared pleased that I'd picked up on his subtle metaphor. Heather dispassionately rearranged the lettuce in her salad.

"It sounds... interesting."

"Thanks, B. I showed the script to the president of the Black Student Union. He's a drama major and would be perfect for the lead. Now, I just need someone for the female role." He turned to Heather. "Do you think Baldwin or Reed would be interested?"

Heather pushed away her untouched plate of food and shrugged. She scratched her shoulders, and her low monotone could have come from another table.

"Here's a script idea for you," she said. "You have a man who's obsessed with women behind partitions. You know, like glass, something transparent but that can't be penetrated."

"You mean like women in subway token booths?"

"Yeah or the women at the DMV."

"Toll booth operators?"

"No, that doesn't quite work. Not much chance for interaction. Although that could be the last scene. Here's another one: You have a guy who always remains in bad situations because he doesn't want to admit that they're bad, that life in and of itself bites like Cujo. So, he stays in college when that's not working out. He stays married when that's going down the toilet. His kids are all grossly deformed, but he still takes them to Little League and ballet class even though they're just lab experiments. See, he'd rather be positive than negative, but he's really just an idiot because his life *is* negative. He's the positive-negative man."

"That was an episode of *The Avengers*," I said. "The title at least."

"Whatever."

Andy stuck his spoon into a cup of orange sherbet. Once it reached his mouth, he gagged, spat it out, and clawed at his tongue with both hands. Heather slid her lime sherbet to him. Orange remains still clinging offensively to his spoon, he reached for Heather's.

She smacked away his hand. "Jesus H.! Use a napkin, you fucking baby!"

After devouring Heather's discarded dessert, Andy went to the restroom. She immediately handed me a folded piece of paper. The off-centered type read:

Your eyes, an azure sky in the heat of summer
Your skin, as clear and fresh as filtered water
Your lips, two pink salmons swimming in opposite directions
And your hair, darker than the Devil's domain, but just as irresistible
To say you are beautiful would be a pleonasm

I studied the "poem" with mounting concern.

"You want a critical assessment?"

"God, no, I didn't write it. I'm not *that* far gone. I've been getting this crap since Valentine's Day. They just show up in my mailbox — never stamped or addressed, which means this perv knows where I live. I don't want acid tossed in my face!"

"Who would do that?" Andy asked.

"No one. Carlton and I were just..." The color rushed from her face and she left the table in pursuit of it.

Andy sat down. "I guess you're next. This could be another script idea: *The Restroom of Doom!*"

Turning around, I saw Jaye Goetz waving at me through the window. She came inside with a black guy and a small, platinum blonde rounding out her group.

"Hey, it's my favorite writer!" she said. "These are my friends, Nick and Marie."

I shook Nick's hand, pulling away before it could evolve into an attempted soul shake, which I would only mangle. Taking my hand, Marie shared with me the touching story of how the Spaghetti Store was the first restaurant in which she'd eaten in Athens.

"I was with my parents," she said. "We all loved the sherbet."

I introduced Andy, who gave Nick the soul shake I'd prudently avoided. Andy admired Nick's Tribe Called Quest T-shirt and asked him if he were going to see the group in Atlanta. Nick said he was planning on it. He was about my height and build but with a confident stance, dreadlocks, fashionable clothes and glasses, and a thick goatee. I considered him the Bizarro Me.

Jaye placed a red-nailed hand on my shoulder.

"I think you took off before I could get your number," she said. "I'm having a party — really tiny thing, I know no one — this Saturday."

Heather skulked miserably back to the table. There was evidence in her face of a self-administered pep talk. Her hair had been touched up in the desperate manner of someone who forgot to bring a comb and now cursed herself for it.

She groped for her wit. "Meeting of your fan club, Carlton?"

"He's just the best, isn't he?" Jaye said — unaware that Heather felt every word like a kiss. "Nothing's sacred with him."

Jaye's hair was pulled back from her oval face, and her glasses had been swapped out for oversized shades from the '80s. "Classic 67" was stenciled across the front of her purple sweatshirt, which she'd unzipped, so the statement was divided. The blue letters were faded and beat-up. The "A" and the "6" fared especially poorly, and the "7" was now almost more of a slanted "I."

"Hey, you're in Cofer's class, aren't you?" Jaye said to Heather, causing life to appear in her livid cheeks. "The final's turning me gray."

As her natural color was a mystery, this could very well be true.

"You could always study together," I said idiotically, but I felt less foolish when Heather smiled at me in a very grateful way.

"I wish," Jaye groaned. "I could use the help. But it's Open Book Suicide. And we won't know what the essays are until the day of the final. If only it were something like 'blank is the cruelest month.'"

"April," Andy said helpfully.

"I was born in April," Marie said. "I don't think it's cruel at all."

"Maybe you could recite another poem for extra credit."

Heather bit her lip, because she'd just told Jaye how she felt and everyone present saw — except for perhaps Andy, who was scooping out the last bits of sherbet from his cup.

Flattered, Jaye slipped her hands over her round hips into the back pockets of her jeans. "God, you remember that? I was so bad. I couldn't stop popping my fingers. I sounded like such a Valley Girl."

She still did but adorably so. Every sentence ended like a question — "I was so bad?" and "I couldn't stop popping my fingers?" She wrote her number on the back of a take-out menu. "Here. It would be so Fab Five Freddy if you all could come. Like I said, it's no big thing."

Andy and Nick exchanged numbers, as well, along with cementing plans to see the Tribe Called Quest concert.

"Oh. My. God." Heather exclaimed once they were gone. "I just want to die. Really. Die. Did someone replace my brain with a cabbage or something? Jesus H.!"

"Big B.!" Andy slapped my arm. "I'm telling you, there's no way that Jaye could want you more. You're going to be wearing her panties on your head by the end of the week."

Heather ran back to the bathroom.

"What's with her lately?" Andy asked, but I had no answer he would understand.

Perhaps my memory overdramatizes the evening, but I felt a suffocating gloominess the night of Jaye's party. Never being a fan of warm weather, I attributed it to the onslaught of spring. Indeed, the air had thawed enough that jackets could be left in closets.

Andy and I saw *Glengarry Glen Ross* at Tate, after which Heather was to meet us downtown — though I would not be convinced of this until I saw her myself. She'd called me in hysterics Friday night.

"I can't do this! There's no fucking way! I'm so on crack!"

I could hear PJ Harvey in the background promoting Heather's despair. Once the 7:30 p.m. showing let out, we joined Eddie Munster at Peppino's for what was intended to be dinner but had the aftertaste of a wake.

Eddie looked sick with grief, and it affected his appetite. He guzzled Tums, and his meatball sub, unable to arouse any desire from him, lay on a bed of grease untouched.

The cause seemed obvious to me. The two things he loved most were in jeopardy: The recently finalized Tate Theater calendar for Spring Quarter was littered with dubious selections, including *Ice Castles, The Cutting Edge,* and *Pete's Dragon.*

However, Eddie was still devoted to Cinematic Arts and wanted to restore it to the condition it was in when they'd first encountered each other, but he had reason to fear this wouldn't happen.

"Travis is gonna be editor in chief in the fall. There's no way around it. He's shadowing Lori all the time — like he knows he has the job. And she's even going to let him sub for her when she's in Augusta for a week next month. It's the end, just the end."

I actually didn't think Travis's hard line on the division between the *Red & Black* and CA was that unreasonable; I was prepared to return to the role of passive Tate Theater viewer in the fall, but it was fair to say that my sanguine disposition was due to both *Bride of Frankenstein* and *Victor/Victoria* making it onto the Spring schedule. I couldn't wait to tell Janet, who I hadn't seen in days. I was used to the occasional fallow period, though, and during this latest one, I'd actually opened my battered geography book in preparation for the upcoming final.

"How can you put fucking *Ice Castles* on the schedule and not *A Clockwork Orange?*"

"It's an alternate," I offered consolingly.

"Yeah, for when they have trouble locating that very rare *Animal House* print," Andy replied bitterly.

"We never would have had two ice-skating movies on the same schedule, unless it was part of an overall theme," Eddie said wistfully. "I wish you guys could've been here for Doppelganger Week last year — Weekday, Weekend, Midnight, *and* Foreign. It was beautiful."

Eddie popped another Tums as Tom Cody, who gave Cinematic Arts its first drag of a cigarette behind the bleachers, entered Peppino's. He was with Amber Grant and Molly Sherman. I remember seeing Heather talking to them at her Halloween party before I'd stopped remembering much of anything.

The silver buttons on Molly's denim jacket jangled when she rushed past us to inspect the interior of the cavernous restaurant. The green-and-red striped walls made her recoil, and she stared in visible disgust at the one lined with photos of Italian soccer teams.

"It's just like you said, Amber," Molly stated; her face set in a perpetual glower. "It's... *repulsive*, but not deliberately so. It's like a big... urinal. It's perfect."

"Isn't it?" Amber agreed. She held Tom's arm, but his smile embraced Molly. Whoever cut her dark hair must have specialized in twelve-year-old boys with attitude problems, and the thick black belt looped through her jeans was wider than she was. Amber, whose hair was fire red on one side and skunk black on the other, had a slight pot belly that kept peeking out from below her Sub Pop T-shirt as if to periodically join the conversation.

"We're gonna look into shooting the cover for their single here," Tom explained.

"You're in a band?" Andy asked.

Amber chuckled — eliminating Andy from the discussion based on his question. Tom was almost gracious.

"They played at Allen's last month. I think Heather was there. You two hang out, right?"

"Yeah," Andy said. "We're seeing her tonight."

"At a party?"

Andy nodded. Tom's smile returned.

"Then maybe we'll see you later. We're about to go hit a few."

I didn't bother to correct Tom, but I presumed any party that Jaye Goetz, who "knew no one," could throw would not appear on his social calendar.

"You going with them?" Tom asked Eddie Munster, who was picking at his rejected meal.

For obvious reasons, I'd not told Eddie about Jaye's gathering. Heather's self-esteem was fragile enough right now without having someone darting into the nearest room with a toilet whenever he saw her.

"No, no," Eddie replied. He mentioned something to Tom about *Evil Dead 2*, which was the weekend's midnight movie.

Molly drew Tom's attention to the slices of red-and-green fluorescent lights that surrounded us.

"Forget the single," she said. "We should shoot a video here. It would be totally some awe."

Some awe? I couldn't tell if Molly had a learning disability or was just an idiot.

"He's the guy you should talk to." Tom pointed to Eddie, who was avoiding eye contact with both Amber and Molly. "He knows Lance."

"Really? I love what he did with Jim Easter's song... and it sucked. He'd be great for us."

Eddie informed his lukewarm meatball sub that Lance would be at *Evil Dead 2*.

"That so? We were thinking of seeing that, weren't we?" Amber and Molly smiled and nodded obediently. "Maybe we can all go out afterward." The back of his hand waved at Andy and me. "We might even meet up with these guys later."

To my surprise, as Tom's plans would involve Amber and Molly, Eddie Munster said yes. Andy and I offered our seats at the booth to the girls; Tom slid next to Eddie. As we left, I heard Molly say, "I think a video would pave the way for us to no longer be students who play music but musicians who take classes."

OK, definitely an idiot.

We turned right out of Peppino's and headed up Broad. Approaching Jackson Street, Andy pointed to the grimy marquee for the strip club Toppers, which directly faced the *Red & Black* offices.

"Girl in my epistemology class works here. She says it pays better than waitressing at The Grill and the frat boys are better behaved."

We found Heather in College Square, leaning against one of the black lampposts. Her posture implied that the glowing ball above her was self-generated. She was dressed for battle: Her armor was a vise-tight black dress and black high-heeled pumps. It even extended to her rather overdone makeup, which I'd never before seen her wear.

"Rope a dope!" she screamed at us. "What were you two doing in Greekville?"

Heather had recently made a point of never crossing College Avenue to the east. I wasn't sure when this invisible wall was erected, but it ended our Taco Stand picnics.

I told her about our encounter with Tom Cody at Peppino's, which was on the wrong side of the wall.

"It's his War of Indie Aggression," she explained as she snapped her black-nailed fingers and danced to a rap song, which played from a convertible paused at a red light. A burly black man stood up in the backseat and moved along with her. "He thinks his crowd and the townies can take downtown and force the tailgaters back to Steverino's. His family's from Philadelphia originally so that's how they roll." She cocked her head to the north. "I'm parked in the deck."

I could have closed my eyes and still followed her from the sound of the click-click-click-click of her heels, but then I wouldn't have seen Janet's '50s-style safari hat through the window of The Grill. She sat unaccompanied at a far booth, her back to us.

"Train's leaving the station, Carlton. You coming?"

I mumbled something about giving my regrets to Jaye.

Heather nodded, digging her nails into the skin on Andy's arm before he could say anything.

"Catch you on the flipside," she said coldly.

Janet and I exchanged a tense, polite salutary greeting, almost always a prelude to unpleasantness. It was the first time I could recall words not coming easily between us. We could have been talking to anyone.

Her last meal lay before her, if she were being executed by acute indigestion. The Big Molly platter, a half-pound double-cheeseburger that would give a Georgia linebacker trouble, fought for space on the table with a plate of fries and feta cheese, a chocolate malt, another plate that displayed the remains of apple pie à la mode, and five empty bottles of Killian's Red, the sixth helping to wash all this down.

All I could think to say was, "You don't eat meat."

"That's true," she agreed, "but it turns out I *really* enjoy it."

She motioned for me to sit down with a precarious swing of her knife. A simple action best reveals intoxication. She was bombed. Heather had been sober as a Quaker the other night compared to what I confronted. This was the kind of drunkenness one revisits, with increasing levels of homesickness between stays. Heather might never be as drunk as she'd been at Gina Sloane's, but this — my God — this was something horrific.

"Do you mind telling me what's going on?"

"I've been avoiding you," she said, surprising herself. She took a swig of her drink. "Was that a straight answer? Must be my time of the month."

"Have I done something to offend you?"

I phrased my words with care. I couldn't allow myself to say whatever came to mind. My mental mediators had to intervene.

"Mr. Waldorf called me last Sunday. *Molto* upset. Claims you attacked his… whatever." She dipped the last bit of her burger in a cup of feta and lobbed it into her mouth. "Funny thing is he knows he'd ram her ugly face into a wall himself if I promised to do that thing with my tongue again."

"I didn't attack her. I was just… "

"Defending me!" She pressed the beer bottle to her chest. "How *sweet!*"

"I lost my temper. It was dumb. She wasn't worth it."

She took off her sunglasses. A drought had struck her eyes — there was no physical evidence of it anymore, but I could tell she'd been crying and was crying still.

"But…" She paused. "You want to know if *I* was worth it, don't you?"

I didn't respond — how could I? — and she repeated herself more forcefully, her raised voice attracting the attention of the people at the opposite table.

"Is that what this is all about?" I said with the confidence of someone who just didn't get it and was about to prove it. "Do you really think I believed a word that lunatic said? I know it's all garbage."

She winced as if I'd punched her and then clucked like a chicken: "Suck. Suck. Suck. Suck. Sucker!" She leaned toward me. "It's all true, *kiddo.*" The last word struck me like a gob of spit. "Every word that little troll told you is true — and more. She just scratched the surface, which is more than you ever did."

Etiquette could only go so far. I could feel something very precious and vital to me slipping away, as I held on like the losing team in a game of tug-of-war, sliding further into the mud.

"She didn't have to tell you, though. That was cruel of her." She swallowed a cluster of fries. "Not for him. She could have him. I didn't care. He didn't mean this to me." She snapped her fingers. "But you… she didn't have to tell you."

I whispered her name — this caused her to pound her fist against the table and begin to sing "Day Tripper" deliriously off-key before her voice drifted off, breaking up like a radio station going out of range.

The waiter placed another beer in front of her, bringing the tally up to an unlucky seven.

"Don't give that to her! Can't you see she's drunk out of her mind? And she's underage!"

"Don't listen to him. He has a vivid imagination. Not that his tattling matters much." Her beerless hand reached for the waiter's. "Neil's a dear friend of mine."

"Greg."

"Huh?"

"My name's Greg."

"Oh, how silly of me. It's just that you *look* like a Neil."

"Neil works on Tuesdays and Thursdays."

"Yes, yes he does, doesn't he? Well, he's not as cute as you, Greg, with your long, blonde hair..."

"I'm getting the manager," I pronounced.

"I am the manager tonight," Greg replied.

"I'm taking you home."

"But you haven't even bought me a drink! I don't think he's done this before, Greg. Besides, it's *slightly* possible I'm too drunk for you to try to pick up."

Greg glanced at his boots, looking a bit guilty about his plans for the evening. He left to wait on other customers. Janet insisted, "He just doesn't look like a Greg, does he?"

"You're drunk, and I'm taking you home. And we're going to talk about this..."

She saw that I would never believe the terrible things Evelyn Wilson had said about her and that made her angrier.

"You just don't get it, do you? Look, she told you and it's gone... gone! Shattered. Once the little red-haired mutt pulled back the curtain..." Inflamed by her metaphorical ramblings, she continued. "You think you're different, but you're not. Maybe I wanted to believe in you... in something... in me maybe...even in Beatles." She snickered. "But there's nothing. I tricked you, OK? You were had. Now go. Try to leave with some of your dignity."

"Why do you keep talking to me like I'm not here?" I snapped. "Like I'm just anyone. I'm not, and it's wrong for you to think that. Maybe I see things differently!"

"Don't… don't… don't make this so hard! You don't see things at all!"

She lifted her head. The sadness in my eyes, tinged with pity, infuriated her.

"You think you know everything about me, kiddo," she slurred. "Well, I know things about you." She pointed her finger at me like a pistol, the others curled around her Killian's. "I know why you got stinking drunk at Kermit's Halloween party, and I also know the *incredibly* stupid thing you were about to say to me on Christmas Eve."

She could have just shoved her plate into my face. My mouth opened and closed silently.

She threw down her napkin and hobbled away from the table — the front window's flashing "Open 24 Hours" sign drenching her in neon. I squeezed an abandoned fry between my thumb and index finger, the grease oozing down my palm. Fifteen minutes passed, and Sunday began with someone angrily shouting, "Aw, fucking hell!"

A waitress marched up to Greg, her nose ring trembling as she wiped her hands with paper towels.

"Some dumb bitch just threw up all over the restroom. It's fucking disgusting."

I teleported inside. Janet lay sprawled over the toilet, convulsing and choking, unable to stop. Her seventeen-course meal, mixed with the reddish hue of Killian's, painted the wall. I pried her limp, hacking frame from the toilet. She jerked away from me, rushing into the corner.

"Still won't go away, will you? Such a sweetheart." I moved toward her, and she turned away, facing the wall. "Don't… don't touch me, OK? I'm such a fright." She took in the full spectacle of her handiwork. Her whole body shook as she laughed, a haunting sound like bone being scraped. "Oh, how funny! I didn't even have to do it myself this time."

SPRING QUARTER '93 PLAYLIST

Michelle Shocked, "It Must Be Luff" — Heather and Jaye
Al Green, "Call Me (Come Back Home)" — Brad and Janet
Velocity Girl, "Pop Loser" — Tom and Dana
Michael Jackson, "Wanna Be Startin' Something" — Andy and Jaye
The Police, "Hole in My Life" — Brad
Carol Haney, "Hernando's Hideaway" from *The Pajama Game* — Janet
Fred Astaire, "Never Gonna Dance" from *Swing Time* — Brad
Doris Day, "Tea for Two" — Janet
Prince, "17 Days" — Heather
The Smiths, "Rusholme Ruffians" — Brad and Heather
Etta James, "I'd Rather Go Blind" — Janet
Sebadoh, "Soul and Fire" — Eddie
The Pretenders, "Message of Love" — Brad, Janet, Heather, and Andy

1

Ninety-nine miles separate Athens, Georgia from Greenville, South Carolina. Years later, when I returned for my mother's funeral, I made the journey alone for the first time. It took just under two hours, which is not how I remembered it. At the time, it always felt like the difference between life and death.

My memory of the rest of that night at The Grill is equally impressionistic. I recall it as snapshots in some macabre scrapbook: Cleaning the sick off Janet's mouth; placing her on her roommate's bed and closing the door behind me; sitting very still and very silent in the middle of the quad until well into morning on damp grass that stained my pants.

I didn't see Janet for the rest of the quarter. She didn't answer her door or her phone even when her lava lamp flared red from her window. As I was in no condition to do anything more productive than lie on my bed and stare at the ceiling, I fortunately was not required to work at the *Greenville News* during Spring break. I believe the assumption was that I'd embrace tradition and spend the week off having "fun." It was an expectation my parents — in a display of irony that would shame O. Henry — shared, as well.

Melinda Miller didn't push the fun button when she called for a mostly one-way conversation during which I contributed only few mumbled "yes, ma'ams." I appreciated that — even more so when she whispered, "It'll get better. You'll see. And stop calling me 'ma'am'" before hanging up.

The next day, a postcard, sent from San Francisco and bearing a photo of Marilyn Monroe at the Golden Gate Bridge, arrived like bait on a hook:

Honey Pie —
Can't wait until we're back home at Tate and the Seventh Floor.
Kiss me deadly,
Mahogany

Early afternoon on Sunday, the crunch of wheels on gravel drew me to my bedroom window. Peering through my blinds — and briefly suffering a Lugosi reaction to the sun, I saw Heather Aulds round the driveway and politely ring the front bell.

"Howdy, I'm going door to door selling Girl Scout Cookies." She took in the living room with the plastic slipcovers over the furniture to prevent any actual living from taking place. "So, this is the old homestead, huh?"

She'd just escaped a harrowing family affair at their place in Hilton Head. "Too many Aulds farts in one place," she explained. I knew I should invite her inside and offer her tea or something, but no living, breathing thing belonged within these walls. So, instead, I left a note for my middle-aged roommates on the kitchen table:

To whom it may concern:
I'm going out to have FUN!!!

I drew a circle around the last word. They would be pleased to know I'd lied to them for the first time. It was the sort of normal, teenage behavior they'd always wanted from me.

"What do you do for fun around here?" Heather asked.

"Nothing," I stated honestly as we drove by my old high school.

We passed grazing cows and Mom and Pop grocers before reaching the twentieth century. We cut through a neighborhood where families of modest means would often bring their children on Halloween for more lucrative trick or treating.

"Spencer's brother Robert is thinking of moving here. He says Atlanta's getting too cosmopolitan." She winked knowingly at the coded language. "Jesus H., Carlton, you're supposed to say, 'Bob's your uncle?'"

I weakly complied.

She threw up her hands, abandoning the wheel, and cried, "Too late! Too late!"

While I wouldn't say there are fun things to do in Greenville, there are pleasant ways to pass the time, depending on the company. Taking a spare racket from her trunk, I played a few sets of tennis with her at Cleveland Park. Her backhand and serve were too accomplished for a real match, so she spent a futile hour improving mine.

"I'm thinking of switching from history to pre-med," she told me over the mating call of an African elephant in the Greenville Zoo. "Dr. Heather Aulds, Veterinarian. What do you think?"

She threw her arms around my neck, clinging to my back like a cloak as we trotted to the lions' den. Passers-by found this more peculiar than anything the lions were doing.

"I wonder what will freak Karen out more? Having a job... " She gasped in mock horror. "Or being a dyke? Maybe I should tell her all at once. No, she'd keel over. That would just devastate Spencer." She shattered the fantasy of a loving couple who couldn't live without one another with her next sentence: "His 'friend' would be after him to make her an honest woman."

A lion and his female companion slept peacefully under a golden blanket of sun. A nearby child stomped his foot impatiently.

"But they're not doing anything!" he complained.

"Oh, well, you see," I explained to him, "lions actually sleep twenty-one hours out of the day, hunting and eating during the other three."

He stomped his foot again. "But they're not doing anything!" His mother smiled wanly and expressed gratitude for my clueless attempt at pacifying him.

A pack of brutes, hats turned backward on their dark heads, overhead my impromptu lecture and proceeded to mockingly imitate my mannerisms and speaking voice.

"Hey, fuck you!" Heather shouted.

"It's no big deal," I said. "This happens all the time."

She looked at me, then at them, and screamed louder, "Fuck you!"

We ordered double-cheeseburgers — hold the meat — to puzzled looks at BB's Restaurant on Laurens Road and ate them in the neon-bathed parking lot. Munching her fries with ravenous glee, Heather looked radiantly happy and eager to tell me why. I offered her my now cold fries as an apology for not noticing sooner.

❧

Jaye Goetz lived in the Players Club apartments a few miles from downtown. When Heather and Andy arrived, there were four people present at the "party," only one a stranger to them.

"I'm so glad you came! Can I get you anything?"

Jaye wore just an oversized *2001: A Space Odyssey* T-shirt — to Andy's cultural and Heather's carnal delight. She took them into the kitchen to meet an olive-skinned brunette named Christine, who was at work making a bong out of a pipe and a plastic bottle of Mountain Dew. She looked at Heather and Andy and smiled searchingly.

"So, do you guys like... marijuana?"

The living room was filled (as decorated was not quite the right word) with assorted clearance items from Walmart. All the furniture seemed unstable and likely to collapse with the slightest provocation. This included Marie, who was rooted to the floor. She shared a joint with Nick and the way her eyes frosted over when she looked at him indicated she wished to share more.

Jaye asked about me, and Heather opened her mouth to provide a polite, non-revealing explanation but instead belched loudly. It was only slightly less embarrassing than when she'd "become a woman" during a middle-school tennis match.

Andy planted himself in the dirt brown carpet with Nick and Marie. This created a comical triangle to which he was oblivious: Andy desired the pixie-haired Marie, who would like nothing more than to subsist on a steady diet of Nick, who found Andy far more appetizing than his roommate.

The black butterfly chair in the corner had swallowed up Heather to her knees as if starving for functionality. While Heather strategized how to get out of the chair without federal assistance, Jaye came over and sat next to her on the floor; Heather instantly noted this was as close as they'd ever been. She smelled like Lux soap and cigarettes, which made Heather's toes curl inside her high heels.

"I've never thrown a party before," Jaye stated miserably. "Although I'm not sure this counts."

Heather felt an overwhelming urge to console her.

"It's nice. Very... mellow."

Jaye pointed at Heather's shoes. "Then why don't you stay awhile?" There was an audible clump as Heather allowed them to slip off to the carpet.

"You were at Noel Hartigan's party, weren't you?"

Heather could only nod in response.

"I thought you looked familiar when I saw you the other day. You changed your hair. I like it."

Heather now could only blush in response.

"Do you go to a lot of parties?" Jaye asked.

"Yeah," Heather whispered, "but this is my favorite one so far."

It was such an absurd statement that its true meaning could not have been clearer.

"That's a really cool tattoo."

Jaye's middle finger traced the image of a purple dove on her ankle. It was possible that what was left of Heather would spill over the sides of the butterfly chair.

Marie burst out laughing. Heather felt for a moment that she was the obvious source of ridicule but realized that Marie had reached the point where everything was funny.

Between giggles, Marie lifted up her shirt to reveal to Andy and more importantly yet pointlessly to Nick that her nipples were pierced.

"This is getting rowdy," Jaye observed. "Let's go someplace a little more quiet."

Jaye scooped Heather out of her chair and led her to the bedroom she shared with Nick.

As they left, Christine paused during a conversation with an invisible guest on the other side of the window.

"Am I high or is there a Porsche in the parking lot?"

"I told you Ronnie was dealing," Marie answered.

"Well, duh, he's the one who sold us this."

"Oh." Marie paused. "It's good shit."

The only items of furniture in Jaye and Nick's room were two beat-up dressers and two twin mattresses lying on the floor. Above one were posters of A Tribe Called Quest and Digital Underground.

"That's Nick's," Jaye said. She stooped to light a strawberry-scented candle on her dresser. "He's the perfect roomie. He's neat and we... like different things, so no drama."

Heather joined Jaye in a pool of red sheets beneath posters of The Cure and Nick Cave. A heated volley of topics began that included concerts they'd seen and favorite albums, all of which were the last things on Heather's mind, but they kept her from sharing the actual feelings swimming furiously in her head.

On that confusing, frightening Valentine's Day a month earlier, Heather had tried to drown Jaye's persistent image in her mind with bourbon before passing out in front of *Jeopardy!* Now, the long, thin fingers she'd first seen in Cofer's class were entwined in hers, and she thought she might pass out again. Instead, she pulled off Jaye's glasses — the most audacious act of her life — and traced the fine scar above her black eyebrow.

"Chicken pox?" Jaye said in her delightful upspeak. Whenever she spoke, it sounded like an overwhelming question.

Heather knew if she kissed her, the formlessness of her life so far would suddenly solidify, but this neither confused nor frightened her. Perfectly sober, she leaned in to that lopsided mouth.

When Heather finished her story, we'd long since left BB's and had driven through my neighborhood twice. Her Porsche moved through the dimly lit streets like a flying saucer. We pulled into my driveway and as I unbuckled my seat belt, I realized something I had to do.

"I shouldn't have just left you like that," I said. "I'm sorry."

"Disappointed that you didn't get to see Marie's tits?" She shrugged. "Expert opinion: They're *aw-right*."

Her levity ended with the music. The porch light carved white lines into her maple skin. She gripped my wrist as another song began.

"What the hell did It do to you?"

I hadn't intended to tell her anything. My theory was that nightmares only became real when you shared them. Yet words welled up inside me and flowed out in a stream of consciousness that for the first time in my life was not carefully composed and arranged.

She remained silent during my verbal meltdown, her face as impassive as a figure on Mount Rushmore. Finally, when I was done, she turned suddenly and pulled me close to her. Stroking my head, she held me through two Al Green songs.

"I love you," she whispered.

There was neither a rush nor a push from her words, and they were as soothing as her embrace.

"Now get the fuck out of my car."

The first of April, on my way out to the *Red & Black*, I encountered a weight on the other side of the door, pushing it shut. I struggled with the lock for a second before hearing Janet's voice plead, "Don't come out yet, OK?"

She sounded like a Billie Holiday record. She'd traipsed through winter in bare legs so it seemed typical of her to come down with something just as the grass began to green in the quad.

"Don't say anything until I'm done, please. You saw something you shouldn't, but I forgive you. What we have is so divine, and I don't want to lose that. And we will unless we just forget what happened. Don't talk about it. Don't mention it ever again. Don't even think about it. If you do, I'll know and I'll never speak to you again — ever. And I couldn't bear that, so please, honey, promise me you'll do this for me... for us."

She was kind enough to make her request without my seeing her, but there was no resisting that voice, that music playing in her throat. In the end, I was too selfish, needed her too much, not to open the door.

"Oh, there you are," she murmured, and I'd never loved her more.

My eyes raced to hers, but she slipped on her sunglasses before they could meet. Her wild curls had been tamed somewhat into a 1930s-style finger wave. A black cloche with an elaborate raspberry bow covered her head.

I thanked her for the postcard, which produced a smile from her, then expressed my wish that she had called. The smile remained, but a raised eyebrow added an element of deviousness.

"I was three whole hours in the past, kiddo. I was busy getting into my corset and carriage. Have you been to San Francisco?" I shook my head. "It's divine. It's all so deliciously noir-ish. We should take a trip back in time together. I just know you'll love it."

I do in fact love San Francisco, and I spent my first trip a few years ago tracing Janet's spectral steps from her week there alone in late March of 1993. She had no photos because she hadn't planned on going. Janet hated plans.

"It's the future conspiring against you," she once told me.

Janet had been waiting for her flight to New York at Atlanta International when it occurred to her that this was the first time she was ever early for a flight. Normally, she was rushing to board before they closed the gate or at least as close as she ever came to rushing for anything. She considered this a sign, so she traded in her ticket for one to San Francisco.

"How did your parents react?"

"Mother was Mother." Janet performed her Abigail Tomalin impersonation, which involved a lot of censorious finger wagging: "'Janet, you are *so* irresponsible! We were worried sick!' I thought I'd been *very* responsible. I called them as soon as I checked into my hotel." The devious smile returned to her lovely face. "That way they wouldn't cancel my credit card."

She put her arm through mine, and we ambled through the wooded areas between the dorms, always off the path. She spoke only through the squeeze of a hand, a smile, a wink, or the bittersweet murmuring of whatever song the moment inspired.

Reuniting with Janet had buoyed my spirits and made me believe in the promises of the upcoming season. There was no logical reason to think everything would be just as it was, but walking with her, I felt like it would be and that was enough. She may have had no proven power over the gravity that bound us to the earth, but she certainly did over the internal forces that struggled to control my emotions.

"It's so hot! I miss winter already!" Janet cried. She still clung to the season in a knee-length black day dress. "Why is it that I only truly appreciate something when it's gone? I'm always confusing beginnings with endings. That's my problem… with spring, I mean. I think it's just so *cocky*, so certain that it's all going to begin again. I don't like cocky." An appropriately dramatic pause and then the giggle for which I had no defense: "That's why I adore you."

Stopping suddenly, she wet her index finger and tested the air with it.

"Oh yummy, it's Ice Cream Season!"

"Ice Cream Season," according to her, never started before Easter, which was two weeks away, nor extended beyond Labor Day — unless the ice cream was especially yummy and then an exception was made.

She practically skipped into Hodgson's Pharmacy on Milledge Avenue where a 1950s-style soda fountain was tucked away past shelves of medications and assorted items for the infirm. I questioned its reality for a moment; it resembled a bit of set design that Janet had constructed from the theatre of her imagination. I expected the people around us to burst into song and dance.

"What's your poison, kiddo? My treat."

It has since become a victim of inflation, but at the time, Hodgson's sold scoops of ice cream for a quarter. A man who I fancifully suspected might actually be Donald O'Connor scooped up two small mountains of vanilla in time to Janet's tuneful murmur and heaped them onto the old-fashioned sugar cones he handed over to us. Janet smiled at him as if he'd invented ice cream and brought it over to the New World. He'd never seen a smile like that, nor would he ever again.

We headed downtown while enjoying slow licks of our melting mountains.

There was no strangeness between us, as though that awful night had never happened. It was exhilarating to know that what we shared couldn't be broken even under the weight of Evelyn Wilson's sobering truth.

Janet must have sensed it herself because later at Rocky's she leaned back in our booth and began to giggle uncontrollably.

"Oh sweetie, you've made such a mess!"

I glanced down and saw a sloppy trail of marina on the front of my blue shirt.

"That means seven weeks bad luck or six more years of winter... or something like that." She stood up to announce, "We need to get you presentable for Fred and Ginger."

We'd planned on watching *Swing Time* that evening at Tate. It had been "movie nerd" Claire Simone's farewell addition to the schedule before leaving Cinematic Arts at the end of Winter Quarter. It was my first Fred and Ginger film. I did a lot of things for the first time with Janet — even the things I'd done countless times before.

She led me down the street to The Gap where her aubergine nails tapped a rumba on hangers in the shirt racks. I reached for a button-down that was essentially identical to the one I wore, but she found that distasteful.

"You can't just *replace* it. You shouldn't be so fickle."

She held up shirts of many colors against me like paint swatches. I made a few Madonna-video-inspired poses, and Janet's laughter poured over me like hot fudge.

Then as if someone had switched out a recording of *La Cecchina* for *Tosca*, her laughter ended and I almost thought she was about to cry in the middle of the store.

"None of them are right!" A chestnut spread collar fell in a rejected heap to the floor. "It's always *so* hard to get exactly what I want. I should get used to it, but I never do."

A sales clerk with dark blonde hair approached us — her black-and-white striped shirt and relaxed-fit navy jeans were both from The Gap. She reflected the store's image so well I thought she'd stepped out of an advertisement.

"Can I help y'all?"

Recovering herself slightly, Janet explained our dilemma. The clerk took this opportunity to promote the store's merchandise with an enthusiasm that was as unfashionable west of College Avenue as The Gap itself was.

"I know just the thing!" she said.

Janet smiled politely.

"It has to be *perfect!*"

I admired the girl's pluck because I doubted that she'd produce anything that would satisfy Janet right now.

She reached into the rack and perhaps while silently saying "abracadabra" pulled out a light purple shirt I could have sworn Janet had rejected previously, but this time it defined perfection for her.

"That's it!"

La Cecchina was playing once again.

The clerk rang up the button-down and offered to let me change into it in one of the fitting rooms. I came out to find Janet dancing a polka near the wall displaying men's T-shirts.

"It's better with two people," she explained, absently fingering the ends of her ruffled Peter Pan collar. "Shall we dance? That's *not* the one we're about to see — though it's divine."

I took her hand and yet another thing I did with her for the first time was to glide cheek to cheek out of the store and down Jackson Street, and none of the many extras we passed on the way intruded on our daydream.

We cut through what I thought was a park — the proscenium overrun with grass and the chorus line of trees waving its branches in the wind — but the crop of ragged tombstones growing from the lawn identified it as a cemetery, which Janet called "Ye Olde Athens Cemetery."

I thought it best not to subject the dead, who had suffered enough, to my amateurish foxtrot. Janet agreed and even turned off the jukebox playing in her head. She shifted from one patent leather heel to another before finally reclining against a decaying gravestone as though lying on a chaise lounge.

"My sociology professor last quarter would bring us here for lectures when it was warm enough. It was lovely, but then he started talking about *society* or something like that, and I lost interest." She pulled a tape from her bag and placed it in my hand. "This is for you. Made just last night. They're our love letters, aren't they? I prefer them to the ones with rambling metaphors about cake and ice cream. Miss Campbell showed me this letter she'd gotten from an RA she's seeing. Indiscreet, yes, but it's her first so forgivable just this once. It was the biggest bunch of hooey I'd ever read. There were all these... *words.* Four pages! Front and back. Who needs words? They're so dreary and serious. That's why I adore sad songs and movies. I love a good cry. I would sometimes spend whole days in my room listening to sad songs, watching sad movies, and crying to beat the band. Mother got so mad once, but I suppose it *was* my birthday party and there *were* guests. She likes things to be perfect. She can't understand that a good cry *is* perfect. You're a good cry, kiddo."

She folded my hand over into a fist, and her thumb stroked my knuckles.

"I know I'm not supposed to talk about... it," I said.

Her grip on my hand tightened.

"But I just want to say that none of that matters. All that matters is that you were on the other side of my door when I opened it today. And when I listen to your tape later... well, all my life, everything that's meant something to me has been strange or different or just wrong, but I never have to explain myself to you, and I think it's because you're the only person in the world who, deep down, is just like me."

It was the most idiotic thing I could have said. I thought I'd insulted her and was about to apologize when she stripped off her sunglasses and stared at me with those dark, bare eyes for an intense moment... and suddenly it was clear we were about to kiss — wildly, hotly, and decidedly unfriendly. It felt like we already were and just needed to punctuate it physically.

Then just as suddenly, a will asserted itself — certainly not mine, as it was desiccated. What self-control I had left was now buried somewhere deep in this cemetery.

Janet had sprung to her feet, and it appeared that she was actually running in place.

"We are *very* late," she said. "And the beginning of *Swing Time* is my favorite part... other than the middle and the end."

The pleated hem of her dress dipped and twirled as she raced away from the reddening sky. A hand waved above her, providing a butterscotch beacon for me to follow to the Tate Theater. I headed after her, careful not to tumble over tombstones in the darkening cemetery, but she left me in her dust.

2

One of my obligations as a member of Cinematic Arts was to tear tickets for two movies each quarter. Before the midnight showing of *Valley Girl*, Janet came by to help me. More precisely, she placed her purple bowler on my head (yes, I looked ridiculous), slipped her arms through mine (also ridiculous), and gamely attempted to accept tickets from the steady stream of patrons. We were not as efficient as a unit as I was alone, but I couldn't deny the rush I felt from her breath against my neck.

As the last of the ticket holders entered the theater, she retrieved her hat, adjusted her sunglasses, and declared, "You're more fun to watch than that movie will be." She was not a fan. Neither was I, but Debbie Tyson had pushed hard for its place on the schedule. She was not in attendance, though, because The Veldt was playing downtown at the Shoebox and she was really into them that week.

Lying next to Janet on the quad, I wanted nothing more than to talk to her about our near kiss in the cemetery. But while I searched for the right words, she plucked a dry blade of grass from the ground, tickled my face with it as my ear filled with her musical laughter, and I was done thinking for the night.

If I had stayed for *Valley Girl*, I might have had a chance to catch up with Eddie Munster, who was working in the projectionist's booth. I had a more respectable class schedule this quarter and didn't get to the *Red & Black* until noon most days. I also missed the first CA general meeting, because Janet came by my room and announced with much fanfare that it was now "Swing Season." We went to the playground where I'd spent part of Valentine's Day and took turns pushing each other well into the night.

I would not see Eddie again until the following week, when I was having lunch at Gyro Wrap with Andy Razinski. We'd not been there long when Eddie passed by our table outside with Tom Cody and Dana Weichman.

"Captain! Andrew! How's it going?"

Tom nodded at us. Dana, her loose bun brushing his shoulder, pursed her lips; I thought she was about to whistle. Instead, she murmured, her eyes on the brick wall behind us, "Do you think I could have a curly fry?"

This was asked of me because Andy's plate was empty.

"Sure, help yourself."

Eddie had gotten a haircut recently — perhaps his first since high school — and looked almost normal. He even seemed relatively comfortable in Dana's presence.

"Cody's joining our film union!" Eddie announced. "Cool, huh? Just wait, Fall Quarter's gonna be the best yet."

It took a moment for me to adjust to Eddie's newfound optimism. Licking ketchup off her fingers, Dana informed us of a party she was having that weekend.

"Swing by if you can."

"Should be fun," Tom added. "Heather and Jaye will probably be there. They've been making the rounds."

"Thicker than thieves." Dana smirked as she snatched the last fry from my plate.

When Andy's three large Pepsis sent him away from the table, Dana turned to us, her voice full of alarm.

"You don't think *he'll* come, do you?"

I pointed out that her invitation might have confused him.

"Well, it's only right to invite him. He's in CA. But that's different from expecting him to come."

Tom absently stated that it wouldn't matter if he did.

"That's fine for you to say. You can just leave if losers start showing up."

Tom shrugged.

"So can you."

"Oh, that would be lovely!" Dana exclaimed in agreement with Tom's chic rudeness. "To just walk out of my own house and leave it to the Georgia Theatre crowd."

Tom's smile lit on Eddie.

"So I heard from Pete. The Movie Dope gig is yours if you want it."

This surprised me. Eddie was always critical of the *Flagpole's* bullet-length movie reviews. Also, he knew Andy had applied for the open position.

Tom noticed the party across from us leaving.

"Should we grab a table?"

"I've gotten my fry fix," Dana stated, "so let's just go to The Grit like *people.*"

"Come with us, Captain. We can talk about the *Flagpole*."

"Yeah, you might want to consider trying for a better readership," Tom said with a smile.

"I wouldn't touch the *Red & Black* at gunpoint," Dana said, "but I'm told you're funny in an edgy way that I would definitely think about checking out in an appropriate venue."

Her statement was only in the crack neighborhood of a compliment, but I thanked her anyway and said I'd see them later. The three then left for hipper cuisine.

"Where did they go?" Andy asked upon his return.

"Not far enough," I replied, surprised that I'd included Eddie in my dismissal.

Dana's comment about Heather and Jaye reminded me that the new couple had been busy hitting all the hot spots on downtown's west side. So much so that I'd only seen Heather once or twice since Spring break. However, the next day, I ran into Jaye Goetz herself coming out of Wuxtry Records with Heathers Baldwin and Reed.

Waving me down in the rain, she ran up to me on Clayton Street.

"Aulds and I were just talking about you," she said, her smile as lop-sided as ever but somewhat more focused now. "You and Andy are such good friends of hers, so I'd love to get to know you a little better."

I guessed that was why she was out with Baldwin and Reed, who were busy discussing their newly acquired Velocity Girl album. She was far more patient than I.

"Why don't you two come over Saturday afternoon? I'll make lunch and we can do whatever later."

Recalling Heather's description of her apartment, I assumed her meal would be cooked in one pot, served on paper plates, and eaten on the floor, but she clarified that this would be at Heather's place.

It was still raining, almost torrentially so, a few days later when Andy and I walked over to River Mill just before noon. My glasses got so fogged from the hot shower outside that I couldn't see more than two feet in front of me.

"I think Heather and Jaye are dating," Andy announced as we avoided small wading pools on Sanford Drive.

"That so?"

"Yeah, I've got pretty good gaydar," he explained. "My sister goes to McGill."

Before I could explore the relevance of that statement, we were at Heather's apartment. Jaye opened the door on our second knock. She wore an apron, which made it seem for a second that she had on a dress. Her bare legs were unblemished and resistant to tan. Their only splash of color was the light red on her toes.

"Hey guys! Come on in!"

She held our rain jackets on one arm while pulling us each in for hugs with the other. Up close, I mentally agreed with Heather about the enchanting effect of Lux soap and cigarettes.

The living room was cleaner than I'd ever seen it. It was all so spotless I wondered if Alma had come up for the weekend. The only out of place items were a pair of discarded black Adidas soccer cleats next to an armchair. The feet they once covered rested on the ottoman. Columbia the cat skittered across a brown-legged tightrope and settled into Heather's lap.

"What can I get you?" Jaye asked from the kitchen. "A beer? Soda? Ice tea?"

"I made the ice tea, Carlton, so it's Dixie-approved."

"Is that how it works? Jaye does the cleaning and you make the ice tea?"

"Are you implying I'm not domestic, Razinski?"

"No, I'm stating it."

Months of debris had been cleared from the coffee table. The now visible surface held a neatly arranged display of exactly one month's worth of *Flagpoles*. The rattle of ice in tumblers preceded Jaye into the room. She handed us our drinks. I sat on the sofa with mine and skimmed over last week's *Migraine Boy*.

"So... you spend much time here, Jaye?" I asked.

"A little."

Jaye gently combed her fingers through Heather's dark hair, which made her purr as contentedly as Columbia.

"It's closer to everything," Heather explained with her head leaned back and her eyes half-closed. "And her roommate situation isn't that great."

Jaye agreed: "It's turning into *Melrose Place*. Christine's high all the time, and it's not like it's something she does once or twice a week. It's a lifestyle. She might as well start listening to Phish. And dear Marie is just crazy about Nick. She must have the same gaydar as whoever married Liberace. I'm not sure what she believes he does when he brings guys over — maybe she thinks they're talking about comic books while playing very loud and graphic video games."

Jaye had leaned in so close to Heather their noses almost touched.

"I should go finish up. Everything's almost ready."

She kissed her, and Heather responded with an intensity that implied she feared she wasn't simply leaving the room but might vanish forever after entering the kitchen.

Heather pressed her ice tea against her face as red fought with brown for dominance on her skin. She looked almost charred. Her mind slowly eased back into her body, as if stepping into a scalding bath. She didn't speak, but I imagined her thoughts matched the sentiments expressed on her T-shirt, which read, "She's a WOW."

After emptying her glass in one long swallow, her voice returned.

"Need any help?"

Heather looked at Andy and me with an expression indicating she wouldn't know what help to provide if asked.

"No, I'm fine," replied the pleasant voice from the kitchen. "Just relax and watch the game with the boys."

There was no game to watch, so Heather put on a CD. It was the Vigilantes of Love, which pleased Jaye, who set the table while swinging her ample hips to the beat from the stereo.

"Atlanta might have won on Monday, but I still think this is the Cubs' year," Andy said to Heather. "They're gonna go all the way." No response came as the lifelong Braves fan watched Jaye in a total fascination that had nothing to do with the art of place setting.

I recall it being the fanciest, almost formal, meal I'd ever had in someone's home: There was a salad course with salad forks and separate plates and silverware for the main course. There was no reason for this to impress Heather or Andy, but it was all very new to me and apparently Jaye, as well.

"My first big meal! I'm so excited." She rubbed Heather's back — more purring came. "My brothers and I always ate in front of the TV. Pizza and hamburgers and KFC. Mom would just stop at the drive-thru on her way home from work. I got so sick of food in boxes."

I took a few tentative bites of gnocchi and quickly realized that Jaye was an awful cook. I felt the need to offer something encouraging, so I said in all honesty, "This looks and smells great."

Jaye beamed at the compliment, not seeming to notice my lack of comment on the actual substance of the meal itself. I then attempted to put a respectable dent in what had been served to me before giving up. Across from me, Andy had emptied his plate. I found myself wishing that Heather had dogs.

After lunch, Jaye cleaned up — refusing any offers of assistance in the kitchen — and the three of us sat in the living room and talked over the sound of dishes being washed and put away.

"God, I think it's gonna rain all day," Andy complained. "I hate feeling cooped up."

"Don't you belong to film club and spend all day watching old movies?"

Andy attempted to rationalize this apparent inconsistency as Jaye entered. She took a long drag from Heather's cigarette and collapsed next to her on the sofa with a yawn.

"Tired, baby?" Heather asked, stroking Jaye's shoulder. "Not *too* tired, I hope."

"Silly! Not in front of the boys."

"Fuck the boys!" Heather exclaimed. "Well... probably not."

The boys talked movies for a while as our hosts cuddled on the sofa. The storm made early afternoon look like evening, and the room simmered with light from strawberry candles.

"What should we do with the rest of the day?" Heather wondered, boredom stalking her as always. "Remember when Saturdays were a big deal? Now, you can make every day Saturday, which makes them all feel like Wednesday."

"Someone's cynical," Jaye noted.

"I've been reading Carlton's columns."

"You have?" I asked.

"Of course." She shrugged. "They should put it on the same page as the crossword, though."

"Or in the *Flagpole*!" Jaye suggested. "No one really reads the *Red & Black*. If you wrote for the *Flagpole*, you could own this town."

"I'm not sure what I'd do with a whole town."

"It'd be awesome if you wrote for the *Flagpole*," Andy said. "When I'm Movie Dope next year, we'll be this unstoppable force, laying waste to complacency."

Embarrassed by all the attention, not to mention Andy's delusions, I clumsily changed the subject.

"I read in the *AJC* today that we're going to have a very hot summer because of all the global warming."

"Really?" Heather said. "You keep that up and they'll give you a diploma in three years."

Jaye's lopsided smile regarded the spectacle outside Heather's window.

"I love the rain. The one and only thing I miss about Nowhere, California is the beach. It was great on a day like today. We lived in this crappy apartment in a building where most of the units were rented out to tourists. It was quiet for about eight minutes on a Tuesday in February. The rest of the time was a big ole party. But Mom liked being near the beach. Not that she ever really went. She was always at work, but she liked seeing it through the window. My brothers and I would go there whenever we could and pretend we were tourists — not just nobodies. When it rained, we'd have it to ourselves."

Heather looked at Jaye without the concealer of irony and her bare face was never more beautiful. I imagined she now considered all that had brought Jaye from an unnamed town in California to lying within the crook of her arm on her sofa.

In September of 1991, Jaye Goetz journeyed against the historical flow of westward migration and arrived in Athens, a town that at least had a name, one she knew intimately through the music she loved.

Once here, she was content to tread the waters of the Classic City — a party here, a concert there. Then came her sophomore year and she happened to meet the girl whose athletic command of the waves far exceeded her humble breast stroke.

Together, they floated into deeper waters, until she could no longer see the sands on the beaches she'd abandoned in her pursuit. She found she didn't really miss them; her dreams had been so completely realized.

However, Heather would deny her nothing — not even the past.

"OK, baby, you don't have to ask me twice." Heather pressed her lips against Jaye's milky forehead. "Let's go to the beach."

Which beach now became the question, as there were a few options within driving distance. Tybee Island in Savannah was rejected with a look from Heather that resembled my reaction to Jaye's gnocchi. She eventually settled on Hilton Head, and I almost thought we'd end up at the Aulds's vacation home there. However, Heather remembered that the house's staff had the weekend off, and she wasn't interested in "roughing it." This was when it was decided to "crash" at some hotel on the beach.

Jaye and Heather went into the bedroom to change, which delayed our departure significantly enough for me to suspect that there was more going on behind the closed door than wardrobe consultations.

I used part of this time to discreetly — or so I thought — call Janet from the kitchen phone. I told myself it was to let her know I might not be back until mid-afternoon Sunday for our Rocky's brunch. She didn't pick up, and she'd turned off her answering machine shortly after her roommate all but officially moved in with her boyfriend. When I was there the past week, even the sheets on the bottom bunk bed were gone.

Heather — freshly showered — emerged from her bedroom, now wearing a green button-down shirt and jeans. She smiled like she was about to offer me religion. Jaye — who quite possibly was in the same shower — swept through the room blowing out candles. She paused to extinguish one next to Heather, who brushed a strand of red hair off her face when she bent over. Her propinquity was too much for Heather, and as soon as the candle was out they were kissing again.

I checked my watch.

"It's almost 4."

"All right then," Heather said absently, "everyone in the station wagon. Let me just get my keys."

"They're in your hand."

"Oh, so they are."

Andy and I exchanged a look that silently wondered if Heather should be driving, especially with her very distracting girlfriend next to her.

"Why don't I drive!" Jaye offered merrily. "Andy can stretch his legs in the front seat, and you and the celebrity can take the back."

Heather handed her the keys.

"I didn't know you drove stick."

"Oh, I prefer it! It's not really driving otherwise."

I'd ridden in Heather's Porsche many times by this point, but with Jaye behind the wheel, there was the sensation of being inside an expensive and private amusement park ride. She let out a giddy "Whee!" as she barreled down rain-slick streets and hugged corners with undue familiarity on the way out of town.

The storm had lessened everywhere but inside my own head. It bothered me that I couldn't reach Janet, and I wondered where she was and who was with her. The almost-kiss that replayed in my mind was now a definite one, but some stranger had replaced me in the image.

"You look like a puppy someone left in a car at Kroger with the windows rolled up." Heather nudged me in the ribs. "Stop playing hide-and-seek. Try to go a whole evening without thinking about It."

But I realized that was impossible, and I began to doubt the feeling was mutual.

Once we'd reached a cruising altitude on the interstate, Jaye popped in a CD, and music from our childhoods escaped the stereo.

"Michael Fucking Jackson?" Heather groaned. "Can it get any whiter in here?"

"This is popular again — as long as you don't take it too seriously. It gets all the guys at Boneshakers on the floor shaking theirs."

Andy attempted to moonwalk while seated. Jaye's cigarette-dependent arm bounced on the air outside the window.

"Yeah! Yeah!" they shouted in unison.

Thriller provided the soundtrack as Jaye casually recounted the circumstances that led to her meeting me and ultimately Heather.

So, basically:

Jaye was roommates her freshman year at Creswell with Christine Weiss. Christine was supposed to room with her friend Marie Peterson, but she'd forgotten to fill out the appropriate paperwork (Pot use might have been responsible for the memory lapse.). Christine and Marie had both grown up in Little Rock, Arkansas.

This caused me to unconsciously hum "Two Little Girls from Little Rock" from *Gentlemen Prefer Blondes*, which Janet and I had seen on the seventh floor of the library the other day. Heather elbowed me in the ribs again.

Marie was roommates with Noel Hartigan, who was in an art class with Nick McKee. Noel thought Nick was hot but was not inclined to cross certain boundaries. This didn't concern the immediately smitten Marie.

"I'm down with the brown," she'd explained to Jaye and Christine.

A wave of laughter flooded the car.

Marie apparently had a plan for seducing Nick that was so lengthy and complex she should receive a law degree upon its completion. Everyone else seemed aware as time went on that Nick was gay, but Jaye thought it kindest to not puncture Marie's fantasy. Jaye also enjoyed having Nick as part of their foursome.

Once they all started living together this year, what little social lives they had came from Nick. Marie was unaware, but Noel had secured the college passport for crossing boundaries and hooked up a few times with Nick during his bi period. Nick was also good friends with Gina Sloane, whose similar passport was almost full, but she was willing to make room for Nick. Unlike Marie, Gina's overtures were more obvious and uncomfortable, so that's why Jaye and Christine went to her party alone.

Jaye thought that Nick's own popularity was inevitably winding down.

"As soon as he comes out, it's over," she said ruefully. "Straight guys will be wary, and no girl wants to be seen as someone's fag hag, no matter what Evelyn Wilson says."

Just the odor of that name was enough to put me off the conversation. I rolled down my window and felt the usual sense of dread I experienced whenever I crossed the state line into South Carolina. This time, though, it stayed with me all the way to Hilton Head and even when Jaye turned the corner into the hotel Heather had chosen for us to "crash."

There were not enough stars in the heavens to adequately rate this hotel. A family reunion of sorts waited for Heather's Porsche in the parking lot. A valet took Heather's keys, and she took Jaye's hand as we entered the columned lobby and walked a city block across cool, mosaic tile to the front desk. A couple, one in impossibly high heels and the other in a blue blazer with gold buttons, stared at Heather and Jaye with the offended expressions of people who feel they own the exclusive rights to certain forms of affection.

Noting their disapproval, Heather snarled, "Looks like someone got lost on their way to Charleston."

The clerk didn't seem that pleased to greet us but became appropriately obsequious when Heather's platinum card introduced itself.

"How may we assist you?"

She winked at Jaye.

"Shall we get the honeymoon suite?"

Jaye pulled free of her, turning to all of us to suggest gaily, "Let's just get one big room. We'll stay up and hang out all night!"

"Oh," Heather said hesitantly. "I thought we'd put the boys in their own room — they can talk about comic books and video games."

"This'll be more fun. It'll be like a big slumber party."

This wasn't quite what the rest of us had in mind, but no one wished to cool Jaye's enthusiasm.

She was only more excited when she saw the room, which was nothing like the Days Inns I remembered from trips with my parents.

"This is larger than our house!" she exclaimed.

This was likely not hyperbole. It was a massive suite with two queen size beds with plump blue pillows and comforters gorged with down; a separate sitting area with an upholstered sofa bed, deep, inviting armchairs, and a marble-top dining table; plus a balcony with a sweeping view of the ocean. Everything looked as if you were the first to see or touch it, and once you left, the hotel management would replace everything so the wondrous effect could be repeated.

"My dad once went after a corporation that was dumping waste in the river but sending their execs to places like this for conferences," Andy said. "Great view, though."

"Yeah, it's swell," Heather replied with a yawn. She slid casually into a plush chair and looked as comfortable as someone in her own living room.

Andy turned on the air-conditioning unit full blast. He spread out his long, thin arms and the rushing air whipped up his short-sleeved dress shirt.

"What are you, a goddamn dry-aged steak?" Heather shouted. "Turn that shit off. It's not even that hot."

"Are you kidding? It's an oven. I'll just set it at sixty."

"Sixty?"

"Just for a few minutes."

"Get the fuck out of here!"

She pulled a bottle of bourbon from her backpack.

"Haven't you Yankees heard of drinking to cool off?"

"Should we make mint juleps?" Jaye teased.

"We could."

"You know how?"

Heather nodded: "Electric Boogaloo's a big fan — her grandmother in Kentucky has one every night before bed. But we're not in our nineties, so let's go with Maker's and Blenheim."

Heather called down for the Blenheim and was insistent that no other ginger ale would do. "If they bring up Schweppes, it's their ass," she said. She also ordered multiple items from the room service menu, creating a buffet line on the dining table.

They mostly ate just enough to keep the Maker's and Blenheim company. In between rounds, I continued my vain attempts to reach Janet. I gave up by the fourth round and sat down at the mahogany executive desk, where I had a drink for the second time in my college career.

Enjoying the view from the balcony, Jaye said, "I just remembered: Dana Weichman's party is tonight."

"Oh?" Heather responded with the regret of someone who missed her own beheading. "Another Cody-sponsored bash. I would've needed to get my thigh-high hip waders back from the cleaners."

"Didn't you used to run around with him, though?"

Heather wrinkled her nose at the curdled gossip.

"I never so much as developed a heated trot with Tom Cody. Who told you that?"

"Oh, Baldwin and Reed said..."

"Those Nobel Prize laureates? Yeah, they love to claim they're down with T-O-M — you know them. We used to come up to Athens for the weekend last year to see shows; sometimes we'd wind up at one of his parties. Keep in mind, Cody doesn't throw parties. Usually, it's some chick he's seeing — or just finished seeing only she doesn't know it yet — but it's billed as his party."

"Didn't he throw that after party for Stan's band at Georgia Theatre?"

"Yeah, he wanted one night where it was worth being seen there. He likes to show off. His dad's a Coke exec, which Spencer still thinks is an 'upstart company.' I didn't go to that one, but I heard Suggs got wasted and started a fight with Bracy."

"Suggs?" Andy said incredulously. "Is that a person's name?"

"Yes, *Razinski*. Suggs is from Disgusta. He and Cody roomed together their freshman year at O-House. I was at one Cody party at Crumbley's place last year, and Baldwin and Reed were barely conscious. I'm holding them up like two ventriloquist's dummies. Cody comes over and gives me the full court press. He wants me to come back to his apartment downtown. I remind him I have Heckle and Jeckle with me, but he says they can crash at Crumbley's. She's delighted, of course. I told him I'd only do it if Suggs came along and made it an amazon's three-way. I think Cody was considering it, but Suggs wasn't so adventurous."

There was more idle gossip, which I ignored until the spotlight fell on me.

"So," Jaye said, "you gotta tell me about Janet Tomalin."

The room froze with silence. I was the first to speak.

"Excuse me?"

"I still can't believe I wasn't near the main stage during the throwdown with Evelyn Wilson. I hear you tore her a new asshole, which is awesome. Everyone hates her."

Heather agreed:

"Someone needs to drop a fucking house on that bitch."

Even after almost a year in Athens, I couldn't fathom why someone as universally loathed as Evelyn Wilson was freely invited to every social event in the city.

"Wilson is going around saying that Tomalin is your queer peer or something, and that's how she was able to run around on Waldorf for so long."

"B. isn't gay," Andy said with McGill-honed certainty.

"No one really believes that!" Jaye corroborated with a lopsided smile. "They know Wilson eats Crazy Flakes for breakfast. She's just burned that Scott's music has only gotten better since Tomalin dumped him. He was doing all this power pop stuff before, but now he's moved into wounded angst. It's like how Dion became The Wanderer after he met Runaround Sue." She pointed her still-full drink at me. "I think it's romantic. She's your muse, right? Your Zelda Fitzgerald or Holly Golightly... which one was real?" Stumped, Jaye shrugged and said, "Doesn't matter. Anyway, she's probably great material."

"She's not material."

"I'll say," murmured Heather.

"We're friends."

The absurdity of what I'd just said was now the fifth guest at this party. I should've offered it a drink.

Jaye nodded solemnly, as if hearing some secret meaning in my words. Andy studied the room service menu like there'd be an exam later. He finally just threw it against the wall and started to laugh. This unsettled Heather and me; Jaye simply settled into a chair as if in third row center at Tate.

"Why do you keep saying that?" he asked me. "Why can't you just admit you two are a couple? Is it because you'd have to accept that she's the fucking worst girlfriend on the planet? What sucks most, though, is how she treats you. You've been trying to call her all night, haven't you? But God knows where she is."

"Probably not at Engine Room," Jaye said. "Waldorf's roommate is a bartender there. Wilson says she was banned." She lowered her voice dramatically. "She claims there won't be a bar west of College Avenue where Tomalin can show her face."

"Next stop, HO'Malley's," Heather predicted.

"This isn't funny!" Andy said, although he was the only one who'd laughed recently. "Can't you see what she's doing to him? Half the town thinks they've got some *Suddenly, Last Summer* thing going." He aimed his next words at me directly: "You even wound up taking Introduction to Paint Drying 101 for jocks last quarter because of her."

"I was being existential," I said with all possible contempt.

He ignored my insult and, red-faced, continued on, "She's your top priority, B. You follow the first and only commandment of Janet Tomalin: 'Thou shalt have no other gods but her.' You even blew off Jaye's party just because you saw her at The Grill."

"Drop it, Razinski!"

"Is this an intervention?" I asked heatedly.

"If that's what it takes. Don't you see? That girl is poison!"

I got out of my chair.

"That's enough!" Heather commanded. "And really? You're quoting Bell Biv DeVoe?"

"The Nietzsche garbage was annoying, but at least it was literate," I said. "If you have any more opinions formed from the wisdom of dead Germans or inner city thugs, keep them to yourself. I couldn't be less interested."

My verbal punch was flavored with Schweppes, but the shaking hand by my leg craved the spice of Blenheim.

"It has disrupted our happy home enough for one night," Heather said decisively, and with a slight wave of her golden hand, she imperiously banished the subject.

I could not let it go so easily so I took it with me, without a word to the others, out of the room and out of the hotel. I stormed onto the beach, collapsing on the sand.

After what seemed like hours of desultory sulking but was probably more like twenty minutes, Heather appeared and sat next to me. My khakis made it look like I'd been buried up to my waist.

"I told Razinski to take the sofa. I figured you wouldn't be up for cuddling. Look, about what happened..."

"He was right."

She looked as shocked as I was by what I'd just said.

"But I can't stop needing her and wanting her and... I have sand in my pants."

I stood up. Heather's hands squeezed my shoulders as she set her patrician gaze on me.

"Listen, Carlton: It screwed Razinski. It screwed Waldorf. But It is *fucking* with you. You've gotta exit the theater of this horror show."

Jaye strolled across the sand to us.

"Hey. So, I never knew Andy dated Janet, too."

"We don't talk about that," Heather said — there was almost a tone of annoyance in her voice.

"Wanna go swimming?" The invitation was offered to both of us. "It'll help to cool off."

That was the last thing I wanted. There was also the small fact that I would drown.

"I don't swim."

"Scared of the water?"

"I don't know."

Jaye pulled off her shirt. It was a clinical sight. I loved Janet so much no one else registered, and it ate at me that I didn't think the reverse was true.

"I didn't bring a swimsuit," she said as she unzipped her shorts, "but it's so late I don't think anyone will notice a quick skinny dip, do you?"

"Yeah, should be... fine," Heather whispered — her voice now smoothed of any edge like an expertly cut diamond. With some effort, she turned away from the bare skin gleaming light blue from the moon and asked me, "Are you gonna be all right?"

I responded with a gruff "yeah" and started off toward the coldness of the full moon — wandering further down the beach until I could no longer hear their laughter amongst the splashing of water.

3

When I returned to my dorm room Sunday afternoon, the red light on my answering machine blinked furiously at me.

"Honey, where are you? I'm listening to the tape you left for me, and... oh, gosh, you... you *really* need to be here. Just come down, please... we'll listen to it together... oh, sweetie, there is *nothing* I want more."

I had no messages when I checked them after I returned to the hotel room at just before 2 a.m. I sometimes wondered when Janet slept.

Then:

"I ordered some pizza from Gumby's, and it is chewy and frightful and I'm gonna eat it *all*."

And finally:

"Yes, there is pepperoni on this pizza, and it is divine. Yes, I am eating meat. I won't say *again* because *again* always sounds like I failed. Mother says *again* a lot."

Whenever I missed a call from Janet, I found myself resenting whatever else I had been doing. This time was no different, and I'd picked up the phone to call her when a black guy knocked on my open door. His thick body blocked out the empty space to the hallway.

"Hi there, glad I finally caught you. I'm Derrick, your C.L.A.S.S. advocate."

C.L.A.S.S. stood for "Continuing the Legacy of African-American Student Success," according to the many leaflets and flyers left under my door that ended up in the trash.

"May I help you?" I mumbled absently.

"Well, you see, the Black Student Union is having a..."

My mind drifted back to Janet's voice on the answering machine. I was so deep in self-loathing for not being there when she wanted me that the next words I heard Derrick say were, "So, will you come?"

I wanted to ask, "To what exactly?" but I figured he'd already told me that during his initial sales pitch.

"I don't know. I'm pretty busy right now and..."

"It's important for our people to be united."

This guy was a moron. He had to be to espouse such a bogus concept as unity, something I'd never experienced.

"I'm not much of a joiner."

"I know, I know. I read your columns — really cynical stuff, bro." *Bro?* "You have a really strong voice, though, which you could use to..."

I began to consciously ignore him, as if I could will him away with some as-yet undiscovered telepathic power. Once he finally left, I threw on my robe and headed for the shower. After scrubbing off the persistent sand, I crossed the hallway to find the equally persistent Derrick cornering Janet by my room. When she saw me, she walked through him like he was the choppy image from a filmstrip projector.

"Get dressed, kiddo." She wielded a rolled-up copy of the Tate Theater calendar for the quarter as if it were the Olympic torch. "We have something very important to discuss."

Soon the calendar was spread out on our table at Rocky's like blueprints to a bank while Janet studied it as though planning the perfect heist. She dangled a sparkly "Judy" on the tips of her toes. I kept waiting for the shoe to crash to the floor, but she always caught it just in time before repeating the process. I was too entranced by the spectacle to notice the obvious metaphor.

"So, where oh where had my kiddo gone last night?"

The wide brim of her lampshade hat spoke to me as she focused on her task. Occasionally, she'd use the pen I'd given her to circle a film that we "had to see." I noticed there'd been more circles on the Winter Quarter calendar.

"I was at Hilton Head with Heather, Andy, and Jaye."

I spoke the names with escalating annoyance, which Janet noticed before I did. She lifted her head to smile at me and said over the rumbling thunder outside, "I bet you would've had more fun at 393."

That was her room — directly below mine. Some nights I'd lie in bed, listening to one of her tapes, and consider how she was only a few feet away yet somehow still just out of my reach.

"I tried calling you before I left. I called you a lot, actually."

"I was probably napping. Springing forward always exhausts me. Going forward at all is just dreary."

She had a way of looking at me that generated an immediate and prominent physical reaction, and there was something in her voice that screamed of her full awareness of this effect.

"You must have *really* missed me."

Her "Judy" now hung off one solitary toe. This only further heightened that physical reaction, but I chose to concentrate on my frustration.

"I just wish things weren't always on your terms." Then my blood-starved brain allowed me to foolishly say, "Were you really asleep all day? Or..."

Her "Judy" hit the floor hard. Her smile melted like butter in a hot pan.

"You think I'm lying?"

Ice tea washed down the final slice of black olive and mushroom that she'd just stuffed in her mouth. She slammed the now empty glass onto the Tate calendar — creating an unintentional circle around *Animal House*, which neither of us had any intention of seeing.

"No, of course not... what I meant was..."

She slid her foot back into her shoe as she stood up from the table.

"Excuse me. I need to powder my nose."

That expression no longer charmed me. I grabbed her arm.

"You don't have to do that."

A staring match began.

"I think I do," she said coldly. "I drank a lot of ice tea."

"*Please.*"

"Let go."

I couldn't, but I soon fell to the glare of those sunglasses. I released her and watched her disappear into Rocky's restroom. When she returned, the smell of Crest toothpaste was noxious.

❀❀

After work on Wednesday night, I stopped in Espresso Royale for a medium hazelnut to go. Nick McKee and Marie Peterson were seated at a round table near a small gallery of local art on the wall. I hadn't planned to intrude until Marie called out my name.

"How are you?" I asked.

"Wonderful." She did not take her eyes off Nick as she spoke. "Never better."

Two worlds coexisted at their table: There was Marie's, where reality could be seen only through an ultra-high-powered reflecting telescope and where Nick was so attentive to her needs that he always took her cup up to the counter for refills without being asked. Meanwhile, on a world that more closely resembled the planet Earth, Nick was openly flirting with the male counterperson.

"Have you seen Jaye?" Marie asked as Nick made a return trip to the counter. Such devotion would likely keep her up for days.

"Not recently."

"Yeah, she's all in love now, which is wonderful."

"Sure."

"I know you're not big on love." She took a sip of the coffee Nick handed her. "What was it you wrote last week? Oh right: 'Love and astrology are for teenage girls.' But *I* believe in the power of love." She gazed at Nick as though he could be wrapped in parchment and inhaled. "If you see Jaye before I do, tell her we should talk. If she's never coming back, maybe we could trade rooms." Nick looked unaware of this plan and swallowed uncomfortably. "Christine snores, so..."

I thought Nick's bedtime activities might disturb Marie more than Christine's sleep apnea. I left them to their separate worlds and took my coffee out onto Jackson Street. The air had cooled in the past few hours, so I welcomed the hot stream from my cup as I headed back to Myers.

Crossing through Tate Plaza, I decided to stop in to see Eddie Munster. The lingering warmth in my body vanished when Debbie Tyson opened the door of the projectionist's booth.

"Hey! Come on up."

I was as shocked as if I'd accidentally walked into the ladies room. Eddie Munster swung around on his stool to greet me.

"Captain! Long time no see."

I wasn't at the last Cinematic Arts meeting or more accurately, I pushed through the crowd of new members that made me think I was entering the 40 Watt and saw that the only free seats were next to Andy Razinski and Evelyn Wilson. Neither option appealed to me, so I'd left.

"If you can't make it to the meetings," Debbie said, "you should still come to the after parties."

"The after parties?"

"Yeah, it's sort of the real CA — everyone old school. Tuesday, we went to The Grit and then Engine Room, but Dana thinks that we might hit Taco Stand first next week. Cody says Stipe hangs there, so the least we can do is take it back from the Greeks."

I suppressed a sigh as I turned away from her to speak to Eddie.

"How's the *Flagpole?*"

"Great, Captain! Should've done it a long time ago."

I wondered for a moment if The Movie Dope position came with a total makeover: His somewhat soft and gooey center was wrapped in a crisp, untucked, short-sleeved periwinkle button down. The red from his pen had left no pockmarks on his cuffed jeans, which rested above black, Doc Marten boots.

I suppose he must have had contacts previously, because now his full face wore thick, black-rimmed glasses like Elvis Costello's. He'd also shaved somewhat successfully (there was just one nick near a difficult area by his chin). A tuft of dark brown hair fell over his forehead in that trendy, undetermined space between deliberate and natural.

The makeover also extended to the room itself. It was tidier... more professional, like it was no longer Eddie Munster's tree house.

Debbie picked up a portable tape recorder from the projectionist's bench and started to talk into the attached microphone.

"Nothing makes sense in this movie," she said — her voice shifting from conversational to dramatic to news anchor as she spoke. "Characters react without motivation and spout sluggish, cliché-ridden lines of dialogue. Scenes come and go — neither entertaining us nor progressing the storyline."

These were not Debbie's own critical observations but a passage from the last movie review Eddie had written for the *Red & Black*.

"Debs is auditioning for co-host of *The Film Thing* once Robertson leaves."

The look on Debbie's face seemed to say, "Yeah, he calls me Debs."

I didn't give a damn about Andy Razinski at this point, but I still asked, "Andy's also up for this, right?"

"Yeah," Eddie said absently, "but Cody thinks a female voice will attract more listeners."

Debbie's speaking voice could be used in place of fire alarms, so I questioned the merits of this decision.

"I didn't know you and Cody had gotten so close."

"Totally!" Debbie said proudly. "Cody, Eddie, Brian, and Kevin are like the Fab Four."

I had no idea who Brian and Kevin were and was annoyed enough to be snotty.

"What about Suggs?"

"That bastard?" Debbie said with obedient distaste. "Dana told me he was a stalker."

"So, Captain, you wanna stay and watch the film with us?"

"Yeah," Debbie said, as she placed her hand on Eddie's shoulder. "Dana says *Ice Castles* is a great *date* movie."

I had earned enough college credits to determine I wasn't wanted.

"I need to go, actually." I flailed around for a suitable excuse and failed spectacularly: "I have a poppy seed stuck in my teeth."

I was almost through the south exit to Sanford Drive when I heard Debbie Tyson cry out, "Hey!"

Outside the theater, I could see how unevenly she tanned. Her face looked like a poorly peeled potato.

"Thanks for being so cool back there." She'd raced to catch up with me and was panting and sweating slightly. "I didn't mean to be rude or anything. I just figured you'd be uncomfortable with all the sexual tension."

Sweet Christ.

"But we should totally double."

"Excuse me?"

"You're seeing Scott Waldorf's ex, right? That's what Jaye says."

"Does she?"

"And who cares what Evelyn Wilson thinks? It'll be fun."

The setting of this "fun" event was the following week's screening of *Bride of Frankenstein*, one of the films circled on Janet's Tate Theater calendar. I couldn't think of any way out of it (I'd already played my "poppy seed" card), so reluctantly agreed and let Debbie return to the hot, tension-filled projectionist's booth.

I mentioned the upcoming "double date" — casually and almost as a joke — to Janet the next day when we were settling in to watch *The Philadelphia Story* on the seventh floor.

She twisted open a bottle of Strawberry Yoo-hoo and offered me a swig. She'd been so undauntedly giddy recently it was hard to believe our last brunch had ended so stormily.

"Hold still, kiddo."

She waved her hands over the TV set as I hit play on the console. She did this when we saw movies in theaters, as well. I liked to think it was her way of magically allowing my fascination for her to temporarily include the image on the screen. If so, it was a kindness, as I recall the films we watched together as vividly as I remember her perfume.

Once the credits started, I alluded again, this time in a whisper, to our *Bride of Frankenstein* doubles match. She could skip through topics the way a child skipped through puddles, so I wanted to confirm she was okay with this plan.

"Does it even matter if we're with two other people or 200 when we see a movie?" She put two red-nailed fingers to my lips. "Now, hush!"

The "double date" was also a double feature: *Frankenstein* preceded *Bride of Frankenstein*. However, after the ticket tearer left and the theater doors closed, I began to suspect that there'd only be a double feature. I spent most of the first film outside by the box office waiting for Janet. Punctuality was not something I expected from her when it came to anything else, but she'd never been late before to a film we were seeing.

Eddie Munster appeared behind me and patted my back consolingly.

"She blow you off, huh? Yeah, I heard she was a little flaky. No offense. And here you are missing some Karloff goodness because of her." It was almost 10. There was no one else in the immediate area, but Eddie still looked around furtively as if about to hand me confidential documents. "So, look, man, we need to talk. You and me. Not now, though. Later... without the ladies."

He moved his clenched fists around in a circular motion as he said the word "ladies."

"We're halfway there already," I said bitterly.

"Yeah, man, I hear you. That's the kind of crap that keeps me from dating."

He couldn't possibly be this clueless.

"You do realize you're on a date *now*, right?"

"Huh? Debs? No, we're friends. She's a *friend* girl. Not a *girl*friend. She's cool, but she's too normal."

"Really?"

"Yeah, I like weird girls. Weird girls... move me."

Debbie Tyson walked out of the theater, rubbing her eyes.

"God, no one said this was in black and white. It's giving me a head-ache." Thoroughly Normal Debbie turned to Eddie. "Do we have to stay for the other one? I might have a seizure."

"You gonna stick around?" Eddie asked me.

"For a few more minutes."

"Let's go to Uptown. Dana and Patty said they might be there around 11."

"If your lady ever shows up, you should join us, Captain."

Debbie made a face before catching herself, and I knew her lack of concern for what Evelyn Wilson might think existed only in the neutral zone of the Tate Center.

"That's fine. I'll probably just go home after this."

Eddie and Debbie headed out in the drizzle toward downtown. I waited through intermission and then went inside, without my mate, to watch *Bride of Frankenstein*.

I left the theater convinced that Janet was under an Orbit bus some-where. A cold sweat of irrational fear insulated me from the warm mist out-side. There was no light in Janet's window and no answer when I pounded on her door as if the building was ablaze. My phone, however, rang violently no more than two minutes after I'd entered my room.

"Hey, poopsie!"

My mind quickly wrapped chains around my elation at hearing her voice.

"Where are you?"

"Hernando's Hideaway!"

"What happened? You were supposed to meet me at Tate."

"Huh?"

"We were going to see *Bride of Frankenstein*."

"Oh… right. Have we missed it?"

"It's after midnight."

"Well, I miss *you*, poopsie. Come keep me company."

There was no Hernando's Hideaway in Athens, so her "poopsie" met her at a dive on Washington and Thomas. Evelyn Wilson and her broom had swept Janet deep into downtown's east side.

The wind overpowered my cheap umbrella, so I walked into the bar damp and irritable. I quickly spotted Janet at a grimy booth in the back near a jukebox that played what was asked of it but with almost visible shame. She was not alone. Clinging to either side of her like musty sweat were two guys in wrinkled cargo shorts and faded polos with turned-up collars. They were indistinguishable from the other screaming roughnecks in the bar, so I don't know how they were selected to join her. Maybe they were just the first to sit down.

I never learned their names. I doubt Janet even knew. "Jed," the one on her right, had offered as tribute his UGA baseball cap, which Janet wore in an absurd pairing with her red-collared gray dress with black polka dots. "Jethro," the one on her left, played with the fancy red bow at the end of her short sleeve and ogled her like a present he couldn't wait to take home and unwrap. They were drinking beers that Gina Sloane's refrigerator would have asked to leave. Janet raised her bottle when she finally saw me.

"Poopsie! Sit down. Join the party."

Jed and Jethro took their attention away from Janet long enough to greet me with the "wink-and-trigger."

"Sorry about the movie, kiddo," she said — a weary emptiness streaming through her sunglasses. "I just couldn't bear all the darkness and the noise."

We were currently in a dark and noisy place, where Jed now smelled the black hair pouring from his baseball cap.

"Hmmm, you smell so nice, you know?"

"Of course, silly, I'm a girl!"

Jethro fondled the tawny skin on her arm.

"You're real soft, too."

"Still a girl! Not rocket science, boys."

The three took shots of Jägermeister. Jed offered me some of what he called "Bambi blood," but I declined.

"Hey," Jethro said, "you're that guy from the paper, right? You're pretty funny."

I gave no response.

"Kinda angry, though," Jed added.

"I wanna dance!" Janet announced to no one in particular.

"Aww yeah," Jethro shouted, "play that funky music!"

Janet went over to the jukebox as if learning to roller skate. Jed turned to me.

"You know, she's really something."

"That so?"

"Yeah… kinda sexy… kinda *wild*."

I wanted to slam his face into the wooden table until his nose spurted blood and his teeth cut through his lips. Instead, I got up and grabbed the sexy, wild one by the arm.

"What the hell is this?"

I was so furious my words came out like Western Union telegrams: "What. *Stop.* The. *Stop.* Hell. *Stop.* Is. *Stop.* This? *Stop.*"

"Why so grumpy, uh…" She couldn't think of a word that rhymed, so she started to tango to the music in her head. Jed and Jethro demonstrated their appreciation with claps and whistles.

"You blow me off tonight to come here. And then you want me to *watch*? Is that what you think of me? Am I some loose tooth you like to wiggle and push around?"

"Oh, let's just dance! I know you wanna dance." She winked at me. "You always do. I can tell."

She pulled off her heels and stood barefoot on the dirty floor.

"You're tall," she whispered in my ear. Then she giggled: "But I bet you're not as tall as they are."

If I'd spoken, the next words to flow from my mouth would have been molten and savage, so I said nothing and simply walked out of the bar. I was sick of her and sick of myself for not feeling ill sooner.

☙❧

The next morning, campus transit replaced its buses with arks that could more effectively transport students through the near-flooding streets of Athens. After class, I waded over to the *Red & Black* and sat there in the first room of the office pounding keys with an intensity that any passive observer would probably correctly describe as dementia. I can't even remember what I was writing, but I knew it would be as angry as the paper's readers had come to expect.

From my desk, I heard the creaking and wheezing of the stairs as people came and went. It was easy enough to ignore after a while, but at one point, I noticed something different — a tunefulness, an elegance to each step, and as the glass door opened, I knew Janet was behind me.

"Hey, kiddo."

She was soaked to the skin. She didn't wear a coat or carry an umbrella; her cherry red hat hung limply in her hand like a wet dishrag. Her sunglasses were so streaked and steamed, I doubt she could see through them.

"It wasn't very nice what you did. You just left me."

I activated spell-check, my face not veering from the screen. My rage was my only defense against her voice, but I knew I couldn't look at her.

"I can't talk about this right now."

"When do you want to talk about it?"

That was a reasonable question, I suppose. I felt the urge, the necessity, to have it out... but not here. One our way down the stairs, we passed a porcine sports writer whose name I have chosen to forget. Pausing to let us by, as well as to collect his breath, he waved a nicotine-stained hoof at me, his chubby fingers a veritable crime scene of untimely deceased, high-calorie meals.

"Shit, man, she's with you?" he said about Janet. "And you bitch and moan about life!"

"Go to hell."

He laughed. There was something about testosterone that made guys think insults were endearing.

Janet and I swam upstream to Rocky's. We even took our usual booth. I watched the train. I counted cigarette burns in the tablecloth. Janet was the first to speak.

"Are you mad at me?"

Her voice quavered like Jell-O. I knew if I made eye contact, I'd do the same.

"I'm not mad." This was a lie. "So, who won the toss-up? Jed or Jethro? Or was it an amazon's three-way?"

I was being unforgivably cruel. Only now am I able to see that my love had boiled over to the point where I couldn't control my feelings or myself, and the power she had over me made me hate her.

"Why are you being so mean?"

"I'm not." Another lie. "I'm just... tired. Tired of pretending we're just friends. Although, frankly, you kind of suck at that, too."

I still boldly addressed the tablecloth. Janet's wet hand was moving toward me. If she touched me, it was over and I'd only find new ways of apologizing to her. I shifted away. I think this surprised her because I detected a note of desperation in her words.

"Honey, why don't we just finish our drinks and then go to the seventh floor and watch *Bride of Frankenstein*? We'll make our own double feature."

"No." I was drenched in sweat. "You think it's that easy? You think *I'm* that easy? You must think I'm an idiot. Of course you do. Because I *am* an idiot. It's not a complicated logic problem. Everyone sees that. It's like what Heather says..."

The glass of ice tea in Janet's hand began to shake.

"You've been talking to *her* about us?"

The youth had been twisted and wrung out from her voice like a mop. "She's my friend."

"I know! And she's just so *friendly* — always whispering into your ear about how awful I am. And how everything might be better for everyone if you just got rid of me."

"That's not entirely true."

"Stop! I know how it works. First hand." Our waitress waited by the counter for a calmer moment to take our orders. "I haven't changed, but suddenly that's not good enough for you. And it's so unfair because I've always loved you for who you are."

"Yes, an idiot, who tags along while you rub my face in guy after guy and whatever those two were last night."

"How can you say that? I've shared with you things I've never... You were the first. You're the only one in my life, you're all there is."

"That's demonstrably untrue."

I always used big words when being a jackass.

She slammed down her glass, sending a wave of ice tea over the table. Soon a shower of crumpled bills sprinkled over it. A damp Andrew Jackson seemed to sneer at me and mock my inability to let her just walk out the door. I called out her name and she spun on her heel, tottering slightly as if perched on the end of a diving board.

"Fuck you!" Anger scarred her face. "Why don't you go get a boyfriend or something and leave me the hell alone!"

My next memory was sinking below the back of my seat at the booth. I recall staring at the brick wall behind the register. Then I stared at the train tracks and the peeling wood panels beneath them that had buckled from moisture over the years. Finally, I stared at the empty pale-green vinyl cushion in front of me.

The waitress crossed the ford to my table.

"Uh, would you like anything?"

"No, thank you."

"Oh, man, she left me way too much money."

"Keep it."

She slipped the bills into her apron pocket and said brightly, "Look, all couples have fights! Don't worry, it'll be fine."

I almost laughed. That was funnier than anything I'd ever written. No ending had been more final than what she'd just witnessed.

4

My phone was silent those first few days after Rocky's. My head was not so tranquil. It rumbled like a growling stomach that couldn't be filled, and whenever I tried to get out of bed, the floor seemed further away, as if the mattress was rising upward on a column of unstable air.

Eventually, ringing began to fuse with the pounding in my head; the answering machine clicked on as though triggering an exploding shell, and Janet's voice — perhaps believing me suitably chastened — filled the room.

"Hey, kiddo, I can't stay mad at you, especially when you haven't seen *The Awful Truth*. Come down to 393 and we'll pop some popcorn — shh, don't tell the RAs! — and watch it together."

I couldn't reach the phone. My floating bed almost touched the ceiling. The ringing at some point turned into a solid rapping at the door — recognizably melodic at first and then painfully insistent, but I didn't move. Hours passed — possibly enough to be divided into days — and then I heard...

"It's like you don't even own a telephone, dear. Not that it matters. You won't see me. *You won't see me.* Guess you never really did. But you're missing tea for two! Except I don't think this is tea, and it's just me... alone."

The scent of her lilac perfume could not carry over the phone lines, but the smell of alcohol on her breath did. A gusty wind brought the phone up to me. I was very close to calling her when I fell out of bed. I think I stayed on the floor for a while and watched the stucco on the walls peel in rippling waves. I later saw my roommate's face over me asking if I was all right. I gave him the "wink-and-trigger." He put searing notes from the door in my hand and vanished between flashes of white and the rumbling of the phone.

And sometime later:

"Honey, you just... you just can't *do* this to us. Oh, you big liar, you pushed me right off that mission. I never had a chance."

The phone was in my hand. I'd dialed all but the last digit of her number before forcing myself to remember that if I gave in... that if I crawled to her, as I so desperately wanted to do, how I felt now would just be how I'd always feel eventually.

I couldn't sleep so I went downtown, shamefully staying on the west side, where I knew Janet wasn't welcome. I even sat through an impromptu marathon of bad movies at the Classic Triple. The dollar movie house was a safe space because the only films released in Janet's lifetime that she'd seen were *The Muppet Movie* and *Victor/Victoria*.

I'd stumbled out of the last showing of *The Bodyguard*, almost slipping on the floor as the janitor mopped and landing with a splash on a vintage video game. I couldn't go home. If patheticness is an object spherical in shape, my next action circled its globe: I walked into The Grill. It was the last place Janet would come. Evelyn Wilson's bullying wasn't necessary to banish her when Janet herself had made the dubious choice of going home with two of the restaurant's shift managers in the same week.

Cool tiles of black and white spread across the walls, ceiling, and floor. The tables were black, as were the cushions in the booth. The plates were white with a black trim. Waitresses in black miniskirts and white button-down blouses poured black coffee into my white cup. The coffee was bitter, and no amount of the white crystals I sprinkled into it seemed capable of sweetening the taste. It kept me awake, though, which was my sole focus, because sleep was the rip current that would pull me out to the one place I couldn't escape Janet.

I was aware enough of the rising and falling levels of patronage to time my food orders accordingly, so it wouldn't appear obvious that I'd become as much a fixture as the World War II posters on the walls. I only touched a few bites of anything I was served, but I sampled everything on the menu except for the Big Molly burger.

There were some small scatters of color — a neon cursive "The Grill" sign in the window facing me and a tiny red jukebox attached to the wall by my booth. It played no music, though, at least none I could hear anymore.

Overcast with sleep, my eyes picked out two girls floating through the doors on clouds, one a fluffy white and the other a thick black. It was not until they'd parked their conveyances and sat across from me in my grim booth that I recognized them as Heather Aulds and Jaye Goetz.

"Jesus H.! You've really gone to seed."

My mouth opened to respond, and the creaking of associated muscles indicated that I hadn't spoken for quite a while.

"I talked to your waitress or concierge or whatever the hell. Do you know how long you've been here?"

"I'm not sure," I said truthfully.

"Three days, motherfucker!" Heather smacked my hand away from the knob on the jukebox that adjusted its levels of silence. "So, I guess you finally broke up with It."

I tried pointing to an item on the menu but realized that wouldn't work for this conversation.

"Yeah... no... I mean... we were never really together."

"So you wised up."

"How did you know?"

"You're living in a theme restaurant!" Heather looked around contemptuously. "Where's the singing bear?"

"The LaBrea Stompers ate here after a show last month," Jaye said pleasantly.

"Why didn't you come to me?" Heather demanded.

"It was weird," Jaye noted. "You vanished around the same time as Andy... but he just got a girlfriend." She ordered a vanilla malt and as the waitress left, quickly added, "I'm sure there's no connection."

"I'm handling it," I said to Heather.

"Really? You look like Hobo Jenkins with that ridiculous peach fuzz on your face. You getting ready to ride the rails?"

Jaye's malt was presented in a steel container that glistened with drops of water. It tumbled lazily into a cone-shaped paper cup tucked inside a chilled metal stand.

"Want some?"

I didn't answer. Heather shook her head. Jaye pierced the malt's heart with a straw and wrapped her lips around it.

When they'd spotted my remains, Heather and Jaye were on their way to see Dashboard Saviors at the 40 Watt. Afterward, they planned to drop in at Annie Battaglia's May Day Party (somehow May had arrived and somehow, it was safe to presume, irony would be involved in the May Day Party). However, Heather was now insistent on not leaving until I did.

"You don't have to do that," I said.

"Hey, why don't I give you two some privacy," Jaye said graciously enough that I felt guilty about my lingering resentment of her. "I can roll with Baldwin and Reed."

There was a quick caress of Heather's dark hair and a lopsided smile at me, and Jaye unhitched her low-hanging cloud and drifted out onto College Square while sipping her frosty malt in a to-go cup.

"Look, we can stay here as long as you need to," Heather said softly, squeezing my hand. Then to the waitress who looked at her expectantly: "I'm not eating this shit. Just bring me an ashtray."

A crushed pack of Marlboros and my cold fries and feta lay on the black slab between us as a dull fog began to cover my eyes. Someone at another table, who didn't appear drunk, was quietly eating eggs. It must have been morning.

"You should get some sleep," Heather insisted.

"I'm not tired."

A truck barreled past me, sending a splash of water in my face.

"That'll start for a shower — we just need to scrub you down with some soap."

"We're not at The Grill," I said, slowly comprehending. I'd passed through North Campus in a haze. I stepped back onto the sidewalk. The Journalism Building was across the street. I remembered racing out of it with Janet on the first day of class. The sun was burning off the morning mist, and the somber building glowed brightly in the reflected light — just as I did with her. Now its colors seemed to have faded to a sunken orange, and inside were just rooms and hallways, empty and absent of all joy.

I was now propped up against the door to my room at Myers.

"Seriously, get some sleep."

Heather sounded very far away, but I could feel her hair falling on my shoulders like black sheets of rain.

I shivered slightly and said, "No, I'm good."

"If you're worried about It annoying you..." She held up her fists. "I'll stand outside the door with Frazier and Ali."

I thanked her, told her not to worry, promised to go to bed… but first a shower… maybe even a shave. I'd call her later. I'd be fine, well-rested.

Heather left reluctantly. I stumbled to the shower. At one point, I found myself on the cold linoleum with water streaming down my bare chest. My hands were also tingling, so overall I thought it best not to handle a razor right now.

I'd dressed and was on my way to class when I realized I couldn't fully recall what classes I was taking… also, it was Sunday.

"You stopped answering your phone."

Andy Razinski's voice gusted over from the far end of the hallway. There was an aggressive rustle of long limbs and he was suddenly facing me.

"What do you want?" I asked.

He crossed his arms and frowned.

"If you're pissed at me, fine. But you should still go to the CA meetings. I know you like them."

"I did."

"Yeah, I know it's weird now, but I don't go for the people — other than you and Eddie. It's just fun to talk about movies."

"They still do that?"

"No, not really." He paused. "Hey, come with me to the Kangaroo."

Outside was sticky and humid, as though every molecule of air was bursting with moisture. I thought I was still in the shower until a blast of cool air struck me as we entered the convenience store. Andy bought two Tabs — one for me, as I needed caffeine and the coffee percolating behind the counter resembled crude oil.

"Have you read Eddie's stuff at the *Flagpole*?" Andy asked. "He's really improved *The Movie Dope*." He seemed genuinely pleased for Eddie. "I haven't had a chance to talk to him much lately. He tends to leave with the others after CA now."

I nodded and, perhaps eager for another topic, said, "Jaye mentioned you're seeing someone."

"She did?" Andy tore open a bag of Skittles as we stepped back into the steaming shower. "Yeah, so..."

◑◐

Myrtle Adams approached Andy when he was tearing tickets for the midnight showing of *Animal House*. Andy's set pre-film routine had him settled in his third-row center seat with a Tab and a pack of Skittles before the trailers started, so he never tore tickets for a movie he wanted to watch.

Myrtle was in his philosophy of the mind class. She was not a philosophy major but was interested in things that challenged her perspective. Andy immediately noticed the many other ways that she was well-rounded — her elbows were like tiny dimples in her lush arms, and her rosy cheeks would eclipse her eyes whenever she smiled or laughed — so if she enjoyed *Animal House*, it was possible she'd see very little of it.

"In class the other day, you claimed God's existence could only be proven through circular reasoning," Myrtle said as Andy dropped half her ticket into a long metal tube. "And I thought... well, I'm gonna have to have dinner with that man and set him straight."

Andy's metabolism craved both debate and food, so he waited by the concession stand with Skittles and a Tab until *Animal House* ended. Myrtle's friends rode off on wheels of knowing giggles to the Georgia Bar, where they were meeting another group, and Andy chivalrously adjusted his pace to Myrtle's Southern saunter as they moseyed up to Taco Stand.

"It's still nice and hot out," Myrtle said, "so let's go eat on the lawn."

The North Campus grass, fresh and warm, appeared to grow out from the sides of her tan feet. As the bustling noises of downtown faded, Myrtle's voice mingled casually with the remaining sounds of nature around them.

"See, I'm a materialist," Andy said through bites of burrito, "so the mind *is* the body, and the body's the mind. It's all connected."

"The mind's connected to your body, sure, but it's separate. Like my daddy says, your soul's not something you can put in a jar." A bit of cheese from her burrito spread on her cheek in a primrose pattern. "In my biology class last quarter, they showed us a brain — it's just this little, shriveled-up old thing. Who can really believe that's *you*... everything you feel and think? No, that's just being stupid to try to be smart."

It was sometime before 6, when morning was close but still looked far off and remote, that the impulse seized Andy to kiss Myrtle. He didn't dwell on the girls he'd kissed or hadn't kissed in the past or what it would mean once he kissed the one in front of him. He was fully in the moment, and as he savored the satisfaction of living authentically, Myrtle pressed her pear-shaped face against his.

"Just felt like doing that," she said.

"B., you just don't know, she's so... she's so..." Andy slapped his hand against a stop sign on Lumpkin. "Who needs fucking words, man?"

Andy Razinski usually had words to spare, but this morning, he was simply a blur of rapturous movement. Meanwhile, I struggled against the advance of sleep and its regiment of brutal dreams. I almost nodded off on the way back to Myers, but I snapped back into semiconsciousness when Andy said something that's always stuck with me.

"It's like my dad told me once — you've gotta be true to yourself. That's all that matters."

That's advice my own father would have never given me — the conventional wisdom of an unknown multitude was the quicksand on which he thought you should build your personality, your life, your entire reality — and half-awake, I must have confessed this out loud.

"What does he know?" Andy said. "Don't overthink that shit. You see *Dead Poets Society?*"

I gazed up at what seemed like a limitless number of moldy stairs, silently wishing Myers had put in an elevator during our walk. Before pushing on upstream, I turned to Andy and shook his hand.

"Thanks for the Tab."

I realized, in my near delirium, that I'd never thanked him for anything, not really, and it seemed long overdue.

The answering machine glared at me when I plodded into my room — growling as its tape sped backward before playing an elegy.

"You... you've ruined *Swing Time*! I can't even think about it without... oh, God, you are *so* cruel. You took everything! And I'll never forgive you... never!"

She was sobbing, and unlike when she wept in my arms on Valentine's Day, I was the source of her pain and not her solace. I have never hated myself more, and so I did another thing for the first time with her — I cried.

I cried because the dream was over but so was the fantasy that I could ever stop loving her, that I could rewind my feelings to a time before I knew her. So I cried until exhaustion finally overcame me and I was conscious of nothing but her absence. I cried because the world had ended and we were the only ones who knew.

❀❀

When I woke up, it might have been hours or days later. I didn't bother or care to check. The grass in the quad was being mowed, and each cut blade reacted so volatilely that the stifling air was filled with the stench of their anguish.

My hands fiddling pointlessly with keys and change in my pockets, I walked through the Myers parking lot and came upon Eddie Munster, leaning against his car and punctiliously smoking a cigarette.

He looked like he'd been waiting for me a long time, although we had no plans to meet. He put out his cigarette with the heel of his sneaker, wiped his dry hands on his red-and-blue plaid shirt, and took several quick steps forward to hug me.

"Captain! My Captain!"

Releasing me, he stepped back and patted the hood of his car.

"What do you think?"

It was a bright, flaming red; even with the lingering overcast, I had to shield my eyes from the glare. Of course, I'd seen his car before — often, in fact — and had ridden in it with him on several occasions, including to a sneak preview in Atlanta of *Indecent Proposal*, which we mutually jeered in a clever (at least to us) co-written movie review for the *Red & Black*. I think he presented it to me now, as something new, because it had somehow become for him more than just a means of transportation.

"It's an '88 Dodge Shadow ES!" he said proudly. "It's a classic... well, in fifteen more years. Wanna go for a ride?"

"I'm heading to the office."

"I'll drive you."

That seemed absurd — it wasn't a long walk (and with traffic, was quicker on foot) — but he appeared so desperate for my company I thought he might pull me into the vehicle by my shirt collar.

I usually had to clear some random take-out food bag or candy wrapper from the passenger's seat, but the car's interior no longer contained evidence of Eddie's appetite.

"Debs sometimes rides with me," he explained as we started up Lumpkin.

"How is your friend girl?"

"She's good, she's good. We saw Mudhoney at the Masquerade last week."

That explained the noises coming from his stereo. He used to only listen to movies he'd recorded with a tape player pressed up against the TV. Once, he'd demonstrated how *Annie Hall* was still just as effective without visuals and that *Taxi Driver* was compellingly nightmarish when you only heard Bernard Herrmann's score and De Niro's eerie voiceover.

"So, I heard you were living at The Grill for a while..."

"Not exactly..."

"Hey, I get it, it has air conditioning. You know, I tried the Myers thing my freshman year, too... now I'm over on Pope and Baxter, which is nice. You should come by sometime."

"Sure."

"So, we really need to talk." He gripped the burgundy steering wheel as though it was the looming topic. "Let's get lunch later... at The Grit."

"The Grit?"

"Yeah, it'll be great. See you there at noon?"

He dropped me off outside the *Red & Black* office. I saw Gwen Lupo timorously stepping out of Espresso with a cup of coffee and her usual slightly terrified expression. Saying hello as I opened the door for her, I watched Eddie's red wagon pull itself up Jackson.

Three hours later, I passed under the hanging metal globe bearing the words "The Grit" and spotted Eddie Munster sitting at a booth with a similarly dressed man of around fifty, who he introduced to me after an especially crushing hug as Pete.

I thought for a moment that the balding man was Eddie's father or a more liberal faculty adviser than mine, who always wore a suit, but he shook my hand in a way that indicated he wanted me to consider him a peer. It's the type of handshake that makes every teenager instantly feel a member of the secret society of adulthood.

Eddie and Pete were drinking glasses of carrot juice. Pete offered me some of his.

"Fresh made. Best thing for you."

I didn't know a polite way to refuse, so I accepted his offer through a nearby straw.

"I come here for the juice," he said, adding almost wistfully, "but I like the food down the street better."

"Where's that?" I asked.

"Bluebird Café," Eddie answered.

"Yeah," he said with a touch of the local's surprise that his vague terminology wasn't sufficient. "They make a great avocado omelet."

There was a brief moment of silence for the omelet, and then Pete looked at me as if remembering something.

"You know Tom Cody, right? Eddie said you were friends with him."

"I know him."

"He's a good guy to know," Pete insisted. "Really has his head screwed on tight for someone so young. Some of these kids involved in the scene here... they never leave Athens. Not Tom. He'll go far."

He finished the rest of his juice and slid out of the booth.

"I have to get back," he said. "I'll let you two enjoy your lunch. Try the staple... or the hash if they have it today."

Eddie looked at the pink menu in his hands and cast a glance at the specials board.

"I don't think they have the hash," he said glumly.

A waitress followed a snake-like tile pattern to our table. We ordered perfunctorily and our lunch soon arrived in blocks of invisible ice.

"That was Pete," Eddie explained, "from the *Flagpole*."

"Oh."

"I've been talking to him about maybe doing some *real* articles — not just *The Movie Dope*."

"That's great. I always liked your movie reviews."

"Well, they wouldn't be about movies... more music-focused like the rest of the magazine."

"Really?"

"Yeah, it's what this town is all about, you know? It's the language of Athens."

That sounded like a bumper sticker, so I figured he'd heard it from Tom Cody.

"You wanted to talk?" I said curtly.

He tried to look casual, but his tense bearing, the tremble in his voice... I began to suspect he'd invited me to lunch to ask for a kidney.

"Yeah, yeah... so, uh, you going to the prom?"

Having graduated high school almost a year ago, I thought this question nonsensical until Eddie provided some background: The "prom" was Debbie Tyson's upcoming party. She had not attended her own prom, which was as shocking as a sunrise, and she and her roommates had conspired to throw their own "cool" version in a few weeks. Considering his growing involvement with Debbie, it didn't surprise me that Eddie would go or would ask if I planned to do so, but what he said next did. "Do you think Heather will come?"

This threw me for a moment. He'd never said her name — only ever referring to her as my "weird friend."

"I don't know."

He stared for a long moment at the accordion row of T-shirts on the opposite wall underneath unfinished wood letters spelling out "Bakery"; then he fumbled for a while with the maroon slats on the window blinds.

"I think... I think I might have handled things poorly at *The Crying Game*. Does she say much about it?"

She didn't like the film, and she didn't know Eddie was alive.

"No," I said as delicately as possible.

"I figured... see, I'd hoped she'd join CA... everyone else in her crowd was starting to... and that was my home base... it would've been good. But when she didn't, I guessed she was freaked out by how I acted. That's why I started writing to her."

Random events began to take a cohesive shape, and it was ludicrous yet horrifying.

"You sent her those..." I caught myself and paused for a moment to season my block of ice with salt and pepper. "You sent her love letters?"

"That was just Phase One."

"There are... phases?"

"I thought the letters would make it clear that she was welcome."

The letters were unsigned and invoked salmon. I wasn't sure what he hoped to communicate. Fortunately, he'd moved on to whatever the next "phase" was before Heather called the police.

"Remember at the end of last quarter when we were at Peppino's? I was really stressed about it. She hadn't responded, so it hit me... I should be a gentleman... go where she's comfortable. But she wasn't at any of the parties I went to with Cody that night. Debs was at one of them, and she heard me *casually* talking about Heather with him. She told me how Heather was thinking of joining CA but not until it became more..." He plucked the word from the air like an overripe piece of fruit. "...*fun*."

Eddie didn't realize Debbie wasn't even talking about the same Heather.

"So, you let Tom Cody turn CA into an amusement park on the off chance that Heather might show up? You were wasting your time."

"C'mon, man, who cares if they show *Pete's Dragon*? I mean, I loved CA. It was great, but to make it something she would like... that she'd come to and enjoy... Don't you see? That would be *everything*."

"Is that the only reason you sponsored me in the first place?" I suddenly believed him capable of anything. "You thought I'd bring Heather?"

"No! No, I never brought her up to you because I didn't want to put you in a tough position."

"But you told Tom Cody?"

"Sure... I knew he could help." He leaned toward me. "He knows a little more about girls than we do."

"Yeah, he's full of great ideas. Where does dating Debbie Tyson fit into all of this? What 'phase' is she?"

"We're friends. Good friends — she's helped me out some..." He gesticulated to offer his clothes and hair as examples of this "help." "Now, it might look like she's into me..."

"Because she is."

"I know that rumor's going around, but Cody says not to worry about it. It's actually not that bad if Heather thinks I'm with someone else. Cody says it just makes me look more appealing."

"No, it makes you look like an asshole. In fact, it *makes* you an asshole." I shoved away my block of ice, and our waitress carried it off with tongs.

"I don't understand," I said quietly.

Eddie squeezed my forearm; the expression on his face widening the year separating us into a gulf of decades.

"It's OK, Captain. True passion makes no sense until it happens to you. It's like watching *Kagemusha* without subtitles. You can sort of follow along, but you don't really get it. I remember when we did the final votes for the Spring schedule. The way you argued for *Victor/Victoria* — it was like your life depended on it. I used to be like that, but who gives a crap about movies when she was so close I could taste it... I wasn't going to lose that again."

I was furious now and in no mood to be delicate.

"No, Eddie, what I don't understand is how you could be this obsessed over someone you met for about five seconds a few months ago."

Eddie shook his head vigorously.

"That's what you don't get, man. Heather and I have known each other for years."

The mystery of his statement failed to compel me. I just considered him deranged — I'd read his poetry, after all — and wanted to leave. I asked for the check, which I insisted on paying.

"I'm not sure what you want from me," I said.

"I'm a little desperate. See, we keep missing each other at these parties. She didn't go to Dana Weichman's last month... and everyone went. Debs and I were there all night, but she never showed. And I was certain she'd come to Annie Battaglia's, but her friend Jaye said she couldn't make it."

"You talked to Jaye?"

"Yeah, she's cool," he said dismissively because we'd veered too far from the subject that consumed him. "Cody and Dana took her off my hands, though." He drummed his flat paws against the table. "I wanted to stay focused in case Heather showed up."

I again felt the urge for delicacy.

"Look, Eddie, the thing is… Heather's… seeing someone else. She has been for a while now."

There was another tumultuous shake of his head.

"Where'd you hear that? It's not what Cody says. He thinks now is the best time. That's why I'm helping Debs with the prom — you know, going in on the food and drinks and all that. Cody says he'll be there, which means everyone else will. It'll be huge. If you could just get Heather to come, I can finally…" The concrete settling of his actions melted into the abstract. "…it'll be perfect."

I stared at him for a moment with cold distaste.

"You want me to bring Heather to a party you're throwing with another girl so you can make your big move on her?"

I thought the vileness of the concept, once uttered aloud and accumulating some sort of reality, would smother his fantasy like grass under the first coat of snow, but it only evaporated on contact.

"Yeah, yeah, that's all I'm asking…" His pleading faded into an idle fiddling of the window blinds. "…well, there's just one other thing… and it's more for Debs."

How thoughtful of him to consider her.

"Don't bring Andrew."

"What?"

"Debs hates him. I guess he pissed her off at CA." Eddie paused to recall a relevant incident. "He did say nasty things about *Valley Girl*. She loves that movie. Anyway, it's not like he fits in with our crowd."

The way he said "our crowd" felt like he'd included me in a police lineup.

"And I do?"

"Oh yeah! Debs thinks you're awesome, and everyone loves your stuff even if it's for the *Red & Black*."

"That's… really… something." I got up from the booth. "OK, here's what I'll do for you: Debbie won't have to worry about Andy going to her party, because I won't be there, either. And if you want Heather to come, send her an invitation... but I'd leave seafood out of it."

My conversation with Eddie Munster ended as abruptly as someone hanging up the phone — even The Grit's front door slammed shut with a sharp click as a line was permanently disconnected.

⊙⊙

I floated around for the next few days like dried wood. I avoided calls from Heather, because I didn't know how or even if I should tell her about Eddie Munster's twisted affections. Andy wanted me to meet Myrtle Adams, but his descriptions of her forecast such unrelenting sunniness, I didn't have the stomach for it.

Heather and Andy were other halves of couples now, and Janet and Eddie were both sealed away in my past. So I hunkered over my desk at the *Red & Black* and wrote review after review and column after column. It felt like the paper was the only thing I had that was mine, so I suppose it was inevitable that when I arrived in the office one late afternoon in mid-May, I discovered what looked like a crime scene.

Writers from all departments moved in slow motion through the office's three narrow rooms. They would whisper to each other and occasionally react with the expression of melodramatic shock from a silent movie.

Pushing through the yellow tape I felt was strewn everywhere, I looked around — specifically under desks and behind coat racks — for Gwen Lupo but couldn't find her. Aside from Eddie, she was the only other *Red & Black* staffer I knew. Jennifer Howard had moved on somewhat predictably to advertising. Curiosity overwhelmed me, so I approached one of the sports writers. An assemblage of long hair, round glasses, and long arms, he'd stopped me the other day to compliment a favorable review I'd written for the new PJ Harvey album.

When I asked him what was going on, his response was terse but comprehensive: "Travis got screwed."

The *Red & Black* board — in that secret, slightly sinister room up the stairs — had just announced their selections for editor in chief and managing editor for Fall Quarter, and Travis Richards was neither. The resulting ripples of panic and confusion were less about Travis, though, than the disruption to the overall order of things — he'd been the next in line, the most likely

choice, and the new editor in chief, Dan Buchanan, was a newspaper management student who had never worked at the *Red & Black* until this quarter,
when he'd churned out just enough mediocre articles to qualify him to apply
for the top position.

The board's choice for managing editor — one of the last living girls
named Daisy — was a nondescript younger version of Lori O'Brien who'd
written nondescript articles about the nondescript actions of student government for most of the year. If someone had sneaked in one night and scooped
out Lori's brain, leaving behind only the charming rattle — more pronounced
now because of the excess space, this would be our new managing editor.

"It's an invasion," the sports writer said with a flair for the operatic.
"See, the board's putting in all of Grady's golden kids. We might as well
move into a room in the Journalism building — if any of us still have jobs."

There was the sickening sound of tortured movement behind us. It
came from the sports writer who I'd passed on the stairs that last day with
Janet. Two sagging mounds of flesh, mercifully though not completely hidden behind a sweat-stained jersey, imprinted themselves in the desk as he
leaned forward to speak.

"Hey, Big Shot, I bet they give your Friday column slot to Simon!"

Peter Simon wrote pleasant, Lewis Grizzard-inspired pieces about the
crowds at football games and frustrating experiences on the Orbit bus. They
weren't controversial, unlike mine, which was never my *intent*, yet each week,
after reading my latest column, Lori O'Brien said she'd pray for me — and
she was Catholic so that was a significant time commitment.

"Yeah," I said absently. "They should do that."

"No way," insisted the sports writer next to me, "that guy sucks."

I left thinking that maybe Eddie Munster was right to head west —
symbolically if not literally, as the *Flagpole*'s offices were to the east of Jackson, but, regardless, it was at least run by a guy who admired someone my
own age, even if it was the mostly detestable Tom Cody. The *Red & Black*'s
management thought so little of us it had installed fresh-scrubbed puppets
to keep the staff in line.

I walked south to my dorm, the burning gold windows of Broad Street's
row of restaurants and bars receding like a hairline with age. Without the
distraction of the Tate Theater, the trip was brief, ending well before my
morose thoughts did, so I lingered for a while outside Myers with them.

Eventually, I noticed what looked like an abandoned car in front of me on Lumpkin. It seemed to sit on concrete blocks with a tarp of gloom over it, but after a few confused blinks, I began to recognize it as Heather's Porsche.

Tinted windows rolled down after my knock on the driver's side.

"Was... gonna... come... up..." Heather pushed the words out of her small mouth with a Sisyphean effort. "I...I..."

"You're wet."

She looked like she'd jumped into her car directly from the shower. Her hair ran in blue streaks down her face, and her billowy, gray T-shirt was damp as a towel... and all she was wearing.

"Get in, please."

Heather stared at the dashboard for a moment as if she were seeing it, seeing everything, for the first time. Her bare foot pressed the accelerator and the car stumbled off its concrete blocks and plunged forward into the pool of darkness.

The radio was on a gospel station, which I assumed was a mistake, but Heather claimed it was the only thing she could listen to because all other music, including silence, reminded her of... and before she could finish she began to convulse like she was drowning. I thought she might pull over, but she continued on, occasionally spurting out disassociated words that I attempted to reassemble.

Heather hadn't seen Jaye in days. She'd stopped spending the night at Heather's apartment and was distant and noncommittal over the phone. Heather rationalized all this as stress from midterms, which had just ended, or finals, which were coming up, or maybe she was freaked out because of what happened on a muggy Thursday afternoon the last week of April... they'd never left for class that day and as her hands explored Jaye's white skin, she'd wondered how a body functionally the same as hers could so effortlessly make her shiver. The sensation was palpable; Jaye noticed and asked if she was cold. Heather's response was a sudden and breathless exclamation: "I love you" ... but Jaye didn't seem freaked... no, she'd smiled, and her lopsided mouth echoed the words before it moved in closer to Heather and stripped away the chill.

Funnel clouds of confusion and doubt carried Heather downtown. She'd called Jaye at a payphone underneath the faded orange and blue sign for

Horton's Drugstore, checked her messages again to see if Jaye had returned her increasingly anxious calls — she hadn't. She was calling too much. She was certain of it, but she didn't know what else to do. It had been seven days.

Heather didn't want to think anymore so she met up with Baldwin and Reed at The Globe. Before opening the bank-vault heavy front door, Heather passed grad students out on the patio discussing Faulkner under the shade of a striped awning. Inside, the heart pine floor trickled around battered wood tables, and Baldwin and Reed floated on the dark brown patina of two leather sofas. Their poses implied attendants would soon sweep into the salon and keep them cool with tuft fans of peacock feathers. They'd dyed their hair recently — not green or black but the same multi-shaded red as Jaye's, which Heather sullenly thought was also noncommittal of her.

"Have the Glenfiddich," Baldwin offered, extending her whisky tumbler to Heather.

"Then drink some of this water." Reed pointed to a glass on the oak coffee table between them. "Then try this Talisker." She paused, her chin almost touching the antique bike that hung from the ceiling. "That's how you do it."

Heather was too nervous to drink. Her head spun from Baldwin to Reed as if watching a tennis match, but she was actually looking out the panel of windows behind them for red Chuck Taylors, a Whitman's sampler of red hair... any indication of Jaye.

"...so we figured you wouldn't mind..."

This splatter of conversation struck Heather like wet mud.

"What?"

"We did offer you one of the bedrooms when we first got the Boulevard place..."

"Yeah, but you wanted privacy," Baldwin corroborated. "*Very* only child... though, I guess you're not one. Anyway, we weren't offended." She shrugged as her hair appeared to join the embers of the sun through the window. "I kept my bike in there."

"You probably still can. Jaye won't care. She had a junkie on her kitchen floor."

"That was one of her roommates... the one I made out with... the floor was better than that ratty mattress."

Reed's eyes widened.

"Nick?"

"No, Nick prefers to sip through the straw rather than lap up from the bowl." Baldwin smirked as she revealed a new stamp on her college passport. "It was Christine."

"Stop!" Heather broke in violently. "What were you saying about Jaye?"

"Calm down," Reed said reproachfully. "This isn't the Georgia Bar."

"Jaye's moving in with us once her lease is up in shanty town." Baldwin's sandaled feet pressed into the sofa's armrest. "We told her we'd double-check that you still weren't interested."

Heather felt sick. She sank into the rocking chair opposite them. Jaye had never said anything about moving in with Baldwin and Reed. Why would she? Heather had just assumed once Jaye's lease was up... yes, her place wasn't big enough for two people long-term, but they could find something larger... together.

She bit her lip and clenched her fists as she willed her eyes to stay dry.

"Wait... you saw Jaye recently?"

"Yeah," Reed said. "You just missed her. Cody came in to see about using the second floor for Grant and Sherman's record release party." She waved her empty tumbler in the direction of the tattooed man behind the brass bar. "Jaye was with him. *She* liked the Talisker."

Baldwin glanced at Reed questionably.

"Oh, she was bound to find out eventually," Reed insisted. "And it's for the best," she said to Heather, "You were way too mopey over Cody. It was getting all Dylan and Brenda."

"What?"

"C'mon, you were a wreck at Gina Sloane's party. Waiting for him like he was... well, something you wait for until you get as drunk as a skunk and leave without saying goodbye."

"We're your friends," Baldwin declared. "We notice these things."

"Don't be pissed at Goetz," Reed said, blithely misinterpreting Heather's pallid expression. "She didn't pounce. That's what Weichman thinks. But Cody just saw what he wanted and went after it. How could she resist?"

Heather had stumbled out of her chair and collided into someone entering the bar. He bent to pick up the books that were scattered around her feet.

"Where did they go?" she demanded.

Reed shrugged indifferently.

"I thought they were heading over to Weaver D's," Baldwin answered, "There aren't as many *Automatic* tourists these days." She quickly responded to Reed's cold stare, "She was going to find out eventually."

Heather headed east on Broad until the trees started to overtake the street lamps. For a moment, she thought she was walking through an especially fierce rain but then realized she was crying. At the end of Broad Street, overlooking the Oconee River, was Weaver D's, which gleamed brightly against the surrounding foliage. A simple cinder-block building, its white bricks culminated in a ragged triangular peak — a sort of permanent bad haircut. The flat scaffold of an awning formed a scowl over the two large windows.

As Heather approached the restaurant, she remembered that Baldwin and Reed were idiots. She'd known that for years, and the upside of that reality was they could just be wrong again... their simple minds having twisted what they'd seen into something suitably salacious, and Heather held onto that comforting, dried stalk of a theory until she saw through a window, underneath the plastic "Open" sign, Jaye and Tom Cody... no, not Jaye *and* Tom Cody... Jaye *with* Tom Cody. That was a more accurate and yet devastating description.

They sat across from each other at the end of a long, communal table shrouded in a red-and-white checkered oilcloth. There was a plate of fried chicken, macaroni and cheese, and collard greens between them, which they shared, along with a gallon-sized glass of ice tea.

Wiping her eyes but never averting her gaze, Heather stared at them from a patch of focused sunlight on the sidewalk. It was Tom Cody who finally noticed her; his hand held Jaye's and from the way he whispered to her, one might assume this was a scene they'd been expecting.

The fragrance of Lux soap and cigarettes, now mixed with the immolated carcass of chicken, joined Heather, who had slumped onto a bench at a picnic table outside.

"So..." Heather could hear Jaye idly stirring the ice in her drink with a straw as she spoke. "...this is obviously the worst way we wanted you to find out about... everything."

What Heather said could not charitably be called words, but after an intense struggle, she managed to surface for air and gasp, "Jasmine." It was Jaye's full name; Heather had previously whispered it to her as they drifted off to sleep or exclaimed it in moments of ecstasy. Now, it was spoken in confusion and despair.

"I know this must be a shock, but it's not something we planned. It just sort of... happened." She took a long sip through her straw before adding, "Chemistry, you know?"

Jaye squeezed her shoulder, and Heather hated herself for still savoring her touch.

"Look, we'll see each other around. I think you're awesome. That hasn't changed, and we had a lot of fun together."

There was a sly verbal wink to the word "fun" that made Heather wince.

She watched Jaye go back inside Weaver D's, through the rosewood front door that looked like it would open into someone's cozy living room, and a weakness flooded Heather that almost caused her to cry out how much she loved her, as if that would return things to normal, make her understand, but she knew those words would have been nonsensical to Jaye.

Now there was nothing but a soggy pain coursing through her, and she felt if she got up and walked as far away as she could from the source, it would lessen. She was watching the cleats of her black-and-white Adidas bite into the grass when she heard Tom Cody call her name. He said it repeatedly because she didn't respond, and he had to walk beside her because she wouldn't stop moving.

"I hope you don't blame Jasmine for what happened." The way his tongue caressed the full length of Jaye's name made her want to drop him with one delicious punch in the face. "She told me how close you two had gotten, and honestly, I'd hate to see a friendship end because of me."

She stared at him with puzzlement that growing realization turned to disgust. Could he really look at her face, battered by a downpour of tears, and think *he* was capable of destroying her so completely? She wanted to sit him down and tell him all about her "friendship" with Jaye Goetz, and she'd include dates, times, and positions.

But Heather wasn't about to entertain him with previews of coming attractions, so she kept walking on Wilkerson until Tom Cody stopped following her and returned to Weaver D's where his new girlfriend waited for him.

Heather's dark blue car had at some point become part of a funeral procession led by a creeping Orbit bus, which had completed its circuit through campus and returned to the desolate, paved area where the buses were interred until the cycle began anew the next morning.

We were parked not far from the passenger-less buses that I thought looked somewhat sad in their emptiness, once their purpose had been removed from them. There were no solemn rites or customary observances once the vehicles rattled to a stop and spilled red onto the gravel as the drivers exited — temporarily relieved of their purpose, as well.

Heather wept steadily into the gray wreath hanging on the dashboard. Toward the start of her disjointed, sepulchral narrative, I'd tried to offer words of consolation, but they felt a meaningless ritual, like pebbles on a grave, so I just kept quiet and listened. It was late now, and I decided to pull Heather out of the marsh of this awful day and take her home.

She was in no condition to drive, but I had observed her operate the manual transmission enough times that I gambled on my successfully trans-porting us to River Mill. We traded seats, and after I'd flooded the engine to the point that my feet felt damp, the proud Porsche lurched forward with the poise of a Plymouth Scamp.

Curious thoughts often arise as necessary distractions, and as I battled with the clutch, I considered how this 1993 Porsche Carrera Coupe — a few weeks shy of its first birthday — was not intended to grow old. Its particular purpose, at least for its owner, was its lack of antiquity and permanence.

Slumped against the window, Heather cried along with the wailing gospel music she'd never changed on the stereo, and I sat on the tiled floor next to her tub as she cried in the hot bath I ran for her. And I lay beside her in her bed, holding her hand as she cried into her red pillow case — part of a set that Jaye had picked out to "warm up the place." She cried for the first time in her life that night because something wasn't permanent... and maybe that was a "good cry," though I ached as I remembered Janet saying those words.

5

I opened my eyes the next morning as a slow tide of orange sunlight drifted over Heather and me from her bedroom window. She lay pressed against my side with her small brown hand on my chest. During the night, she would sometimes moan a particular name and either whimper from its loss because it described something that no longer existed or, depending on how cruel her dreams were, smile as if Christmas morning waited for her in the next room.

I had an 8:55 class, which gave me just enough time to head back to Myers and shower before the humidity drenched me again on my way up to Park Hall. Not entirely asleep but not ready to face being awake, Heather grasped my hand as I got up to leave. I whispered to her that I'd be back later in the afternoon and, using a clump of tissues I'd pulled from a box by her nightstand, I dried her soaked cheeks.

In the Myers lobby, TV Guy watched an infomercial about a miraculous hair relaxer product. Sitting in an armchair across from him was Eddie Munster. His eyes were on the door and not the twenty-six-inch screen so almost instantly I saw my jaded face reflected in his glasses.

"Your roommate said you didn't come back last night. I checked The Grill, but you weren't there, so I thought I'd wait here." He suddenly sensed that if he wished to halt my progress, he should move on to the point, so he hastened to add, "I did what you said."

I looked around. We were still in Myers rather than one of Dante's nine circles of hell, so I don't think he followed my instructions.

"We sent out invitations to everyone," he went on. "Debs loved the idea. She thought it was really retro."

"Great."

I turned to leave and Eddie followed me to the south stairwell.

"I know why you got so mad," he claimed. "Heather's your friend. I respect that. You don't want some loser mac daddying on her if she's already got a daddy mac. But I confirmed again that she doesn't."

"From Tom Cody, right? Funny how he knew that."

"So, uh, I thought I should reassure you of the honorability of my intentions toward Heather." Whenever Eddie said her name, his face reddened and expanded like a balloon about to take flight. Then he abruptly fell to earth. He held my arm with a force that was almost painful. "There's just one thing, and I have to ask. See, I heard you stopped seeing that girl you were always at Tate with."

A long moment passed before I answered shortly, "Yeah."

"So, you know, Debs was talking about her the other day, and well she thinks she's kind of weird."

"That's her opinion."

"Yeah, yeah, but if you like weird girls... well, God... I'll just ask you straight: Are you in love with Heather?"

I actually laughed in his face. His understanding of the situation was similar to a student's command of a subject for which he'd read only store-bought and poorly written class notes.

"Heather and I are friends."

My proclamation renewed springs of faith and trust that now fountained into a sticky embrace. I felt his day's growth of beard against the fuzz on my own cheek.

"Sorry to put you on the spot like this, Captain."

He slapped me on the back. Gushing with enthusiasm and hopefulness, he dragged me out the back door of the lobby. "I need to tell you something." TV Guy — the only person in the lounge separating us from privacy — was far more engrossed in the benefits of the advertised hair relaxer than I presumed he'd be in whatever Eddie had to say, but we went outside regardless.

Hot gusts of wind flogged us and carried over the quad the smell of baking piles of garbage that hadn't been removed yet from their tin can ovens. I sat on the bench with my back turned to him. It wasn't an intentional slight. I just couldn't bear a direct view of Janet's window. I don't think Eddie even noticed. He started to speak to me through a curtain of sticky humidity, as if we were in a church confessional.

Summer was a month away. Eddie loved that time of year: He could spend all day at the movies, and his favorite comics came out twice a month (not *Daredevil*, unfortunately, but *Spider-Man* and *X-Men*). So it had pained him when his parents sent him away to an academic retreat, the Senator's Academy for the Arts, back in July of 1988.

He never had many friends beyond the movies and the comic books. His parents, well-meaning enough people, probably thought he would easily make some amongst the kids nicely designed brochures claimed were just like Eddie… although, he wasn't Eddie Munster then; he was still George Meyer, and what Mr. and Mrs. Meyer failed to grasp was that the reason George didn't have friends was not because of what he liked but because of who he was.

Once at the Senator's Academy, George discovered that kids who weren't normally popular tended to react to a rare taste of social acceptance like a starving man handed a loaf of bread… gluttonous and not interested in sharing. And because popularity as a commodity only has value if someone present is unpopular, it wasn't difficult to cast George in the necessary role.

It didn't really bother him because he'd made better friends — John Cassavetes, Nicholas Ray, and Vittorio de Sica among others. They provided more than the superficial charm of the anonymous blockbusters he used to watch in a cold theater; there was the emotional depth of a true, life-altering relationship.

However, when the lights were up, and literature and art were discussed, his focus drifted to one of the three blondes who had set themselves apart from the other students. This was Heather, and from their described obnoxiousness, I recognized the other two as Baldwin and Reed. For them, the Senator's Academy was not a pinnacle of summer achievement but merely a scholastically impressive requirement they endured until they could spend the dying summer days anywhere else. And it very well could be anywhere else. Gold skin, gold hair, golden girls… they were so unlike the other kids from Macon, Valdosta, or even George's hometown of Lawrenceville they could have been subjects of study at the program rather than fellow students.

He'd never noticed girls before — they'd always seemed somewhat unreal and incomprehensible, but Heather Aulds immediately stood out to him as delightfully strange. He liked to think that inside that stately and symmetrical exterior, there were trick mirrors, shifting floors, and anything else you could imagine that would shock, challenge, and amuse.

He admired how her quirky comments and observations might generate bemusement but never mockery. She possessed the freedom of speech and movement of someone who never had to impress anyone because everyone was trying to impress her. This included the otherwise dull, golden brown wings on either side of her — the only connecting link their common backgrounds and their parents who either golfed or lunched together.

Yes, she was beautiful, but there was something more, something he grew to love and perhaps even covet. Other kids her age struggled with their changing bodies, but an awkward stage was something Heather had avoided like an ill-conceived fashion craze. And if Heather had been surprised by her own recent explosion of femininity, she never showed it. She wielded total command over her brash, steely figure.

It was during the final week of the program that she'd yawningly asked him, "Hey, Eddie Munster, can I borrow a pen?" Her extemporaneous substitution for his own name was reasonable shorthand for the canine tufts of hair on his cheeks. It was those recent indications of maturity that she'd acknowledged and used to define him, so it wasn't difficult for him to prefer "Eddie Munster" to short (he wouldn't achieve his current height until two years later), fat (he had achieved his current weight two years earlier) George Meyer.

He never worked up the courage to say anything — not a bold proclamation of devotion or even a mild expression of gratitude for not knowing his name. The program ended and she was gone, along with George Meyer. He'd given up on seeing her again, returning to the comforting escapism of movies and comics with only that one, lasting souvenir of his time with her, and then suddenly there she was in third row center of the Georgia Square Mall's 8 p.m. showing of *The Crying Game*. It didn't matter that the hair and clothes had changed, and almost five years had passed. When those two frozen ponds looked at him, he knew now was the moment.

"But you hid in the bathroom," I said.

"Yeah, yeah, but I had to... *prepare*," Eddie explained. "Prepare to seize the moment."

This was when I should have set everything straight with Eddie Munster, but either I was still so angry with him I couldn't be bothered or I recognized enough of my friend in the hip new clothes to not want to extinguish his dream as mine had been. Let him hope a little longer... what harm could come of that? Because once it was buried, nothing would be left but the ashes.

"So, you'll come to the prom? And make sure Heather comes, too?"

He was desperate — the wisps of summer might carry her off forever and leave him floating lifelessly on the first chills of autumn.

"If it means that much to you, I'll go, but I can't guarantee anything else."

My measured response did not prevent him from hugging me boisterously. Then he went off through the flowering shrubs to wherever one goes to wait for paradise to finally admit you inside.

Strangely, I didn't have to ask Heather to attend the prom, because she asked me herself. I don't know if Eddie had personally mailed out all the invites, but he'd been reckless or bold enough to address Heather's in the same hand that composed the poetry she'd inspired.

"Debbie Tyson, of all people, is having the event of the season."

She waved the shiny gold invitation at me.

"And you actually want to go?"

She shrugged.

"It'll be good to get out."

She said this while sitting on her leather sofa wearing the same plaid robe she'd had on all week; her hair was unwashed, and her legs were unshaven. She was rather proud of the latter: "This is some serious sasquatch shit going on here."

She hadn't left the apartment since I'd steered the bucking Porsche into its parking space. I'd picked up and dropped off assignments for her, and we were now on the Christmas card lists for the deliverymen from Steverino's and Gumby's. I'd even handed her the bundle of mail that had included Debbie Tyson's invitation.

Although I still went to class and to the *Red & Black*, from an emotionally functional standpoint, I was at best Bette Davis to Heather's Joan Crawford. I changed clothes and showered at Myers but hadn't slept there in days and woke up each morning to an unconscious kick from Heather's scruffy bare leg. There was an intimacy, a comfort between us, especially during this mutually difficult period, that I'd define as familial. This shocked me because I'd never previously considered family, the strangers who share your surname, as a source of comfort.

There was no question that I'd take her to Debbie Tyson's hokey affair if she wanted, but I needed to ask her something. We were listening to Prince's "17 Days." She'd dubbed the LP single onto a cassette where it played repeatedly until the tape ended and she'd rewind and start again. To this day, I can recite the lyrics from memory.

"Are you going to be OK seeing her?"

We both knew that was her only motivation for leaving the safety of her apartment and the sensual understanding of Prince. Jaye Goetz would be there, of course, in her debut, her formal coming out, as Tom Cody's girlfriend.

"I have to, Carlton... I..." She briefly inspected the chipped black polish on her nails. "The worst thing is knowing that if she were to call me right now, I'd be over at her shitty apartment on my goddamn knees. I have to be able to look at her and not feel a thing. I have to beat this. I need to be me again."

So that's how I wound up attending the prom with Heather Aulds — a concept I would have considered akin to science fiction a year earlier. Baldwin and Reed had somehow persuaded Heather to give them a lift, and we picked the two up Saturday night outside The Globe, where they stood on the patio in their gowns like twin stems of AstroTurf. The pre-gala tour of downtown in semiformal wear was "part of the fun," Baldwin explained, "because it was clear who's going to the party and who's, you know, lame."

Baldwin and her choppy waves of chiffon spread out over Heather's backseat; Reed had chosen to ride in front on the lap of my rented tux. Her hair smelled like soft plastic roses with pepper sprinkled on the petals, and the strands that wound up in my mouth tasted the same way.

"Aulds, are you wearing your gown from last year? That's genius!" More of Reed's hair slapped my cheek as she turned slightly to address Baldwin. "We should have gone retro, too. It would've been a thing!"

"I'm not wearing taffeta again," Baldwin declared. "I'm nineteen. I'm past that."

When we arrived at Debbie Tyson's house in Normaltown, the reddish sun had slipped behind a thick curtain of foliage, perhaps out of embarrassment for what it was witnessing — this rehash of the past, not with any egalitarian goal but simply to recast the victors.

We walked out onto the grassy promenade and wandered within the large fenced-in area that tiny blue lights temporarily wove into the trees. Baldwin and Reed's bare shoulders swanked past the thrift store suits and dresses that likely cost more than my tux rental.

"So, if you go up on Talmadge until it crosses Prince and becomes Park, the neighborhood gets better," Reed explained, "but this is fine for a party. No one cares what you do."

"Yeah, but then it's sort of bland," Baldwin said. "Remember the party in that barn on Satula? Someone starting wrestling in the front yard..."

"They had a keg. They might as well have painted Greek letters on the aluminum siding."

"Yeah, but they got a written complaint from the landlord. That's awesome. That's like receiving a positive review in the press." Baldwin looked at me demandingly. "Who does the party reviews for the *Red & Black?*"

"We don't write party reviews."

"Yeah," Baldwin scoffed, "but you find space for football games and student council. And those stupid quotes with the nicknames on Fridays..."

"Give it a rest," Reed said. "Carlton can't change that rag by himself." Her bronze fingers squeezed my arm in a show of solidarity. "We're *all* persecuted minorities in this town."

Several people from separate directions converged on Heather, Baldwin, and Reed, and I took advantage of the confusion to escape.

The grass beneath my dress shoes was dry and felt prone to ignite from the heat. The air, though, was musty, as if the party was taking place in the attic of an old Southern home, still in despair from the loss of the war.

"You're here!"

It was Eddie Munster — skulking in the shadows like he was standing lookout for a crime in progress.

"Where's Debbie?"

"She's around. Playing host, you know."

I struggled with the appropriate acknowledgement for Eddie's efforts in assembling this multi-ringed circus.

"It's... nice."

"Yeah," he said miserably. "I cut the grass."

Debbie Tyson's back lawn was as freshly shaved as Eddie, who was covered in Aqua Velva and a glittering tinsel tuxedo jacket with wide, black peaked lapels.

"Want some punch?"

He forced into my hands a blue plastic cup that smelled like he'd dumped the rest of his Aqua Velva into it.

"God, she is so beautiful."

His eyes flew from his dilatory body and buzzed deliriously in the air around Heather, pausing to soak in the sweet visuals she produced: Her

black hair was parted in the center, twisted, and pinned back from her tren-
chant face, which was whiter now due to her recent springtime hibernation,
but her exposed arms were as taut as ever and lay folded over a navy blue
bodice with short, puffed, red-dappled sleeves. Two young men performed
before her, and their self-esteem swelled the longer they could hold her
attention, which they struggled to maintain with the most strenuous verbal
contortions.

"It's like... like she's... she's... it's just..." He laughed at his own speech-
lessness. "There's no one else here, man."

My mood softened.

"Look, Eddie, it's not what you think."

I was about to finally settle the issue when Debbie Tyson stepped out
onto the back porch. Below her round face and a fortunately modest expanse
of self-induced brown skin was a dress the color of cheese melted on too high
a microwave setting. Specks of green were sprinkled throughout like chives.
She accessed those assembled in the yard with the eyes of a jewelry appraiser.
When she saw Eddie and me, she scooped up the hem of her dress and took
several careful steps over to us.

"This is so much fun!" she announced. "Everyone's here. The guys from
Jim Easter even showed up. They said they might play later."

"They have their instruments with them?"

I wasn't the least bit interested, but I wanted to divert Debbie's attention from Eddie's adoration of Heather, whose shimmering gold skirt flut-
tered in the stale air as she approached us.

"There's my mandingo!" She threw her arm around my neck and
leaned in to whisper, "I'm not just miserable but all its associated synonyms,
as well."

Debbie complimented Heather's dress, which put her in the position
of having to acknowledge the tasteless monstrosity Debbie wore. I quickly
repeated my earlier question.

"Yeah, they've got their instruments. It's all in the back of Zach's van.
They drive around in that van like those guys in that show with the weird
dog."

"*The Partridge Family?*" Heather asked with false innocence.

"Yeah, right, that's the one..." She straightened the bow tie on the
besotted statue next to her. "You know Eddie, right?"

"Sure," Heather said, referring to an event five months — not five years — earlier. She shook his hand with the same affection as a colleague at a business dinner, but Eddie looked as if every dream from his past had arrived at this moment.

"Whoop! Whoop! Cute couples alert!"

A short, bearded young man danced around us as he spun an invisible noisemaker and blew into an equally imaginary party horn. The cup in his hand, however, was quite real.

"Cute couples! Cute couples!"

"Having a grand time, Rogers?" Heather asked.

"Damn right!" His wide shoulders started to shrug off his disco-era sport coat. "Can we take off our jackets now?"

"You can if you want," Debbie said. "Some of the girls ditched their heels already. I'm so happy we're reaching the point where everyone's kinda fucked up."

Noticing Eddie was still attached, Heather let his hand drop and took a drink from the plastic cup in mine. He swooned at the sight of Heather's lips on the same rim he'd drunk from not so long ago.

"Wow!" Heather shouted — her head spinning like she was the subject of an exorcism. "Jesus H.! This is gasoline."

Debbie smiled and nodded in agreement with Heather's review.

"Right, huh? It's like if you'd spiked the punch at a high school dance. That was Brian's idea."

Brian Dean, whose perfectly coifed head resembled Mickey Mouse ears, was one of Debbie's roommates. He stood in the center of the yard with an unlit cigar in his mouth next to a fully lit Cecily Allen, their other roommate.

"Come on." Heather took my arm, and I handed Eddie's drink back to him. I imagined him rushing to preserve it under glass.

We headed to the outskirts of the yard where a pair of Adirondack chairs rested under the sparse shade of a withered white oak. The night was bright from the full moon and still broiling hot, so I removed my jacket. After about an hour alone with just our wry observations of the evening so far, we were accidentally enjoying ourselves when I looked up and saw Janet standing not more than ten feet away.

She looked directly at us. Her carriage was stiffly formal, as if her black gown was made of iron. My eyes were tangled in the barbed wire of her sunglasses and from the scorn smoldering behind the lenses, I thought she'd walk off with them still attached. Instead, she threw her shoulders back and came over to us, her hand casually pulling her companion along with her like a rollaway bag.

I rose from my chair, and we stared at each other with contained surprise. Neither of us had expected to see the other here and felt caught in a hailstorm wearing only Bermuda shorts.

"Miss Aulds," she said to Heather, who neither got up nor put out her cigarette, "it's been forever."

"Alas, no."

"You two look so *friendly*." She turned to her companion, a pop-eyed young man with curly dark hair. "Don't they look friendly?"

"Sure."

"I'm being rude. This is Frank Curry."

"Francois," he corrected.

"I know. I just sound so pretentious when I say Francois."

"You wouldn't want that," Heather said.

"And this is Heather Aulds and..."

"I know you," Frank interjected. "You're pretty funny. One question, though."

"What's that?"

"Why so cynical?"

"Oh, he's just a critic... a cynical critic. That's who he is." She raised her plastic cup. "To the friendly couple!"

The sentiment or the words themselves seemed to scratch her throat, so she quickly sent down Debbie Tyson's punch to soothe it.

I thought I knew every expression on her unsmiling face, but there was another, different one there now that I didn't recognize, and I stood confused for a moment, as I watched her wander off with Frank Curry.

"It is *jeal* to the *us*," Heather said. "You took Its ball of yarn away. I don't think anyone's done that before." She punched me in the shoulder. "Cool."

Seeing Janet again had unleashed a cataract of emotion and I felt dizzier and sicker than if I'd actually drunk Debbie's toxic brew. I stumbled off into the dark with only a mumbled explanation to Heather.

The chains linking guests to their individual consortiums had loosened, and there were random flights from one group to another. Based on criteria I was not adept enough to comprehend, some were caught and seamlessly allowed to mingle, as though they'd been there all along, while others were ignored and left to plummet onto the hard ground of irrelevance.

The screen door was propped open by a drunken wedge with a thick mustache. He had not only removed his jacket but his tie and shirt, as well, and held the door in place as if performing a great feat of strength.

"He always takes it too far," Cecily Allen slurred. She stood next to Debbie Tyson and Brian Dean in a shadow of light cast from the open door.

"The worst thing is that I don't think he's that drunk," Debbie replied. "He's just weird."

Evelyn Wilson's stubby legs carried her aggressively toward them. She held up her dress to avoid tripping and falling face first into the grass — a sight that would have pleased me far more than I'd like to admit.

"What's that bitch doing here?"

Apparently "bitch" had a specific definition in Evelyn's deranged language.

"Huh?" Cecily mumbled. "Oh her? I think she came with Curry."

"Who invited him?"

"I did." Debbie straightened up — very proud of herself. "I wanted some diversity. He's a French exchange student."

"Frank Curry?"

"*Francois.*"

"Bullshit!"

"No... no, it's true," Cecily insisted. "He goes back to the... to the..."

"Sorbonne," Debbie said helpfully.

"Yeah, he goes back... there in the fall."

"Is that a community college in Alabama?" Evelyn snorted. "Have you heard him talk?"

"Yeah," Cecily replied. "I think it's just wonderful how well he's picked up the language."

"Do you even know you're alive?"

"Look, I don't know why you're being such a snob about it," Debbie said. "Scott's not even here, so it's not like you have anything to worry about."

Brian Dean quietly took his plastic cup into the house. The patch of light that had dared approach Evelyn's pallid face quickly retreated, as well.

"What?"

"Hey, I don't think you're afraid Scott still wants her." Debbie chugged her punch as her free hand appeared to feel around for a Bible to rest on and solemnize her statement. "I even told Dana last week that 'Brown-Eyed Baby, Please Please Please Come Back' is probably about you."

Evelyn's green eyes regarded Debbie in scornful silence before she turned and spoke into the air, "I wonder how the hell she met Curry anyway. Maybe he just tripped over her in the Mellow Mushroom men's room."

I'd headed on a course to capsize Evelyn Wilson and take us both to the depths of my crushing rage, but Heather's strong arms anchored me to the ground.

"No rematch tonight, Carlton. She's not worth it. Neither of them are."

We moved toward the house, passing Baldwin and Reed, who danced to the '80s funk song currently playing. They shuffled side to side in unison — their hands flat on the front of their waists — and occasionally would exchange low-fives.

"Let's get out of here," Heather said. "This is dead. And the Wonder Twins over there can either come with or hitch a ride with their new roomie."

I suddenly recalled the point of this evening.

"Have you seen Jaye?"

"No, and honestly I don't care."

Her voice disputed the actual honesty of her words.

"Looking for your little friend?"

The arctic blast came from Dana Weichman. She put her hands several inches from her sides to simulate wider hips than nature had granted her and slithered over to us. Even in caricature, I recognized how Jaye Goetz walked.

"But she's not exactly little, is she? And you two aren't exactly friends."

Heather ignored Dana's rattling of the lion's cage.

One side of Dana Weichman's wavy black hair spilled over the front of her red satin dress, which had a neckline that plunged dramatically but revealed nothing. Multiple layers of lipstick and gloss imposed a gargantuan effect on her mouth. She had fake red nails, fake dark eyelashes, and perhaps an equally artificial interest in her date, a fellow with close-cropped brown hair and the demeanor of a future banker.

"Suggs," Heather said to him. "Flying standby, I see."

Suggs offered me his hand, which I accepted reluctantly.

"Guess you two have never officially met," Dana said. "Of course, he's read your column."

"I saw you the other day, actually," Suggs said obligingly. "You came by at the end of classical mythology."

"That's right," Dana said — clearly remembering. "It was so nice of you to drop off Heather's paper for her." She ran her hand in circles over Suggs's back while taking long swallows from her blue cup. "Having a real gentleman around is a change of pace for both of us, isn't it?"

"You feeling better?"

"I'm fine," Heather said shortly.

"Oh, you've just missed a lot of class." If I looked closely, I could see Dana's hand operating Suggs's mouth from his back as her lips moved imperceptibly. "I thought you were sick."

"I'm sorry to hear you weren't well," Dana said, not sorry at all. "You've always been so..." She flexed the muscles in her thin arms. "...*sturdy*. Whatever you caught... must have been *devastating*."

Heather looked ready to breathe fire.

"You can really stop watching *Dynasty* now, Weichman. You have enough attitude."

Dana had always seen Heather as a rival and although her vision had cleared enough to realize this rivalry existed only in her mind, she was small enough to find pleasure in any blow to Heather's brick facade — even one caused by the girl who'd also vandalized her own, far less impressive dwelling.

I'd begun taking broad steps toward the house with Heather, whose skin was hot to the touch. Dana called out pleasantly to us.

"If you are looking for Jaye, I saw her on the front porch with Tom. It's the perfect match: He likes big butts — no lie! — and she likes guys who are a little less... *sturdy*."

I pulled Heather inside to the kitchen, and as soon as I released her, she slammed her fist into the refrigerator, permanently injuring a few of the magnets.

"Weichman's just begging for me to tap dance on her face."

I repeated Heather's own words: "She's not worth it. Neither of them are."

"Fuck that! I'm sending the bitch to Gilbert Health postage due."

There was a school of glittery silver cardboard fish hanging from wires on the living room ceiling, and whenever someone went out the front door, the fish would splash against the blue walls. Although I presumed the intent was to recapture the look of a high school gymnasium during a school dance, I felt like we were inside an aquarium.

Baldwin and Reed accompanied the echo of high-heeled footsteps down the stairs.

"Hey, hey, hey!" Reed said. "What's happening?"

She'd been drinking the punch.

"We're thinking of leaving."

"Yeah, it is getting close to lame-o-clock," Baldwin agreed.

"Leaving? Who's leaving?" Eddie Munster demanded from the foyer. He was still carrying his blue cup, but I don't think he'd taken more than a sip all night.

"We probably should get going," I explained, "but thanks for everything."

"Oh, it was all Debs, but..." His pleading eyes looked directly through me to Heather, who examined the blue lava lamp on the coffee table in disbelief. "Did you have a good time?"

"Sure."

"So, stay!" he insisted and then added, like a grandparent trying to extend a child's visit with the promise of candy, "Uhm, I think Jim Easter's about to play."

"Oooh, Jim Easter!" Reed exclaimed. "I'd love to open for them."

She exchanged another low-five with Baldwin.

Heather squeezed the lava lamp like it was Dana Weichman's neck.

"You can stay if you want, but Carlton and I are out of here."

"I just bet!" Reed said with a wink. "Don't worry about us. We might stick around for a song or two."

"Whatever."

I finally got the lava lamp away from Heather before she'd shattered it. Following Heather to the front door, I placed the lamp on a black hutch that was a foundling home for blue plastic cups. Eddie Munster rushed to my side, reminding me again of Jim Easter's performance and how they'd probably play that song about people skating that everyone liked. He was begging me to do something to stop Heather from leaving, but I didn't think there was any force on earth that could until her aggressive tread halted so suddenly, I almost swallowed one of her bobby pins.

Dana Weichman was right: Tom Cody and Jaye Goetz were both inside the screened-in front porch. Tom's only real acknowledgement of the evening's theme was a white boutonniere in the lapel of his tan blazer. Everything else — the blue button-down, even the patterned tie — was not so different from how he normally dressed. Sitting very close to Tom on a wooden swing, Jaye strained the confines of a high-neck, sleeveless dress with abstract swirls of blue splattered on a white canvas. In the dim light, the powdery white of her dress and her skin made it seem as if the blue collages were all that separated her from exhibitionism.

Amber Grant and Molly Sherman stood over them like silver sparklers, and although there was no natural breeze on the porch, their heated bombast was sufficient to gently rock the swing.

"They can't go around calling themselves the 'cutest band in Athens.'" Amber cried. "*We're* the cutest band in Athens."

"That's our tagline," Molly insisted.

Jaye tapped her blue nails against the long neck of a beer bottle.

"I think they're just going for irony," she said genially. "You know, cute like a puppy."

Tom nodded.

"Jasmine's right. You're not jokingly cute. You're the real thing."

Someone in shorts and sagging crew-neck socks opened the porch door to ask Amber and Molly if they wanted to fly a kite with him. The ladies declined.

"He lives down the street," Tom explained. "Brian says he has a great collection of vintage kites, including one from *Sesame Street.*"

"Hey guys," Jaye said to us. I could feel Heather tremble. "You staying for Jim Easter?"

"They totally should, right?" Eddie said, the desperation in his voice rising.

"We might even play later," Molly said almost violently casual.

"*If* those guys can keep the crowd motivated," Amber stressed.

Heather stared at the girl she once knew and still loved. She'd attended this carnival to prove to herself that her feelings for Jaye Goetz had cooled, that she was herself again — the Heather Aulds she now remembered only vaguely — but instead her stomach twisted every time the blue shadows over Jaye's gray eyes rose and fell, and she knew that person was gone forever, along with the faint hope that her presence would at least provoke *some* reaction from Jaye — discomfort, embarrassment, and, much to her shame, perhaps some small remnant of love. But all she got was that lopsided smile — the perfect complement to Tom's.

Debbie Tyson stepped onto the porch and pulled on Eddie's arm to get his attention, which wasn't possible as long as Heather was there.

"Hey, babe..." This was the after midnight and a few drinks preview of an endearment. Much like opening a show out of town, if the reaction wasn't positive, the fallout was less severe and there was time to retool and try again. "Do you wanna help me get Dana upstairs to my room? She's a little..."

"To' up from tha flo' up?" Amber interjected. "I saw her earlier. Someone needs to introduce her to Step One of Twelve."

Tom shook his head sadly.

"That's a shame. Suggs shouldn't let her drink so much."

I didn't think there was a limit to my capacity to dislike him.

Jaye patted his knee.

"I wouldn't worry. He's just so happy to be with her again."

"He shouldn't let her run wild," Tom said decisively. "But I do think it turned out best for both of them that I got out of the way."

"Yeah, Cody," Heather said, "they should really get you fitted for a cross."

Jaye laughed.

"I love your sense of humor!" She pointed her bottle at us. "I bet she helps with your columns, right?"

Tom seized on Jaye's remark.

"So, I heard a little about what's going on at the *Red & Black*. It's getting real corporate, huh?" There was another sad shake of the head from Mr. Cody. "Let me know if you'd like me to talk to Pete. Eddie told me you two met. I think you'd be a great fit at the *Flagpole*."

For all I knew Dan Buchanan was going to bar me from the Op-Ed page, and after replacing Gwen Lupo with an entertainment editor bold enough to stare down a rabbit, I'd go back to writing the random CD review if anything at all. There was no good reason for me to remain at the *Red &*

Black; I had no insight into the future, so I didn't know about Amy, Wendy, Trent, Marc, Eric, Crystal, Kim, Keith, Carrie, Todd, Beth, and Ann — all the people I'd never meet if I left. No, what loomed in my mind at that moment was how Cinematic Arts was no longer recognizable to me. It was no longer an organization that would show *Vertigo* and maybe that angered me more than it should. Then I thought about the girl in front of me, and I was certain that the last thing I wanted was to owe Tom Cody a favor.

"I'm happy where I am," I said brusquely. Then to Heather, "Let's get out of here."

"Don't go!" Eddie exclaimed. With great effort, he pulled himself from the deep end before anyone noticed. "Hey, Captain, let's all go downtown to..." The destination didn't matter, just the prolonging of the evening and his dreams. His hands moved frantically like he was juggling countless objects that he feared would soon drop and shatter. "I'll drive. After party, huh?"

"It's too late."

I spoke so rigidly as to cut him off completely. I expected Heather to burst into tears any second now and I'd be damned if I'd let these people see her like that. She squeezed my hand tightly as I led her outside. We'd gotten halfway to her car when I realized she wasn't going to make it. She wobbled in her high-heeled pumps as though about to implode from an explosive demolition.

Without thinking, I spun her around and pulled her close. She was crying now, but no one could hear that over the music. They only saw her face buried in my chest, our arms wrapped around each other as we appeared to dance to The Pixies on Debbie Tyson's front yard.

"Thanks," she whispered as the song ended.

"Any time," I replied.

Our own after party began with a circuitous drive through Athens at its darkest and ended at the Waffle House in Five Points, where two native Southerners had a breakfast of cheese grits and hash browns.

"I'm thinking of apple pie with some à la mode action," Heather said; her shoeless feet swayed next to me. "What say you?"

I didn't have time to reply: An embalmed Janet stumbled to our booth. She pointed at an empty pocket of air, perhaps addressing the third me.

"You used to be so sweet. Now you're so sour — a big sourpuss." She glanced at Heather. "Maybe it's the sour pussy. Meow."

Heather dropped her fork.

"Look, sister, the shoes are already off so we can get down right now."

Oblivious, Janet continued: "You know, he... he may pretend that he's different, that he cares, but he doesn't. Nope. Not even un poco." She whispered confidingly to Heather: "He dropped me. Like an old brown shoe. Like I was nothing. Like I never even mattered to him."

I stared at my plate — anything to avoid looking at her. Like a coward, I'd tried to run from her, from us, from myself and now she was going to confront me with the pain I'd so carelessly caused.

"Just tell me, be honest for once: Because... I gave you *everything*, but if I'd given you what you'd wanted, the only thing you probably ever wanted, would you have stayed?"

Nothing she could have said would have hurt me more. I think Heather sensed this because her eyes, still red from tears, seemed to burn in their sockets when she spun around to confront Janet.

"We've had enough of *Drunk Bitch Theatre* for tonight. Take it to another table."

For an instant, it looked as though Janet was reaching out for Heather's arm, and if she had completed that action, based on Heather's expression, I was convinced I'd end up testifying at an inquest.

"I just wanna help — one woman to another. I'm just trying to *warn* you, Miss Aulds."

"Don't call me *Miss Aulds*!" Heather spat at her. "God! Are you really so pathetic that you can't handle just one of your victims getting away before you've sucked them dry? Do you have to come back and gnaw on the goddamn bone? I'll let your sorry ass walk away this one time. But if you come near someone I care about again, I will fucking finish you!"

Janet backed away from us. She put her hand to her mouth and suddenly looked so unwell, I thought she was going to be sick. Heather suspected it, also, because she instinctively moved from what would be the line of fire.

I knew, though, that Janet was not reacting to Heather's outburst. The entire time she spoke, Janet's eyes were on me, waiting and hoping. Those eyes replayed our brunches, movies, late-night phone calls, and now looked expectantly for me to lash out at Heather, to defend her as passionately, as desperately as I had attacked Evelyn Wilson for her vile screed in Gina Sloane's living room. Instead, those eyes saw that no matter how upset she could still make me ultimately my loyalties would lie with my friend... with Heather.

The sight appeared to generate instant sobriety, but she still slumped next to Frank Curry.

"What's going on?" he asked, almost close to concerned. "You said you were just going to the bathroom."

"I did. I did." She winked at me. "I'm not making a scene. I just wanted to chat with some friends of mine. Make new friends, Mr. Curry, and keep the old... or something like that. Right, kiddo?"

"Please make sure she gets home all right."

Frank nodded at me in confirmation.

We paid our check and left. I watched Janet get into Frank Curry's car and ride off but not in the direction of Myers.

I sat in the passenger's seat of Heather's car, her high heels in my lap, as she turned the key in the ignition, and Morrissey announced that "The Queen Is Dead."

"It is *high*-larious."

"Don't call her 'It.'"

There was no argument or response other than a soft stroke of my head.

The Porsche roared to life, and as we drove off into the morning, I thought about my recent actions regarding someone with whom I'd shared so much and claimed to love, and I realized with great despair that I was no better or perhaps even worse than Tom Cody.

6

The humidity that had threatened to drown Athens during May briefly ended a few days before June, but it was rather anticlimactic. It didn't retreat, broken and shattered, from the cracks and flashes of a storm but just simply faded away, and as this happened, the city itself prepared to do the same.

Athens during the summer is often compared to a ghost town, with its zombie population of graduates who never leave, and there is that quality of abandonment... of lost purpose... even if only seasonal like that anonymous town on some nameless beach where Jaye Goetz grew up.

But if the campus is a haunted house, the effect is cumulative and constant, with more ghosts lingering each year. On one of Athens's many muggy days, it felt as though I could almost see them through the haze, as they crowded onto Tate Plaza or North Campus or an especially itinerant Orbit bus. There are only ever 30,000 students wandering the halls and corridors of the University of Georgia, but the spirits mount with the crushing advance of years until they have long since surpassed the current population who are unaware of their existence... their struggles, their joys, and their tragedies, which are forever echoed but never fully repeated.

Athens became a permanent ghost town for me after my freshman year. Perhaps I was too attuned to the apparitions surrounding me, whose time here had been no better or no worse than my own, or maybe I'd prematurely joined them.

The last Wednesday in May was dry and scorching, and the newspapers were soaked with stories of an imminent drought. Andy Razinski and I had gone to see *Last Tango in Paris* at Tate, and on our way out of the theater, he was telling me about his girlfriend, Myrtle Adams, and how, apparently, we had already met.

"You probably don't remember, I mean, she doubts it, but she works at The Gap and I guess you were in there with Janet once. She said you two looked so crazy about each other, she couldn't believe you were the same guy from the paper."

We were so fully in our own world when together I never considered how we'd appear to anyone else.

"There is always some madness in love, but there is also always some reason in madness."

Andy instantly recognized these words.

"*Zarathustra*! You've read it?"

I nodded.

"Look, B.," he said quietly, "if you'd just told me..."

"I know," I said, "but it makes no difference now."

I noticed Eddie Munster walking toward the north exit of the Tate Center. Just a few months ago, he might have been leaving the theater with us, but now he was deep in conversation with Debbie Tyson and Cecily Allen, whose shark-like smile was more intimidating when she was sober.

Despite the company, I wanted to speak with him, and so I called out his name. When Eddie saw me, he barreled forward like an out-of-control car and punched me square in the face. The blow was crazed and wild but sufficient to send me crashing to the floor of the Tate Center.

Andy was at my side before I reached the ground.

"You all right, B.?"

"Ow."

There was blood on my fingers when I pulled my hand from my mouth.

"What the hell are you doing?" he shouted at Eddie.

"Your friend here's a fucking asshole!"

"What are you talking about?"

"You must think I'm pretty dumb," Eddie yelled down at me. "I confide in you and then you sweep in behind my back and make your move like a goddamn vulture!"

"What daytime soap are you watching?" Andy demanded. "B. wouldn't do that."

"You weren't there, man! I saw him and Heather at the prom. They were all over each other."

The victor of this epically brief *Thrilla in Tate* looked close to tears.

"He stole her! He stole her!"

"You are smoking crack," Andy said. "Not that you'd have a chance in any scenario, but Heather's gay."

"That's a lie!" Eddie cried ferociously. "Jasmine told me that was just some sick rumor her stoner roommates were spreading."

"You believed that bitch? You are dumb."

Debbie Tyson had watched this scene play out as a pitiable realization boiled her spud-like face. She responded in the only way that made sense for her.

"Don't try to deny it! Everyone knows they're an item now. They practically live together." She whispered to Cecily, "Aulds is down with the brown."

Andy had helped me to my feet, but I could only see talking blurs. My glasses were still on the floor, the right frame twisted grotesquely and the left lens shattered on impact. Fortunately, my right eye was the weak one, so while I could still see, my damaged glasses wobbled precariously on my face as if punch drunk, and my left eye shut instinctively to avoid the bright flash from Cecily Allen's great, white teeth.

"I'm gonna go," I said.

I'd been friends since January with George Meyer, who adopted a different name five years ago but otherwise remained the same; he then spent five frantic months trying to become Eddie Munster, because of some incoherent belief that this transformation would deliver to him the girl he desired. Once that failure was finally clear to him, the crack of his fist against my mouth was my friend's last act, and now Debbie and Cecily carted him out of Tate like pallbearers who'd never actually met the deceased.

"You sure you're OK, B.?"

It was strange. For the first time since *Vertigo*, I was able to look at Andy and not see Janet.

"I'm fine, thanks," I said absently — still somewhat fascinated by the sight of my own blood. I'd never had so much as a nosebleed as a kid, and reading in my room with the door shut did not pose a high risk for scraped knees.

Andy stood there with me for a while, as though it were the scene of a car crash and we were waiting for the police to arrive. Eventually, once assured there were no further injuries beyond what was apparent, he said goodbye and headed toward the south exit to Myers.

I stepped through the sliding doors out onto Tate Plaza. This area thrived with activity during the day — the screaming preachers offering both fire and brimstone at a special group rate; the "tasty dog" cook-offs to promote racial harmony and gastrointestinal distress; the overwrought rallies for social and political causes that the participants will most likely abandon if not outright denounce within a decade. Now it was desolate and covered in a thick cloth of black with small circles of artificial light burning through the fabric.

I'd just lost a friend because he'd long since lost himself, and now I sat out on the same steps where I'd met Janet, who I lost through my own immeasurable stupidity, lost her because I was afraid of losing her. I didn't understand that loss, like flowing water wearing down rock, is inevitable and defines being alive.

Janet had recognized what Melinda Miller had fancifully called my "aura" — that undefinable difference in me that had for so long pushed people away but instead pulled her to me. She'd never demanded, expected, or wanted me to change and because of that, I had. It was so overwhelming a gift I didn't know I'd received it until this moment.

A dull ache vibrated through my mouth. The wind murmured a steamy torch song. My impaired vision delivered new, captivating images from the shadows, as a night bus routinely grunted to a halt and then groaned away on Sanford. For the first time, I didn't feel like a spectator but truly part of it all, part of this singular instant that no one would experience again.

Despite my near blindness, I picked out the colorful floral bouquet in the brim of a large felt hat that floated toward the wall of cash machines next to the University Bookstore. Without any awareness of movement, I soon stood behind Janet as she inserted her card into an ATM. The fluorescent light cast a dream-like shadow, and I thought for a moment this was a possible concussion-related hallucination, but her pounding of the ATM's face was too aggressive for any fantasy.

"What's wrong?"

If she was surprised to see me, she held her emotions behind a steel dam. As offensive as she found the ATM, she preferred to direct her words to it instead of me.

"The stupid machine won't give me any money."

It couldn't have been because she had none. I'd seen her balance once, after she'd carelessly dropped her receipt to the ground, and it was more than my father made a month. No, it was more likely that she'd forgotten the PIN. She did that a lot, which always amused me because it was her birthday backwards (271301)... or seen through a mirror, as she liked to say.

"May I help?"

She didn't answer, but I entered the correct PIN for her. As she took the dispensed bills, she saw me fully in the ATM's glow.

"What happened to your face?"

"I was in a fight."

I couldn't even say it without laughing. A trickle broke through the dam: Her soft fingers touched my now swollen lip, but she quickly withdrew them and spoke dispassionately, like when I'd confirm the cause of death for an obituary.

"Are you all right?"

"Yeah," I said and then after some consideration, "I had it coming."

Janet nodded in agreement.

"All along."

She noticed the ruins of my glasses.

"You didn't win this fight, did you?"

"I was sort of caught off guard..."

She waved her bills from the ATM.

"I guess I owe him a drink, don't I?"

She dropped the money in her purse and started off in the dark toward downtown. I'd called out her name before I even realized what I'd done. Her back stiffened. There was no warmth or melody in her voice.

"You really hurt me when you left. But I don't care about you now. I'm free of you. You can't hurt me anymore."

"I love you."

My timing was worse than my self-defense skills.

She turned around slowly. Her hat was in her hands, as though she were about to hear the national anthem.

"You... you've never said that."

"I thought you always knew."

She frowned.

"You probably make all As and got a 16,000 on the SAT or something like that, but you are truly the dumbest boy I've ever met. No wonder people go around breaking your glasses."

"I suppose I didn't say anything because I was afraid of how you felt, and I don't know why I thought that would change anything." My words stumbled out of my mouth, slick with the red on my lips. "I just... I've loved you from the moment I saw you, maybe even before, and I'll never stop. I love you so much I realize I haven't learned a damn thing this year other than that. I've been such an idiot, and I'm sorry, and you have every reason to hate me and you probably do. I don't blame you. I hate myself and I hate how my whole life was wasted because I wasn't prepared for you."

She stared at me incredulously.

"You think I was?" Suddenly, I realized how unfair I'd been. "I just came here to get away... but I found you and I fell so hard and so completely and my God, what we had was divine. Why did you have to spoil everything! It's like in *Vertigo*, when Scottie has Madeleine again and they're both so happy, but he can't accept that she's Judy, too. Even though if he just loved her enough, it wouldn't matter."

"Madeleine wasn't real," I said. "She was fake."

"She is so real! And so am I! Just because I'm not perfect all the time doesn't mean I'm rotten every other second. After what happened at The Grill... you *promised* me you'd forget, but you didn't. You are such a liar. But it doesn't matter. I can't be perfect for you... or my father or his wife... or anyone else. And I won't! I'm me. That has to be enough."

I wanted to apologize, because I had lied to her and to myself... because I never should have promised to forget anything about her. It was all precious to me... every perfect imperfection.

Months ago, during our first brunch at Rocky's, Janet Tomalin told me about Mahogany Slade, but what she'd actually done was ask me to love her — the woman underneath the hats and behind the dark curtains of glass; the woman who heard music when no one else did and was compelled to dance to it no matter where she was; the woman who always wept exactly three minutes and fifty-four seconds into Miles Davis's "Fall"; the woman who only shared the same form as the starlet from my dreams.

I didn't understand it at the time. She probably didn't either. Now all I wanted was to finally answer that burning request, to tell her how much I loved her, *all* of her — even Mahogany Slade, the person a sixteen-year-old Janet tried to escape in a tub of red water, but I didn't have the words. So I just took off her sunglasses and gently pressed my bruised lips against each of her eyes.

"Oh... my," she said, "how long have you wanted to do that?"

"Forever..."

"Well..." Her lips brushed mine with each word. "This is what I want to do right now."

The distance between us vanished, and our kiss was as tender and as passionately exploratory as one shared at an actual high school prom — something neither of us had experienced. We'd both been removed from the world when our peers danced without a care under a paper moon, so we held each other now on Tate Plaza — so tightly and desperately that we must have known the future was coming for us.

Eventually, we returned to her room and scaled to the top bunk together. We lay in the dark, her fingers stroking the erect hairs on my forearm, and listened to the mixtapes she'd made for me during our time apart.

This was the happiest I'd ever been — and though it's not entirely appropriate for me to admit now, it was as happy as I'd ever be. Occasionally, Janet's face would turn to mine — the light of her smile an able substitute for the lava lamp — and I could tell she felt the same way. There is no greater sensation than mutually shared bliss.

"Hey Bulldog" by The Beatles started to play, and I told Janet how I almost put that on a tape for her.

"Why didn't you?"

She'd turned around now, and her hands caressed my back.

"Oh, I don't know... I guess I thought..."

"You think too much, Brad."

The way she said my given name, the love that echoed in that one syllable, made every previous "kiddo" or "sweetie" sound as formal and reserved as "sir" or "mister."

"Oh, there you are," she murmured as her lips found me in the dark.

The next morning, which was more like a grudgingly acknowledged early afternoon, Janet took me downtown to get new glasses. Through a miracle of science, the archaeologists at the store on Clayton were able to derive a prescription from the cracked right lens and the shards of glass remaining from the left. Janet and I browsed the racks with all the focus of two people in love who were recently reunited. Sometime later, she'd selected a pair of full-rimmed frames that were identical to my old glasses except for their reddish-brown tint.

"I think these are lovely," she said. "Just like you."

She was in my arms, and I told her again how stupid I'd been.

"Don't talk so much," she said with a kiss that greatly reduced the market value of conversation. "It's all right. We have time..."

And she described a costume party (just the two of us) in San Francisco for her twenty-first birthday with a double feature of *North by Northwest* and *Notorious* ("highly alliterative," she giggled), then Thanksgiving at Brennan's — her favorite restaurant in New Orleans, Christmas among the lights of Rockefeller Center after seeing The Rockettes, and New Year's... I wish I knew what New Year's would have been. I've imagined those other dates so clearly and with such relish over the years, they are as real as any actual memory.

I missed her plans for New Year's because I'd noticed that none of these fantastic events took place in Athens, and when I asked her about it, her smile said everything, but I still waited for the words.

"They have this weird insistence that if you want to be a student here you have to attend the classes or something like that. I thought about getting a place of my own, you know, maybe even above Rocky's. We'd be so close." That was too painfully wonderful to contemplate, so she quickly moved on. "But I'm sure Mama Carlton wouldn't want her only son shacking up with a townie drop-out. Besides, Mrs. Tomalin has summoned me back to New York. Maybe it won't be so bad. My father doesn't look directly at me anymore, but he does try to look out for me."

Still in shock, I started to write a check for my new glasses. It would empty my account, which I'd have to explain to my parents. However, Janet had already put down a gold credit card.

"Early birthday present. My parents are used to my shopping binges. I almost got the people at Almanac to sell me that cute horse outside their store." She looked at me crossly. "We would never ride it. That's just mean. We have perfectly good legs."

"You certainly do," I whispered into her ear, feeling free to express myself without the security blanket of a song.

She laughed, long and loud, and once we left the store, she stopped to trace my eyebrows with a red nail.

"I love your eyes. There are so many sweet thoughts in them."

Those "sweet" thoughts involved the top bunk bed in room 393 at Myers. A little embarrassed, my eyes began a dim inspection of the storefront for Foster's Jewelers across the street.

"I'm not so sure about that."

"Sweet things can be hot, too," she insisted. "Like chocolate, which is so yummy. I like it almost burning. You know, the way it feels when your tongue gets numb? It's..." I kissed her. "If you're gonna do that whenever I start to ramble... well, that'll just be divine."

We spent the hour or so before my new glasses were ready at Rocky's, at our old booth, sharing a pitcher of ice tea and a pizza that hosted an orgy of mushrooms and black olives. I'd abandoned the twisted wreck I'd worn into the eyeglass shop, and my blurred vision matched my delirious joy. I was so happy at this instant that I buried any thoughts regarding Janet's upcoming departure. Besides, we'd have time, she said, and those words assaulted any potential gloom.

Janet was the only mirror I required when I tried on my new glasses later that day. She puckered her lips, her eyes narrowed in powerful concentration for a minute, before softly exclaiming, "Perfect!"

The promise of more time gave me the strength to leave Janet's side long enough to finally have a more extended meeting with Myrtle Adams. This opportunity came about because Heather had discovered I'd never been camping ("I'd expect that from a Yankee," she'd said, "but not from one of my own.") and decided to rectify this horrific lapse in my cultural experience as a tribute to my upcoming birthday. So, Friday afternoon, the four of us drove down to the Skidaway Island State Park in Savannah.

There were showers and toilets closer to our tents than the common baths at Myers were to my room; Heather thought this "sissified camping" would prove less a shock to my "khaki-clad system," and when she told me how camping worked *without* access to showers and toilets, I was inclined to agree.

The temperature skulked in the nineties, so I'd left my blue button-down in the closet and instead wore Heather's *The Queen Is Dead* T-shirt. During my brief career as an obituaries writer, I'd filled paragraphs with how fine Southern ladies had led their churches to spiritual touchdowns against Satan, the North, and progress. Obituaries, I realized, were the self-indulgent exception to all journalistic tenets, because when you die, everything you were doing is suddenly everything you'd done, and the only relevant news to communicate were the same four words found on my T-shirt.

Heather and Myrtle got an impressive blaze going while Andy and I, both hopeless suburbanites, tried to look useful. Andy gushed warmly about Myrtle, who I agreed was charming. Her birthday, he told me, was a week before Heather's in July, so we "should all do something." He was working at Blockbuster over the summer, but he could take some time off and fly down.

Andy's plans for the next few months all seemed plausible and lacked the dream-like quality present whenever I imagined Janet's description of our reunion by the fountain in Central Park.

Spotting a large spider on my thigh, I sat up with a noticeable lurch, but the venomous creature revealed itself as a shadow cast from the fire. I wiped dirt from my pants, and Myrtle, whose honey blonde hair had curled in the heat, turned to me.

"Those are nice khakis," she said. "If you ever need a new pair, I can get you a discount at the store."

"Thanks."

"Some people are crazy enough to go camping in jeans or even shorts," Heather noted.

"I don't like jeans."

"They're not for everyone," Myrtle agreed. "And those baggy ones look silly on most people. That's what I tell folks: Just don't look silly. That's my only fashion rule, and you'll get it right every time if you just wear what feels right for you."

Myrtle was named after the beach in South Carolina where her parents had met, but she was "boan en razed," as she put it, in Milan, Georgia, which was in the county of Dodge, so when people move away, which happens with the regularity of Halley's Comet sightings, everyone likes to exclaim, "Get the hell out of Dodge!"

Her drawl was several tax brackets removed from Heather's, but when Myrtle gently interrupted one of Andy's anti-Christian diatribes, I detected something familiar under the slow-tongued sweetness.

"If existentialism is all about choice," she said, "then sometimes you might wanna choose not saying exactly what you're thinking. You don't have to lie or anything, but you don't have to share, because if you always choose to do that, then it's like there's no choice at all."

"Yeah!" he shouted. "That would be... *deterministic!*"

Heather would have told him to just "shut the fuck up," but the effect was the same, and I was glad that Andy had found someone so essentially like her in Myrtle. Their greatest dissimilarity at present was stark but temporary: Heather had shaved her head the day after the prom, and there was now just thin blonde fuzz atop a deep brown face and piercing blue eyes. We'd gone for a walk on the nature trail to escape the fire's aphrodisiac effects on Andy and Myrtle, and I asked her what she planned for her next color.

"I might keep it blonde," she answered. "The Manic Panic's getting a little old."

We shared swigs from her flask. Bourbon wasn't so bad when you weren't drinking just to get blind.

"I'm kinda touched that you got into a fight over me, even if you were One Punch Carlton."

"Isn't a fight supposed to be announced or something?" I protested. "You can't just start swinging, right?"

"You expected pistols at dawn, Lord Darcy?" She stood on her toes and kissed my cheek. "Happy birthday. Nice specs, by the way. So, how is Janet?"

The bourbon was the sudden lead in a spit-take.

"C'mon, those glasses are from the Elton John collection. Who else?"

I explained to her how different and wonderful things were now, and she listened patiently to my lovesick ramblings: Yes, Janet was leaving, but she said we'd have time (somehow, those three big words had more buoyancy than the three little ones), and who knows, maybe I could transfer to NYU or Columbia on a Magical Fairy Dust Scholarship. I was being absurd, which is the only possible state for someone who achieves happiness beyond his previous ability to even conceive of it.

"Jesus H.! You've got cartoon birds circling your head. If you do go to New York, you might want to try lasting more than one punch... maybe even two. I can give you some lessons this summer. I expect to see a lot of you. I'm getting the Hilton Head place for my birthday — 7/17, it's all mine or part of my trust, I guess. Got this guy Eisenberg who's supposed to try and explain it to me. All I know is I have to host the Labor Day barbecue this year, which, based on how Karen does it, involves making two phone calls in July and getting a mani-pedi the morning of, so, bottom line, pretty sweet." She handed me the flask, and a slight nod stated I should finish it off. "She is gonna fucking break your heart. Awesome."

I began to argue against her prediction, but her hand quickly covered my mouth.

"No, really, it'll be good. Best thing for you. Sort of like the carrot juice at The Grit but it won't taste like ass. And in her fucked-up, self-involved diva way, she probably really loves you. Anyway, that's what you and I have in common: We both were a TKO in round one."

"I'm sorry about what happened with Jaye..."

"Fuck her! I was in love. That's more than she'll ever have. Besides, I listened to *Automatic* for the first time since I bought it and I kinda like it. It just makes sense now. Even *Out of Time*, which I thought was too crossover poppy but..."

We hugged.

"Think of all the new music you get after being dumped. Karen and Spencer's wedding song was 'Unchained Melody.' So vanilla. Who needs that? I love what I can hear now. I wouldn't go back if I could."

She demonstrated with an a cappella rendition of "Losing My Religion" as we ventured further into the unknown darkness, and I tunelessly joined her for an encore.

❦

Outside Barnett's Newsstand in College Square, there was a faded beige sign bearing the image of what Janet had titled two "his and her pipes over a book opened to the most scrumptious part." The city was haunted this way with every nickname she'd given to every dentilled cornice and stone balustrade.

As a child, Janet would extend this familiarity to the gothic towers and blinding white brick buildings in her neighborhood, and she'd receive her mother's reproach gift-wrapped in that inescapable steel blue voice: She was being "silly" and being "silly" was not how the Tomalins managed to live on Fifth Avenue.

Athens had been a relief for her, a place where she could jump on the bed, so to speak, where pretty things could be *touched*, and where imperfection was prized. And now she was leaving it behind.

I'd paused here on my way to the *Red & Black*, intentionally delaying my arrival, because that Monday was when Dan Buchanan and Daisy Summers announced their editor selections for Fall Quarter, and this procrastination was why I saw Jaye Goetz.

She'd just left Wuxtry Records, and as she crossed the street, her sundress gave off a spectral shimmer. There was no breeze so the white fabric fell over her like cool sheets that were rumpled after a steamy evening. Light perspiration from the day's almost tropical heat covered her bare skin like drops of water on china. She opened her arms to greet me, but I abruptly stepped back, indicating that I'd prefer the oncoming traffic on Broad to a hug from her.

Ignoring the rebuff, Jaye proceeded with innocuous pleasantries before commenting on my most recent column, the first written with the aid of my new glasses.

"It was almost... *sentimental*," she said cheerfully. "Cody and I couldn't figure it out, but then we realized you were just being sarcastic. Kind of like Swift and the tomatoes."

I didn't respond and was content to just walk away, but I remembered something Eddie Munster had said when I last saw him. It struck me that although Eddie was definitely disappointed when Heather and I left Debbie Tyson's, the rage that twisted his face that night at Tate could have come from nothing less than the sudden and unanesthetized extraction of his hope.

"What did you tell Eddie about Heather and me?"

My unhip directness startled her, but she quickly recovered. I think she realized any outright lie wouldn't hold up. Too many people had been present, and she needed to make sure that her story, while ultimately self-serving, still wove seamlessly into the overall tapestry of gossip.

Debbie and Eddie, Jaye said, were about to take an almost disembodied Dana Weichman upstairs when Dana wrenched free and hobbled over, wearing just one red shoe, to her and Tom Cody. They braced for a confrontation, but instead, Dana pointed to Heather and me on the front lawn and mawkishly cried, "Oh, how cute! She's... she's moved on... from one little adventure to another."

"No, no," Eddie broke in. "They're just friends. He told me himself."

"It's good, you see, so good... because I hear she was just so heartbroken before... just *heartbroken*."

I imagined that Tom was smugly blind to the direct line from Dana's words to Jaye, but Jasmine Goetz saw and quickly spoke. She had to, after all, before the innuendo developed into something worse than rumor... the truth.

Of course, she said nothing about Heather and me that wasn't the truth, but true statements, carefully selected and deliberately without context, are as effective, if not more so, than lies. And it wasn't long before Eddie Munster found himself on the outside of an inside joke. He had to stand there and watch Heather... not with Tom Cody or even Brian Dean but with me, someone similar enough to him that he probably felt as if he'd been recast in his own dreams.

Jaye finished her Cubist version of events with a defiant, "Look, what kind of friend is he if he can't be happy for you guys? I mean, I totally am."

I wanted so badly to respond with a column-worthy rejoinder, one she'd never describe as "sentimental," but I could only feel sorry for her. She was so desperate to be the person she was now with Tom Cody that she sacrificed the person she'd been with Heather. I wondered if she was even aware of the loss.

This time I let her hug me. It meant so little, and her arms seemed to cut through me in their transparency. Then I left my fan on College Avenue as I headed east to Jackson Street.

The *Red & Black* offices were as fractious as I'd anticipated that afternoon. I'd missed Dan Buchanan's motivational speech with lots of MBA buzzwords prior to the announcements, but I did manage to catch Daisy Summers's invitation to an end of quarter party at the apartment on Milledge she shared with the just-named news editor.

Gwen Lupo observed the meeting from a swivel chair with her chin resting on her knees. Compared to everyone else, she was remarkably calm, and she remained her naturally nervous self, revealing no sense of relief or enthusiasm, even after she was again named the entertainment editor. The opinions editor was the only other appointment that concerned me, and Buchanan had selected Nancy Blackwell, who no one else on staff much liked but who apparently liked me and looked forward to more of my columns.

Writers from all departments went to Taco Stand to commiserate over beers, and the new editors, excluding Gwen, stopped a few feet closer to the office at the restaurant with white tablecloths and stemmed water glasses that Janet and I had peeked into last October. Someone told me this was the first time the staff had celebrated separately. I didn't know if that was true or not, but regardless, the board had succeeded in making the *Red & Black* very much like a real job.

I walked over to Espresso with Gwen, and as I watched her fill a sixteen-ounce cup with equal parts coffee and sugar, I began to suspect that her constant jitteriness was at least in some part artificially induced.

"We're entertainment. No one notices us." The chair supporting her rattled as she drank her coffee. "You know, you technically can only be an editor for three quarters? Fall will be my fourth, and no one cared. But no one else applied, so that's probably it. Anyway, next year is my last so if you stick around, you're the obvious choice to replace me."

I thought that was the last thing I'd want, so of course, I eventually wound up doing it.

☙❧

The next week was finals and shortly afterward, parents would come up to remove students from campus like tinsel and garland off a Christmas tree, which would remain untouched in the center of Athens's living room until decorated again three months later. In a few weeks, I'd dress in a shirt and tie and cover random acts of violence (Melinda Miller had warned me that crime spiked in the summer — no holidays at the beach for murderers and thieves — but I should look forward to the clips). Today, though, I walked down Lumpkin in khakis, *The Queen Is Dead* T-shirt, and a thin blazer. It was too warm for the blazer, but Janet sometimes got cold in the air-conditioned Tate Theater.

We were seeing *Victor/Victoria*, and if it seems too perfect for the film to have played on my birthday, my only defense is that's how it happened. Janet stood on the concrete steps outside Tate wearing black slacks and a vest buttoned over a patterned tie and white shirt. The bright red heels obliterated any masculinity the outfit might have conveyed.

"I *had* to wear my 'Judys'," she said. "It's your birthday."

She rolled up her sleeves, stepped forward, and greeted me in a manner that has never been equaled on any of my birthdays since. This greeting lasted through the previews. Whether we were the only people in the theater literally or merely figuratively I can't recall and ultimately was a meaningless distinction.

"We're gonna miss the movie!" She giggled. "But then... I've already seen it."

I would eventually get around to watching *Victor/Victoria* — on my first Thanksgiving in New York, three years later. It was one of those cold days when Janet had crept up on me with a phantom tap on the shoulder, and I saw her uncovered eyes above the Marquis Theatre where I worked and heard her laugh amongst the eternally young Columbia undergrads near my first New York apartment. I felt the need to be close to her, so I went into the Blockbuster on 96th Street and rented *Victor/Victoria* from a clerk not so dissimilar to Andy Razinski. I ate (shockingly bad) pizza in a room about the size of the one I'd left at Myers just a few months earlier. It wasn't Crepes Fitzgerald at Brennan's, but I like to think we spent the holiday together.

Rain had come and gone while we were in the theater. The streets were slick, and puddles had formed in small, uneven recesses along the north lawn. Whenever we'd walk around one, Janet's tongue would strike the side of her mouth and make dripping sounds.

The slam of the screen door — it always slammed, no matter how gingerly you opened it — welcomed us back to Rocky's, and I recall feeling the simultaneous excitement and regret that comes with opening your last present on Christmas morning, which was the first time I'd felt something in metaphor without ever having experienced it in reality.

"I love that movie," Janet said between sips of ice tea.

"*Victor/Victoria?*"

"Yes, although not as much as…" She winked, and my cheeks caught fire. "But I meant the one on your shirt."

I hadn't known the image was from a film. I presumed it was someone from the band, but Heather would later explain that Morrissey was never so prosaic as to do that.

"It's yummy black and white and noir-ish, well, not *ish*, it actually is, and it's French. That's always good." She raised her hand and lowered a finger with each word: "Fries. Dip. Vanilla. Toast." Her thumb wiggled as if she was hitching a ride. "And something else."

We considered it for a moment before the subject of her leaving, the only one she wasn't able to drop with disinterest, came up. That was my fault. I kept hoping I'd misheard her, and she'd return in the fall, the star at the top of Athens's Christmas tree.

"The movers came yesterday and took everything I couldn't put in my bags. Now, all I have to do is show up at the airport tomorrow." Her fingers took great interest for the next few minutes in the small burn on the back of my hand — the only visible scar from my childhood. "*Everyone* goes to New York. It seems unfair to overwhelm it. No one ever goes to Cincinnati, Ohio."

"There are probably reasons for that."

"Well, that's silly. You know it never rains there in the summer? That's a fact." It was not even remotely factual. "Let's go! I'll trade in my ticket for two."

An apple is not tempting. It's often mealy, dense, and dull... so I have no sympathy for Adam, but getting on a plane somewhere headed to *anywhere* with this woman epitomized temptation.

I struggled to speak, to think of her and not of us.

"New York's not so bad."

"New York's cold and demanding," she said decisively. "Even in June, it's just... rigid and brittle."

"I don't think your parents expect you to turn up in Cincinnati."

"Oh, I'm sure that's what they expect... or something like that."

"Then surprise them."

"You're so *serious*."

"We'll have time, right?"

"And you remember the things I say. That's not very romantic."

She released my hand and leaned against the booth's vinyl cushion. The beach ball she balanced on her nose soon crashed almost audibly.

"I'm impulsive. That's one of the things about me on the list to be fixed." She mimed unrolling an endless scroll. "I've never seen the list, but Mother has it stashed away someplace in her office, I'm sure. It's all very civilized and unbearable. And it's been tried before. There are these pills that are supposed to fix everything or something like that. They're like M&Ms, but they're *not*. I know because I took M&Ms instead once and everyone got upset."

So, around 8 p.m. on my nineteenth birthday, I mentally regressed a decade and began viewing Abigail Tomalin as the cackling Disney villain responsible for our fairy tale's unhappy ending. I saw her obsessively checking her list — once, even twice — and doing everything in her power to ensure that her only daughter was perfect, suitable for display in that gallery of a Manhattan apartment. She failed to comprehend the beauty in Janet's imperfect spirit and would try to cage it inside her perfect shell. If she succeeded, only the shell would remain.

Suddenly, Cincinnati didn't seem like such a bad idea.

"It's time for presents," Janet announced with a laugh that shifted the mood with a tectonic force.

She handed me a mixtape that her unique swirling script — more like musical notes than letters — labeled "Fats Love," and she explained it was all Fats Waller songs, which were "divine," or songs she was sure he would have liked. Next from her peddler's pack came a square of red cardboard. A black-and-white photo of Janet, which looked like she'd taken it herself with a disposable camera, was pasted onto it, along with a lock of her hair; written on the back in that musical handwriting was *"a relic of me so you'll know I exist."*

"I know. I'm so *vain...* but you already knew that, and I wanted you to have something tangible because memories are so fickle." She looked up as the train chugged along past us. "I wish I could give you more. If I could, I'd ride around in that train with you until the world ended or they stopped making pizza, whichever came first — although, I don't think I could live without pizza."

Morbidly linear thoughts overwhelmed me, and whatever time we might have later, I wanted right now. I couldn't even wait for the plane as I imagined us swimming across the Ohio River to a new life together in Cincinnati. I wasn't afraid of the water anymore, and I was about to tell Janet this when I felt her beside me in the booth. She pressed two fingers against my lips.

"Shhh," she whispered. "Let's just watch the train."

My eyes followed hers to the wall, but first, they stopped at the final gift she'd placed on our table: In a sealed Ziploc bag was a leaf picked from North Campus on a Sunday late in October, the first time we came to Rocky's. The leaf had fallen early, far too soon, and was still green with only flecks of autumn red.

On the first day of June, the leaves cling to the North Campus trees with no consciousness of their impending plummet to the earth. The students who gather on the lawn, preparing for finals but unprepared for any true endings, aren't so different.

Some of the students clearing out of the dorms now will never return, but new students will arrive in just a few months, buoyed upon their unique ambitions and dreams. Most will storm this beach of red, yellow, and green as they claim the campus as theirs, oblivious to the falls that preceded them, but occasionally, someone special, someone irreplaceable, will try to preserve the moment when our ambitions and dreams aren't just memories but are as numerous and attainable as the leaves at our feet.

I held Janet's hand in our booth for the rest of the night, which went on into memory. Rocky's is gone now, whisked away on one of those falling leaves, but the tracks are still on the wall, and as long as they make pizza somewhere and I can still feel her hand, we will ride in that train forever.

14786418R00139

Made in the USA
Charleston, SC
01 October 2012